FOREWORD

Almost everyone on the trail is given a trail name, mine is Box Turtle. (YouTube - *Box Turtle on the AT 2018*). My journey began on April 4th at Amicalola Falls in Georgia and ended at the summit of Mount Katahdin on September 27th. Twice I had to leave the trail due to injuries (four weeks), but when I did hike, I averaged fifteen miles per day.

The trail is 2200 miles in length and the constant elevation changes add up to climbing Mount Everest sixteen and a half times. It felt like I was training for a marathon every day. I never wanted to quit, but many times I wished I were finished because often the conditions were miserable due to cold rain, snow, heavy winds, lightning, heat and humidity, blisters, and injuries. The hardest part was being away from my family for so long. The scariest part was the lightning storms while on top of the mountain ridges. The best parts were the trail angels who provided, at no costs to the thru-hikers, food, drinks, rides, and encouragement.

I documented my saga using a smart phone so that I could share my experience with family, friends, and other interested parties. A thru-hike is not for everyone. Section hiking is preferred by most due to time constraints and the wonderful option of going home whenever one felt like it.

This book is dedicated to my family, friends, trail maintenance crews, and trail angels of the Appalachian Trail. The names of the hikers are fictitious as are most of the characters. The places and trail angel names are real.　April 2021

TRAIL MAGIC

DAY 1

Early in the morning, she pulled into the state park parking lot, selected a space facing the visitor center and then turned off the engine of her white Jeep Compass. "Is this the place, Dad?"

"Well, I've never been here Madison, but from all of the YouTube videos I watched, this looks like the place."

They both exited the vehicle slowly. The all-night ride from Ohio took two hours longer than they had planned due to road construction on I-75 and their muscles were stiff. Sonny retrieved his backpack from the back seat and put it on. He had worn it numerous times the past year during training hikes at Oak Openings Preserve, but practice was over. This was now very real and as they walked towards the Amicalola Falls Visitor Center, his trepidation increased. When they reached the front of the wooden building, he hung his pack from the hook of the spring scale and then checked the weight reading on the dial. All of his gear, including food and water, registered thirty-seven pounds. He intended to carry all of it on the trail from Georgia to Maine and document the adventure with photos and videos.

Once inside the building, they viewed the oversized vintage black and white photos and displays of heavy, outdated hiking equipment. At the counter, he registered and was handed a NoBo (northbound) thru-hiker plastic tag that he immediately tie-wrapped to his backpack. He was directed to an outdoor educational area to await final instructions from a ridge-runner (A person who patrols a section of the trail, maintains privies and shelters, and advises hikers).

They exited the building through the back door and immediately saw the famous stone arch where many hikers over the years had started their journeys on the Appalachian Trail. There was still five minutes before the lecture on trail protocol began, so they used the time to take pictures of each other under the arch. After they sat down on wooden benches near two young male hikers who were wearing running shorts, the ridge-runner arrived and introduced himself. He was a lanky man in his fifties with gray scruffy hair and a beard that hung lazily down to his midsection. Everyone laughed when he said his trail name was Billy Goat. He spoke of the importance of leaving no trace behind, erosion control, and the proper procedure when pooping in the woods. He praised the hikers for walking the 8.5-mile approach trail to the official beginning of the Appalachian Trail at Springer Mountain. Half of the hikers usually rode up to the start.

During the presentation, Sonny noticed that both of the young hikers had evaluated his daughter. The ridge-runner concluded his talk by well wishing the hikers. Then he pointed at the arch and said, "Mount Katahdin is that way."

After Sonny and Madison passed under the arch, the two other hikers caught up with them. One of them asked Madison what her trail name was and when she said that she wasn't a hiker, the young men moved on. The father and daughter had had long and sometimes emotional discussions on the drive down from Ohio, but now both were solemnly quiet as they approached the base of the falls.

Amicalola Creek was narrow and unimpressive until its elevation dramatically dropped 729 feet. The waterfall was comprised of numerous cascading sections over bare protruding rocks. The wooden staircase that intertwined with the falls consisted of 604 steps and led all the way to the top. Sonny and Madison took their time ascending and stopped every so often to take in the view, catch their breaths and savor the remaining time together. Sonny knew that although this climb was tough, what lay ahead would be much more difficult. He also knew that when they reached the top, he and his daughter would say their goodbyes and go their separate ways. Upon accomplishing the climb, both tried to hold back tears. Sonny had so much to say to his daughter, but the words wouldn't come out. Madison simply said, "I'm proud of you, Dad."

All that he could summon in response was, "Thanks... for everything."

Madison kissed her dad on the cheek and said, "I'll see you in four days at Neel Gap."

She then headed back to her Jeep. Sonny watched her descend the steps for a while and already missed her. With long blond hair, she looked so much like her mother. He couldn't help but think how symbolic it was that someone he loved was leaving him again. Sonny knew all of his other family members wished they could be here for his send-off and he felt grateful for all they had done for him the past two years. But, Springer

Mountain was still about seven miles away and he wanted to get farther than that on his first day. He turned around and began walking north.

The fourth of April was looking promising with the sun and warm air prodding nature to come alive. Much of the ground around the stones and leafless trees was covered with a variety of early season plant life, some with blooms. Sonny would stop and take pictures of the flowers with his first ever, recently purchased smart phone. The blossoms reminded him of his wife. She had loved flowers and he wished he could share them with her. The trail was rolly and pleasant and it allowed Sonny to ease into the adventure. Already, he was monitoring his condition to avoid over-use injuries. His hiking shoes felt comfortable because they were broken in during the training sessions. He drank water and Gatorade from plastic bottles that were attached to the straps of his backpack. Using his trekking poles, he fell into a smooth efficient rhythm and began to make miles.

Sometime in the afternoon, he grew hungry and stepped off the trail to a small clearing where he sat down on a log and ate the sandwich and an apple purchased earlier that day. When he was finished with lunch he packed away the litter in a gallon plastic bag designated for garbage. After he perused the area for rubbish, he continued walking. A light wind had begun, the temperature dropped, and he was no longer sweating. The weather report called for evening showers and he hoped he was in his tent before the precipitation arrived. Now and then, a younger, faster hiker would pass him headed for Springer Mountain. He would remind himself that this wasn't a race, but the thought of not getting a good tent site near the shelter increased his pace slightly. His mind wandered to the unhappy events of a couple years earlier, but he was released from the torment when he arrived at Springer Mountain.

There were a few hikers basking on the rocks and enthusiasm radiated from their fit bodies. Sonny signed his name and recorded the date in the notebook that was installed in back of the rock with the bronze plaque. The view was pleasing and the hikers took turns taking pictures of each other. Many of them settled on staying at the nearby campsite. At his feet, Sonny noticed the first white blaze painted on the rock. The vertical 2x6 inch white symbol would be the mark that he would look for to ensure he was on the right trail. It was late afternoon and the sun was dropping, reminding him that he still had a couple of miles to go to reach the next shelter.

The Stover Creek Shelter and surrounding campsite was packed full of hikers. Sonny noticed that the two young guys he had met at the visitor center earlier that day, occupied prime real estate near the shelter as their tents were pitched on a flat clearing devoid of any debris. The best campsite that Sonny could find was not flat, but after clearing away the sticks and stones, he put up his blue ultralight tent utilizing his double-purpose trekking poles to support the tent. There was a dead tree nearby, but it was leaning away from the place where he intended to sleep. Next, he selected a freeze-dried packet of food from his food bag, dumped its contents into his titanium pot and added water. He cleared the dead leaves from a spot on the ground a safe distance from the tent, unfolded his tiny stove, and screwed it into the canister of fuel and then placed it on the ground. After turning the valve and lighting the isobutene with a mini lighter, Sonny carefully balanced the pot of beef stew on top of the heat source while stirring the luscious meal with his titanium spoon and watching it come back to life. Following the ingestion, he washed the pot and spoon, brushed his teeth, and then returned the items to the backpack. All of his remaining food was hung in a bear bag from a nearby tree. He looked over and noticed the setting sun and saw there no longer was a line at the privy, so he grabbed his roll of TP and made use of the facility. He returned to his tent and washed up. With all of his work done for the day, Sonny put on his hooded sweatshirt and headed to the shelter.

The typical shelter was a three-sided stone and wooden structure with a raised platform, large enough to accommodate several sleeping bags. Tired hikers occupied all of the spaces and many more sat at the picnic table or milled around the campfire. Sonny smiled and acknowledged those around him, but mostly he listened to their stories of the day. He felt like it was the first day of kindergarten. Everyone was a little nervous and no one wanted to look foolish. Each one dealt with the situation in his or her own way.

Some of the hikers talked loud and bragged about their accomplishments. Others were more sedate and weren't afraid to ask for advice. Sonny tried to resist the urge to prejudge his fellow hikers, but he failed. He thought he could get along with almost all of them, but there already were a few that annoyed him.

Only twenty percent of the people who attempt a thru-hike of the   A. T. are able to complete the task. People leave the trail for a variety of reasons, some get called home for emergencies, portions get injured, and others just plain quit. Sonny studied the group and tried to decide which ones were going to make it to the end.

As he walked back to his tent in the dark, he realized he should have carried his headlamp and was grateful for the moonlight showing the way. Once he was securely in the tent, he removed his shoes and pants. The wind increased and the temperature had dropped so he left on his sweatshirt when he crawled into the mummy sleeping bag. The goose down bedroll was lightweight and had a rating of 30 degrees Fahrenheit. He was tired, but concerned about being visited by a black bear. Every twig that fell from the nearby trees spurned his imagination. Suddenly, the rain came down hard and he used his headlight to make sure no water found its way into the tent. The squall didn't last long and Sonny fell into a deep sleep.

Some time around midnight he was awakened by a scream. He sat up wide-awake and listened. The loud noise repeated several times in a tree branch directly over his tent. He recognized the sound from videos he had watched as a barred owl. It was mating season and the bird was working hard to locate a spouse. Eventually Sonny passed out, but due to the cold air, he woke up and shivered until he was warm and then fell asleep again. That sequence repeated itself until morning.

DAY 2

When darkness gave way ever so slightly, birds of all kinds began to sing in earnest. Sonny did not feel rested, but he was excited about breaking camp and starting day two. A few of the other hikers were preparing their breakfast meals near the shelter and Sonny joined them. He heated some water on his little stove and then added two packets of maple-flavored oatmeal to the pot. The other hikers were doing the same or eating Pop Tarts. Most were quiet out of respect for those campers who were still asleep. Some of the hikers were discussing how far they intended to walk and where they would camp at the end of the day. Sonny knew that if he stayed in the bubble (a large group), he would end up with a poor tent site every night since most of the hikers were faster than him. But, he wasn't going to increase his daily mileage until after meeting his daughter at Neel Gap. He returned to his tent, washed his pot and spoon and stowed all of his belongings into his backpack.

The air was still cool as Sonny began walking, so he retained the sweatshirt for an hour and then when the sun warmed him, he stuffed it in the large net pocket on the back of his pack. The lack of leaves on the trees provided no shade, but allowed terrific views of the gaps between the mountain peaks. His goal was to go thirteen miles for the day. Where he came from the Earth was flat, but in Georgia he faced climbing and then descending switchbacks, one after another. All morning long, hikers passed him.

For lunch he stopped at a shelter and had a chicken and rice freeze-dried meal that he washed down with Gatorade. Some of the other hikers at the picnic table already had trail names. Sonny, who was the only one wearing long pants, told them that his real name was Alexander Toth Jr. One of the young girls named Dirty Knees suggested that he should be A. T. on the A. T. One does not have to accept a given trail name and Sonny passed on that one and then washed his pot and spoon. After using the privy, he washed his hands and saw that all of the barelegged hikers had moved on. Sonny followed and only stopped to filter water into his plastic bottles or take a pee when necessary.

The campsite at the Gooch Mountain Shelter was overflowing. The three-sided structure, which was stuffed with tired hikers, reminded Sonny of the beehives that he maintained on his minifarm back in Grand Rapids, Ohio. Due to erosion control, much of the surrounding area of the campsite was cordoned off with yellow plastic tape. Once again, Sonny pitched his tent on one of the less favorable sites and then headed to the shelter to prepare his supper. He recognized many of the people from the first night. Throughout the day, most of them had passed him on the trail. More of them had been given trail names resulting from various incidents that day. Earlier in the morning, a young woman had donned a cold and wet white tee shirt and was given the name Perky by her male cohorts. One of the young men couldn't take his eyes off of her and was hence referred to as Ogle. Sonny enjoyed the banter between the groups, but there was a crude looking, forty-something man from Alabama who had no filter. His name was Potty Mouth. When the oaf began sharing his political beliefs, Sonny said goodnight, went back to his tent and quickly fell asleep.

Due to his sixty-year-old enlarged prostate, he woke up every night at least twice with the urge to urinate. During the camping practices on his front lawn a year earlier, he had experimented with different nighttime peeing procedures. He had tried kneeling near the open tent door and watering the grass with an unsteady stream, but settled on utilizing a collapsible plastic bottle. The container had a wide opening and at night, he kept it at a reachable distance outside the tent door. In the morning he would discreetly empty, rinse, and put it away in his pack.

DAY 3

When nature's alarm clock, the singing birds, woke him up, Sonny dressed in all of the outer clothes that he had worn the previous two days. Although he ate three meals a day and devoured healthy snacks and junk food all day long, he was still hungry. Today's breakfast consisted of blueberry Pop Tarts, hot chocolate and raisins. At the shelter he was able to secure a spot at the picnic table where he sat and enjoyed the feast. For half of the hikers, there was a sense of urgency in the air because they were going to push it all the way to Neel Gap for whatever pleasures of civilization could be found there. Sonny envied them, but knew his reward would come the following day when he would reunite with his daughter. His plan for the day was to hike 10.4 miles to Jarrard Gap. Between there and Neel Gap a bear canister was required to spend the night and very few hikers carried such a bulky item.

The day felt like Christmas Eve and there was a bounce in his step as he anticipated the break from the trail. Although Sonny was only into his third day, he could feel an amplification of his emotions. The successes and joys of his life brought a smile to his face, but the regrets and sad memories made him gloomy. Before leaving the campsite, he had opened his AWOL guide and read about lodging near Neel Gap (Both AWOL guide and Guthook app were valuable resources that provided information about the lay of the land ahead including elevation, sources of water, food, lodging, campsites or shelters, privy locations, and trail highlights).

As he crested a hill, he made his daily morning video and then noticed that the signal on his phone was

powerful enough to place a call. Referencing his
Guthook app, he found a place in Blairsville with a good
review. The phone at the Misty Mountain Inn was
answered on the third ring by a friendly woman's voice.
There were two cottages available and Sonny reserved
one for the following night. Next he called his daughter
and found that she was still enjoying her visit with a
cousin in Roswell, Georgia. He told her that he was
descending into a gap and might lose phone contact at
any time. Madison assured him that she would be at
Neel Gap by noon the following day and that she had a
surprise for him, but before he could respond, he lost
service.

About one o'clock, Sonny stopped at a stream near a
small waterfall and made water, filled all of his bottles,
and added a scoop of the lemon-lime flavored
electrolyte mix to the wide mouthed bottle. He felt
serene and decided to have lunch at the picturesque
location. After adding hot water to a bag of dried
mashed potatoes, he used his spoon to mix in a packet
of diced chicken breast. A cold can of pop was what he
desired, but he again settled for Gatorade. After he
cleaned his spoon and packed away the trash, Sonny
carefully crossed the creek using existing, well-placed
stepping-stones. As he climbed up the bank, he spotted
a cluster of bloodroots and crouched down to get a
picture of the wild flowers. The stems contain an
orange blood-like substance that he used to squeeze
out onto his hand when he was a boy. When he stood
up and resumed walking, he was distracted by the call

of a pileated woodpecker, tripped over a root, and fell face first.

   He was stunned and found himself on the ground starring right into the face of a dogtooth violet. The yellow flower, also known as a trout lily, reminded him of home. As Sonny lay there in the red dirt, he took inventory of his body and found that he was uninjured. When he reviewed the falling incident in his mind, he began to chuckle. Eventually, he rolled onto his back, gazed at the treetops and laughed heartily at himself. He could not recall the last time he had laughed, but he did remember how good it felt. Finally, he shook his head, took a picture of the flower and then climbed the next mountain peak.

   Sometime in the afternoon, he arrived at Jarrad Gap and although he saw many tents and hammocks, he found an available flat spot, kicked away some stones and set up his tent. After inflating his mattress, he used the remaining sunlight to record his daily wrap-up of the day's events, and then combined pictures and videos and created movies for each day. When he was finished, he considered the remaining contents of his food bag. For supper he ate a bag of almonds, the left over dried apricots, and a Payday candy bar. The Kind bar and Almond Joy candy bar would have to hold him tomorrow until he made it to Neel Gap. Because he felt sticky from the dried sweat on his body, he made his way to the stream where he washed up, brushed his teeth, and filtered just one bottle of water. He then headed back towards the campsite counting his steps.

When he reached seventy, he knew he was at least two hundred feet away from the water source. After making sure the coast was clear, he discreetly used his titanium cat hole shovel and dug a depression eight inches deep. After assuring himself of privacy, he pulled his pants and underwear down to his knees and squatted over the hole. When he was finished he wiped, dropped the toilet paper into the hole, and pulled his pants up. Next he covered the fecal matter with soil and disinfected his hands with sanitizing lotion.

Walking toward the crowded campsite, Sonny saw that there were two groups of hikers socializing. The nearest congregation was standing around an oversized campfire. Three of the young men were either mesmerized by the flames or bored by the lecture they were trapped at. The speaker was Potty Mouth who alternated between drinking beer and ranting. The slob then tossed the aluminum can into the fire and Sonny veered off in the direction of the larger assemblage at the far end of the tenting site.

The smell of burning marijuana saturated the atmosphere. Sonny was offered a joint, but did not partake. He told the participants that he was trying to cut down and they laughed at his joke harder than a sober person would have. A cold breeze swept through the group and Sonny observed that Perky was among the group and still living up to her name. Ogle was close by her and asked Sonny, "Hey A.T. on the A.T., do you have an acceptable trail name yet?"

Sonny said, "Not yet Ogle, but I'm sure I'll receive an appropriate title soon enough."

Ogle took a drag of the evil weed, passed it to Perky and said, "Well, two of my new friends got their names today. You see that guy over there with the bright orange shorts and shirt?"

Sonny looked in the direction that Ogle was pointing and saw a short and very obese young man. "You mean the one with the green knee-high socks?"

"Yeah, that's him. Guess what his name is."

Sonny thought for a moment and said, "Pumpkin?"

Ogle and those around him roared with laughter and then Perky volunteered, "His name is Stinkfinger. You want to know how he got it?"

Sonny said, "No, I don't think so."

Perky snickered and said, "It's not what you think. He told us that he was off the trail taking a dump and when he finished, he realized that he forgot to bring his toilet paper with him, so he improvised with some nearby vegetation. Except the leaves couldn't handle the job and then..."

Sonny tried to interrupt the story with, "Okay, I get it."

Ogle didn't take the hint and continued with another story about a young woman with long dark braids who was standing next to Sonny. Apparently, she too had tattled on herself, but to her credit, seemed embarrassed. At that moment, Sonny wished he was asleep in his tent, but grinned and listened anyway. Laced with irrational bouts of laughter, Ogle pressed on with the tale. Sonny learned that the poor woman suffered a similar fate as that of Stinkfinger, but with the additional trauma caused by a handful of rash producing leaves. Her original name, which was more descriptive, was later shortened to just plain Itchy. Sonny was rescued from any more narratives when a sudden rain began to fall and he scampered to his tent.

DAY 4

Sometime during the night the rain stopped, but in the morning, Sonny saw that the wind had blown moisture into a corner of the tent where his pants were stowed. He had to wring them out before getting dressed and even though he was a little sore from the fall, his spirits were high because Neel Gap was only five miles away. He wasted no time taking down the tent and packing his gear.

As he carefully ambled along the trail, he made his typical morning video where he stated the date, location and plans for the day. Sometimes he would elaborate about trail life, his memories, or philosophies. Today the views were non-existent due a thick fog, which severely limited his vision and saturated his clothing. He ate his last coconut Kind Bar, drank a few gulps of water, and pondered the upcoming climb to Blood Mountain. The steep climb up was tough enough, but he had learned from others that going down the far side would be harder. The stone Blood Mountain Shelter had two rooms and was the oldest one on the A.T.

When Sonny arrived, he spoke with two young ladies from London, one of whom said that she recently had a tick attached to her face. Sonny had doused his clothing with repellent and was not concerned with that happening to him. He walked through the shelter and recorded the landmark and then savored the Almond Joy, his last item of food. The descent was mildly treacherous compared to what lay ahead.

Before he knew it, the fog had cleared and he heard traffic and saw the Mountain Crossings outfitter and hostel across the road. He walked down the slope, crossed US-19, and gazed at the large oak tree that was loaded with hiking boots hanging from its outstretched branches. Twenty-five percent of thru-hikers, who make it that far, decide to surrender there. It was a tradition of the quitters to remove their shoes, tie the laces together, and throw them up into the massive tree. There was a plaque nearby which stated that the Creek and Cherokee Indians fought with each other prior to the arrival of the White settlers.

The establishment was a group of connecting buildings with opposing rooflines. Sonny had time to kill before Madison would arrive, so he looked around the store at the items for sale on the shelves. There were hiking and camping supplies, food, and souvenirs, including a collection of small, brightly painted, bobble head turtles. He selected a green one as a gift for his daughter, loaded up with dried packets of food, and as he paid at the counter, he noticed a guy behind him with a steaming pizza. Sonny listened intently to the directions to the freezer and microwave. In a short time, he found himself outside at a picnic table with a cold can of Coke, wolfing down a brand of pizza he used to not think very highly of.

Just before noon, the white Jeep pulled into the small parking lot. Sonny watched his daughter step out of the vehicle and look around for him. She spotted her dad at the picnic table and ran to him. Thru-hikers don't hug or shake hands because they are filthy animals and don't want to spread any viruses; instead they fist bump. Madison hugged her father and then backed away and said, "You need a shower."

Sonny did not disagree. Madison carried his pack to the Jeep and sat it in the backseat. Sonny opened the passenger side, but could not sit down because there was a large cardboard box on the seat. Inside the container was a cute Weimaraner puppy that appeared to be overjoyed to meet him. Madison said, "This is the surprise. Peaches is your new granddogger."

Sonny had been praying for a different kind of surprise from his daughter. She had married five years ago and two years later her only pregnancy ended in a miscarriage. He smiled and lifted the dog and held her to his chest. Peaches wagged her tail rapidly and then peed on him.

In twenty minutes, Sonny was taking a real shower in a two story cabin. Peaches was fed, watered and taken outside to relieve herself, on the grass this time. The four-day-old hiking clothes were churning in the washer. When Sonny had finished dressing in the civilian clothes that Madison had brought along for the day, all three of them went to a restaurant in Blairsville.

Copeland's boasted of burgers, shakes, fries and beer and Sonny ordered them all. Madison had a taco with iced tea. The puppy slept on her lap the entire time and no one complained about it. In between bites, Sonny answered numerous questions from his inquisitive daughter about the trail. She was really curious about the people he had met. He told her about some of the characters and their suitable trail names, but she didn't seem satisfied and said, "Dad, why are you still wearing your wedding ring?"

He gave her his standard answer. "I'm just trying to keep the babes off of me."

Madison frowned. "Mom's gone, you have to let her go and move on with your life."

Sonny sighed. "I wish you wouldn't bring that up every time we meet."

"I miss her too, Dad. We all do."

Sonny pushed his plate away. "You want any of these fries?"

"No I'm stuffed."

"Me too, let's go back to the cabin, I'm pretty tired."

They rode back in silence. Madison tended to her dog while Sonny made a video, created a movie, and began uploading his first of four movies on YouTube. Madison put the clean clothes in the dryer, took a shower and then went to bed. Sonny got in his bed and quickly fell asleep, but every time that his bladder woke him, he uploaded another movie.

DAY 5

In the morning, they were both in better spirits. As her dad marveled at the bobble head turtle on the dashboard, Madison drove them to a Catholic church in town. This time, she left the dog in the Jeep with the windows partially opened. Afterwards, they stopped at a breakfast restaurant that the priest had recommended. Sonny's appetite had returned and he ordered a large orange juice, over easy eggs with sausage, and pancakes. Madison had an omelet and a glass of water. Before heading back to continue the journey, they stopped at a grocery store where they each picked up submarine sandwiches for later. The drive back to the trail at Neel Gap went too quickly. Sonny stopped thinking about his own woes and put himself in his daughter's shoes. After all, she no longer had the support of her mother and recently, her first Weimaraner had died. Madison was moving on; maybe he should too.

Back at Neel Gap, another hiker took their picture together beneath the only underpass on the AT. Sonny tried to be patient and show more compassion for his daughter. He gave her one last hug and said, "Okay, you're right."

He handed her his wedding ring and for the umpteenth time in her life, she said, "Thanks Dad."

This time, she watched him walk away.

A zero is a day when no hiking is done and Sonny did not want any of those. His long distance racing days ended ten years earlier, but his competitive spirit was still alive and he fought the urge to push the pace. Instead, he cautiously watched his footing to avoid an injury that might halt the adventure. The past two years he had been very reclusive and the time with Madison reminded him that he was on a mission. Madison and her two younger brothers had repeatedly urged him to get out and socialize more. They had suggested he join the senior center, a garden club, a bowling league, a curling club, and a yoga class. But when he jokingly said that he didn't have time for those activities because he was going to hike the Appalachian Trail, they all laughed at him.

The sun was out, but the temperature was in the forties and although he was loaded down with food, he felt comfortable and strong going up and over the repetitive hills. One of his biggest fears was running into a black bear, especially a female with cubs, and every shadow or dark tree stump ahead of him caused a tinge of anxiety. In the front utility pack that was attached between the arm straps against his chest, Sonny carried snacks and his phone for quick access. At one point he came across a tiny and colorful pixie village that someone had set up next to the base of a very large tree. The small ceramic structures were surrounded by a ground cover of a cluster of bluets. He took pictures of the small flowers; each had four periwinkle petals and a yellow center. Because of the late start, Sonny only covered 6.7 miles before stopping at Whitley Gap. There was a side trail, marked with blue blazes that led down a steep path to the shelter 1.2 miles away. Going there and back would be a waste of time and effort, and he noticed a couple of other guys were camping on the narrow ridge, so he did likewise.

The next thing he knew, he was not in his tent sleeping safely on a ridge, but was on the edge of an unknown town being pursued by soldiers in a truck. He and a handful of others were running for their lives. The truck stopped abruptly by some very tall grass, and the men hustled into the cover and scared three people out into the open where they shot them. Sonny observed that the attackers could not see their prey if they did not move. The killers then turned their attention to him and another man as they sprinted into the town. They turned around the corner of a brick school building as the armed men caught up with them. Sonny reached out and grabbed his colleague by the arm and stopped him saying, "If we don't move, we are invisible to them."

They both froze in place and the assailants arrived and shouted at them trying to make them flinch. They did not, but a girl standing nearby panicked and ran. She was gunned down immediately and then the evil men moved further into the town. Sonny then entered the school and went to an office and closed the door. The landline phone on the desk began to ring and he picked up the receiver and talked to an old friend who had died the previous year. Before Sonny could ask him any questions, the birds began to sing and he woke up.

DAY 6

The day started off cold and foggy, so he again wore the sweatshirt along with a stocking cap and glove liners, but at least he didn't have to hike the 1.2 miles up from the shelter. Sonny had looked forward to the large blueberry muffin and even though it was squashed, he did not pass judgment as he ate his breakfast.

Along the way, he saw more than one tree that looked like it had a moose head growing from its trunk at the lower branch level. He took pictures of them and thought they would make a neat calendar. When he stopped to make water, the sound of the splashes reminded him that if he were at home he would be fishing for walleye in the Maumee River. Much of the trail traversed through a tunnel of rhododendron bushes that would all be blooming with large aromatic lavender colored flowers in the upcoming weeks. Any trees that had fallen across the trail were cleared away as soon as possible by trail maintenance crews, which made life much easier for the hikers. Sonny realized that without these volunteers, the trail would quickly fall into disrepair and whenever he met the workers, he always thanked them. He savored the pleasing weather as it was cool enough that he didn't sweat much and the lack of rain kept his feet dry and free of blisters. Days of lousy weather would eventually find him, soon enough. He stopped for lunch at the Blue Mountain Shelter, thought about his family, and then feeling a little melancholy, moved on. After 15.9 miles, he stopped for the day on Rocky Mountain. There was no privy and the only other campers there were a young couple. She had a trail name, but he maintained his real name and together they were known as Forever and Everett.

DAY 7

The following day was again cool and sunny and although he was the first to leave the campsite, the young hikers soon passed him on the trail. After he had climbed Tray Mountain, he hoped for a reprieve of effort that a long and level ridge provided, but that was not the case. So, before he took on the steep descent, he rested and enjoyed the view. Sitting there on a nearby rock was an older man who had hiked a majority of the trail forty-three years earlier. In his sun-weathered hand was a vintage Appalachian Trail hiking guide and Sonny talked with him about the many changes that had occurred during the past decades. The gear was lighter now and the trail was made a little easier. There was better information and more opportunities for acquiring food and hostels for showers, laundry, and healing.

In the afternoon, he took a break and a picture near a round granite rock that was engraved with the name Round Top. The leaves still had not emerged on the branches and this allowed for good views for Sonny as he strode over Kelly Knob. He decided to call it a day after 14.1 miles and set up his tent in Moreland Gap. The site was a former location of an old farmhouse that was rumored to be haunted and all other hikers passed it by. This was the first time he camped alone, but he was so tired that he had no problem sleeping.

DAY 8

At dawn, he unzipped the tent screen and photographed the rising sun and then sent the picture to the foreman on his last construction job. Dicks Creek

Gap was only a mile away and once there, he came out on US-76 and began walking towards Hiawassee, Georgia. In no time, a car pulled over and the driver offered him a ride. The older man's trail name was Encourager and during the eleven-mile drive, he told many stories. He was a former local politician and current hiker and minister and as he gave recommendations during the city tour, Sonny asked him about hitchhiking protocol. Encourager was also an entrepreneur who created a bright pink laminated hitchhiking sign for A.T. thru-hikers. Before exiting the vehicle at the Ingles supermarket, the minister asked if he could bestow a blessing on the hiker. Permission was granted and Sonny thanked the trail angel (a person who provides trail magic) and then went shopping.

After packing away his supplies, he walked down Main Street and sat on a park bench at the town square. There he enjoyed a sandwich and cold bottle of pop as he took in the landscape. Red tulips and other spring flowers adorned the area around the gazebo, and as he turned to look at the buds on the trees behind him, he saw the lake. Lake Chatuge, which had 132 miles of shoreline covered with expensive homes, was formed in 1940 when the TVA finished construction of a dam for flood control and electric power.

After lunch, Sonny decided to make some calls to family members. First, he contacted his aging mother, who still lived in the homestead in McKee's Corners and filled her in on his whereabouts. She told him about her vegetable and flower gardens and her many social activities. After he hung up, he thought that his mother might possibly outlive him and then he called her next-door neighbor. His oldest son August, was the middle child who followed in his father's footsteps and became a union electrician in Toledo's local. Besides working in the industrial and commercial construction field, he maintained and rented houses in his ever-growing Wood County neighborhood. August was glad to hear from his father and said he hoped to walk 'a few miles' with him. With his workload, wife, and three kids, Sonny doubted it would happen, but he did enjoy hearing about the grandchildren. The next call was to his youngest. Henry had taken his grandmother's advice and graduated from Ohio Northern with a doctorate in Pharmacy. He and his wife were the proud parents of four little ones, whom Sonny didn't see much since they lived in Colorado. Henry said he also would love to join his father on the trail, but they both knew it was never going to happen anytime soon. Finally, Sonny called Madison and as the phone rang ten times, he thought about the last time he saw her and remembered that she hadn't consumed any alcohol. Just when he was about to hang up, she answered. "Sorry, Dad. I was in the middle of cleaning up a mess on the carpet."

"That puppy of yours sounds like a real pain."

"It wasn't the dog Dad, it was me. I didn't make it to the bathroom in time and I threw up in the living room."

"Oh... do you have the flu or something. I hope there's not another virus going around."

"No Dad, I'm fine. In fact, I've never felt happier."

"Maybe you should get a check-up, just to be sure."

"I just came home from the seeing my doctor and Dad, you should be happy too."

"Madison, what are you saying?"

"I'm telling you that you are going to be a grandfather again."

For a few seconds Sonny couldn't catch his breath, but then he managed to say, "That's wonderful news, Madison. I'll be on cloud nine for a long time. If you were here I would hug you."

"I don't know, Dad. When was your last shower?"

To celebrate, Sonny stopped at the Dairy Queen and ordered a banana split. While eating the delicacy, he remembered where Encourager told him he could purchase the hitchhiker sign. Soon he was standing by the side of the road facing traffic with both hands displaying the pink sign while counting the number of vehicles that passed by. Number twenty-seven, a black Ram pickup truck pulled over and Sonny hurried to the passenger side and spoke through the open window.

"Hi, my name is Sonny and I'm looking for a ride back to the trail."

The rough-looking driver smiled and said, "Yeah, I saw your sign. Put your pack in the back by my tools and hop in."

Sonny had not hitchhiked since he was a teenager and was worried that an unscrupulous driver might drive off with his gear. But he had to work on his trust issues and this was a good time to start. The man was a local construction worker who enjoyed swapping tales about the building trades. Sonny had retired only two weeks earlier, was loaded with stories, and enjoyed his company on the eleven-mile ride back to Dicks Creek Gap. By early evening, he had managed to lug his pack laden with food, nine miles to Bly Gap in North Carolina. One state down, thirteen to go.

The campsite was known for its landmark twisted oak tree and once again all of the prime tent sites were occupied. Sonny drifted down the side of the trail to an overflow area and settled for an unleveled spot covered with sticks and stones and dead leaves. He had a daily routine for breaking camp each morning and setting up his campsite every evening and after clearing the ground, he began. For easy access, his tent was on top of his food bag in the backpack. The clothes bags, both clean and dirty, were in the middle and the sleeping bag was on the bottom and all were used to create comfort by keeping hard surfaces away from his back.

Prior to the beginning of his adventure, he had been given much advice by many well-intended associates. He was advised to travel with a friend, carry a handgun, and a large knife, but Sonny considered all of the suggestions to be unnecessary burdens. The blade that he carried was a two-inch Swiss Army knife that had a pair of scissors, tweezers, and a toothpick. A firearm was much too heavy and if necessary, he would use his trekking poles as weapons. Having a friend to keep him company and share the decisions might make his life easier, but he didn't want to curtail anyone's effort, and he did not want anyone to slow him down either. Some hikers had camouflaged items, but Sonny had purchased brightly colored gear so that he could easily find them among the earthly hues of the trail.

After the tent was erected, he inflated his mattress, rolled out the mummy sleeping bag, ate, cleaned dishes and self, brushed teeth, urinated, hung the food bag in a tree away from tent, made a video, charged his phone with his portable unit, and said his prayers before drifting off.

DAY 9

The morning routine was much the same, but in reverse. After the birds brought him back to reality, there was just enough light to look at the Guthook app on his phone and the paperback AWOL guide. He had a quick breakfast, put all of his belongings in the pack and walked north.

Before lunch he began the climb over Standing Indian Mountain. The peak was over 5400 feet and known for its gemstones. Along the way he stopped and talked to a couple from Dayton, Ohio, who spend their yearly vacation in the area prospecting for rubies. They cracked open the hard red granite rocks and exposed spots that glittered with red specks. Some of the rubies, which were larger than specks, were harvested for sale. Sonny continued up the mountain until he couldn't resist the urge to stop and break open several rocks of his own.

On the way down the other side of the peak, he was halted by two southbound day hikers, who gave him a bag of candy bars. He thanked the trail angels for the treats, but secretly yearned for the day when hamburgers and hotdogs were offered and he often sniffed the air in anticipation.

His day ended after 15.3 miles at Carter Gap. Following the completion of his camp chores, Sonny made a wrap-up video of the day as the sun disappeared, but instead of going to bed, he decided to socialize with the group. The wind had increased and they were huddled around a campfire near the shelter. He recognized some of the hikers and introduced himself to the others. A lanky young man with long stringy hair had just received the trail name of Tripper and Sonny assumed it was because the guy smoked pot, but that was not the case. Tripper was a curious fellow who liked to look around when he hiked and this caused him to trip over roots and rocks and so, he fell down a lot. One of the younger women stood back from the group. She was overweight and shy and seemed out of place. Sonny asked her what her name was and she said, "Shelly."

A Minnesota man, who went by the name Uncouth from Duluth, spoke up and said, "Her trail name is Fiona, you know, like Shrek's girlfriend."

A few people chuckled and Shelly walked away. Sonny was about to chastise the offensive guy, but a tall blond woman named Athena beat him to it. Sonny just shook his head and walked back to his tent. Before he unzipped the door, he heard the sounds of a woman softly crying in the distance and carefully approached her. There was just enough light so that he could recognize her. "Are you okay, Shelly?"

She felt embarrassed and wiped away the tears and said, "I'm sorry. Am I keeping you up?"

"Don't be sorry. That guy is a jerk and you don't have to accept a trail name that you don't like."

"I have no business being here. I should just go home."

"Shelly, they say 'Never quit on a bad day'. If you really want to leave, that's okay, but that needs to be your decision. Don't let anyone bully you into giving up. You had a good reason to take on this challenge; stick with your plan. If I can do it, then so can you."

Shelly couldn't look at Sonny when she replied. Instead, she stared into the darkness. "I have a twin sister who is nothing like me. She is skinny and cute and garnishes all the attention. I have always been pushed to the background and I thought if I could only do something that she hasn't done…"

Her words trailed off and she began to cry again. Sonny wanted to hug her, but knew that he couldn't. "Shelly, tomorrow you and I are going to summit Mount Albert. That's the hundred-mile mark and your sister won't be there. When you get there, you're going to experience a feeling of satisfaction that no one can take away from you. If you decide to continue the journey, your sense of pride and level of confidence will grow. The good days will make up for the bad ones and I promise you, if you keep going, you will be a better person."

Sonny held out his clenched fist and Shelly bumped it with hers. She tried to smile and then said, "Your trail name should be Real Nice."

"Thanks, but that one has already been taken."

DAY 10

During the night, the wind increased and caused the tent to shake, but when the morning arrived, conditions improved. Sonny did not see Shelly at the campsite, but he hoped that her attitude had improved. The sunny day was just warm enough and the grade of the switchbacks wasn't strenuous. The area that he had hiked through the past couple of days had been part of a major forest fire. The air still smell like charcoal and when he reached Betty Gap and found someone's abandoned smoldering campfire, he doused it with his water bottle. At the next water source he filled all of his containers. The flow of water from the creek was weak and someone had used a small stone to hold a rhododendron leaf over a rock edge. This engineering feat created a small narrow waterfall, which made it easier to collect the liquid.

About midday, Sonny saw the fire tower in the distance. The steepness increased and the last three-tenths of a mile were bare rock. When he arrived at the peak of Albert Mountain, a smiling young woman who offered a fist bump met him. Shelly had gotten up before sunrise and headed north. "For now, I've decided to keep the trail name Fiona. I'm going to use it as a motivation to keep going."

"Whatever works for you, Fiona. I have faith in you."

"When I first dreamed about hiking the A.T., I watched many YouTube vloggers (video bloggers), but my favorite was Dixie of Homemade Wanderlust. She is my idol."

Sonny gazed at the panoramic view of continuous mountain peaks and then said, "I first watched Red Beard, then I learned a lot from Bigfoot. Spielberg had the best videos, but the guy I could relate to the most was Box Turtle."

They had another hiker take their picture together at the base of the tower and then Shelly said, "Athena is taking me under her wing so I have to get going now, but I'm sure I'll see you on the trail again. Thanks for believing in me, Sonny."

Before she left, Sonny told her, "Fiona, after you summit Mount Katahdin, *you* are going to be someone's idol."

Sonny videoed the climb up the fire tower, but because the brim of his gray Ohio State cap blocked his vision, he banged his head on the locked metal door of the tower floor. When the pain subsided, he went down the stairs, sat on a rock and ate lunch.

The beginning of the trail north of the fire tower was an actual creek with an ankle-deep flow. When the trail eventually turned back into dry land, he observed another hiker soaking his feet in a deep pool. Sonny decided to join him and hung his own socks out to dry over nearby branches.

He ended up covering 12.1 miles and stopped in early evening at Rock Gap Shelter. The structure was already full, but he didn't care because he preferred his tent, so he ambled down the hill to an area where a few hikers were already set up. Early at night, he was entertained by the barred owls, but then they left and he fell into a deep sleep until the monster arrived. At least that is what it sounded like. Whatever it was, it came up from a creek far below, crossed the road, strode by the tents, passing the shelter all the while making eerie sounds ranging from a raspy bark to a screech and the scariest, a snarling roar.

DAY 11

In the morning, Sonny looked around, but only located one blurry track. An old timer who camped up by the shelter said it was a bobcat. The weather, which was calm, cool and sunny, was very conducive for hiking. The trees were still without leaves that would block the views and the scenery that was rather bland, consisted of dark tree trunks on a bed of gray rock and faded brown dead vegetation.

The four miles to Winding Stair Gap at US-64 went by quickly and Sonny had a feeling that something good was going to happen that day. As he approached the road that led to Franklin, an older section hiker named Coach passed him. Sonny learned that Mrs. Coach was waiting for her husband at the parking lot and they were going into town and offered him a ride to McDonalds. He accepted the ride and was given Rice Krispy treats from a trail angel named Grace. Sonny felt a strong appreciation for the automobile as the ten miles, which would have taken him hours to walk, was driven in minutes.

At the fast food restaurant, he ordered coffee for the Coaches and breakfast for himself. He learned that McDonalds and the local libraries had strong Wi-Fi and used it to upload his videos. Then he walked up the hill on Main Street into the well-kept downtown section of Franklin. The small city street was lined on both sides with two story businesses, made from a variety of building materials that were maintained and clean. Most of the vintage buildings had large windowed fronts with colorful awnings. Sonny used the time to window-shop and call family members. All of them had watched his initial videos and had questions, but he sensed that they were preoccupied with their own lives and he was left with a slight feeling of abandonment. Madison seemed the most interested, but her biggest concern was whether he had met a 'nice lady' yet.

The call ended abruptly when Madison had to tend to her puppy that was on a chewing binge and Sonny found himself at the front of an outfitter store. He left his pack outside and entered the outdoorsy looking business. While purchasing his hiking meals for the next several days, he overheard a familiar unpleasant voice. Potty Mouth was with a couple of guys at the back of the store speaking with volume about going to a nearby brewery and this disheartened Sonny for he had planned to dine there. It was a burger and beer joint situated next to the Little Tennessee River. He ended up walking a couple of blocks to a place called Root and Barrel.

As he stood in the front holding his pack in his arms waiting to be seated, he saw that all of the prime seats with a view of the street were taken. One of the tall stools was occupied by a woman who was fit enough to be a hiker, but whose superior hygiene disqualified her from the title. She was pretty and slender with shoulder length light brown hair and just a few strands of gray and she was alone. As he tried to determine her age, the hostess interrupted him and sat him in the back where he ordered a beer, salad, prime rib with mashed potatoes, green beans, and pecan pie, plus a ham sandwich to go. While he waited for his order, he sipped the beer, responded to comments on his YouTube channel, and stole glances at the fascinating woman up front. Just after his food arrived, the woman walked past him on her way to the restroom. She smiled at him, but the feeling of joy was quickly squelched as he noticed a ring on her finger. A few minutes later, Sonny sighed as he studied her movements while she strutted out the front door. He finished the meal and checked the weather report. A storm was due to strike in a couple of hours and with any luck, he hoped to be in his sleeping bag before then. On the way back down Main Street, he bumped into a small group of thru-hikers that he knew and one of them was Fiona.

After the customary fist bump, Fiona updated him on her recent activities. There was a breakfast for thru-hikers at a local church that served pancakes and eggs, which she planned on taking advantage of in the morning. She seemed more confident and happier and heard that there were no vacancies anywhere due to the impending storm. "Sonny, did you get a room? I may have gotten one of the last ones?"

"No, I thought about it, but I think I waited too long."

Fiona hesitated, but then said, "I'm sure one of us would be willing to share a room with you."

"Thanks, but I'll be all right. Besides, it will give me a chance to try out some of my adverse weather gear I've been toting around."

Sonny did not hear her response because the woman he recently saw at the restaurant distracted him. The attractive lady was speaking to other nearby hikers and Fiona stopped talking and looked in the direction of Sonny's gaze. Eventually, Sonny realized he was being rude and said, "I'm sorry, Fiona, what did you say?"

Fiona grinned and said, "Her name is Lily. She is a trail angel. She's 51 years old and has spurned every guy that has hit on her, that I've seen."

Sonny sheepishly asked, "Is she married?"

"Couldn't tell you. We just met and besides, it looks like she is leaving with somebody now."

Sonny watched a male hiker and the woman walk around the corner and out of sight and then he said goodbye to his fellow hikers and walked down to an area that was more conducive to getting a ride. He found that it was best to hold up his pink sign at a spot where a driver had ample time and room to pull over safely. As he stood there alone, the skies darkened, the cold wind increased, and he wished he had reserved a room for the night. He put on his raingear and in a few minutes all traffic was nonexistent so he began walking back towards the trail in a torrid downpour. After he had walked about a mile, he saw headlights from an oncoming SUV that slowed to take a look at him. A decision was made and the green Chevy Equinox made a U-turn and pulled over to a stop. The passenger window lowered and he saw that smile again. "Need a ride?"

"I sure do. Back to Winding Stair Gap, please."

"Well, you know the routine. Stash your pack in the back and hop in."

After he put his seatbelt on, she handed him a dry towel, turned up the heat and then offered her left fist. She had small hands and there was definitely a ring, but it was only a plain white gold ban with no gemstones. She slowly pulled out onto US-64 and began the drive back to the trail and said, "My name is Lily."

"My real name is Alexander Toth Jr, but my friends call me Sonny. I don't have a trail name yet."

The windshield wipers were working hard to keep up with the rain. "Well, Sonny, I have a question. Why didn't you stay in town and avoid this bad weather?"

He looked at her sadly and said, "Because I'm a moron."

She laughed, which only enhanced her allure. "Tell me about yourself."

"I'm a 60 year old recently retired electrician from Grand Rapids, Ohio, who has a daughter, two sons and seven and a half grandkids." As an after thought he mumbled, "And I'm single."

"Who's having the baby?"

"My daughter. It's her first one."

Lily concentrated on her driving and Sonny noticed that her green eyes twinkled like stars. There was a short lull in the conversation so he asked, "What about you? Are you a hiker? What's your story?"

"Oh yes, I thru-hiked the A.T. in 2017. My real name is Lillian Gish Velker and I was given the trail name of Trout Lily, but that one only lasted until I reached Clingmans Dome where I promptly sprained my ankle and had to leave the trail for a week. When I returned, I was renamed Miracle Lily."

"Lily, you have neither a New England nor a Southern accent, so I'm guessing that you hail from somewhere in the Midwest."

"Good guess, Sonny. I'm from a small farm in Brown County, Indiana."

Sonny noticed that she didn't share her marital status or mention family. He waited for her to surrender more personal information, but instead she added, "I came here to get away and give back to the trail. This is my first time back since my thru-hike and I want to return on a regular basis to follow the bubble whenever I can get away from the demands of the farm."

They arrived at the drop-off point much sooner than Sonny had wanted, but the rain was letting up and he put on his pack. He walked to the driver's window to thank her and ask for hints as to where he might run into her again. Her smile gave him hope, but it was short-lived because she replied, "I'm not sure at this point. I'll be back, but tomorrow I have to go home and take care of Harry and the kids first."

****

The four-mile hike to Siler Bald Shelter began with a small waterfall and ended with the sun peaking out at the end of the day. He stopped at the occupied shelter to sign the logbook and say hi to the hikers there. One of them was the man who had left Franklin with Lily, and Sonny tried to glean information from him about her. He was small in stature, and his trail name Imp, was an accurate description of his personality. Lily had rejected the mischievous man's advances and he decided to save face by having fun at Sonny's expense. The man used double entendres to convey Lily's relationships, including one involving a neighbor who helped her on the farm. He never even hinted to Sonny that Lily's kids were actually young goats and Harry was a seven hundred pound, well-endowed Poland China hog used exclusively for breeding.

Feeling more curious and confused, Sonny chose a level spot for his tent, ate the ham sandwich, and then performed his evening chores. The temperature dropped, but before sleep came, he remembered the blooming serviceberry trees and felt secure knowing that spring would soon arrive.

DAY 12

When he awoke the next day, two inches of snow was covering the tent and according to the weather app, it would continue to fall, and the wind would blow all day long. His wet shoes were frozen, but he put them on along with dry socks, long underwear, a hooded sweatshirt, a puffy jacket, glove liners, and a stocking cap. He shivered as he struggled to pack things away. The knot in the rope that held the food bag was frozen and he had to use the screwdriver tip of the Swiss Army knife to untie it.

All day he alternated holding his trekking poles in one hand, while warming the other in his pocket and found that if he kept walking his toes didn't hurt. He intended to walk continuously just to stay warm. His meals consisted of Kind and Clif Bars, candy, and dried fruit. Before noon, he reached the Wayah Bald stone tower where he entered the room of the lower section to get out of the wind and make a video and a tribute to his mother. His face was red from the cold and his eyes were misty from homesickness, but he continued the video up the two flights of stone steps. The second level had a four-sided wooden hip roof sitting on strong corner posts. The information sign below boasted of *Fabulous Views*, but the fog kept them a mystery, so Sonny climbed down and continued on his way.

In midafternoon, the sky was still dark and the howling wind was blowing the falling snow sideways. Visibility was poor and traversing the trail during the blizzard-like conditions was hazardous. He did not meet a single hiker on the trail the entire day and he felt so small among the imposing trees and rocks. His biggest fears were frostbite and falling in the deep snow that hid rocks and showed no tracks of any kind. All other creatures, animal and human, had enough sense to get out of the cold and he had never felt more alone. Sonny stopped at Cold Spring Shelter to call ahead for reservations at the Fontana Lodge in three days. He could barely hear the receptionist, but was able to secure a room and looked forward to the luxury. He thought he might enter the shelter to warm up, but when he pulled back the blue tarp covering the front, he saw four hikers already in their sleeping bags glaring at him. No one welcomed him so he said, "Don't worry, I'm not staying."

He pulled the tarp closed and continued his hike in the storm until he reached Wesser Bald (A bald is a peak without trees to block the view). He removed his backpack and sat it on the ground with the trekking poles at the base of the metal fire tower. The steps were covered with ice, but he carefully climbed the structure to the wooden deck on top. From there he could see a fuzzy outline of the peaks nearby and down below all of the brush was covered in hoarfrost. A mile later, he reached the Wesser Bald Shelter, tired, cold, and hungry. He set up his tent in the snow, prepared a warm meal and went to bed contented that he had covered a new record of 17.4 miles. He slept with all of his warm clothes on and when he emerged from his mummy sleeping bag the next morning, he knew that the worst would be over by 10:30, the sun would be out, and warmth would return.

DAY 13

The next day was sunny and bright, but still cold. Sonny took the time to heat oatmeal and a cup of hot chocolate mix. The views were finally clear and as he descended the five plus miles to the N.O.C., the sun warmed his part of the Earth and he took pictures of purple bleeding hearts and white trilliums.

The Nantahala Outdoor Center was a long two story wooden building with a green metal roof and was situated on the shimmering Nantahala River. Several adventure packages were available including whitewater raft and kayak trips. There was also a hostel, but Sonny was interested in only food so he left his gear outside and entered the River's End Restaurant where he was given a table with a view of the river. He ordered a beer and a pork chop meal that came with wild rice and a medley of vegetables and again, he got a sandwich to go. During the lunch, he uploaded videos and afterwards purchased a few items at the general store and then crossed the footbridge over the rapids to continue on the trail.

The climb out of the N.O.C. was about seven miles. Along the way he saw groups of dwarf purple iris and his day ended with 12.8 miles at Sassafras Gap Shelter where he pitched his tent in front of the inhabited structure. None of the hikers from Franklin had caught up with him yet and he did not know any of the ones at this campsite, but all were quite welcoming. Sonny sat at the picnic table and exchanged stories with the group. He was most impressed with a forty-something man with long unruly hair. The man was in excellent shape, had good manners and was respectful to all of the others. A couple of years retired from the marines, he had decided to attempt a thru-hike and because of his wild mane was ironically named Crew Cut. About an hour after all were quiet at camp, a bouncing headlight arrived followed closely by a young guy. He wanted to hike farther, but had just met up with a black bear on the dark trail. After negotiating his way around the male bear, he decided to spend the night around other people.

DAY 14

The morning hike was predominantly downhill and it was a windy and sunny day that provided clear views of the gray and brown hilly landscape. He noticed more wildflowers along the way and stopped to take a picture of a trillium that had small yellow petals and multi-shades of green leaves. Lunchtime found Sonny at Stecoah Gap resting at one of the two nice picnic tables, eating energy bars and trail angel provisions of apples and bananas. The rest of the afternoon was pleasant and the terrain was not strenuous. Before he finished the 15.2 miles to Cable Gap Shelter, he could see the trail winding through the peaks and caught a glimpse of Fontana Lake in the distance.

During the last two hours of hiking each day, Sonny would listen to music from his collection of over three hundred songs on his Spotify app, while traversing about four miles. He arrived at the fairly crowded campsite feeling sad as he listened to Cat Stevens' song - *Miles From Nowhere*, but the melancholy sentiment disappeared when he realized that Fontana Village was only five miles away. That night, the barred owls in the area held a concert with two encores as the hikers tried to sleep.

DAY 15

Spirits were high among the hikers in the morning, for most of them had made reservations for a night or two at the village. The young couples, who passed Sonny during the five-mile descent, appeared to be skipping in anticipation of wondrous activities soon to be had. Pictures were taken of deep red trillium with solid or two-toned green leaves. Hikers were afforded a panoramic view of the dam and its resulting lake as they approached the resort and most arrived in the late morning.

When Sonny came out onto NC-28, he collapsed his trekking poles, attached them to his pack, and displayed his hitchhiking sign. He was soon rewarded with snacks and a ride to the village by a trail angel named Eddie who was on site supporting his wife's thru-hike. The lobby of the lodge combined wood paneled walls with local stone and a fireplace with several couches and comfortable chairs strategically separated.

After Sonny entered his room, a pack explosion occurred. That is, all of the contents of his backpack were emptied out onto the bed and floor. He stripped naked and then dressed himself in only the rain pants and jacket and his camp flip-flops. Next he washed his silk sleeping bag liner in the sink and then gathered his dirty clothes and put them all into a washing machine.

He uploaded videos during the washing and drying process and then he showered, dressed, and headed to the grill for lunch. Having had only a cup of Earl Grey tea for breakfast, he ordered a tall glass of beer, an elaborate salad of greens accompanied with strawberries and feta cheese, and a fish sandwich with onion rings.

Afterwards, he walked back to the lodge, but stayed outside and phoned family members. He learned that his mother had fallen and broken a wrist, but stubbornly continued on with all of her activities. August checked in on her daily and was working overtime on his construction jobsite. Henry was building a swing set for his youngsters. The final call of the day worried Sonny. His daughter began by saying that she was bedridden for two days until her husband came home from a business trip and a neighbor girl was dogsitting Peaches. Madison went on to say that she was spotting and concerned about another miscarriage. She tried to put on a brave front, but her shaky voice gave her away.

After the call, Sonny retreated to his room, sulked, and took a nap. He awoke a few hours later feeling better and then walked to the general store to buy provisions. On the way back, he took a picture of the 1875 Gunter Cabin and then entered the restaurant and ordered a dark ale, a baked fillet of trout with grape tomatoes on diced red potatoes, and asparagus, plus a sandwich to go. Back at the room, he climbed into bed and tried to watch a televised sporting event, but he soon fell asleep while thinking of his daughter.

DAY 16

Before he left the resort in the morning, Sonny sat down at the restaurant and ate over easy eggs with sausage links, diced potatoes, toast, and a large orange juice. It was a beautiful day and the trail followed the shoreline of the clear and calm Fontana Lake. He stopped at the Fontana Dam Shelter, which was known as the 'Fontana Hilton' due to its size and the amenities it provided: indoor toilets and showers, water spigot, trash bin, and solar charger for electronic devices. While savoring the view of the lake, he overheard part of a conversation from some young thru-hikers who where preparing to leave the shelter. One of the guys had just been notified that his girlfriend was pregnant and he had reluctantly agreed to quit the trail and find a job. The others teased him and called him 'Daddy'. Sonny moved on towards the visitor center and was once again reminded that life was not fair. Some people, who don't want children, get them. While others who want children, can't have them.

The Fontana Dam Visitor Center, made of concrete and large windows, showcased the history of the dam and a volunteer gave Sonny the lowdown about the seventy-miles of the trail through the next national park. The white blazes led him across the dam and back into the woods, but he missed the turn because someone had parked their SUV there. After the path dwindled away, he turned around and walked back to the vehicle where he then spotted the permit box and deposited his registration form.

From the dam he had seen a fire tower on the next peak that was four miles away. He was loaded down with food and although the climb was steep, he was excited about being in the Great Smoky Mountains, but not overjoyed about having to stay in the shelters at night. The Shuckstack Fire Tower was made of wood on metal with wood-paned glass windows. Sonny recorded the views from all four directions and did not hit his head on the door that time. At the base of the tower was a crumbling foundation and chimney where he sat down and ate his sandwich on a swath of green grass.

The afternoon brought ridge walking through sections of ground covered in flowering spring beauties, so thick that they looked like snow. The day ended after 16.5 miles at the scarcely filled Russell Field Shelter. Due to its close proximity to Cades Cove, the shelter was equipped with a corral for horses that were allowed on the trails in the area. There was no privy, but a long, wood-handled shoveled leaned against the shelter, for those in need of it.

DAY 17

He awoke the next day feeling grateful that no mice had invaded his pack or climbed across his face during the night. One guy had tossed a granola bar out on the dirt in front of the shelter to appease the rodents. Sonny felt that the offering might have selfishly profited that group of hikers, but the feeding might have enhanced the population of mice for a later bunch of campers. He thought that a mousetrap, which weighed about the same as the snack, might be a better option.

Avoiding 'road apples' deposited by the horses, Sonny enjoyed an easy three miles and then climbed to views of Cades Cove and Gatlinburg from Rocky Top and Thunderhead Mountain. Again the climate was comfortable and there was no wind when he stopped for lunch at Derrick Knob Shelter.

He asked a southbound hiker how far away Tennessee was. The man told him that he was probably in and out of Tennessee and North Carolina the past two days depending on which side of the path he was on, since the state borderline was the mountain ridges. The evergreen tree population was increasing and he ended his day of 15.8 miles at Double Spring Gap Shelter. The shelter was full, so he was allowed to pitch his tent and avoid any snorers.

DAY 18

He slept with his puffy jacket on and wore it with his sweatshirt during the cold morning, three-mile hike to Clingmans Dome where he walked up the spiral ramp to the top. There were no views due to the heavy fog, which really did look like smoke, but he had a young couple take his picture anyhow, since it was the highest point of the trail at 6643 feet. The visitor center was a half-mile down the hill and Sonny decided to walk there for a cold pop. He was disappointed to learn that none was available, but was told if he stuck around, a herd of elk might be seen.

Many hikers were taking advantage of the free shuttle into Gatlinburg to avoid an approaching storm, but Sonny wanted to avoid that tourist trap and headed back to the trail being careful not to sprain an ankle like Lily had done there. Soon he reached the 200-mile mark that someone had designated with the number written on the ground using stones. The next few miles were eerily dark. He did not see another hiker and he had the feeling that he might run into a bear.

In midafternoon, he crossed a busy US-441 at Newfound Gap. There was a sign announcing trail magic (gifts from trail angels which included food, drink, rides and other donations), but he did not see any. The wind was picking up and any remaining hikers were getting rides to Gatlinburg. Sonny climbed the stone steps above the parking lot and had his picture taken there. The rain started as he was beginning to hike the five clicks (five kilometers) to spend the night at Ice Water Spring Shelter, but another hiker warned him that the whole shelter was already reserved by section hikers and staying in a tent would be dangerous in a seventy mile an hour wind storm. He reluctantly went back to the parking lot and displayed his pink sign and Anthony from the U.K. offered a ride.

A young female hiker missed her shuttle ride and Sonny asked the trail angel if there was enough room for one more. The three of them headed for Gatlinburg, but along the way Anthony stopped twice during the fifteen-mile winding road drive to photograph scenic locations, pictures he would later sell.

The woman hiker wanted to be left out at the Holiday Inn where her boyfriend had reserved a night and Sonny took a room there also. He washed some clothing in the sink and hung them at various locations to dry and then showered and walked to the Cherokee Grill where he had prime rib with mashed potatoes, green beans, and a draft beer.

After dessert, Sonny strolled the streets and made his daily wrap-up video of the events during the 10.5-mile day, picked up snacks and a sub for the next day, and retired to his room. He phoned his mom and his sons, but hesitated to call his daughter, hoping she would call him with some better news. He uploaded videos while watching a televised Detroit Red Wings hockey game. While wondering if Lily had provided the trail magic at Newfound Gap earlier in the day, he fell asleep.

DAY 19

The birds did not awaken him, but Sonny rose early enough for the all-you-can-eat breakfast and then carried his pack down the street towards the mountains he had left. He stopped at the outfitter store and rocked in a chair on the front porch waiting for the shuttle. The Sevierville Baptist church offered free rides back to the trail, but Sonny was early and he took the opportunity to take a picture of a rainbow that formed in the distance. He hoped it was a good omen and as he contemplated his day, Madison called. "Hi Dad, everything is good. I was worried, but we're okay and I hope that I didn't upset you."

Sonny was so relieved he wanted to do a backflip. "That's great news Madison. Don't worry about me. If you're good, I'm good."

"Okay, enough about me. Have you met anyone who interests you?"

Sonny chuckled and said, "You never were very subtle."

"I care about you, Dad."

"All right, I'll give you an update, but don't get your hopes up because I haven't."

"What do you mean?"

"Well, I met a woman who I find fascinating and I can't get her off my mind."

"So what's the problem, Dad?"

"She might be married."

"She *might* be? Didn't you ask her?"

"No, but she wears a ring and talked about somebody named Harry and I think she has kids too."

"Dad, it sounds to me like she's married, so you need to look elsewhere."

Sonny sighed and said, "Yeah, you're probably right."

After the ride back to the trail at Newfound Gap, he thanked the driver and tried to hand him some cash. The driver appreciated the offer, but assured him that the ride was free and declined the offering until Sonny insisted it was a donation.

The light cold rain continued all day. He stopped to eat his sub next to the trail instead of going four-tenths of a mile to a shelter and ended up at Tri Corner Knob Shelter after 15.7 miles. The structure had two levels of sleeping platforms and the lower one was full so he laid out his mattress and sleeping bag on the last remaining spot up top. Packs were hanging from the rafters like cured hams and someone was struggling to keep a fire going with wet wood in the stone fireplace. Many faces of the hikers had a look of desperation, which if verbalized, would say - 'I want to go home.' Sonny couldn't look them in their eyes. Instead, he pulled back the tarp that fought with the wind to cover the entrance, and searched outside for more firewood. Although the rain pounding on the metal roof drowned out much of the human nighttime noises, he did not sleep well. Twice he woke up to empty his bladder. With stealth like procedure in the dark, Sonny climbed down from his perch, went outside and then snuck back up again. The older woman next to him snored like a yodeling bullfrog all night long and he searched in vain for his earplugs.

DAY 20

The rain was still falling in the morning as he ate Pop Tarts and milk. It made no sense to put on dry socks because the trail was underwater. His shoulders ached, but he was reminded that - 'Discomfort is temporary, but quitting is forever.' He had read that there were fifteen hundred black bears in the Smoky Mountains and hoped not to meet any of them as he sloshed down the path. The rained stopped and he recorded a male, black, white and orange towhee singing from a bush next to the trail. Before he stopped at Crosby Knob Shelter, he took pictures of several wildflowers including Dutchman's breeches and a small white and pink orchid. After lunch, the rain came again and he hiked by many moss covered areas and waterfalls. He called ahead to a hostel and reserved a place in the bunkhouse.

Shortly after crossing the bridge over the Pigeon River, Sonny arrived at Standing Bear Farm. The hostel was his first and operated on the honor system with each hiker keeping a running tab that was paid before departure. The property consisted of several small rustic buildings on a narrow strip of flat land with a creek running through the center. Sonny secured a bunk, took a shower, bought supplies, and ate pizza and beer, all in separate buildings. The 18.1 miles for the day was mostly downhill and the wet conditions were starting to take a toll on his feet. On the bright side, he was out of the Great Smoky Mountains National Park.

DAY 21

Once again a bird awakened him, but this one was a black and white rooster that thought it owned the place. Sonny dressed and packed his gear and then went to the kitchen building that was decorated with pansies planted in old hiking boots, next to the deck railing. There he had tea and donuts and drank a can of V8 for its nutritional content. The forecast called for rain the next couple of days and when he left the hostel, Sonny missed the white blaze and walked about five minutes before he checked his Guthook app and turned around.

The first four miles were uphill, followed by a two and a half mile downhill. Then came another climb and a descent. He was beginning to notice a pattern. It rained off and on all day, but he took the time to take a picture of a three inch black centipede with pink legs. He climbed the steps made of short logs cut into the trail and made a windy and foggy video of the bald peak called Max Patch. There were areas protected with fences to safeguard the golden winged warblers that nested on the ground.

Lunch was an apple and a banana that were eaten on the go. When he had a good signal, he made reservations in two days at Elmer's Sunnybank Inn of Hot Springs, North Carolina. Sonny's shoes stayed wet all day and the last two miles were muddy, but after 15.5 miles he replaced them with his flip-flops and tented at Roaring Fork Shelter.

DAY 22

At the end of each day of hiking, he was tired and expected to sleep well, but during the previous night, another variable entered the equation. Potty Mouth showed up late with his cronies and interrupted the calm. They built a roaring fire and did not honor the code of ethics for thru-hikers. Hiker Midnight is at sunset. You don't have to go to bed at that time, but you need to be quiet for those who wish to sleep. Simply stated: Sunrise-get up, Sunset-shut up. The party lasted until midnight when the dope wore off.

At daybreak, before putting on his Darn Tough socks, Sonny wrapped tape around his two middle toes because the tops had been rubbed raw. He thought about waking up the inconsiderate people in the shelter, but he let them sleep in and walked away. The first three miles were downhill, often next to a raging stream and purple, yellow, or white violets. Rhododendron buds were swelling and the brush was just starting to leaf out. Sonny was astonished to hear juncos singing from the bushes. The black, gray, and white songbirds with pink beaks were frequent winter visitors in Ohio. Back home, the snowbirds would feed off the ground near the base of the feeders, but would never make a sound. Sonny invited them to spend the winter in his yard.

Around noon, he stopped to take a picture of garlic mustard, an invasive plant, which he tried to eradicate from his property. When he summited Bluff Mountain, the rain came again and the raincoat was put on, again. The streams he crossed, had glistening minerals in the water that looked like gold, but were probably just bits of mica. Due to lack of sleep he felt cranky, so he made a video where he complained about the noisy campers. His attitude improved when he finished the 14.7 miles at Deer Park Mountain Shelter because he was only three miles away from Hot Springs.

DAY 23

Normally, on a cool morning he had oatmeal and hot chocolate for breakfast, but he had scalded his pot while making Alfredo noodles for supper. Sonny didn't want to make the burn marks any worse, so he skipped cooking and only drank Gatorade as he walked down out of the mountains and onto the edge of the town.

Hot Springs had been a health resort since 1800 and the trail led right through the town. Sonny stopped along a stone wall and took a picture of one of the A.T. symbols emblazed in the concrete sidewalk. The grass was green, the trees had leaves, and the azaleas were displaying their purple flowers. Elmer's Sunnybank Inn, with white siding, a red metal roof, and ample porches, was the oldest house in town, and sat up a hill on a large corner lot. Sonny found the Victorian house and then crossed the street and entered the Smoky Mountain diner for a late breakfast of eggs, hash browns, ham slices, and orange juice. The meal also came with biscuits and gravy, something that he would never order, but he ate it anyhow.

Sonny climbed one of the elaborate staircases and found his room. It wasn't the haunted one and he had to share a bathroom, where he shaved, showered, and then videoed the home. Elmer had filled the place with antiques and artwork by Vincent Van Gogh. The walls were all wainscot with period looking wallpaper. There was a library and a room filled with a large selection of musical instruments that tenants were encouraged to use, but only if they played well. Many rooms had fireplaces and all had crafted trim work and floors that were made of wood and partially covered with area rugs.

Sonny scrubbed his cooking pot clean and rested on the bed while a video was uploaded and then he went across the street and bought supplies at the Dollar General. After he stowed his purchases in his room, he grabbed the dirty clothes bag and walked further into town to the Laundromat.

While his clothes were in the washing machine, he walked to the Bluff Mountain Outfitter and then to the library for their strong Wi-Fi. Later, he put the clean, but wet clothes into the bag and then found an outdoor seat at a restaurant next to Spring Creek. There he sat alone, rested, and ate a salad, burger, and beer.

Back at Elmer's, he hung his clothes on the line in the backyard and then went to his room for a nap. He was in a deep sleep when his alarm woke him up in time for supper. Eight people sat around the table and were served a vegetarian meal of soup, salad, couscous, stew, and lemon tea, while Elmer encouraged conversations.

Later, Sonny wanted to sit on the second level front porch, but it was occupied, so he stood out on the corner under the full moon to check in with his family. His mother wasn't answering, so he called August who informed him that everything was okay. "Grandma went bowling. Someone needed a substitute and she volunteered."

Apparently, her wrist was healing fast. "Nothing she does ever surprises me anymore. I really appreciate you looking after her."

"It's not a problem, Dad. She's the best neighbor I have." He paused, and then added, "I'm serious about going out there to hike with you."

"Well, Augie, I'd love that."

"So, what I was thinking is that I'd go there when you get close to McAfee Knob."

"That sounds great. I'll look forward to seeing you."

"Okay, well I'll pay close attention to your videos to keep track of your progress and I'll see you then."

"Thanks Augie, I needed that."

The call to his other son was shorter. The daughter-in-law and her youngest child were at the grocery store while Henry played outside on the swing set with the other three children. They were climbing up the slide and when they summited, each one would turn around and raise their fists over their heads pretending to be holding up trekking poles on top of Mount Katahdin. Henry was making individual videos of the epic event and promised to send them to Sonny.

Sonny looked up at the moon with misty eyes and then called his daughter. She and her husband were sitting on the deck enjoying the night sky. Peaches was growing fast, but still chewing and had to be watched constantly, lest she damage the furniture. The baby was developing and healthy; everything was good. "Dad, I think I worry too much. I wish I could be as calm and under control as you."

Sonny thought - *If she only knew I was just the opposite*, but he said, "Madison, over the years when I reached different plateaus in my life, I thought 'Now I don't have to worry anymore,' but concern and even anxiety never really go away if you are a caring person."

DAY 24

After breakfast, Sonny walked through town for the final time. Good weather was predicted for the entire week. The sky was blue and his feet were dry as he walked past the resorts with the hot springs. He crossed over the French Broad River that was high and flowing fast and then resumed climbing mountains with a backpack heavy with food. Along the way he spotted a black and white warbler and asked the feathered friend if he was going to Ohio for the Big Bird Week at Magee Marsh on Lake Erie, but the songbird just flew away. The terrain leveled out somewhat in an area called Mill Ridge. Many years ago, the fields were planted with hay and tobacco, but later the land was purchased by the U.S. Forest Service and changed into brood areas for grouse and turkey.

The next ascent took him to the Rich Mountain lookout tower. The frame was in the process of being repaired and painted, but the graffiti-covered top had dangerous spots on the floor from either rotten or missing planks. The views were worth the climb and Sonny could see for miles. Due to the lower temperature at the higher elevation, the trees were still leafless. He sat down near the base of the tower, ate a sub, and watched the videos of his grandchildren.

He resumed hiking feeling strong and content and took pictures of a pink and white fern and two contemporary granite grave markers, decorated by hikers with coins and stones. He wondered if the bodies were beneath the stones or if only their ashes were scattered there. Just before the end of the hike for the day, he fell for the second time. The gravel was loose, his feet shot out from under him and he fell on his back. The backpack took the brunt of the impact and he was not injured. Although he was startled, his biggest concern was for the snack he had placed in the rear, mesh pocket. To his relief, the bag of Fritos was unharmed. He dusted himself off, crossed Paint Creek, and after 15 miles, made camp at Allen Gap.

DAY 25

Sonny woke up on a ridge where he camped alone. During the middle of the night, he had put on his sweatshirt, peed in the bottle, and went back to sleep. All of his water bottles were empty, and he had to hike over four miles to the nearest source along the trail. He stopped to photograph a yellow lousewort and then he ate raisins and a Clif Bar for breakfast.

At Little Laurel Shelter he filtered water, made Gatorade, ate a Zero bar, and made use of the privy. He stopped at Big Firescald Knob and looked back at the observation tower he had climbed the day before. Another hiker, who was attempting to fly a kite, took his picture for him at the scenic spot. The path going down was rocky and narrow and Sonny crossed the

300-mile mark. He stopped at Jerry Cabin Shelter to eat his large meal of the day and make more water. A trail angel and hiker named Bernie, who had with him two large black Great Danes, was there and passed out Snickers and oranges to the small group sharing the picnic table. While Sonny gave the dogs a lot of attention, he ate mashed potatoes with chicken. After the trail angel left to continue his hike, the older dog snuck back for another rubdown.

The natural landscape of Bald Ridge was pleasing to the senses and Sonny savored the area. He was making good time and rewarded himself by listening to music, but the song by Five For Fighting - *Superman*, made him melancholy. While passing over Big Butt Mountain, he saw a male black-throated blue warbler and then stopped to visit the Shelton Gravesites. The two Union soldiers, who were brothers, were buried on the spot after they were shot and killed while visiting relatives. Because of his early start, Sonny covered 18.6 miles, a new record, and made camp at the Flint Mountain Shelter.

DAY 26

It was sunny and cool, another pleasant day for hiking. Sonny ate vanilla wafer cookies with hot chocolate and began the gradual descent of the first three miles. When he reached Devil Fork Gap, he climbed up and over a wooden set of steps that led into a fenced-in pasture where he saw wild turkeys on the other side of the ravine. He stopped to take a picture of a deep purple larkspur and then missed a turn of the trail. He continued on up a path that turned into a creek bed and then he checked his location on his Guthook app. After he made his way through the brush and back onto the trail, he met an ex-cop who gave him trail mix. He enjoyed some easy walking and as he looked up ahead towards another bald mountain, he was reminded that at one time, the Appalachian Mountains were more majestic than the Rockies. Many eons later, erosion smoothed out the peaks and made them much shorter and easier to walk over. To help make it up to the 5500 feet elevation of Big Bald, he put in his ear buds and listened to a variety of inspirational music from a duet of Patsy Cline and Jim Reeves singing - *I Fall To Pieces,* to Metallica - *Fade To Black.* The reward of a hostel the following day pushed him to 19.2 miles for the day where he stopped at Piped Spring.

DAY 27

The good weather continued the following morning. Sonny started his hike before seven o'clock because he wanted to complete the 16.5 miles before five o'clock when the shuttle left the hostel bound for the town of Erwin, Tennessee. The terrain for the day was a sequence of short climbs followed by long descents like giant stairsteps. At midmorning, he took a break near a small waterfall, ate a raisin and walnut energy bar, and took pictures of white azaleas and odd looking purple flowers that resembled airplanes with propellers. A woman hiker came by and told him that those flowers were called gaywings.

By the afternoon, he looked down from 1000 feet above the Nolichucky River and saw bridges, kayakers navigating the rapids, and the town in the background. He knew he was close and his anticipation grew. Once the epitome of hostels along the Appalachian Trail, its quality took a dive after the owner's death. Uncle Johnny's was now under better management, the washing machine was up and running, and the septic system had been upgraded. Upon arrival, he had just enough time to check in at the general store, toss his dirty clothes into the washer, and shower in the bathhouse. He skipped shaving in favor of a beard. His room for the night was the last one available. Cabin H was poorly lit with wood paneled walls and no amenities save a small microwave oven. The best feature was the green stained glass box turtle lamp. Although the bed was worn, anything seemed luxurious after camping in the woods. He hung his wet, clean clothes around the room to dry and then headed to the free shuttle where he waited at a picnic table in front of the bunkhouse.

A small group of young co-eds were selecting bicycles to ride to a restaurant in town. Sonny recognized a couple of them and when Fiona saw him she smiled and walked over to talk. She decided to skip the bike ride and go to supper with Sonny. When she informed Athena of her change of plans, Sonny noticed that one of the men looked brokenhearted. The white van dropped them off at a Mexican restaurant where Sonny ordered burritos, tacos, chips with salsa, and a large margarita. Fiona had the same, except half the portion. She sighed and told him, " I don't get it. I work as hard as all of the guys, but I haven't experienced the weight loss like they have."

Sonny assured her, "Shelly, I mean Fiona, I can see that you are already in better shape now than when we first met. You are definitely burning off the fat, but now you are getting muscles. That's a good thing. Muscle weighs more than fat. You look good and I'll bet you feel stronger too."

"I do."

"Good. Don't worry about weight. You're making good progress, so just go by how you feel and keep going."

Sonny felt like he was lecturing his kids so he changed subjects. "So Fiona, who was that one guy back there by the bikes?"

"Which one?"

"The one who was bestowing you with adoration."

"Oh him. That's Tom. They were calling him Tommy Boy because he's overweight. He's kind of like the way I was, he didn't believe he could make it the whole way, so I named him Doubting Thomas."

"He looked pretty disappointed when you didn't go biking with him."

Fiona smiled and said, "I think he likes me."

DAY 28

During the night, Sonny slept like a sixty year old log and stayed in bed as long as possible. There were no birds to awaken him and he dreamed of home until his phone alarm went off. He dressed, walked to the front of the hostel, and took a seat in the van. At nine o'clock the half-full shuttle left for town. The occupants were dropped off at McDonalds for one hour. Sonny ate a large salad for breakfast and then strolled to Walgreens to add to his supplies. Before taking the ride back to the hostel, he re-entered the fast food place and ordered a hot fudge sundae. When he arrived back at his cabin, he quickly packed his gear, anxious to get back on the trail. Before he left, he stopped by to say goodbye to Fiona. She told him that her tramily (trail family) was taking a zero (day off from hiking) and that she had heard of trail magic just across the river at the Chestoa parking area.

The Nolichucky River was running high and fast. For his morning video, Sonny recorded the flowing river as he crossed the bridge and shared the two stories told by the van driver. The toothbrush was invented in Erwin, Tennessee. If it had been invented anywhere else, it would have been called the teethbrush. The second tale was about an elephant.

According to legend, a circus came to town in 1916. An angry elephant killed the trainer and then went on a tirade that injured people in the crowd. The citizens of Erwin put the elephant on trial, found it guilty of murder, and sentenced it to death by hanging. During the first attempt, the chain broke. The second try was successful, but the elephant struggled in vain for an hour before it succumbed to death. A large hole was dug and the body was buried and forgotten. In 1960, a construction crew inadvertently unearthed the remains. They thought the bones were from a mastodon and called in an anthropologist to authenticate the find, but then someone remembered the story about the circus elephant.

When he reached the parking area there was no sign of any trail magic. A kayaker said that he was staying at the hostel and only crossed the bridge for the free bacon and eggs. Sonny asked him, "Who was the trail angel?"

"Well, she just left about five minutes ago. I don't remember the woman's name, but I can tell you she was nice looking and friendly."

"Was her name Lily?"

"That's it. Do you know her?"

"She gave me a ride back to the trail a few weeks ago, but then she was needed back home in Indiana. I would have liked to have seen her again."

"You may be in luck. I didn't remember her name, but I do recall that she's planning more trail magic."

Sonny stood in the parking area under the beating rays of the sun and applied sunscreen to his face and neck and thought about the woman. If only he had known about the trail magic sooner. He would have skipped the fast food and gotten to see Lily again.

He started walking along the river and fought the urge to take a dip to cool off. For the first time on the trail, he saw poison ivy and was glad he wore long pants. When he came to the railroad, he looked both ways, crossed, and began a climb that grew steeper as he went along. The warmer weather had brought out the reptiles. He saw a santeetlah dusky salamander, five lined skinks, and a non-poisonous snake. A white trillium with purple veins caught his attention. He sweated more than usual and on his way up to the bald named Beauty Spot, he listened to Johnny and June Cash perform the duet - *If I Were A Carpenter* and then Mercy Me sang - *I Can Only Imagine.*

Sonny savored the view and the cool breeze near the top and then the ascent continued. The surrounding ground was covered in trout lilies and he hoped it was a good omen. Just before he reached his campsite he stopped and took pictures of an evergreen that was decorated like a Christmas tree. He ended his day at 13.1 miles (a half marathon) on Unaka Mountain in a dense spruce forest. The trees reminded him of a section at Oak Openings Preserve in Ohio where he had trained and he felt homesick. He was not hungry, but he drank water, Gatorade, and pop before going to bed in the warm tent.

DAY 29

The birds woke Sonny and he felt refreshed after sleeping on his mattress and a thick layer of evergreen needles. The air was cool when he began to walk and without wind, the only sound came from the busy birds. The weather report promised good conditions for the next two days, followed by several days of rain. Before lunch, he came to a deserted orchard of standard sized fruit trees. Sonny watched golden finches fly into the apple trees that were full of small white blossoms.

By the middle of the afternoon, he had stopped at Little Rock Knob and videoed the views of the roads and farms below. At one point he noticed he was walking south and had to check his Guthook app to be sure he was still northbound on the trail. He took a picture of a chimney remnant from a former cabin and then stopped for the day with 20.9 miles by Roan High Knob Shelter at an elevation of 6193 feet. A few miles back, he had been invited to camp with a couple from South Africa named Antelope and Lioness, but he graciously declined the offer saying, "Thanks, but I have to keep going. I made a promise."

Inside his tent, he laid in his sleeping bag that night, content that he had kept his promise to his grandfather.

The man who had given his life to save his own son had died decades ago, but it was his birthday and Sonny wanted to honor his memory by setting a new mileage record. He fell asleep recalling a childhood memory of sitting in his father's lap watching his grandfather's favorite video. The recording was from the 1972 Olympics in Munich, Germany, where American Frank Shorter entered the stadium alone for the last two laps of the marathon. When he crossed the finish line, the athlete had raised his arms over his head in victory. Sonny dreamed of striking the same pose on top of Mount Katahdin.

DAY 30

In the middle of the night, he awoke to the screams of two young guys who were evicted from the shelter by a mouse. In the morning he began his hike with sore muscles and again, missed a turn on the trail and ended up on a road. He backtracked and continued on. Along the way, a trail angel had left a six-pack of beer on the ground near the parking lot at Carvers Gap. There were only two left in the pack and Sonny grabbed one to drink with his lunch. Less than a mile later he stood on top of Round Bald. While resting, he videoed the views and had his picture taken on his phone.

Close to lunchtime, he followed a blue blaze (side trail) towards the Red Barn, an old structure where many hikers liked to camp. In a cold creek before the famous landmark, he hid his can of beer. The ample structure was recently renovated and had multiple string, pack hangers with shields attached to discourage mice. When he was finished documenting the barn, he retrieved his cold beer from the stream, sat down and drank it with a bag of corn chips. He soaked his feet in the stream and then taped his damaged toes.

He later listened to CSNY sing, *Ohio,* on the way up Big Hump Mountain. Somewhere on the way down he crossed into Tennessee, leaving North Carolina for good. His day ended after 15.8 miles at Apple House Tentsite. All the other hikers had opted to stay in the nearby town of Roan Mountain. When he attempted to make his beef stew meal, he had a problem that he quickly solved. The butane lighter was empty, but sparks from the striker still ignited the canister of stove fuel. After supper, he washed up in the stream and slept in the lone tent.

DAY 31

Sonny skipped breakfast at camp and hiked a half-mile to US-19 where he tried to hitchhike to Roan Mountain. Ten minutes later, he didn't get a ride into town, but arrived at Mountain Harbour Hostel, an unpainted barn-like building. He entered and sat down to a meal of pancakes, scrambled eggs, and fruit. There was also a vendor in a trailer on the property who made him a sandwich for later.

Back on the trail, he took pictures of many wild flowers including lavender orchids, sweet pepperbush, golden ragwort, moss phlox, and American cancer-root.

Afterwards, while he was alone, he thought about how much his wife would have liked the flowers. The grief overwhelmed him and he dropped his trekking poles, fell to his knees, and sobbed.

When he got control of his emotions, he stood up and looked around, embarrassed. No one had seen him, but still he chastised himself for being weak. The rain was holding off, but he felt he needed a break and booked a room in Elizabethton. As he strolled by Isaacs Cemetery, he read the names on the gravestones and thought that he was only passing through life like all of those buried people had. His thoughts went back to all of the blossoms he had discovered and he realized that he had not seen any honey bees on them. He felt that was symbolic of missed opportunities that all creatures endured.

When he stepped out on Campbell Hollow Road, he was experiencing a new low. But, then he saw the handwritten sign announcing trail magic. His eyes followed the arrow to a green SUV parked next to a party tent fifty yards away. A familiar female voice shouted at him. "Are you a thru-hiker?"

Sonny yelled back, "Yes I am."

He walked towards her listening to the grill sizzle and inhaling the scents of the feast. There were two hikers sitting on chairs stuffing their faces, but Sonny concentrated on the trail angel with the green eyes. He said to her, "Hello, Lily."

She said, "Hi, Sonny, you're making good progress."

"Thanks. Sorry I missed the breakfast in Erwin."

He was rescued from a moment of awkward silence when she said, "Have a seat by these other two and I'll serve you. I have tacos and burgers and pop or beer. What would you like?"

"I'll have a couple of tacos and a beer, please."

She handed him a plate with three tacos and wild rice. At first, he hungrily gulped the food, but then slowed down. He hoped the other two hikers would finish their food and leave. When they accepted seconds, he did the same. Eventually the pair hit the trail and Sonny eyed the ring on her hand and began with a mundane question. "So how is life down on the farm?"

She sat down on a chair next to his. "Very busy. Always so much to do there."

Lily couldn't remember the exact content of her first conversation with Sonny. Normally, when talking about her life, she had always given the same information to the hikers. She would tell them about Harry, her boar used for breeding the local sows and her two kids, which were rambunctious young goats. She assumed those were the same details she had shared with Sonny, but she was wrong. He still thought that 'Harry and the kids' were members of her family.

Sonny asked, "How's Harry doing?"

"Well, he's getting older, but he still can perform."

"Oh?"

"Yeah, he knows why I keep him around. But to be honest, there are times when he's so enthusiastic that I have to call over Alice, the neighbor woman, to help handle him."

"Oh my."

"Thank goodness she's younger than me."

He stared at her with his mouth agape as Lily further explained. "Sometimes I just have to close my eyes until it's over."

Sonny didn't want to hear any more details of the presumed threesome and changed the subject.

"Tell me about the kids."

"Oh, they are both very cute, but they get into a lot of trouble. Sometimes I don't know if they are worth the problems they cause me. I should probably just get rid of them."

With a concerned look, Sonny asked, "How would you do that?"

Lily shrugged, "I don't know. I suppose I could sell the pair or barter them for some tools or something."

Sonny nervously laughed as his opinion of her took a nosedive. She seemed to be enjoying his company and complimented him on his handsome beard, but Sonny became withdrawn, thanked her, and got up to leave. Lily looked disappointed, but said she understood that thru-hikers were always concerned about making miles. Before he left, she told him that she was planning the next trail magic lunch in three days at Low Gap. He forced a smile, nodded, and walked away.

Sonny felt overly stuffed like on Thanksgiving, except he couldn't lounge and watch football - he had to climb the next mountain. He heard splashing water and took a side trail to video the tall, cascading Jones Falls. A short time later, he noticed sticks laid out on the trail signifying the 400-mile mark. He walked along the Elk River and spoke with a trout fisherman who was having fun catching small rainbows. There were yellow daffodils scattered about that suggested the area was once a homestead.

He stopped after 16.5 miles and stealth camped (secretly camped) beside a stream. Because he had eaten so much during the day, he saved his sandwich for the following day and had potato chips, pop, and an apple instead. Try as he might, while he lay in his sleeping bag, he could not get Lily off his mind. He did not know if he was attracted to the woman despite her presumed current life style or because of it.

DAY 32

Twice, he was awakened in the middle of the night by sounds. For a while he was serenaded by barred owls and then later, an hour-long thunderstorm swept through. He began his day with sore ankles and discovered a tree used as a territory marker for a black bear. The bear had reached as high as he could and scratched the trunk to emphasize his stature and then deposited fur and fecal matter on the ground, beneath the marks, for good measure. A while later, Sonny took another picture of a tree with a moose head growing out from it.

After 8.8 miles, he came to Dennis Cove Road. He put away his trekking poles and displayed his pink sign as he walked toward the town. Soon, a Jeep pulled over and Sonny crowded into the vehicle with three young hikers and a driver named Bob Peoples. The three young hikers had volunteered to perform trail maintenance the previous day. Bob, who was a thin man with a white mustache and eyebrows to match, was well known. He was a trail angel, hostel owner, and Appalachian Trail Hall of Famer. He took the hikers to McDonalds for breakfast where Sonny bought him a cup of coffee. Next, they were driven to a grocery store for resupplies. The three hikers were heading back to the hostel, but Sonny was dropped off at his hotel in Elizabethton. There he washed his clothes and showered before walking to a nearby restaurant for a Reuben and a beer. He continued to upload videos and before climbing into the bed for the night, stepped outside to call family members.

Sonny called his mom first. They updated each other on the latest events and he marveled at her positive attitude. Even when she suffered, she never complained. Before he hung up he told her, "You're my hero, Mom."

"Thanks. You're a warrior just like your…"

Sonny interrupted her with, "Just like my father. I know."

She corrected him. "I was going to say, just like your grandfather, Brian Toth."

Sonny ended the call feeling humbled. He called Henry next. Henry was out playing in the yard with the kids again and they took turns talking to him and showing off. Near the end of the call, Sonny heard the oldest child announce that he was going to climb mountains like Grandpa someday. A younger sibling said that she was going to do that also, but then added, "When I'm bigger."

Sonny's heart melted and after the call ended, he felt homesick and had to take some deep breaths before calling August. It dawned on him that he was doing the thru-hike for more than just himself. His oldest son said to him, "Are you okay Dad, you sound a little worn out?"

"I think I'm okay. Some days are rougher than others, but I'm sleeping in a bed tonight, so I should be well-rested and ready to go back to the trail tomorrow."

"Well good, I have my gear ready and I've been training so I can keep up with you when you get to Virginia."

"Thanks Augie, I'm looking forward to it."

Finally, he called his daughter. "Hello, Madison, it's good to hear your voice."

"Hi Dad, you sound sad. Is everything alright?"

"Yeah… just missing the family, I guess."

"We miss you too, but we'll see you and celebrate your accomplishment when you finish it. Keep going Dad. You're doing well."

"Sure."

"Hey, have you met anyone that meets your standards yet?"

"I've met a lot of nice people."

"Anyone special?"

"No, well… I ran into Lily, the trail angel again."

"You mean, that married woman?"

"I'm pretty sure she is, but I'm not certain."

"Dad, why don't you just ask her?"

"Maybe I will if I see her again. But, maybe I won't.
As a parent, she seems kind of irresponsible and as a
spouse… she's a little freaky."

 "A little freaky, *how*?"

"Maybe a lot freaky. I don't have all the facts, but I
know she lives on a farm with someone named Harry
and she has a friend named Alice and…"

Just then the smoke detector went off near
Madison's kitchen due to a smoldering pot. "Sorry Dad,
I have to go. Supper is burning, but I want to hear your
story the next time we talk."

DAY 33

Sonny awoke the next morning feeling refreshed,
but 8.5 miles away from where he had left the trail. He
began walking, held out his sign, and counted the
vehicles that passed him by. Number sixty-seven was a
compact car driven by a young man named Jamie who

gave him a ride to Route 321. A short while later another young guy who went by the trail name of Sartech took him to Dennis Cove Road. That left only 3.8 miles. He walked up the winding road with tight curves for 2.5 miles and just when he reached the highpoint and began the descent, a white truck pulled over. The passenger asked him if he wanted a ride and Sonny gladly hopped in the back of the truck. After he was taken back to the trail, Sonny grabbed his pack and walked to the front of the truck to thank the driver. The driver was Bob Peoples. Sonny wished he had stayed at Bob's hostel near the trail since the return trip from Elizabethton had taken him an hour and a half and wasted much energy.

Laurel Falls was a wide and loud cascading falls that Sonny videoed. The trail after the vertical white water show, led him on a rocky ledge between a rock face and the stream. He stopped to take a picture of a wildflower called woodland stonecrop. The blooms were white and had pointy petals that were speckled with brown pollen anthers. He noticed the leaves on the trees were filling out more as he went up and over a steep mountain. As the temperature rose and he began to sweat, he found himself on the sandy shore of Watauga Lake. At a picnic table with three other hikers, he ate lunch. He did not wait an hour after the meal to go for a swim, but instead stripped down to his swimming trunks (black underwear) and waded into the cold lake.

Clean and refreshed, he continued the hike on the trail along the lake. There were many piles of bear scat on the path and the nearest shelter had been shutdown due to aggressive bear activity in the area. Sonny photographed yellow azaleas and lady slippers and then strode across the dam that created the lake. Near the end of the day he arrived at the Vandeventer Shelter, but it was packed, so he moved on another half mile. He set up his tent on a spot barely large enough, between the trail, and an edge of a cliff covered with poison ivy.

DAY 34

For breakfast, Sonny ate a bag of tangerines. It was his youngest grandchild's birthday and he would miss the celebration. He wouldn't be in any of the pictures of the party, but someday, he would have a story to tell his grandson. He planned to go 22.1 miles and loaded up with water because messages on his app from other hikers informed him that the next water opportunity up ahead was down a long steep side trail. He walked through a pasture of clover, grass, and alfalfa. The dairy cows glanced his way, but continued to graze. The gates, which were designed to keep the cattle in, but allow the passage of humans, were either wooden steps that went up and over the fence or tight angled walkways. Sonny enjoyed the lush pasture and blue sky with puffy white clouds as he listened to the Beatles play, *In My Life*. He thought about what he would do in Damascus, Virginia, the next day and realized he was hungry.

Before he stopped for lunch, he remembered that Lily was providing a trail magic meal at Low Gap. He checked the time and the mileage and realized that he probably would just miss the opportunity. He rationalized that *that* might be best since she wasn't the woman he first imagined her to be. But, after a long drink of water, he picked up the pace and pushed on to Low Gap. He arrived sweaty and tired just in time to see the green Chevy Equinox pulling out of the parking area. He sighed and then looked down at a full bag of trash left from the thru-hikers who were just fed lunch. He was tempted to examine its contents to see what he had missed, but was distracted by an SUV that came to a stop near him. The driver stepped out and Sonny said to her, "Did you forget something?"

Lily said, "Yes, and I'm glad I did. Would you like lunch now?"

"I sure would. I'm starving."

He helped her set up a long folding table and chairs and then unloaded the cooking gear and half-full coolers of food and drinks. She sat him down and handed him a beer as she warmed up a bowl of chili and buttered slices of French bread. "I wasn't sure I'd see you today, Sonny."

In between gulps he said, "The trip to Elizabethton put me behind schedule."

After the meal, he helped her clean up and they put everything back into her vehicle except the two chairs. She told him to sit down and handed him another beer. She sat down close to him and opened a beer for herself. With a serious look she said, "Sonny, when you left the last time, I had a feeling that you were upset with me about something."

Sonny wanted to be careful how he responded. "Lily, I have enjoyed your company and your food, but how you live your life is none of my business."

Lily was puzzled. "What do you mean?"

Sonny was feeling the effects of the beer and became more outspoken. "Look. You can raise your kids anyway you see fit. And whatever you and your husband have going on with the neighbor lady, doesn't concern me."

Lily was flabbergasted. "*What* husband?"

Sonny threw up his arms and said, "Harry... You know, the guy you share with Alice."

Lily looked stunned and Sonny continued, "And where are the kids when this tryst is going on?"

Lily's expression turned from scorn to ludicrous and she began giggling at Sonny. He watched as every attempt by her to talk brought on another wave of laughter. Finally, she caught her breath and said, "Harry is a hog," and her laughing continued.

Sonny felt insulted and got up to leave, but Lily stood up and blocked his escape and stopped giggling long enough to explain. "Harry really is a hog. He weighs 700 pounds, is all black except for a white band around his upper body between and on both front legs. And my kids are baby goats. Have you never been on a farm before?"

Sonny's face flushed. "I feel like such a fool."

"Don't. I think you're adorable," and then she kissed him on the forehead.

They both sat down and chuckled about the misunderstanding. He told her a lot about his family, but the thought of sharing details about the loss of his wife was too painful, so he avoided the topic completely. She told him that after high school, her intentions were to attend Bowling Green State University on a partial scholarship, but she got married to a local farmer instead. They never had any children and he died of cancer two years before she thru-hiked the Appalachian Trail. The farm was struggling to make a profit, but she worked hard to save it. Sonny asked her what she had planned to major in if she had gone to BGSU. "I wanted to study Theater and Film and follow in the footsteps of my namesake. *Lillian Gish* was an ancestor from my father's side who became an actress during the silent movie era. Her career lasted for decades and during that time, she was a major contributor to many humanity causes. There *was* a theater on campus named in her honor."

"What do you mean, *was*?"

"Early in her career, Lillian had a role in a racist movie called *The Birth of a Nation*. Despite all the good she had done in her life, the people in charge at the university bowed to the pressure of a popular movement and removed her name. There wasn't any discussion outside the group; they just went with what was politically correct. Needless to say, I don't donate to them anymore."

She noticed him looking at her ring and said, "I only wear it to fend off the undesirables."

"Well, apparently it works, because it's holding me at bay."

She took the ring off and put it in her front pants pocket. As Sonny thought about what to say next, he noticed the sun was getting low in the west. He looked at the time on his phone and stood up. After thanking her for the food, he put on his pack and turned to go.

Lily said, "I'm needed on the farm again. I won't be back for a while."

Sonny turned around and said, "Lily, can I have your phone number?"

"You silly man, I thought you'd never ask."

Sonny reached his campsite at Abingdon Gap Shelter just before sunset, but he didn't remember much of the five miles he walked to get there. He fell asleep with a sensation he hadn't had for a while - the feeling of hope.

DAY 35

During the night, he heard the calls of whippoorwills. After breakfast, Sonny walked with a bounce in his step. The terrain was user friendly and he was only ten miles away from Damascus, Virginia (Trail Town). Along the way he left Tennessee for good. Three states down, eleven to go.

Around noon, the trail led him out of the mountains and through the town. He had his picture taken beneath the wooden welcome sign by another hiker and then he returned the favor. The sign, which was created by the local Boy Scout Troop #23, stood at the end of the empty vendor area. In a week and a half, the green space would be full of vendors displaying their hiking wares and services during the annual Trail Days Festival. He went by a small park with a black locomotive and a red caboose displayed on short sections of rails. Once on Route 58, he crossed over Beaver Dam Creek where the sidewalk was made from bricks and A.T. symbols. He walked a few blocks until he saw a spinning barber pole. The barber was a little reluctant to cut his hair, but Sonny assured him that he had washed it recently in a local creek.

Afterwards, he retraced his steps and after buying supplies from an outfitter and a grocery store, he stopped for a late lunch at Old Mill Inn. The hostess sat him outside on the deck next to the spot where Laurel Creek ran into Beaver Creek. There, he wolfed down a rib eye steak, fresh mixed vegetables, and a draft beer. He took a similar meal to go and finished walking through the town to a point where the Virginia Creeper Trail merged with the A.T. Before he headed up the next mountain, he stopped at an ice cream parlor, and had a bowl of vanilla and cherry.

Towards the end of the day while he listened to music, Sonny stubbed his toe just as Led Zeppelin began to play an appropriate song - *How Many More Times*. He stopped after 17 miles and stealth camped next to Laurel Creek. When he was finished with his takeout meal, he stripped down to his swimming trunks and submerged himself in the cold stream.

DAY 36

Sonny slept well, but the birds held rehearsals at six o'clock and he began his day walking past a growth of red columbines. He made a reservation in Troutdale at the Sufi Lodge that was 45 miles away. The breeze picked up and clouds moved in and provided a short period of rain during the day that kept him cool during the four-mile climb over the 5000 feet elevation of

Whitetop Mountain. He listened to a song by Five For Fighting - *100 Years.*

Late in the afternoon, he videoed the forest floor that looked like snow on green carpet, but was really fringed phacelia with an occasional purple violet. He saw several tents at a parking area and one of the hikers told him that they had stopped for the night there because of bear activity at the next shelter. Sonny thanked the man for the info, but kept going. He soon ran into a ridge-runner named Okay from Medina, Ohio, who was coming from that shelter and confirmed the news of the bears. The young man suggested camping a mile away from the shelter. Sonny took his advice and put up his tent near a meadow surrounded by piles of pony manure.

DAY 37

Visibility was poor when Sonny crawled out of his tent. A cloud of fog blocked the views and covered everything with dew. He ate breakfast, packed away his wet tent, and headed north. He passed by Mount Rogers, the highest point in Virginia and stopped to talk with those that had stayed at Thomas Knob Shelter. They told him that the bears came by an hour before sunrise and enjoyed a successful raid. Sonny noticed that all of the trees in the area were short. The low hanging food bags never had a chance.

After a drop in elevation, he passed through the rock tunnel known as Fatman Squeeze. He did not have to remove his pack to negotiate the passageway, but then he missed a turn and ended up in an area with several mares with matching colored foals. He did not see any stallions and the young ones were either nursing or lying down near their mothers. Sonny knew enough not to get too close. Back on the trail, he entered Grayson Highlands State Park and stopped to read the sign. It warned him not to feed the horses and to avoid their bites and kicks. He passed the 500-mile mark and then met Fabio.

   The rock star of the wild pony world was brown with a bleach-blond tail and a matching long flowing mane that would make many women envious. From the looks of the markings on the nearby foals, it was very apparent that Fabio was quite popular with the mares.

   Sonny followed a half-mile side trail to a parking lot at Massie Gap. There he called the number for the Grayson Highlands General Store and requested a ride. Thirty minutes later a worn pick-up truck arrived and took Sonny to the store where he purchased supplies and had lunch. The hamburger, hotdog, french fries, and orange cream soda were followed by a banana split with walnuts. Then he used the restroom, got a ham sandwich to go, and weighed himself on their vintage Toledo scale. He had already lost fifteen pounds, which averaged about a half pound per day of hiking. He was given a ride back and finished the day with 16.1 miles. Again, he stealth camped and continued the daily ritual of massaging his leg muscles with a roller stick. The apparatus encouraged the departure of lactic acid and sped the healing process.

DAY 38

A jubilant towhee brought Sonny out of the dream world and back into the reality of thru-hiking the A.T. He began the 6.1-mile descent to Dickey Gap and made arrangements with the owner of the lodge, for a pick-up in less than three hours. It was another cool, but sunny day of maneuvering up and down hills. The decor of the outdoors continued to be brown leaf-covered soil with gray rocks and tree roots. An occasional wooden bridge covered fast flowing streams and waterfalls along a tunnel of flowerless rhododendrons. Just before Sonny reached the road, he slipped on a tilted rock while crossing a stream and fell for the third time. His arm was scraped and his clothes were muddy, but his ride was there waiting for him.

James and Susan had converted a medical center into the restful oasis. Sonny was given room number two where he soaked his feet in warm water with Epsom salt. He talked with a couple that was staying there to recuperate from a hip injury. They were vloggers who had a large following and they gave Sonny advice on how to improve his videos. The meals were healthy and filling and the following day, after an omelet on unleavened bread, he was given a ride back to the trail. Before his departure, the convalescing couple had wished him well and he felt sorry for them and hoped that an injury never took him off the trail.

DAY 39

Sonny made use of the continued good weather and enjoyed another stroll through a pasture of grazing young steer where he took a picture of a blooming lily of the valley. One of the black angus heifers stood in his way on the path, but Sonny held his course and didn't break stride. The young bovine stood its ground as long as it dared and then sauntered away. Had it been a bull, Sonny knew that his route would have been different. After 20.9 miles, he stopped at Chatfield Shelter to camp and make water. For some reason the privy was locked, so he made other arrangements in the woods.

DAY 40

The monotony of the Green Tunnel (miles of trails enclosed in rhododendron, mountain laurel, and other bushes) was broken late in the morning, when Sonny reached the Lindamood School. Built in 1894 and utilized until 1937, it was now an unpainted wooden lap sided museum. The one-room building was painted white on the inside, had a blackboard at the far end, and a small wood burning stove in the center. Upon entering, Sonny saw four coolers filled with pop, snacks, fruit, and hygiene products. He made use of the trail magic donated by the West End United Methodist Church of Wytheville and gave thanks in his video. He sat at one of the desks and ate an apple and then

departed, crossed a railroad track, and walked to
Atkins.

Sonny stopped for lunch at the Barn Restaurant
where he had a large glass of milk with a small BLT
sandwich. He got a small ham sandwich to go and
walked down the road under I-80 until the trail turned
back up into the hills. The temperature and humidity
increased and he visited the Davis Cemetery for its
history and shade. There was a sweet scent in the air
from the blooming bushes. Sonny missed a turn as he
walked through a pasture and felt certain that the cows
under the shade trees were snickering and taunting
him. He ignored them and took a picture of a
buttercup. A wooden sign nailed to a tree indicated
that he was a quarter of the way finished with his
adventure. He walked on boards between the fenced-in
pasture and the stream, but did not make water due to
the higher possibility of bacterial contamination. After
20.4 miles he put his tent up next to Lynne Camp Creek
and ate his small ham sandwich. He could not stand the
thought of climbing into his sleeping bag while covered
with sticky sweat. So, before entering his tent, he
bathed in the stream and listened to the distant
thunder.

DAY 41

The rained had ceased by morning, but the day of
bad luck had only begun. Early in the morning hike, as
Sonny passed under a low branch, he simultaneously
bent over and stepped on a bent stick that flew up and

hit him in an eye. The highlight of the day was the discovery of a lone orange azalea bush in full bloom.

He made a four-mile climb to Chestnut Knob Shelter. The rare four-sided building was created from large rocks and afforded great views of the valleys below. It also had a privy that Sonny wished to utilize. He did not want his skin to touch the seat, but he did not want to waste toilet paper building a nest either. So, he held onto the doorjambs and leaned back towards the pit. After the paper work was turned in and his hands were sanitized, Sonny got back on the trail. He noticed a sharp pain just above his left knee. Hiking the next ten miles did not alleviate the discomfort, so when the day ended at Hunters Camp Creek, he took some Tylenol. He rinsed his body in the creek and limped to the tent.   As the rain fell, he told himself that he would feel better in the morning.

DAY 42

It rained during the night and was overcast the next day. The precipitation had improved the intensity of the waterfalls, but made the trail wet and muddy. Tylenol relieved the pain, but not the swelling. Most hikers seem to prefer vitamin I (Ibuprofen), but Sonny's doctor had advised him to stick with Tylenol because it might harm the liver, but not the kidneys like Ibuprofen did. The doctor had further explained that the liver could heal itself, but the kidneys would not. After hearing the opinion of the medical man, Sonny's final decision was based on something a fellow electrician had once told him. "The liver is a bad organ and must be punished."

Along the way Sonny had run into a vlogger who was hiking to Damascus to sell his miniature Mount Katahdin signs at the upcoming Trail Days festival. He reported to Sonny that the Brushy Outpost had the best vanilla shakes around. Sonny was planning to stop there for lunch and now he drooled in anticipation. In a few hours, he reached the eatery on Route 52 where he ordered a cheeseburger, fries, a vanilla shake, and a burger to go. The cook informed him that they were out of ice cream, but the delivery truck was on its way. Sonny drank a coke with his food and was able to text his daughter. His iPhone's memory was almost full of pictures and videos and he needed more storage. Madison researched memory sticks and gave him suggestions. As he left the restaurant, he watched a Hershey ice cream delivery truck arrive, but he kept walking down Route 612. After crossing over I-77, he called to order a memory stick. He explained to the woman that he was hiking the A.T. and that he lived in Ohio, but needed the item shipped to a hostel in Pearisburg, Virginia.

Once back in the hills, his knee continued to throb. It hurt to bend it, so he didn't lift his foot as high as he normally would and this caused his toe to catch on a rock and made him yelp, every so often. He stopped to take a picture of a blooming pink azalea and stones on the ground signifying the 600-mile mark. Where he intended to camp was full and a young hiker offered to make room, but Sonny stubbornly declined the offer and limped on. He was pleased with the 22 miles he had covered, but was still 34 miles from Pearisburg. The site he defaulted to was covered in sticks and stones. He cleared them away, made camp, took more Tylenol, and went to sleep.

DAY 43

It poured for most of the night and continued to rain the next day. His feet were wet and his eye was red with blood from where the stick had struck him. To compliment the aching left knee, his right calf cramped. He figured he was low on potassium and needed bananas and oranges to go along with his Gatorade. He hoped that the half-mile walk down Route 606 to Trent's Grocery would be worth it. After he crossed another wooden suspension bridge, blooming mountain laurel bushes surrounded him. He stretched his calf and took pictures of the copious cup-shaped white flowers with pink tips.

At Trent's Grocery, he ate an early lunch, drank Gatorade and a can of V8 juice. He bought a few snacks and intended to get the last overripe banana that was sitting on the counter. The banana was in such sad shape that the clerk did not charge him for it. He took it outside and choked it down. Although he was concerned about time, miles, and his injury, he decided to take a side trail to view Dismal Falls. There he sat down to rest his legs and video the site. At the end of the day, the tops of his toes were raw and bleeding.

DAY 44

Before his walk the following morning, Sonny taped his toes. He called the hostel and made reservations for a second night. After seven weeks of continuous hiking, he was going to take a zero. He crossed through a burned out area and was told by a hiker that the fire was started when a tree had fallen on a power line and that rain had later extinguished it. The rain continued to come down making the trail slippery with mud that aggravated his knee. When Sonny reached Route 634, he called Angel's Rest Hiker Haven (ARHH). A young guy named Papa Smurf and his wife Commando ran the hostel. While waiting to be picked-up, Sonny stood back off the road, up on steps made of slick four by fours embedded into the hillside. From there, he fell for the fourth time, which did not help the condition of his knee.

In the suite of the double wide, he lay on the bed and iced the knee. For supper, he hobbled to a Mexican restaurant and had tortillas filled with beef cubes and mushrooms, beans and rice, salsa and chips, and a jumbo margarita. He stopped in at Dairy Queen for a banana split dessert and then staggered back to his bed.

DAY 45

The following day, he moved into the bunkhouse that resembled a garage. Next to the bunkhouse was a newer building that contained three separate restrooms with showers. Unlike a couple of the hostels that he had stayed at, ARHH was very clean. Down the hill on the backside of those facilities was a kitchen and laundry room. Sonny filled quart bags with water and put them in the freezer for later and then shuffled to the Food Lion grocery store and carried back meals from the deli for the day and supplies for resuming the hike. The memory stick had not arrived yet and when he called to inquire about its whereabouts, he was told it was not shipped yet because the shipping address did not match the billing address. He again explained to the woman that he was not at home and asked her to ship it ahead to the Four Pines Hostel instead. The rain fell again while Sonny and a bag of ice lay on a lower bunk for most of the day. He self-diagnosed and concluded that he had bursitis and then opened another bottle of Tylenol. At the end of the day, feeling over optimistic, he signed up for a ride back to the trail in the morning.

DAY 46

Bending his knee was still a problem for Sonny. He savored the flat walkway across the New River on the Senator Shumate Bridge, but felt like a nursing home resident with trekking poles in lieu of a walker. The downhills especially put the hurt to him and after nine miles, he stopped near Rice Field Shelter. He did not walk the extra distance to the shelter, but opted to sit on a rock near the ledge and eat lunch while watching the cloud shadows move across the landscape below.

There were homemade signs on display from a group of concerned citizens protesting a pipeline being built in the area. Sonny saw areas that were cordoned off by law officials and police escorts for the pipeline workers and the construction company equipment. He stopped at an azalea bush to video a red-spotted admiral swallowtail butterfly. After making water, he resumed walking and almost stepped on a copperhead snake. He tried to move the snake with a trekking pole, but the coldblooded amphibian did not wish to leave its sunny location. Sonny warned a hiker that was coming up behind him and then moved on. He videoed a four-foot shiny black, eastern rat snake as it slithered through a patch of wild geraniums. The day ended after only 15.3 miles.

DAY 47

Sonny wrapped his swollen knee with an Ace bandage, struggled to get dressed and took more painkillers. Surprisingly, the milk that he had put into a quart sized plastic bag, was not sour and had not been churned into butter. He poured some of the white liquid into the two small boxes of cereal. After eating those, he had a banana and a cherry pie with the rest of the milk.

The day started off nice, but soon the temperature rose into the eighties and the persistent flies annoyed him. The highlight of the day was seeing a flowering yellow azalea. It rained and he labored over the rocky path. Three times he had to squat to get under fallen trees. Doing so made the injury burn and he halted the death march after 13.6 miles. As he ate his mashed potatoes and chicken chunks meal, Sonny brooded over one fact - he was slowing down.

DAY 48

Getting dressed and breaking camp in the morning was a major effort. He could barely bend his left knee without experiencing a surge of pain. To get out of his sleeping bag, he had to unzip it the entire way and use his good leg to kick out of it. He put on his left pant leg first, keeping the leg straight. The wet sock was difficult to put on his left foot in that position, and the shoe was almost impossible. Once he got moving, tiny gnats took their turn at him. He stopped and videoed an eastern five-lined skink basking on a log and noticed that he had enough bars on his phone to make a call. The Four Pines Hostel, which did not take reservations, was on a first come, first served basis and had plenty of room available.

Normally, he would have enjoyed the hike along the fast flowing streams lined with flowered mountain laurel, but the discomfort took all of the fun out of it. He grew envious of the numerous hikers that passed him on the trail all day. Late in the afternoon as he passed by Laurel Creek Shelter, the occupants called out to him and invited him to stay with them. He intended to make some water at the creek just passed the shelter, soak his knee there for a while, and then join the others. But, while filtering the water, a huge downpour doused him and he abandoned all plans and stubbornly kept walking north. After a half-mile climb up a hill, the rain ceased and he called it a day with only 8.5 miles to show for it. He went to bed early and hoped for a miracle cure.

DAY 49

At sunrise the torment was still with him. By comparison, his right knee looked like a baseball, but his left was the size of a softball. The pain was at a new high and he did not want to bend the joint. Sonny made it out of the sleeping bag and struggled to put on his pants. He pulled on his wet, right sock and shoe and slowly tied the laces, putting off the inevitable left shoe as long as possible. As he sat on the floor of the tent, he looked at all of gear that had to be rolled up and placed in the backpack. The everyday chores seemed insurmountable. He checked for a signal on his phone and saw that he had no bars and couldn't call for help. The realization that he was going to have to save himself took him to a new low. His shoulders sagged as he remembered how it felt to put on his left shoe the day before and his eyes filled with tears for he knew this time would be worse. Somehow he managed to get the sock on and then prepared his mind for what came next. By the time he was finished double-knotting the lace, he had broken out into a cold sweat. He ate a walnut and raisin Clif Bar and began walking stiff-legged.

From his AWOL Guide he knew that the next crossroad led to a town. His plan was to hobble out to the road, hitchhike to a hotel, and ice the knee for as long as it took to heal. Fellow hikers that had stayed at the shelter wished him well and then rapidly walked away. Sonny's envy was only bested by his discomfort. It took almost two hours to cover the 1.9 miles to Route 42, but as Sonny approached the road he saw an SUV parked there. The vehicle from ARHH was letting two German slack packers (hikers who only carry a light daypack and don't camp) out to continue their hike. Sonny pleaded for the driver to wait. The driver, Papa Smurf, recognized him and for the normal fee, gave Sonny a ride to the medical clinic in Pearisburg.

After the knee was examined and x-rayed, Sonny called for a ride back to the hostel. A young employee picked him up, stopped at Wendy's drive thru window and took him back to the bunkhouse. Along the way the doctor called and said that he had expected to see bone chips in the x-ray, but that was not the case. Sonny was relieved with the news and agreed to stop hiking for a week or two. He was issued the lower bunk nearest the door and given an icepack.

While he sat on the bed eating his burger and fries, he thought about going home to convalesce. A younger guy name Pierogi who was on leave from Louisiana State University, told him that he was leaving the trail and going home to help a friend. He also told Sonny that the hostel van was going to take him and another guy to Blacksburg and there they could buy a bus pass that would take them to Roanoke. He was going to the greyhound bus terminal, but the other guy was going to the airport. The wheels began to turn in Sonny's head and he asked, "Is there room in that van for me?"

Pierogi said, "I think so, but you better hurry, we're leaving in ten minutes."

Sonny had not showered since his first stay at the hostel, but there was no time for that. He limped over to the doublewide to speak with Commando. She said there was room for him in the van, so he paid his bill and grabbed his gear. He left the things in the hostel storage room that he felt were not allowed in the airports and gingerly climbed into the van.

When they arrived at the bus stop on the Virginia Tech campus, Sonny handed some cash to Pierogi who went inside the student union and bought him a ticket and some snacks. During the bus ride, Pierogi encouraged Sonny to purchase a two-way ticket since it was much cheaper. Sonny agreed and used his phone to do just that, with a return trip in ten days. Aboard the airplanes, he was seated on the right side next to the aisle, which allowed him to straighten out his left leg. He stood up every time anyone would pass by, to protect his knee from further irritation. During a stopover in Charlotte, he called August and asked him to pick him up at the Toledo Airport just after midnight.

Sonny entered his house and it seemed so big to him. He left his pack on the kitchen floor, limped to the bathroom and took a shower. There was a lone beer in the refrigerator that he opened and carried to his recliner along with a bag of ice.

DAY 50

It was close to noon when he woke up and took some Tylenol. A thawed out porterhouse steak was placed on the grill while he cooked some frozen sweet corn from his garden. After cleaning the dishes, he called LaRoe's Restaurant in Grand Rapids and secured a large table on the deck for later in the week. He then called his family members to tell them that he was home to heal up and invited all to dinner. Sonny knew that Henry wouldn't be there and he wondered how long it would be before he saw him again. Madison and Peaches planned a visit and August said that he would pick up Grandma and bring her over some evening too. Sonny sat back in the recliner and iced his knee. He reviewed all of the events from the past seven weeks and ended up thinking only of Lily. But any feeling of contentment was soon replaced by guilt as his eyes locked onto the smiling face of his wife's framed photograph on the mantle.

DAYS 51-58

Late the next morning after a cup of Earl Grey tea, Sonny slowly rode around on his all-terrain vehicle and surveyed his twenty-acre farm. He had not planted any vegetables for the year. A good neighbor was tending the beehives and chickens and harvesting any honey and eggs that were produced. August and Madison would pick the cherries and peaches from the dwarf fruit trees when ripe, but Sonny was hoping that he would be back home again in time for the apple harvest. He stopped and pulled out a clump of weeds growing next to a fence post and admired the dark Wauseon fine sandy loam soil clinging to the roots. After parking the vehicle in the century old red barn, he went back inside and called Lily. Ten rings later he heard her voice on a recording. He was caught off guard, but after a short stutter, composed himself and told her that he was home with an injury and would call back later. He spent the remainder of the day catching up on things on the Internet and resting under the ice bag.

During the days, he showered frequently and ate foods that he had craved while hiking the trail. There didn't seem to be any improvement of his knee at first, but having had recovered from running injuries before, he tried to be patient. After losing interest in watching TV, he would go out on the deck with a book. From there he could survey the islands of his wife's flower gardens in the yard. He noticed that they had been watered and weeded in his absence. During a visit, his mother never mentioned it, but he knew she did the work. August came over and mowed the lawn whenever he found the time. The previous year, Sonny had performed preventive maintenance on all systems in the home so that no family member was burdened with the upkeep. After a few days, the pain and swelling subsided and his knee became more flexible.

His daily calls to Lily went unanswered, but as he was leaving his home for the dinner with his family, she called. "Sonny, I'm sorry it took so long to get back with you. I've had some problems here and I'll tell you all about them, but first I want to hear about you."

Hearing her voice made him feel even better. He began by describing the incident at the Chestnut Knob Shelter and then brought her up to the present. He assured her that he would be back on the trail the following week and couldn't wait to see her again. Lily told Sonny that she missed him too and was about to expound on the recent activities on the farm until Madison called him. He said to Lily, "Oh oh, my daughter is trying to reach me. I'm supposed to meet my family at the restaurant and I'm late. Can I call you back tomorrow?"

"Of course you can. Go and be with your family. We'll talk tomorrow, Sonny."

Sonny hurried through the restaurant and out onto the deck. There was an empty chair next to his mother who sat next to Madison and her husband. August, his wife, and three children occupied the remaining chairs. They were all talking and eating appetizers until they saw Sonny. He meekly approached the large table. "Sorry, I'm late."

His mother said, "I'm sure you have a good reason."

He hesitated in order to choose the right words as everyone listened. "I was talking on the phone with a woman whom I met on the trail."

Madison chimed in. "I hope it's not that married woman."

Sonny's mom arched her eyebrows as he explained. "Lily is a widow, but she's married to the farm."

August asked, "How does that work?"

Before Sonny could respond, Madison asked, "What about Harry?"

"Who's Harry?" asked Sonny's mom.

Sonny surveyed the river beyond the canal and calmly replied, "He's a hog."

The three adults bombarded Sonny with questions until they were satisfied with the answers. Finally, when all were quiet, the middle child asked the oldest one, what was going on. The response was, "Grandpa has a girlfriend."

All of them had crème brulee for dessert and watched an eagle soar over Wolf Rapids. Sonny paid the bill, left a generous tip, and they all walked down Front Street towards their cars. As the others kept walking, Madison held her father back to talk in private. "Dad, you appear to be more upbeat."

"I didn't think it would happen for me so quickly, but my injury is heeling well."

"I'm not talking about your knee."

"Okay Madison, I can't fool you. Without your mom around, I have been pretty miserable at times."

Madison successfully fought the urge to speak and allowed her father to continue. Sonny smiled and added, "When I'm with Lily, I feel alive again. But, I keep waiting for the other shoe to drop. Maybe our relationship will grow, or it could just fizzle out. So, I just try to enjoy each moment but still brace myself for disappointment."

Madison subconsciously rubbed her protruding abdomen and said, "Keep trying Dad. That's all you can do. It will work out."

Each day the knee felt stronger and Sonny wanted to stray from the house and do some work outside, but he remained loyal to his friend the ice bag, faithful to the end. On Memorial Day, August hosted a family get together at the homestead in McKee's Corners. The younger members of the family insisted that Sonny and his mother just relax outside while the food was prepared and served. Grandma would not hear of it, but Sonny knew they were right. While he reclined on the chaise lounge icing his knee, he observed how radiant his pregnant daughter looked. There was a glow about her that reminded him of his wife. The growing and energetic dog, Peaches, entertained the two oldest grandchildren. August's youngest child came over to keep Sonny company and involved him in a game of catch until the children were called inside to wash their hands. As he sat alone in the yard, Sonny watched an automobile pull down the driveway and park close to the house. A spry elderly man exited the car and walked towards him. Even at a distance and without the white collar, Sonny would have recognized his Uncle Samuel. The retired priest lived and worked at the Haskins House (A work-for-stay safe haven for first-time pregnant, single women) and was an inspiration to all who knew him. "Sonny, I wanted to see you before you went back to the trail."

"Thanks for coming by, but maybe I'll forget about my hike and just stay here with the family."

"We both know you can't do that. You need to finish your adventure."

Sonny only nodded and Samuel continued, "Do you remember our conversation from about a year ago?"

"Yes, you told me that doing penance was good, but I needed to live a full life also."

"That's a pretty good paraphrase of what I said. I think by walking the Appalachian Trail you'll accomplish both goals. I watch your YouTube videos so

I've seen the beautiful mountains and waterfalls; but, tell me Sonny, what's it really like out there?"

"The scenery is better in person. Most of the people you meet are terrific. I get a lot of satisfaction from the mileage that I achieve everyday."

"But?"

"But, it is difficult. I miss my family. There are moments of elation and then sometimes, depression."

"The pain of losing a loved one never goes away, but you can learn to live with it. You have to if you want to remain healthy. Look at your mother. She's lost a lot of family and friends, but she keeps pushing forward."

"She's one of my inspirations, and so are you."

"Thanks Sonny. I pray for you everyday. Hey, I almost forgot this." He pulled out of his pocket a stone and handed it to Sonny.

Sonny said, "What's this for?"

"It's a family heirloom that my mother had saved. This was the stone that your father hurled through a window at the present day Haskins House. I want you to carry it with you and deposit it on the summit of Mount Katahdin."

Sonny held the stone in his hand and he knew his knee was healed.

DAY 59

After a hardy breakfast of fresh, over easy brown eggs laid by his own chickens, hash browns, and orange juice, Sonny sat on his deck next to his backpack. Before showering and packing, he had toured the farm one last time. The scale in the bathroom indicated that he had regained five pounds during his stay at home. Madison would be arriving soon to take him back to the Toledo Express airport. August was joining him for a week of hiking in Virginia. Sonny felt a mixture of excitement and anxiety like he had at the starting line of a race back in his youth. His knee felt fine, but he knew it wouldn't take much to reinjure it. Some scar tissue was like worn Velcro that could be pulled apart with little force. He would have to be careful.

Sonny liked the airport because it was small, not crowded, and very convenient. Madison pulled right up next to the terminal door. But before they exited her Jeep she said, "Keep me posted on current events, Dad."

"Don't you watch my videos?"

"You know what I mean."

"Okay, Madison, if Lily proposes, you'll be the first to know."

"Now you're being silly."

"I've been accused of that a lot, lately."

The trip back was just the reverse of the one from the trail, ten days prior. Besides being accompanied by his son, the only differences were that Sonny had showered and was now pain free. From Toledo, they landed in Charlotte for a short layover. After a lunch of airport food, the pair flew to Roanoke where they caught the bus back to Blacksburg. While they waited for a shuttle back to ARHH, they strolled around the Virginia Tech campus. Back at the hostel, they were dropped off at the bunkhouse where Sonny spent most of the time resting and icing his knee for good measure. August made friends with the thru-hikers and listened to their stories about the trail. For supper, Sonny walked with August to the Mexican restaurant and then they stopped at the Food Lion for some last minute items. On impulse, Sonny bought a lottery ticket.

DAY 60

Surprisingly, he slept well and after a quick breakfast, the father and son boarded the earliest shuttle back to the trail. They were dropped off at Route 42 where Sonny had left the trail eleven days earlier.

The Keffer Oak had stood for over three hundred years at its location next to the trail. Hikers looked like dwarfs standing in front of the trunk with its thick limbs reaching out like the arms of a giant octopus. Pictures were taken and August sent them home to his family. From there, they climbed up a ridge and enjoyed three miles of smooth hiking. Over the years, people had cleared all of the rocks away from the trail and stacked them in heaps on that section. The trail was greener now with all of the trees and bushes leafed out. Sonny was upbeat, but cautious. As he walked, with August a few strides behind, he felt grateful for having a second chance of completing the journey. He wondered if there would be other second chances for him during the remainder of his life. The father and son were quiet for most of the walk and just relished the sights and sounds of the trail. They came to a sign hung on a tree indicating that they stood at the Eastern Continental Divide. Rain that fell there either flowed downhill to the Gulf of Mexico or found its way to the Atlantic Ocean. They took pictures of themselves at the sign and videoed a resident eastern fence lizard. After crossing the Craig Creek Bridge, they stopped for a lunch of potato soup.

At the end of the day, they had covered 12.3 miles and made camp near a small creek. Down in the creek bed, they watched the sunset together. August soaked his bare feet while Sonny knelt in the cold water. As the daylight waned, August said goodnight and went to his tent. Sonny stayed in the therapy pool a little longer and thought about the day. The elastic knee support that he wore during the day helped him physically, but emotionally, having family along was even better.

DAY 61

At seventeen minutes past four o'clock, a whippoorwill decided it was time for the campers to get up. Sonny used his collapsible bottle to urinate in and then fell back asleep. The regular birds began to chirp at five thirty-two, but again the hikers remained in their tents. They stayed put as the rain came down hard around them for an hour and then emerged for breakfast at seven o'clock. August ate Pop Tarts while his father enjoyed handfuls of peanut M&Ms and dried apricots, supplemented with vitamins and Tylenol.

The day began with a humid hike up Brush Mountain. They stopped to visit a monument near the crash site of Audie Murphy. The American legend, who was a highly decorated WWII soldier, became an actor, songwriter, and rancher, after the war. The gray granite marker was adorned with flags, cairns (stacks of rocks), coins, and other mementos. As they continued on, Sonny took pictures of a pink with yellow center swamp rose, a woodland sunflower, a galax, and an eastern newt in its orange stage. They arrived at a jagged outcrop of rocks on Cove Mountain called Ledges (More than one state had sites known as Ledges) as the rain began again, but it stopped when they reached the 700-mile mark. A few miles later, they viewed a monolith known as the Dragon's Tooth. The first mile of the climb down from the site was treacherous. The ledges of the descent were not only steep, but also slippery from the recent rains. The hikers were compensated for the dangers by the frequent mazes of mountain laurel bushes. As the trail leveled out, Sonny relaxed and listened to *Save My Live* by Head East.

After 14.3 miles, they reached Route 624 and walked down it a short distance until they turned into a gravel driveway before four mature pine trees. Like a small farm, the property had several outbuildings and chickens. After passing by the owner's brick ranch home, the Toths made their way to the three-bay brick garage. Four other hikers were leaving when they arrived, so both Sonny and August were able to secure a bottom bunk for the night. The large building contained all the amenities of a good hostel including a wood-burning stove. Sonny dropped enough cash in the donation box to cover his and his son's one-night stay.

While August showered, Sonny asked Joe, the proprietor, if his memory stick had arrived. Joe instructed him to go up to the house, enter the back porch and search through the pile of packages there. He also told Sonny that the keys were in the Suburban and that he should drive it to a popular all-you-can-eat restaurant before it closed. Sonny found his package among the others and then took a quick shower. When he and his son reached the vehicle, a petite young woman hiker was waiting for them. "I'm going with you," she said.

August opened the passenger door for her, but she gave him a dirty look and climbed in the back seat instead. She wore a baseball cap on backwards over her closely cropped hair and had not showered yet. August said, "This is my dad, Sonny, and you can call me, Augie. What's your name?"

She proudly stated, "I'm called Cilantro."

Sonny asked, "How'd you get that name?"

"Well, some people like me and some people don't."

They all laughed and felt more at ease with one another during the drive to the crowded Home Place restaurant. The large white-sided farmhouse had a red metal roof with matching shutters. Its two-sided, pillared front porch had several wooden benches, a white rocking chair, and a porch swing. The hikers thought the property resembled a historical park more than an eatery, until they went inside. There they were seated at one of the numerous tables and stopped talking once the food arrived. Four kinds of meat were served with a selection of vegetables. Although Sonny ate the most, August and Cilantro were close behind. Halfway through the meal, August went to the restroom and Sonny told Cilantro about his injury ordeal. She suggested that, because he came back, he should be named after that mythical bird that rose from the ashes. He told her that he would have to think about it. Sonny and Cilantro got a container of cherry cobbler a la mode for the ride back to Four Pines Hostel, but

August was too full, so he got to drive. Along the way they made a stop at a carryout and purchased supplies and two six-packs of beer.

Upon their return, Cilantro took a shower, August called home and Sonny transferred pictures and videos from his phone to the memory stick. The three of them then joined other hikers outside where they sat in chairs and drank the beer. Cilantro's dog, Charlie, a neutered wirehaired fox terrier, was introduced to the Toths. He had spent the last two hours playing Frisbee with several hikers and was now slightly sedate. Sonny was the first to say goodnight. But for a short while, he stayed outside and made a wrap-up video for the day and then headed to his bunk where he uploaded a video to his YouTube channel. Each time during the night, whenever he got up to pee, he shared an additional video with his subscribers. After thinking about it for several hours he decided to accept the trail name suggested by Cilantro. Sonny was now Phoenix.

DAY 62

For breakfast the father and son ate bowls of cereal, washed the dishes, and then said goodbye to the others. Sonny's knee was a little sore from the climb down the Dragon's Tooth, but the day was sunny and the clouds were attractive, individual puffs. The terrain alternated between steams and waterfalls in the woods and pastureland with evidence of cows. As the morning trail warmed up, August would pull away from his father during the climbs, but would wait at the top until

Sonny caught up. The climb to McAfee Knob was steep, but well worth the effort. Many day hikers had started from the parking lot below and sweated along with them to the top. McAfee Knob was the most photographed location on the Appalachian Trail. The views were outstanding and hikers took turns taking pictures of each other out on the protruding ledge. Some people were known to sit with their legs dangling over or perform handstands near the edge. Sonny and August were more practical. They carefully shuffled out and looked down upon the tops of the trees below and savored the view of the valleys and distant mountain peaks. They videoed the numerous tadpoles swimming in the rock puddles near their feet and added water to them from their bottles.

    The hike down from the popular landmark was more interesting than the ascent. The trail wound through a labyrinth of boulders and tunnels of blooming mountain laurel. They stopped to watch two dung beetles struggle to roll their ball up a hill. Each time the insects almost made it to the top, they lost control and had to start over again. Although they were tempted to help, the hikers did not interfere with nature - this time. The walk along Tinker Cliffs continued to provide good views. As they skirted the edge, they swallowed the last of their water and took a picture of a white bergamot.

    After 16.5 miles, they made camp by a small stream near Lamberts Meadow Shelter, where they replenished their water bottles and themselves with water. Plastic bottles of cherry Pepsi were laid in the bottom of the waterway to chill. Handfuls of almonds were munched on while their dehydrated meals were cooked. The end of the day found the two sitting in the cold water discussing their lives back home in Ohio. That night, rain began at nine o'clock and was followed by heavy winds that dried their tents.

DAY 63

After a quick breakfast they set off looking forward to a lunch in Daleville and whatever interesting things the trail might provide. The weather was good again and neither hiker suffered from blisters. When they reached a natural rock monolith, they could hear the activity of the town below. At Hay Rock, Sonny took a picture of a yellow mushroom while his more adventurous son climbed the landmark for a better view of Carvins Cove Reservoir. As they approached Route 220, the brim of Sonny's hat blocked the view of a wooden sign that had been bolted a little too low on a tree next to the trail. The result was a bump and a gouge at the top of his forehead. After verbalizing his resentment, he took the time to write a request on the back of the sign to have it raised to a safer level.

It was a short walk to the Three Li'l Pigs Barbeque. They were offered outdoor seating, but chose to eat inside the air-conditioned building. The table where they were seated flaunted a brass plaque celebrating a visit by a former U.S. president. After a healthy salad, they ate BBQ sandwiches and drank beer. Thru-hikers were given free banana pudding for dessert. August told the waitress that only his Dad was attempting a thru-hike, but she delivered two servings anyhow. Sonny took advantage of the strong Wi-Fi and uploaded videos. To insure adequate time to finish the process, he ordered more beer. Afterwards, they went back out into the warm sunlight and visited an outfitter and a Kroger supermarket in the same shopping complex.

When they had made it back to the trail, Sonny took a picture of a shasta daisy and later videoed a female box turtle. Twice along the way, they came across fallen trees. The first one, they were able to get around, but they had to go under the next one. Sonny did not risk re-injuring his knee; instead he handed his pack to August and crawled under the obstacle. They finished the day during a light rain after 17.9 miles. The hill leading to the stream was too steep so they washed up at the campsite with their drinking water. Before going to bed, Sonny took some Tylenol and August asked him, "Hey, where's this trail magic I always heard about?"

"I don't always know. Sometimes it is advertised, but other times I just walk down to a parking lot and there it is."

"Well, I sure would like to experience some."

"Me too," Sonny said as he crawled into his tent and he wondered why his attempts to contact Lily went unanswered.

DAY 64

The sun shone through the tent and the birds sang in earnest, but Sonny remained in his sleeping bag, reminiscing and feeling sad. August ate his breakfast and then began packing away his gear. Finally he said to his father, "Are you okay, Dad?"

"Yeah, I was just planning the day. I'll be out in a few minutes."

The Blue Ridge Parkway existed where the A.T. used to be. The present day hiking trail snaked back and forth across the road. The views were spectacular for people in the vehicles zooming past, but they lasted much longer for the pedestrians. They stopped at Montvale Overlook and sat down at a picnic table in the shade for a lunch with a view. The submarine sandwiches and cherry Cokes that were purchased the day before were warm, but still tasted pretty good. August shared a video that Henry had just sent him. Using Sonny's routine, style, and mannerisms, the youngest son, his wife and their four children made a spoof of Sonny's typical daily videos. August and he both had a good laugh, but afterwards, Sonny missed the family even more.

The trail provided many examples of Virginia's wildflowers. Sonny photographed eastern smooth beardtongue, Virginia spiderwort, and grazing doe. Later while admiring the Peaks of Otter they saw zebra swallowtail and fritillary butterflies. After a good day of 19.7 miles, they camped near Jennings Creek. They were too late for a shuttle that would have taken them into the park where ice cream and burgers were served. Instead, they swam in a deep spot in the cold creek near the Route 614 Bridge with the locals and then dined on dehydrated lasagna.

DAY 65

It was another sunny day. After a breakfast of bananas, the father and son continued north through the green tunnel of rhododendron bushes, still in bloom. They both knew it would be their last full day together and they savored the time. At one point August jokingly said, "Dad, I thought this was going to be tough."

Sonny took a moment to consider how to respond. "Augie, the weather has been great and beautiful Virginia makes up about a quarter of the length of the Appalachian Trail, but there are states up ahead that are going to be more difficult for me. Still, the hardest part of doing this thru-hike is being away from the family. So, it means a lot to me that you are here."

At Cornelius Creek Shelter, they made water, ate lunch, and used the privy. As they continued the hike, August seemed unusually quiet, so Sonny put in ear buds and listened to his music. During a steep climb, Sonny asked August if he had ever heard the song, *Wagon Wheel*. "Sure, that's a Hootie song, isn't it?"

"Well, he sang it, but Bob Dylan originally wrote it. Years later, a guy named Ketch Secor added to it. My favorite rendition is by Old Crow Medicine Show."

Sonny unplugged his ear buds and shared the song. Afterwards, August said, "I like that version better. It has more of a bluegrass sound and it helped me up that hill, too."

In the middle of the afternoon, they arrived at another landmark. The Guillotine was like other narrow rock passageways, but it had a small boulder wedged between the top edges of the two rock walls that hikers have to pass under. After taking a photo of a white bowman's root, Sonny resumed listening to his Spotify collection. *Green Grass And High Tides* by the Outlaws helped get him over the last hill of the day, but he didn't share it with August. They stopped after 20.9 miles at Marble Spring. The campsite was crowded with a Girl Scout Troop. After supper Sonny and his son washed up in a creek down below the tents. They wore earplugs in anticipation of a noisy night.

DAY 66

Surprisingly, the scouts were mostly quiet during the night. In the morning, Sonny commended their leaders who thought the girls were really tired from hiking and nervous about nighttime animals. The Toths ate handfuls of dried apricots and talked about what a good week it had been. The seven and a half miles to Route 50, which would lead them to Glasgow, was mostly downhill and laced with blooming mountain laurel bushes. Along the way, August spoke about his plans for the rest of the summer and Sonny added red raspberry slime mold to his pictures of fungi. As they walked the mile along the James River, it reminded them of the Maumee River back home. The current was slow and the water was murky. The walking bridge across the waterway was long and straight. A railroad bridge was nearby, but unoccupied. Sonny asked August if he was going to jump off the bridge when they reached the midpoint. "I will if you will." They both kept walking.

It didn't take long to receive a ride offer. A man named Tom, drove them the six miles into town and dropped them off by a dinosaur. The brontosaurus replica was one of many fiberglass creations of local artist, Mark Cline. In 2003 he placed the prehistoric collection all around town as an April's Fool prank. A man and wife couple from Ireland, with the trail name Lemon and Lime, took pictures of Sonny and August in front of the town mascot. The Irish thru-hikers directed them across a mowed field between businesses, to the town's shelter house. The town now operated the facility, which was originally a Boy Scout project. It had a shower with hot water, a portajohn, and trash and recycling bins on site. Hikers, who milled around the smoldering fire pit, occupied the shelter. One of them was giving another a tattoo on his shoulder. The Toths both made use of the privy and shower and then went to lunch.

They left their packs outside and sat at a booth inside the Italian restaurant. August had the special of the day, but Sonny ordered fish and chips, a hotdog and a double cheeseburger to go. Sonny finished off a sundae for dessert, while August made a call for a shuttle to Roanoke. Afterwards, they went to the small grocery store across the street where Sonny bought supplies and then they stood outside next to Dino. When the ride to the airport showed up, Sonny offered a fist bump, but August pushed it away and hugged him instead. "I think you're going to make it, Dad."

"Right, just fourteen hundred more miles to go."

"I'm not talking about the hike, Dad. I'm talking about life without Mom. You're getting much stronger now."

"Yeah, I'm climbing out of the dark valley; I mean gap."

August got into the car and said, "Keep climbing those mountains. One at a time."

Sonny watched him go and then said to himself, "Okay, son." He then took out his hitchhiking sign and headed back to the trail.

A young couple named Josh and Karen, gave Sonny a ride in a small tired car named Marcel and took him back to the footbridge where he had left the trail. He took their picture on the bridge, said thanks, and headed north. The climb up was made easier by rock and log steps created by maintenance crews from the local trail club. He took pictures of bush beardtongues and yuccas. The humidity increased and when he reached the top of the next peak, the good feeling from the earlier shower had disappeared and was replaced by sticky sweat. The view of the winding James River was hazy. While walking the ridge through a glen covered in knee-high stinging nettles, he tripped on a tree root. His fifth fall came while he listened to Green Day's - *Welcome To Paradise*, which he found humorous. The highest peak of the day was at Bluff Mountain. There was an old foundation, but the tower was no longer there. He stopped after 18.2 miles and put up his tent near the Punch Bowl Shelter. After he washed up in the creek, Sonny talked with a father and son who were the lone occupants in the shelter. There was an old man camping nearby who kept to himself and a young guy who had just showed up and was setting up his tent in the waning minutes of the day.

After sunset, it didn't take long to become very dark in an area that was far away from a city. Singing eastern gray tree frogs and screech owls invaded the campsite and two people were in such awe that they chased them around with their flashlights. Sonny was entertained but did not join the nature boys. When the commotion ended, everyone fell asleep until 10:30. At that time, about ten people arrived, shining their bright headlamps on the translucent tents, making noise and talking loud, oblivious to the existing inhabitants. Around midnight, all were quiet again and Sonny fell back asleep. Periodically, despite wearing earplugs, talking or laughter woke him throughout the night.

DAY 67

When the sun rose, he ate a walnut and raisin Clif Bar and as he packed his gear, considered waking up everyone before he left the camp. Instead, he chose to walk as far away as he could from the inconsiderate people. He knew that if they cared about others, they would have used the red lights on their headlamps and been as quiet as possible at night. Sometimes the only recourse when dealing with bad neighbors was to move away from them. That was what he intended to do.

The day began with a descent and his hip still hurt from the fall. The land leveled out and after passing the 800-mile mark, he crossed over a wooden suspension bridge that bounced with every step. A flutter of summer azure butterflies on the ground caught his attention so he videoed them near a smooth phlox. Sometime during the five-mile ascent of Bald Knob, he listened to *Hang On Sloopy* by the McCoys. On the way down he heard *Moon River* by Andy Williams and as he passed through an area dominated by ferns, the rain began.

After a good soaking, he arrived at Hog Camp Gap. He felt that the 17.7 miles was enough to get away from the rambunctious mob of the previous night. So, while fighting off a swarm of gnats, he set up the tent and then headed to the spring. Three-tenths of a mile later, he filled his bottles and rinsed his body with the very cold water. The rain had ceased, but the sky was dark and he heard thunder approaching.

It was a repeat of the night before. The few campers, who fell asleep when the sun went down, were roused at 10 o'clock by the bright headlamps and noise of a group of bad hikers. An hour later, Sonny heard an angry loud voice from across the field, instructing the idiots to be quiet so that everyone could get back to sleep.

DAY 68

According to the AWOL guide, the hike for the first half of the day would be climbs and descents of five hundred feet or less. Sonny called ahead to reserve a night's stay in Waynesboro. He had three days to cover the 49 miles and the forecast predicted more rain. When he stopped for a picture of Indian cucumber root, a horsefly attempted to land on the back of his neck and take a bite of his flesh, but he thwarted the attack by donning the black veil. He spotted a scarlet tanager near a group of stacked boulders. One of the rock formations was called Spy Rock. Rhododendrons surrounded the landmark, and Sonny made a video of the area including common beargrass and a red lily on the verge of display.

As he climbed a peak named, The Priest, the skies darkened and a cold wind rudely entered the area.

Most people would stop at the Priest Shelter and confess their sins of the trail in the logbook, but Sonny was worried about being on a mountain ridge during a lightning storm. His concerns were not unfounded. Large, cold drops of rain pounded him and the gusts pushed him from side to side as he hustled along the ridge towards a lower elevation. Bolts of lightning cracked over his head followed quickly by claps of thunder that proved the close proximity of the danger. He could smell ozone and during the life-threatening situation, Sonny became more religious. He repeated all of the prayers that he had been made to memorize in his youth, kept his head low, and walked as fast as he dared. An hour later, the storm moved on to harass other hikers.

The heavy rains raised the levels of the streams and increased the intensity of the waterfalls. The constant wet feet, combined with the fine abrasives of the soil, caused much friction inside his hiking shoes, especially during the descents. He could feel the burn on the top of his toes as he crossed the suspension bridge over the Tye River. After 21.8 miles, he stopped for the day near Harpers Creek Shelter by a Boy Scout troop and much scarlet waxy cap fungi. He had almonds and water for supper, washed up in the creek, and then inspected his raw toes.

DAY 69

The first thing Sonny did in the morning was to wrap his raw toes with tape. He did not care for the dried bananas for breakfast, but he ate the whole bag because his food supply had dwindled. Right away, there was a three-mile climb up Three Ridges Mountain, followed by a rolling landscape.

While viewing Chimney Rock, he looked at the weather app and saw that another storm would hit him in the afternoon and he decided to have his large meal of the day for lunch while it was still dry out. But those plans changed when he arrived at Reeds Gap. He saw a patio tent near the road and knew there would be trail magic, but his excitement diminished a little when he did not see the green Chevy Equinox. The trail angels were Michael and two young women named Rambler and Baltimore. As Sonny relaxed in a chair, they served him beer and ice cream. He had two helpings of both entrées, gave thanks in a video, and then walked away. A half mile later, he came to Three Ridges Overlook.

The scenic roadside stop had room for several cars and a garbage can. There was a young couple struggling to take a selfie with the view in the background and Sonny offered to take their picture. Afterwards, he disposed of all the trash in his backpack and headed north, or so he thought. A half mile later, he came to a road and saw a blue patio tent that looked very familiar. He realized that he had walked in the wrong direction and had returned to the trail magic site. For a brief moment he considered having more beer and ice cream, but a sense of urgency drove him on. He fretted over the wasted time and effort, but he knew that if Lily were there, he would have stayed a long time.

In the afternoon, he put on his lightweight rain suit and endured an encore of the prior day's abuse. At the day's end, he had covered 14.9 miles and camped at Wintergreen View. The gnats were so aggressive that he only removed the veil long enough to eat his supper.

DAY 70

In the morning he retaped his toes and put on dry socks. Exiting the tent, he was greeted by fog while eating a Larabar energy bar and after packing away his wet gear, began the 12.3-mile hike to US-250. During the descent of Humpback Mountain, he snacked on Skittles because that was all he had left to eat. The rain came early, but it was warm so he made do with just a tee shirt. A long wall of stacked jagged stones accompanied the ridge trail at times. Sonny wondered about the history of the wall. Who built it? Did soldiers use it for protection during the Civil War?

The skies were overcast all day and the rain continued to soak his world. At Mill Creek, the stepping-stones used to cross were barely visible in the rising stream. He was always drawn to the old graveyards and visited the Lowe Family Cemetery, just off the trail. At the W.J. Mayo home site, he took pictures of the rock foundation and chimney. The word mayo made him think of mayonnaise and reminded him that he was very hungry and he pushed the last three and a half miles to Rockfish Gap.

Hungry, wet, and tired, he enjoyed the shuttle ride to Stanimal's 328 Hostel in Waynesboro. After securing a lower bunk on the second floor with many other thru-hikers, he washed his clothes and took a shower. Finally, he walked to a nearby restaurant and devoured a steak with a baked potato, toast, and milk. After pecan pie for dessert, he took a trip to the grocery store and then bought a ham sandwich from Subway. He made his daily end-of-the-day video outside, in back of the hostel and then began making phone calls. His mom glossed over her recent activities in favor of hearing about his. After he had brought her up to date, she said to him, "I was going through some of your father's things the other day and I found a couple of writings from your grandfather, Brian Toth."

"Letters to God?"

"No, these were short writings to his deceased wife, Linda."

"I never got to meet either one of them."

"Well, I never did either, but I thought you might be interested."

"Mom, I am interested in anything you find regarding their lives."

"Good. Should I send you a copy to your phone?"

"You know how to do that?"

"Sonny, you underestimate me."

"Sorry, Mom. I won't make that mistake, ever again."

"Yes, you will."

Sonny smiled to himself. He was always so proud of her. "Thanks Mom. I'll look forward to reading them."

His call to August was short since the two of them were together for much of the current venture. He thanked his son again for spending the time together and said he felt stronger because of it. Next, Henry talked about his latest project with his children. They had created raised beds for a variety of vegetables and designated one plot for flowers that Henry had told them was 'Grandma's Garden.' Hearing this, Sonny got choked up. Henry said, "Are you still there, Dad?"

"Yeah, I hear you."

"The gardens look good at this point, but we have such a short growing season here. I just hope it pans out so that the kids can enjoy the benefits of their hard work."

Without thinking, Sonny opened up an old wound by saying, "Maybe you should move back to Ohio, we have an adequate growing period and much better top soil too."

The call ended as Henry made an excuse about getting the younger ones ready for bed. Sonny's disposition took a backwards step, but improved when Madison answered her phone.

"Hi, Dad. What's the good news?"

"You go first."

She told him about the good doctor visits and all of the work being done by her husband and her during the nesting period. They had painted the nursery and purchased a safe crib for the newborn. "You wouldn't believe how big Peaches is now."

"Does that animal know that she is going to be upstaged, later this year?"

"I'm starting to think she does, because during the painting, she tried to sabotage the mission by knocking over the paint can onto the carpet."

"That sounds about right. By the way, what color did you paint the room?"

"Nice try, Dad. We painted it a light green. We don't want to know the gender until we get to hold the baby."

"I can't wait to hold your baby, Madison."

"Okay Dad, enough about me. Are you still seeing Lily?"

"How should I put this? I'm not seeing her like dating-seeing her, if that's what you mean. In fact, my calls to her haven't been answered lately. But, I'm sure she has her reasons. The farm occupies much of her time and energy."

"That doesn't sound very encouraging."

"I try not to get my hopes up, but the good news is, I'm going to call her next."

"Well then, good-bye Dad. I love you, too."

Sonny prepared himself for rejection by planning his return to the trail the following day. It was dark now and he looked around the yard to insure his privacy and then he called Lily. She answered after the second ring. "Sonny, I was going to call you," she said with enthusiasm and then added, "What a week it has been."

"Actually, it has been closer to two weeks, but tell me about it."

"Well let's see. I'll start with Harry. When we last spoke, the demand for Harry's services was at its peak. The local farmers had many sows in heat and they were lining them up to be bred. Unfortunately, Harry hurt his back during one rendezvous which hindered his performance."

Sonny was feeling playful and said, "Did you call for back up?"

"No, Harry wouldn't hear of it, but we came up with a solution to keep the production going."

"Who is 'we'?"

"Oh, I called Alice over. John, my neighbor from the other side, showed up too. He always shows up when Alice is here. I think something is going on there, but I can't be certain. Those two are pretty sneaky. Anyways, together we constructed a homemade back brace so that Harry could continue his duties. It took all three of us to put it on him."

"And that solved the problem. Wow! You could be an engineer."

"We farmers have to know a little bit about everything. Things are always breaking down. That being said, I don't know how I would make it without my good neighbors."

"From what I've learned about you so far, I think you'll always find a way to succeed."

"Thanks Sonny. That's nice of you to say, but I'm not so sure how much longer I can sustain my lifestyle.

Harry's injury was a small problem compared to the rest I have."

"Please explain."

"Okay, in an effort to show full disclosure, I will tell you. The farm is in debt to the local bank and I'm not sure how much longer I will own the place. Just by doing the math, I can see it's only a matter of time before there's a sheriff's sale or something."

"Oh my. What are you going to do?"

"I've talked to the creditors and I've worked from sunup to sundown in the fields. I'm exhausted and embarrassed. That is why I haven't had time to answer your calls. I'm sorry."

"Don't be. I think you'll end up on your feet no matter how this pans out. I have my own struggles. That is primarily why I am hiking the trail - to help work out my issues. Maybe I'll be able to show full disclosure someday too."

"I've decided to resume the trail angel circuit. There's no more I can do here now. The crops will either be good or they won't. It's up to the weather now."

"It's in God's hands now?"

"You might say that. Either way, I need a break, so I'm going back to the trail. I'll see you soon."

DAY 71

In the morning, he had a bowl of cereal and fruit in the kitchen of the hostel with a few other hikers who were eager to get back to the trail. He put his pack in the vehicle and was shuttled back to continue on his trek. But, as the driver pulled away, Sonny realized he was missing his gray Ohio State cap. He had placed it on a peg of the bunk's bedpost, but didn't see it in the morning because Ankles, the guy on the top bunk had covered it with his jacket. A call to the hostel owner solved the problem. When the next load of hikers were dropped off, the driver handed Sonny his coveted cap and was rewarded with a nice tip.

A mile later, a kiosk at the start of the Shenandoah National Park instructed all hikers to fill out a permit and leave a copy in the box provided. The hikers were to provide exact information about how long they planned to be in the park and where they would camp every night. Sonny was vague with the details and hoped that he wouldn't be harassed about it. The document was to be displayed on the hiker's backpack, but most hikers were concerned about damage from the rain and carried the paper in a more protective place. The park was known to have many black bears and Sonny kept his eyes peeled to avoid a confrontation with one, but the trail was engulfed in a cloud and visibility was bad. There were no spectacular views to be seen and all of the grass, bushes and trees were covered in dripping dew. The condensation kept his shoes wet and played havoc with his blisters and tormented his feet until the afternoon when the sun came out. More than once he was able to get close to a feeding white-tailed doe. He assumed there were fawns nearby, lying in the grass that the mothers were guarding.

After 20.7 miles, he stopped at Blackrock Hut (In SNP the shelters were called huts). The ground was rocky and the thin layer of topsoil was not adequate to sustain his tent stakes, so he used rocks to support them. He ate half of his ham sandwich along with an equal proportion of a bottle of Coke and then went to bed. The campsite around the shelter soon became very dark as only places away from the cities can and all was quiet. But then, a loud whippoorwill started its relentless chant and Sonny recorded the noise. One young guy, who declared that this was the third night in a row that the birds kept him awake, left the safety of his sleeping bag and began an assault on the birds. He flung rocks and F-bombs in their direction until they retreated. Sonny thought the antics of the madman were humorous, but deleted the foul language from his dark videos.

DAY 72

He taped his raw feet and finished the sandwich and cola for breakfast and started back on the trail that was beginning to dry off. The weather for the week was sunny and the land for the next several hundred miles was beginning to smooth out. Sonny anticipated increasing his mileage, which gave him a good feeling like putting money in the bank. At one point he crossed a field of sharp gray rocks that covered the side of a mountain and he was grateful for those who had cleared a path through the jagged terrain. The trail followed alongside the Skyline Drive and offered panoramic views and camp stores, some with eateries.

After about eight miles, he stopped at Lost Mountain Wayside and purchased supplies, including Moleskin to cover his blisters. The aroma of food had lured him to take a half-mile side trail to the grill where he ordered a BLT, hotdog, garden salad, blackberry shake, and a chicken breast sandwich for later. He considered having a root beer float before he left, but didn't want to overdo it. The meal had made him thirsty and he swallowed much of his water supply. A quarter mile side trail took him to a ranger station where he filled his bottles. On the way back, he took a picture of a morning cloak butterfly flaunting itself on a plant.

The final tune of the day was *Highway Song* by Blackfoot and he stopped after 21.5 miles at Hightop Hut. After brushing his teeth, he used the privy and then rinsed his body with water from the spring. Next, he hung his food bag near several others, from one of the arms mounted high on a metal post. In his tent, he cut pieces of the Moleskin tape and applied them to the tops of his raw toes and on the bottom of both feet in the forefront, just behind his middle toes. He fell asleep with the knowledge that he had passed the 900-mile mark and although he continued to lose weight, he still felt strong.

DAY 73

For breakfast, he added water to a package of granola cereal that contained almonds, dried blueberries, and powdered milk. While eating the mixture with his folding spoon, he searched for and found the source of the knocking sound that he had heard throughout the night. The wind was causing two trees to thump against one another producing the percussion. He discovered that the insides of the SNP privies were painted white, but all other aspects were the same as any other outhouse. Someone had recently written in the shelter's logbook about seeing a sleuth (family of bears) in the area. Sonny remained vigilant on the cool morning and his mood was sanguine until he fell for the sixth time. One moment he was marveling at the audacity of a mole that had dug tunnels in the shallow soil of the mountain ridge, the next, he slipped on a muddy patch and fell off to the side of the trail. A quick assessment proved that he was uninjured, and he stood up and walked on, refusing to wipe the dirt from his pants.

He stopped at South River Picnic Area and ate the chicken sandwich, pecans, and a bottle of root beer. There was no water at the site, but he later filled his bottles at Pocosin Cabin Spring. The PVC pipe for the water source had been broken off and was resting below the spring. While retrieving the plastic tube, Sonny's hand touched stinging nettles, but he quickly applied some jewelweed sap and the pain was averted. He reinserted the pipe between the rocks and was rewarded with a steady flow. He then took nearby rocks and placed them below the small spring to be used as stepping-stones for future hikers.

Later that afternoon, he spoke with a southbound section hiker from Columbus, Ohio. Sonny told the young man that he ran a marathon in that city twice, a few decades earlier. The hiker stated that he was a marathoner too, and soon after he left, Sonny spotted another southbound creature. This one had no legs and gave a warning shake of its tail. The timber rattlesnake was dark, but Sonny could see the pattern on its back and the red tongue that tasted the air as it slithered by, hunting chipmunks. Sonny quickly called back the section hiker, to see the two-foot reptile and then made a video of the thick snake.

Someone had painted small smooth rocks with bright colors and designs and then distributed them along the trail in various locations. Sonny took a picture of one that was pink with the Appalachian Trail symbol on it. Near the end of the day, as Sonny was walking by the cemetery on Tanners Ridge Road, he was passed by a young thru-hiker who said his name was Viper. Less than an hour later, while approaching Big Meadows Campground, Sonny saw his first black bear. It was fifty yards away on the left side. The male was alone and primarily interested in eating grubs from a rotten log. Sonny took out his phone to video the animal and continued walking. When he got within ten feet, the beast looked up, leaped at and bounced off a nearby tree trunk and then slowly walked away. Sonny breathed a sigh of relief and noticed that Viper had stopped up ahead and was gazing to his right. When Sonny caught up with him, Viper said that four bears had just crossed in front of him and were still close by. Viper appeared to be really relaxed and said that he was going on a side trail to a nearby scenic overlook where he intended to smoke a joint, as potheads often did at such locations. Sonny only spotted two of the bears and he anxiously turned down an invitation to join Viper and then walked on, hoping to reach the campground soon. He passed the lodge and as the trail leading to Big Meadows Campground appeared ahead, Sonny froze in his tracks.

Most male black bears ignored the hikers or ran away from them. They were mainly interested in food at that time of the year. Females, on the other hand, were concerned with protecting their young and would attack a man if he got too close. This one had a single cub tagging along behind her. She stopped and assessed Sonny with her dark eyes. He held his breath and didn't move. The curious cub kept looking over at him and Sonny feared that it might run towards him and set off its mother's primal instincts. He nervously whistled The Ohio State fight song as they kept moving past and when Sonny felt at ease, he walked to the ranger's station.

Campsite #11 had a picnic table, a brown metal bear box, and a fire ring that he did not use. He set up his tent near families with RVs, ate at the table, and then locked his food bag in the box. He was tired after the 20.4 miles of the day, but didn't mind the short walk to the shower room. There, he brushed his teeth, used the toilet, and inserted several quarters into the timer in the stall for a five minute hot shower. He basked in the warmth of his sleeping bag, listening to the voices of excited children around a campfire. He thought about the rattlesnake and the five black bears and then fell asleep wondering what tomorrow would bring.

DAY 74

It was another cool and clear morning and the current conditions were optimal for hiking. The weather was perfect, the terrain was not as difficult as it had been or was eventually going to be, and eateries were easily accessible. Sonny was getting spoiled. But then he came to another mountainside that was jammed full of rocks as far as he could see up and down the slanted land. There were no trees, no plants, and no clear path. He could see where the trail picked up again at the far side of the rockslide and had no other choice but to climb though the mess. During the crossing, he almost fell and tried not to think of the consequences of that scenario.

Around noon, the trail led him alongside a U-shaped horse stable where the well-groomed animals swished their tails. The wooden stable, which housed and fed the four-legged occupants, was painted dark brown like most park buildings. Sonny knew that its matching human counterpart was very near and his stomach growled in anticipation. He left his pack outside and was seated at a table inside the restaurant at the Skyland Resort where he took part in the sin of gluttony and then purchased additional snacks for later.

The sightings of wild flowers had diminished and he was left with only the reality of mostly rocks and green leaves. His day improved though, when he spotted a barred owl silently flying towards him. The predator that had awakened him many times at night landed on a nearby branch. Sonny activated the video camera on his phone and quietly stepped into the woods recording the raptor. He expected the mythical omen of death to fly away, but was surprised when, with only four feet separating them, the feathered animal only looked at him and blinked. He felt inspired by nature again and savored the feeling as he made his way to Little Stony Man Cliffs where he took pictures of the view and purple-flowering raspberry blossoms.

Later that day, be walked by bear #6, another male, while on a ridge. Rock Spring hut was already full of hikers when he passed by. Black bear #7, a male, was loitering by the privy that was close to the trail. Some of the hikers at the shelter were trying to scare away the animal by shouting, banging pots together, and hurling sticks and stones. The bear appeared to be standing on its hind legs to get a better view over the bushes. Sonny wished the residents of the shelter would hold off with the antics until after he had safely gone by.

Towards the end of the day, he met a woman and her daughter who were heading south on the trail. They informed him that they had just passed a bear on the trail. Sonny thanked them for the heads-up, but dreaded a confrontation on the very narrow ridge. When he spotted the black male, he again whistled the OSU tune and carefully made his way by the final surprise of the day.

After 19.1 miles, he erected his tent at Pass Mountain Hut, just before sunset. Strangely, he never minded when the owls interrupted his needed sleep, but fumed over inconsiderate campers. A young man and woman had placed their hammocks near his blue tent and talked about nothing for an hour once it became dark. Sonny wanted to be well rested for the next day's effort and eventually fell asleep.

DAY 75

He started hiking earlier than normal because he intended to walk to a shelter that was 23.7 miles away, a new record. After eating only a banana, he set off on a beautiful morning and was serenaded by towhees. He was jealous of the Kentucky eagles (vultures) that covered great distances with very little effort. By midmorning, he arrived at Elkwallow Wayside where he dined on two over easy eggs, hash browns with catsup, sausage, and a glass of mango juice. Still not satisfied, he drank a chocolate shake and just as he was about to leave the restaurant, he observed a display of fresh-out-of-the-oven glazed, cinnamon buns. He started back on the trail, still licking his fingers. For the second day in a row, a barred owl modeled for him as he recorded its screeching calls, perched on a low branch above the trail.

The parking lots were always busy with day hikers on the weekends. Sonny enjoyed talking with the enthusiastic outdoor types. Some of them seemed overjoyed to have the opportunity to speak with a real thru-hiker. Although his ego got a boost by such conversations, he always was gracious with sharing his experiences and encouraged them to hike their own hike someday. He would share his YouTube channel information with anyone who wished to follow his adventure. Before the sun went over the westerly mountain peaks, he reached his mileage goal and camped way down the hill from Tom Floyd Shelter.

DAY 76

As a reward for the prior day's accomplishment, Sonny slept in until seven o'clock. All of the other hikers were gone when he finally walked up the hill to the shelter. The structure was patterned after most of the other shelters, but it also had a wooded deck connected to the front, which provided a much-needed level area. Feeling anxious, like a child serving an after-school detention where everyone else had left him behind, he ate his breakfast quickly. He left his backpack on the empty picnic table and used the privy, as the feeling of abandonment grew. The blisters on the balls of his feet made it feel like he was walking on tacks. He had heard that his feet would swell during a continuous hike and he would need to wear hiking shoes that were a size larger than normal. Some people replaced their shoes every few hundred miles depending on the trail conditions. Sonny knew that between his training hikes at Oak Openings Preserve and the Appalachian Trail, his current shoes had over a thousand miles on them. His toes were feeling cramped and he planned to go to an outfitter in Front Royal and purchase a new pair, a gift to himself on Father's Day. According to his information from Guthook, the store did not open on Sunday until noon. He was less than four miles hiking and a car ride away. Along the way he made video tributes to his father and his two sons, honoring them on their holiday.

Just before VA-602, he carefully crossed a stream by walking on wet stepping-stones. A man, who went by the name Hayseed, gave him a ride all the way to the Main Street destination. Sonny had to ride in the back of the red pickup truck because the passenger side and much of the bed were full of construction materials. After thanking the driver, Sonny checked and found that the outfitter with the A.T. mural and carved standing black bear guarding the entrance was still closed. But, the business next door, with the blue and white striped canvas awning was not, so he went in and marveled at the items for sale there. The Down Home

Comfort Bakery sold him a small pecan pie, a small peach pie, a glass of milk, and a bottle of black cherry soda. He sat in the window seat to watch the activity on the street while enjoying the treats and the air conditioning. With great discipline, he vowed to save the peach pie for later.

Exactly at noon, he entered Mountain Trails Outdoor Store. A woman showed him a selection of trail runner shoes and then asked him how he liked the Merrell hiking shoes that had gotten him to that point on the trail. Sonny said that he liked them, but that the front of his feet were taking a beating. She suggested that he stick with that brand, but in a larger size. He bought a pair that were a half size larger and a set of stiff insert, replacement soles, that would protect his feet from sharp rocks. Since it was lunchtime, his next stop, which was on the other side of the bakery, was the Front Royal Brewery. There he sat at the bar eating a Reuben sandwich with a dark draft beer while watching a soccer match on the screen and conversing with the man next to him who happened to be a native Hawaiian.

After obtaining a sandwich to go, Sonny began walking down Main Street while recording the sites of the town. The downtown area contained well-maintained two or three story buildings that were landscaped and litter free. A park in the center of town showcased a gazebo on an ample surface of laid bricks. The visually attractive structure had seven white columns supporting a bell-shaped, oxidized copper roof. Adjacent to the park was a visitor center that handed out information and bags full of small useful items for the hikers. Outside, while Sonny put on his backpack, a woman named Tina asked if he needed a ride back to the trail.

Heading north again, Sonny felt like things were looking up. Getting rides to and from town was easy, he ate well, was loaded with tasty supplies, and he was wearing new shoes. He stopped under a horizontal branch of a pine tree and after tying together the laces and signing his trail name on his old pair of shoes, he tossed them into the tree. The humidity was increasing and after 13.6 miles he camped next to Manassas Gap Shelter.

DAY 77

The following day was the hottest and most humid one to date on the trail. Sonny started the day off by eating the peach pie with water and a multivitamin pill. When he had a strong enough signal, he called and made a future reservation at a hostel in downtown Harpers Ferry, West Virginia. While he carefully crossed a stream on slippery and moss covered rocks, he was aware of how much better his feet felt. He could feel a storm brewing as he trudged through the Green Tunnel of Virginia, one more day. A trail magic cooler designated for THRU-HIKERS ONLY was full of empty Gatorade bottles, snack wrappers, and other hiker garbage. He took pictures of a flowering skullcap, a white coral fungus, and a leopard frog. The continuous sounds of jets flying overhead told him that D.C. was close by. A hen turkey noisily clucked and tried to lure him away from her chicks that were frozen still in the grass next to the worn walking path. In a muddy area, he was thankful for the double boards strategically placed for the hikers. He decided to eat his large meal of the day for lunch and stopped at Rod Hollow Shelter for a chicken and rice dinner. Afterwards, he entered a section of the trail that consisted of several smaller hills, aptly named the Roller Coaster. Just before his 19.8-mile day ended, he crossed the 1,000-mile mark and then put up his tent at Sam Moore Shelter.

DAY 78

Following a light breakfast of Earl Grey tea and a Clif Bar, Sonny decided to try out his new Feet Saver insoles. It was a wise move on his part because the trail became rocky and the hard plastic inserts with the flexible front, protected his feet from the sharp hazards. The increasing wind was a signal that another storm was approaching. Route 71, which was a busy four-lane highway, bisected the trail and Sonny carefully walked alongside it facing the oncoming traffic and keeping an eye out for the designated spot to cross safely.

Beef stew was again on the menu for lunch and then in the afternoon, a thunderstorm assaulted the trail and its occupants. An hour later when the birds began to sing, he knew he had survived another one. After he made it to Route 9 WVA, he walked down the dangerous edge of the road, to a gas station and deli where he sat outside and ate pieces of fried dark meat chicken, potato salad, a garden salad, a RC cola, and a bowl of cherry ice cream. He carried back to the trail, a foot long submarine sandwich, a plastic bottle of orange crush soda, a bag of chips, and Almond Joy and Payday candy bars.

He ended his day after 19.2 miles, just short of four miles from Harpers Ferry, West Virginia. The following day, after 544 miles in the state, he would leave Virginia for good. He was looking forward to visiting the historic town, but at the moment he had to deal with a problem. The stealth campsite was littered with chips, crackers and chicken bones that could attract scavenger animals of the night. But even worse, nearby where he had pitched his tent was a large rock that resembled a sacrificial altar. On top was a mutilated cottontail rabbit that had blood and entrails seeping down the boulder. It was getting dark and Sonny did not want to search for another place to spend the night. Instead, he took the carcass and hurled it down the hill as far as he could and did the same with the remaining parts and food litter. After he washed up for the night, a local man visited him in the dark. Sonny and the stranger sat on rocks and talked. The man told stories about the area, including one about a cougar whose tracks he saw at that site, the previous winter. After the man left, Sonny laid in his sleeping bag and listened to sounds that only darkness brought. He heard movement on the trail and was concerned until he saw the light from a headlamp.

DAY 79

When Sonny awoke in the morning, there was another tent nearby. He was excited about the city ahead and the food and comforts that awaited. After breaking camp, he snacked as he walked, and soon crossed into West Virginia. Four states down, ten to go.

Much of the trail was downhill until he reached the Shenandoah River. The wide body of water contained many rapids that Sonny videoed as he walked across the US-340 Bridge towards the former Storer College. Red brick and stone buildings with red brick walkways, dominated the campus. He strolled through the school grounds under the mature trees and past the wrought iron fence. Along the way he took photographs of a granite monument that honored John Brown, the abolitionist, and then made his way to the Appalachian Trail Conservancy.

The ATC Headquarters was a two story solid looking building made from dark stones with wide white painted mortar joints. The interior housed contents that were similar to those at Amicalola Falls Visitor Center. For sale were souvenirs, snacks, and hiking gear. Historical displays of pictures and information about the trail were hung all around. Restrooms were available, as was a lounge that contained albums full of pictures of thru-hikers who had stopped in to register over the years. Sonny browsed the 2018 photo gallery until he found the picture of Box Turtle on June 20th. He then searched the 2017 album looking for Lily. The first time through, he flipped the pages too quickly and missed the photograph, so he slowed down and tried again. There she was, slightly thinner with her hair in a ponytail under a baseball cap. He admired her bare muscular arms and legs for a long while and then asked a volunteer to take his picture outside in front of the building, like all of the others had. A scale told him that he had lost twenty-five pounds. He decided that he did not want to carry any souvenirs for the next eleven hundred miles, but would wait and buy some up in Maine, if he made it that far.

The trail wound around the city and along the way, Sonny took pictures of a Civil War cannon, Jefferson Rock, and ruins of an old stone church. Above the downtown area, the trail passed right alongside Saint Peter's Church. It was built tall and beautiful from gray and tan stones with red arches over the large wooden doors and stained glass windows. Had it been Sunday, Sonny would have wanted to attend Mass there. Instead, he made his way to Town's Inn on High Street where he planned to spend the night.

The three story old hotel had horizontal-lain stone walls and white paned windows with several private rooms and suites on the upper floors. He checked in and chose a bunk in the stone walled basement. There was only one other hiker sharing that level and that guy wasn't around, so Sonny took advantage of the vacant shower. Dressed in only his rain pants, rain jacket, and flip-flops, he put his dirty clothes in the washing machine and then sat down in the coffee shop and ordered lunch. Halfway through the meal of a half-chicken on rice with vegetables and a black cherry soda, he put his clean laundry into the dryer and contemplated dessert.

Out on the streets he walked around reading the historical plaques and called his family. His mother asked him if he had received the writings that she had sent to his phone. He assured her that he had, but was embarrassed to say that he forgot about them and promised to read them soon. August reported that he and the family were quite busy with the cherry harvest and that they would have a bumper crop of red haven peaches in about a month also. Henry talked about taking his first vacation since getting married. He had a few destinations in mind, somewhere that his young children and wife would enjoy. Before thinking, Sonny suggested to him that he bring the family back to Ohio and help out with the upcoming peach harvest. After a moment of silence, Henry changed the subject by asking his father about the trail. Madison informed him that all was well with the baby, but that her daily runs with the dog were now only walks.

Sonny arrived at a business that sold ice cream and got in line and scanned the menu. Normally, he would have had a banana split or at least a hot fudge sundae, but he wanted to keep walking and using his phone, so he ordered a large cone that he could handle with one hand. When he checked his list of contacts on the phone, he saw that Lily had sent him a message: **I'm back on the trail. Where are you?** He wrote back: **I'm in Harpers Ferry**. She responded with: **Me too**! Sonny immediately stopped texting and called her.

They met at White Hall Tavern and then walked around the historic town checking out the sites. Eventually, he showed her his crowded accommodations in the basement of the inn. Lily was not impressed. Sonny would rather rest, but she wanted to keep exploring the historical village. While walking down a sidewalk, he accidently bumped her hand and she grabbed his and held on. At suppertime, they found a nice restaurant and ate during a severe thunderstorm. Sonny was glad he wasn't up in the mountains somewhere. Lily felt safe with him and told him so. He walked her back to where she was staying at the Jackson Rose Bed and Breakfast and they entered the parlor. There were two chairs and a sofa and he let her make the selection. She sat on the sofa and he sat next to her. He saw her wince in discomfort and asked if she was okay. She said, "I'm having cramps."

He stood up and grabbed one of her legs and asked, "Which muscle is it?"

She laughed and he worked the other ankle and said, "I'm serious, you need to stretch it, if you want it to go away."

Her laughter increased until the discomfort took the fun out of the moment. She stood up and he released her leg from his grip and faced her. She said, "That's not the problem." She hugged her abdomen and tilted her head "In fact, it has been a long time since *that* muscle has had a good stretching."

"Oh, my."

Lily sighed and said, "Sonny, I had a wonderful day."

"Me too."

"I should probably go up to my room now."

He looked at her with sad eyes and she said, "I'd ask you up for a nightcap, but this isn't a good time."

"I hope you feel better."

"You're funny."

She leaned forward, embraced and kissed him, on the lips this time. He wasn't trying to be funny and became an active participant of the kiss. When she turned to go up the staircase he said, "Maybe you could show me your record collection, someday."

She smiled and said, "I'd love to show it to you, someday."

He watched her ascend the stairs and then headed back to his place. Along the way, he ran into Fiona. She was with her boyfriend, Doubting Thomas, and other hikers Sonny had met earlier on the trail. After fist bumps all around, Sonny said, "I didn't think I would ever see you guys again, after I left the trail."

Fiona said, "We take a zero or two every week or so to heal and enjoy the highlights along the trail. In fact, we're going to take a train to DC. Want to come with us?"

"That would be fun, but at my age, I think I'm better off if I save all of my energy for making miles north. And by the way, I can tell that all of you have lost weight and are much fitter now."

Fiona broke with tradition and hugged him saying, "Thank you. Oh wow, Sonny, you've lost a lot yourself."

"I have and from now on you can call me Phoenix."

Athena said, "You have a trail name!"

Tripper said, "But I thought you were from Ohio?"

Sonny said, "I am. The Phoenix is a mythical bird."

Perky asked, "You mean like Big Bird on Sesame Street?"

"Yes, exactly like that," said Sonny and the other members of the tramily laughed.

DAY 80

Sonny took a seat in the tiny, on-site restaurant as soon as it opened for breakfast. While waiting for his large omelet with mushrooms, tomatoes, spinach, and cheese, he texted Lily and sipped his glass of orange juice. He wanted to know her trail magic schedule so that he could be in attendance at every possible opportunity. They had discussed his hiking itinerary the previous day while shopping for supplies. Today though, she didn't respond and he figured she was sleeping in, so he finished his meal, paid the bill, and put the tuna fish to-go sandwich in his backpack.

He walked down the street and found where he had last seen a white blaze and headed north again. A call to Lily went unanswered and feeling disappointed, he made his way downhill towards the river. There he found a walking bridge that was shrouded with a black chain-link fence and shared a bridge with a railroad. Standing on the bridge was a woman who was looking down at the abandoned bridge abutments in the Potomac River. When Sonny reached the lady, he stood beside her, held her hand, and looked at the merging rivers. Lily said, "Not saying goodbye would be the hardest."

Sonny looked at her and said, "No, not having a chance to say goodbye, is even worse."

"You want to talk about it?"

Sonny couldn't vocalize the full truth about his wife because it was too painful. He looked away and said, "She left me."

Lily waited for more details that never came. She didn't try to hide her disappointment. "Okay, Sonny, I guess we'll talk about it some other time then."

"Sure."

"Well, this morning didn't start out so good. I wanted to surprise you before you got back on the trail."

"Thanks, you did."

They embraced and he tried to kiss her, but she turned her head aside and after a long hug, she silently walked away.

Sonny berated himself for not sharing the full story of his wife's departure while he crossed the bridge. Feeling frustrated, he called his daughter to help solve his dilemma. After talking about everything other than his relationship with Lily, Madison said, "Dad sometimes I sense that you are unable to express your true feelings. Many of the topics we just talked about are mundane things that we both already know about. If you called just to hear a voice from Ohio because you're homesick, I get it. But, I think there is another reason. What is it?"

"Wow, I have to admit, I am a little homesick."

"Years ago, when I had my miscarriage I trusted you to say the things that would comfort me."

"I remember talking to you then, but I don't recall what I said."

"You told me that some angels get to go to Heaven early."

"Well, I guess that's why I'm calling you. I know you would give me good advice, too. I'm having trouble gaining Lily's confidence."

"Dad, if you want Lily to trust you, you have to trust her and tell her what happened to Mom."

On the far side of the river, the train tracks continued straight through a tunnel, but the trail stayed outside, along the waterway. Sonny kept looking for double blazes that signaled a turn up the mountain, but was pleasantly surprised to learn that the path persisted in a flat manner. With the river on his right side and a canal on his left, he felt like he was back home in Ohio, walking on the towpath in Grand Rapids. Mosquitos and biting flies harassed him until he covered his face and neck with the black veil. It dawned on him that he had left West Virginia and was now in Maryland. Five states down, nine to go.

After three miles of easy hiking, the trail turned left and Sonny began another climb. With ten miles under his belt, he stopped for lunch at Gathland State Park. The landmark was famous for its empty tomb and monument that honored Civil War correspondents. The elaborate memorial of arches, statues, and a turret, resembled a two dimensional castle. Sonny admired the stonework of Gathland Hall that was constructed from stones and built to last. He had always dreamed of living in a castle and he videoed the park to savor the design and craftsmanship. While he ate his tuna fish sandwich, other hikers at the picnic table were discussing the tradition on the first day of summer. During the day of the Summer Solstice, the longest day of the year, some people chose to hike naked. Being a pragmatic man, Sonny debated the dangers of such an endeavor with the young men and women having lunch with him. After stating his case, he got back on the trail and wondered if he had convinced anyone.

He stopped at a granite slab that depicted the site where Major General Jesse L Reno had died and took a picture of the monument. More photographs followed when he walked by pink spirea, white yarrow, and a stone church. He did not take a picture of the naked male hiker that passed by. All day long, the sky was overcast and sometimes it rained. In late afternoon, he arrived at the Washington Monument and walked up the interior spiral staircase of the vase-shaped stone tower and took in the view. Near the end of the day, he crossed over   I-70/US-40 via a black fence tunnel on a walking bridge. The day ended after 23.1 miles at Pine Knob Shelter.

DAY 81

The next day was again cloudy and cool with predicted random rain showers. He ate a banana and a Little Debbie oatmeal cookie and followed that with a Tylenol pill because his feet were sore from the trail that was becoming rockier. Early in the day when he stopped to take a picture of a black-eyed Susan, Sonny tweaked his knee on the wet rocks and became very cautious with his foot placement afterwards. During a lunch break at Raven Rock Shelter, he took more Tylenol.

Late in the afternoon, when he reached the sign that marked the Mason-Dixon Line, there was a young female hiker waiting there. She was very tall, sported a black butch haircut and asked Sonny if he would take her picture with the wooden sign. He agreed and asked if she would return the favor. She handed him her phone and proceeded to disrobe. When she was completely naked, save her hiking shoes, she took up a position in back of the sign. The two horizontal painted boards, Mason-Dixon and Maryland/Pennsylvania, were adequately spaced to cover her private parts. When she said she was ready, Sonny took four pictures, each with a different expression on her face. After she dressed, he handed her phone back to her and jokingly asked if she wanted any pictures using *her* phone. She appreciated his sense of humor and thanked him. He turned to resume his hike, until she reminded him that she hadn't taken his picture yet. He stood next to the sign, fully clothed, with a sheepish grin. In the evening, he stopped after 22.7 miles and camped at Deer Lick Shelters. Six states down, eight to go.

DAY 82

The following day was rather bland. Sonny only ate a banana and a vitamin pill for breakfast and then trudged down the trail in his wet socks and shoes. Normally, he liked to look around as he walked to see what nature offered, but on that day, he just kept his head down, stared at the ground and cursed the mosquitos. For lunch, he refused to walk the three-tenths of a mile down a side trail to Rocky Mountain Shelters and ate alongside the trail, instead.

Fall number seven resulted in a cut on the palm of his left hand. He held that hand up beside a white blaze on a lichen-covered tree and took a picture to show the subscribers of his YouTube channel, the reality of life on the A.T. He never wanted to quit, but there were times when he wished it were over.

His spirits were lifted in the afternoon, ever so slightly, when he arrived at Caledonia State Park. Fellow hikers had commented on his Guthook app about the presence of a snack bar in the park. The conundrum was, while everyone boasted about the array of refreshments, no one pinpointed the exact location of the concession stand. Sonny took off his backpack and sat down on a bench hoping to find more details in his AWOL guide. While perusing the guidebook, a young man rode up on a bicycle and before Sonny could ask him for directions, Josh invited him to a feast. His brother and sister-in-law were celebrating an anniversary. They had rented a shelter house, invited family and friends, and brought way too much food. Sonny forgot about the snack bar and walked to the celebration where he was treated like a celebrity.

After being introduced, he loaded his plate with hotdogs, beans, and fruit. A friend named Bobby was interested in hiking the P.C.T. (Pacific Coast Trail) with his father in the future and was full of questions. After having seconds of the food and beer, Sonny was served a slice of Chuck and Nora's cake. Bobby downloaded a podcast app on Sonny's phone for him and then pictures were taken of the trail angels. They packed him food to go and after saying thanks, he reluctantly left.

Two miles later, he came to the nicest shelter on the trail. Quarry Gap Shelters by themselves, were better than most. The dark brown twinplex shelter had an eating area in the center and a cupola on top of its green metal roof. In addition, the oasis in the wilderness was surrounded by rhododendron bushes and landscaped with flowering hanging baskets. There was a spring, a privy, tent platforms, benches, and an additional picnic table in the yard with a bear box, both with roofs over them. Jim Stauch, the Innkeeper, meticulously maintained the paradise. There was too much daylight left, so Sonny walked a couple of more hours and then stealth camped after 19.1 miles. He pitched his tent near a tarp that someone had been recently sleeping under. There was evidence of a campfire that contained foiled wrapped potatoes. Canned goods and cooked ground beef in a pan were left on the ground near the makeshift tent. With no way to know if anyone would return to the site, Sonny left the food where it was, but worried about invading bears all night.

DAY 83

By morning he was still alone at the campsite. Sonny felt that he would have slept better knowing for certain that he wasn't going to be visited by other people or animals. Despite being a little drowsy, his emotional state was on an upswing. It didn't hurt that the sun was out and the birds were singing. He utilized the podcast app for the first time and listened to stories from Dirt Bag Diaries. His senses improved and his appreciation for nature came back. His eyes observed that the rhododendron buds of the northern states were swelling and would soon blossom, giving him something to look forward to. His ears noticed that the crows had a southern drawl. He took a picture of a white azalea and a viper's bugloss and then had a day hiker take his picture at the sign of the A.T. halfway point.

    Shortly after, he walked past the 1100-mile mark that someone had designated on the ground with small stones. Upon reaching the Pine Grove Furnace State Park, Sonny entered the general store. There, he hoped to partake in an Appalachian Trail tradition that was more to his liking than hiking in the buff. At the halfway point of the trail, it was the custom of thru-hikers to accept the Half Gallon Challenge. Upon successful consumption of a half gallon of Hershey's ice cream, the hiker was awarded a coveted wooden spoon trophy. Sonny chose Neapolitan, sat at a table on the front porch and devoured the contents of the carton with ease.

    A nearby clock informed him that the Appalachian Trail Museum was going to close in less than an hour, so he resupplied, tucked away his Member of the Half Gallon Club award, and moved on. The museum, which was dedicated to hikers, was a barn-shaped building made of stones and trimmed in white. Originally a gristmill, the three story structure housed artifacts from the pioneers of the trail and placards that told the stories from the inception of the trail to the present. There was a library on the third floor that was filled with information and stories about the trail. Volunteers handled all aspects of keeping the museum in operation and attractive. Sonny perused the material, but when he came to the vintage Mount Katahdin Sign, he declined to touch it. Normally not superstitious, he decided to hold off making contact with the icon until after he had completed his journey.

The trail wound through the state park and as he walked along the picnic area, Sonny tried to figure out where he should camp that night. He was amused by a group of young people who were involved in a rambunctious game of spikeball. When he stopped to watch, they stopped playing and asked him if he was a thru-hiker. Sonny admitted he was and they awarded him with trail magic and offered a campsite to him. They gave him the number of the tent site and resumed the game. Although there was time left in the day to put in more miles, the thought of a shower enticed him to halt after 14.4 miles and stay at the park. He walked back to the general store and ordered a double cheeseburger and fries.

After the meal, he walked into the campground and met with the group of trail angels. They told him to pitch his tent in the adjacent site and then invited him for dinner. Already full, he graciously declined the meal, put up the tent, and then showered at the free facilities.

Afterwards, he visited the happy campers and listened to their stories. The group had hiked the trail back in 2017 and formed a tramily called Mob of Ponies. They had all returned to the trail to give back for the kindness they had enjoyed during their adventure. Sonny inquired, but none of them could remember meeting Lily. He drank a can of beer and then was offered a bag of potato chips, which he found room for in his stomach. No matter how much he ate on the trail, he always had room for more. After a second beer, he included the group in his final video of the day, again said thanks, and then goodnight.

DAY 84

Sonny woke up the next day feeling optimistic. The weather was perfect, he was halfway finished with the journey and had been enjoying his life on the trail lately. The Mob of Ponies was sleeping in so he didn't bother them. He savored the level terrain of the park and then crossed a small bridge over a stream that fed Fuller Lake. There was a sandy beach at the far end, but he only looked at it while walking past and then headed back into the woods. Eventually, the black flies attacked his bare skin and he put on the veil. He met some day-hikers who quizzed him about his experiences thus far. They asked him why he was doing a thru-hike and he gave him his standard reply, "Because I'm a moron."

He was then asked, what was the best part about the trail. His answer was going to be the wild animals that he didn't normally see back home in Ohio, but upon further reflection, he decided it was the people. "Ninety-nine percent of the people I met are terrific. They love the outdoors and would bend over backwards to help me. My success is important to them and they seem to have more faith in me than I have in myself."

Near lunchtime, Sonny came to PA-34 and knew from his AWOL guide, that food and supplies were less than a short walk away, down the road. The Green Mountain Merchandise Store provided him with a few more items in addition to a meal from the grill and ice cream.

The afternoon began with passages through boulders and then changed to rolly farm ground where he picked and ate wild raspberries. Every so often he would see what looked like wartime foxholes along the way and wondered what purpose they served. The fertile valley was planted with acres of corn, wheat, and soybeans.

After 18.6 miles, he pitched his tent outside the city of Boiling Springs at a campsite with a picnic table and a porta-john. Unfortunately, on the other side of a row of trees, there was an active railroad track that was out of sight, but within earshot. While hanging his food bag from a black walnut tree, Sonny was approached by a ridge-runner named Paige who offered information and advice about the upcoming miles. The fourteen miles after leaving the city contained no access to food or water. There was also no water at the campsite, so Sonny washed-up with his own. Before falling asleep, he felt upbeat and decided it was time to tell Lily about his wife.

DAY 85

The trains woke him up a few times during the night, but Sonny started the day feeling refreshed, nevertheless. It was another sunny day and a brief text from Lily advised him of a chance at trail magic ten miles after Boiling Springs. He skipped breakfast, packed his gear, and headed towards the benefits of the city. After he crossed the railroad track and walked over a one-lane bridge, he passed through a park that featured the remnants of a stone furnace and then found himself next to a clear water lake. The seven-acre body of water was dug out as a reservoir for water used in the iron furnaces. Sonny walked on the fine-gravel path along the lake that was lined with park benches and sugar maple trees. Vintage homes sat high on the hills and there was a gazebo situated on a peninsula. He watched the water boil up from a spring at the bottom of the lake and understood why the lake was given its name.

After a hearty breakfast at Caffe 101, he got a Reuben sandwich and coleslaw to go and then picked up a few supplies at Lakeside Food Mart and TCO Outdoors. Before resuming his hike, Sonny used the outside spigot and filled all of his water bottles at the ATC Mid-Atlantic Regional Office.

The terrain was pleasingly smooth and he stopped at a small cemetery surrounded by a black iron fence. The gravestones were engraved with dates from the seventeen and eighteen hundreds and overgrown with weeds. He was still surrounded by farmland and while passing by dairy cows in a pasture, Sonny took pictures of an Asiatic dayflower, chicory, a monarch caterpillar, and a calligrapher fly on yellow salsify by one honeybee.

Just after noon, Sonny arrived at Scott Farm Trail ATC Crew Headquarters. Lily was there serving sloppy Joes with chips and pop to four other hikers. She wasn't as cheery as she usually was, so after a short hello, Sonny made a plate and sat next to the white barn in the shade. He didn't want his coleslaw to go bad so he ate that also and waited for the others to move on. When Lily was alone, Sonny carried his trash back to the table and properly disposed of it in the available plastic garage bag and said, "Can we talk?"

"You talk. I'll listen."

"Okay, here goes. You were open and honest with me whenever I asked you questions about your life."

"Yes."

"Well, that was a statement, not a question."

"I know. Keep going."

He nodded and said, "I was married to Ellen for thirty-six years and then…"

Sonny looked away, searching for the words. Lily urged him on by saying, "As I recall, you said, 'She left me.'"

His shoulders sagged and he exhaled loudly and then said, "She didn't just leave me. She died in an automobile accident."

Sonny kept his composure until Lily began to weep. When she opened her arms to him, they embraced until the tears stopped flowing. Finally she said, "I'm so sorry, Sonny. Maybe I was insensitive the last time we talked."

"No Lily. You were spot on when you talked about not being able to say goodbye."

She waited and he revealed the details of that horrible day. "It was early October, two years ago and the sun was low on the horizon. She was leaving to go shopping in Bowling Green and wanted me to go with her, but I stayed home to watch a football game. So, she left without me, drove down our road a short distance, and was turning east."

Sonny looked away, stared at nothing and continued. "There was a large van, driven by a young guy who was a new hire and didn't know the route and never saw the stop sign, because the sun blinded him. I heard the crash and I knew. I ran out of the house and could see the steam rising from the accident scene. The driver was traumatized, but I pushed him away and went to check on Ellen. I found the driver's phone in his cab and called 911, but I knew it was already too late."

Lily squeezed his forearms, but couldn't find any consoling words to say. Sonny added, "Before leaving, she would always tell me that she loved me. It didn't happen that day and that's the thing that haunts my dreams; she left without saying she loved me."

"I know it pains you to talk about her, but I needed to know."

Sonny nodded and changed the subject. "Do you want some help cleaning up or are you going to keep serving a while longer?"

"I think I'll pack it in for the day and go to Carlisle and buy some supplies for the next time."

"When and where will that be?"

"I'm looking at Port Clinton in five days. Think you can make it there by then?"

"If I can't, I'll die trying."

She smiled and said, "Good boy. What are you hungry for?"

"Hotdogs sound good."

"Okay, hotdogs it is."

He helped her pack away the food and gear and she rewarded him with a kiss. When she pulled her car keys from her front pants pocket, the ring came out and landed on the ground. Sonny picked it up and slipped it on his pinkie finger. He noticed it fit perfectly and said, "Maybe I should wear this so that people know we are going steady."

Lily held out a hand, palm side up and said, "Give me that. We're not in high school."

Sonny blushed and quickly handed it back.

In the late afternoon, as he began a climb wearing the black veil and ear buds, Sonny stopped suddenly. He thought he heard the sounds of a cicada coming from a nearby tree, but realized the noise was emitted from the ground, right in front of him. He stopped listening to *Cortez The Killer* by Neil Young and began to video the real killer in front of him. It was another timber rattlesnake. The serpent continuously shook its nine-rowed rattle and did not want to leave its sunny location in the middle of the trail. The head of the coiled snake followed him as he carefully made his way past.

After 22.2 miles, the day ended at Cove Mountain Shelter. Sonny signed in at the empty shelter, but camped away from it because there were fresh chew marks from porcupines on much of the structure.

DAY 86

The weather app predicted a lightning storm in the afternoon, so Sonny decided to take a nero (low mileage day) of only 6.3 miles for the day and called ahead to make reservations at a motel in Duncannon. The walking surface was clear and level at the moment, but as he descended the mountain, the trail became rocky. He learned from his AWOL guide, that the dreaded rocks of Pennsylvania had begun.

The city of Duncannon had seen better days. Much of the downtown area and many neighborhood homes were run down. The trail turned off of Market Street at the Doyle Hotel and continued down High Street. Sonny knew about the famous landmark, but had heard stories about the lower hygiene standards inside the building and opted to spend the night at another place. He found a Laundromat and used its restroom to change into his raingear and flip-flops. After his clothes were clean, he packed them away and continued on the trail through the city in his laundry day outfit. He followed the long bridge over the Juniata River and then crossed over a four-lane highway. On the way to a large fuel station for cars and semi-trucks, he passed by businesses that boasted of exotic dancers and twenty-four hour massages. Sonny doubted that they employed authentic Tahitian performers and the thought of a daylong massage did not interest him. The man who answered his call at the motel told him that his ride would be there in thirty minutes, so Sonny went inside the Subway and ate lunch.

At the motel, he lay on the bed and watched a World Cup game while uploading five videos to his YouTube channel. For supper, the owner of the motel recommended and gave Sonny a ride to a restaurant. There he stuffed himself with vegetables and red meat. After dessert, he paid the bill, took his carry out meal outside, and waited for his ride back to the motel.

Once there, he called family members. His mother was battling black spot in her rose garden. August was involved with his kids in baseball and soccer. Henry was coaching his oldest in tee ball. Madison was focused on eating healthy for her growing baby. All were following his journey via YouTube and commenting frequently. Sonny felt he was missing out on many good times and wished he were back in Ohio. His last call was to Lily. After exchanging pleasantries, he asked. "Are you still serving hotdogs in Port Clinton?"

"I am. Are you going to be there?"

"Yes, I will be there. Hey, I've been thinking."

"About what?"

Sonny didn't want to pry into her financial situation so he chose his words carefully. "I was wondering if you would allow me to contribute toward your trail magic budget."

"That's very kind of you. You're probably curious about how I can afford trail magic with the ongoing financial strain of my farm."

His silence verified her statement and she answered his unspoken questions. "I know of many former thru-hikers who want to be trail angels, but they just can't find the time. I give the time and effort, but there is an organized group that generously donates the funds to me. Many of them welcome me into their homes along the way to save money on overnight stays. As you can imagine, they are all great people and I enjoy spending time with them. Before you ask, I only stay in the homes of women. Have I answered all of your questions?"

"I can't wait to see you again."

DAY 87

It was a long walk across the Clarks Ferry Bridge over the wide and shallow Susquehanna River. After Sonny crossed William Penn Highway and its adjoining railroad track, he began a rocky climb. During the night, it had rained a lot resulting in overflowing streams and vicious waterfalls. The temperature and humidity increased and at one point, while wiping the sweat from his eyes, Sonny missed a turn on the trail and found himself struggling to get through a hillside of rocks covered in snarly plants, including poison ivy. When he slipped and twisted his left knee, he stopped where he was and used the Guthook app to locate the correct path. Although a little sore, his knee benefited from the somewhat level terrain for the remainder of the day.

At Table Rock View, he took pictures of the landmark and a Red Elderberry bush. In midafternoon, he stopped at Peters Mountain Shelter and ate the hamburger and RC cola that he carried from Duncannon.

After 16.1 miles, he tented at an unnamed campsite that was occupied by a few other hikers. He ate a day-old submarine sandwich, made water, and washed up down at a spring before going to bed.

DAY 88

Early in the morning, Sonny crossed PA-325 and stopped on the edge of Clark Creek. He could see that the water level had fallen, but was still a foot deep where he had to cut across. He did not want to soak his socks and shoes so early in the day, so he removed them and put on his flip-flops and slowly made his way on the submerged trail. In his morning video, he recorded a blooming white azalea and referred to the area as the Appalachian Swamp. There was evidence of past coal mining, including pits, mounds, and coal dust-covered trails near Rausch Creek. On the other side of the bridge was a plaque that depicted the site of the village of Rausch Gap from 1828 to 1910.

An overflowing beaver dam that covered the trail in knee-deep water, convinced Sonny to change into the flip-flops again. In the late afternoon, he took a picture of butterfly weed and then arrived at his third water crossing of the day. Trout Run was narrow, but deep and fast moving. The boards that had been used as a bridge to a fallen tree across the stream had been washed away. Sonny decided to change into his running shorts and flip-flops and hold the backpack over his head as he made the crossing. Carefully, he stepped off of the bank into the cold liquid. He walked sideways, facing upstream, feeling his way along the bottom while trying to retain his footwear and balance. After a few short shuffling steps, the water was up to his waist. At the center of the stream, the flow was up to his chest and the force nearly knocked him backwards. He began to second-guess his decision, but was already committed and pushed on to the far shore. Once across, he felt a huge sense of relief. He sat on a rock and while the sun warmed his body, he put on his dry socks and shoes. Surviving the dangerous feat made him feel more alive.

The trail led under PA-443 and into a parking lot where trail magic awaited. The trail angels were Craig, whose trail name was River Guide, and his wife Sandy. Sonny sat in a chair and was given a cold can of orange Fanta soda and crackers with peanut butter while River Guide interviewed and made a video of him.   After a short rest, Sonny thanked the trail angels, made a video of them and moved on, carrying extra snacks for later. He left his shorts on, exposing his untanned legs to the elements. The trail crossed over an ornate iron bridge that seemed out of place. Sonny learned that the historic truss bridge had been built in Waterville, Pennsylvania, in 1890 and later moved to Swatara State Park in 1985. When the trail became overgrown with vegetation, Sonny reverted to wearing his long pants. He saw his first porcupine and recorded the large rodent as it flared its quills and scampered up a tree. The day had started at 4:49 when the birds disturbed his slumber and despite the three water crossings, Sonny had walked until sunset and set a new record of 24.9 miles. He camped near William Penn Shelter where he hastily pitched his tent and hustled down a hill to make water with his headlamp on.

DAY 89

The following morning, Sonny's left knee complained when he crawled out of his tent. He immediately formulated a plan for recovery and then called and made reservations at an upcoming hostel. He decided to take his time covering the 13.4 miles to PA-183 and a ride to the healing place. Pictures were taken at scenic overlooks of the farms below and of a granite monument at the site of Fort Dietrich in 1755. A few miles before he reached the state route, Sonny crossed the 1200-mile mark. He had less than a thousand miles left to walk on the Appalachian Trail, and was concerned that another injury would halt the journey again.

Most of the trail during the day was rocky, but the last two miles were flooded. Fortunately, Sonny had learned from his last experience with the injury and this time, his cautious behavior got him to the pickup point without further damage. The Rock and Sole Hostel was situated in a clearing, back in the woods and near a small stream. The property, which was owned and operated by Craig and Jody, was clean, landscaped, quiet, and new. There was a large two story, beige-sided house where the family lived, but the quaint garage-like hostel was set back by itself. Upon entering, Sonny saw a microwave oven and felt the air conditioning from the window unit. He placed his backpack on a bottom bunk and introduced himself to the only occupant. The man was a thru-hiker from New Zealand and informed Sonny that the hostel had just reopened after being closed for a while. Sonny took a shower and placed his dirty laundry in the designated basket near the big house. The two hikers were then given a ride to a store that sold meals and other supplies. Sonny warmed up his chicken sandwich and vegetable plate in the microwave and spent the rest of the night icing and resting his knee.

DAY 90

The hikers ate breakfast on the front porch of the proprietor's house and Sonny broke with his traditional cup of tea and decided to try coffee, like most other people. With cream and a lot of sugar he thought it wasn't so bad. As the other hiker was packing to leave, Sonny had a decision to make. His warrior mentality told him to push on, but the memory of his last convalescence told him not to be so foolish. He decided to take a zero and stay another night. Much of the day was spent sitting on a rock in the cold stream soaking his knee.

DAY 91

The following morning as he drank one last cup of coffee on the front porch, he was pleased with his decision to rest the injury, but anxious to get back on the trail. Heading north again, he met up with another timber rattlesnake in the middle of the path. It was three feet in length, thick, dark and had eleven rows of rattles, which it shook continuously. Sonny left warnings on the trail for any hikers behind him and then gave the coiled snake a wide berth as he passed by the sunny spot.

At lunchtime, Sonny was still full from his large breakfast and was mainly thirsty from the heat. He ate some snacks and drank a lot of water and Gatorade. A trail angel had left plastic gallons of water next to the trail and Sonny filled all of his bottles. The level ground was kind to Sonny all day and the only steep hill was the descent into Port Clinton. He continued to go slow to protect his knee as he came down off of the mountain and crossed several tracks in the rail yard. There was a small train station followed by a green steel bridge, which was held together with large rivets and used by trains, bicyclists, and pedestrians.

After crossing over the Little Schuylkill River, Sonny stayed on the trail into the town until he reached Penn Street. Instead of turning right as indicated by the double white blazes, he went left and walked down to the pavilion. A handwritten sign near the bridge had announced trail magic at the park and the size of the crowd indicated that meals were still being served. Ben and Debbie from Kentucky were hosting the event with their young daughter who was also hiking the trail. They served cold cut sandwiches, potato salad, chips, fruit, beer, and pop. Better than a dozen hikers were sitting at the picnic tables, some still stuffing their faces. Sonny conversed with most of them and thanked the trail angels. Lily was also serving food there.

True to her word, she had provided hotdogs with condiments and pork and beans with bacon. Sonny sat with the hikers and ate a plateful from the first table of food and then moved on to Lily's offerings. He grabbed two hot dogs and covered them with diced sweet onions, catsup and mustard and added a ladle of beans to his plate. Lily noticed that he walked with a slight limp and gave him a bag of ice for his knee. For more privacy, she ushered him to a table in the corner of the shelter house and sat across from him. In between bites he said, "I was worried that I might miss you."

"And the food?"

"That too."

"Well, when I learned that you had taken a zero, I postponed the event for a day."

"Thanks. I'm glad you did."

Sonny could tell that she had a lot on her mind. "Lily, is something bothering you?"

"Does it show?"

Sonny didn't reply so Lily continued, "Maybe a couple of things are on my mind. For one, I need to go back to Brown County and meet with the creditors."

"That doesn't sound good. What else?"

"Just that I'd like to learn more about you."

"I can help you with that. What else would you like to know?"

"Describe to me, your relationship with your wife."

Sonny thought about a good answer while looking at the food on his plate. "We were like this hotdog and bun."

"Which one were you?"

Sonny blushed. "Maybe that's not a good example. He tried again. "We were like an ice cream cone. She was the scoop of ice cream and everyone loved her. I was the cone. Just by herself she was good, but she chose me to hold her and keep her safe."

Lily smiled. "That's good. I like that analogy. When you think of us, what food comes to mind?"

Sonny was on a roll. "Macaroni and cheese."

"I won't ask you who's who."

Sonny explained. "By themselves, they are both good and go well with other foods. But, together they are marvelous."

"Awww, that's so sweet of you to say."

She looked down at the ice bag on his knee and asked, "How was the walking today?"

"I covered 14.6 miles in about nine hours."

"Wow. You *were* being careful."

"Well, that included a lunch break and stops for making water and other necessities."

"Still, that's not very fast for the kind of topography you were on. The upcoming states are brutal in some spots. Maybe you should take a couple of days off to heal-up for the final 900 miles."

"You may be right, but I hate to just sit around. If I took time off, I'd want to go and explore somewhere nearby where I wouldn't have to walk very much."

"There are plenty of neat towns around here that you could check out."

"I have researched the trail thoroughly, but I don't know much about any other places around here. Where would you want go for a couple of relaxing days if you were worn out from hiking?"

Lily thought. "Hmmm. I've never been there, but I heard that Bethlehem is an interesting city."

"Sounds good. But, I'll need a ride to and from the trail."

"There are plenty of shuttle services available. You could probably get a free ride if you stay at the right hotel."

"Lily. The only way I'll agree to stop hiking and go to Bethlehem is if you go with me."

She shook her head. "I can't. I have to go home and talk to the banker."

Sonny only shrugged and Lily said, "Okay. I'll go to Bethlehem with you, but then I have to return to Indiana for a while."

When the sun went down, the food was packed away in their vehicles and the trial angels left. Sonny put up his tent around several others, in a grassy area across from the pavilion near the river. He then changed into his running shorts and waded into and submersed his dirty body in the chilly water. After downing a can of beer, he gladly entered his comfortable sleeping bag. A nearby street light shone into his blue translucent tent, but he was able to sleep except when he was awakened by a jake-braking semi-truck that passed through the town on PA-61. On a few occasions, he heard a train rumble by along the far side of the river, but easily fell back asleep contented with the knowledge that he would see Lily again in a few days.

DAY 92

Early in the morning, Sonny walked towards the business district of the small town. He had planned on obtaining breakfast either at the Port Clinton Hotel or the Peanut Shop. Both were closed, but it was another sunny day and he got back on the trail. The humidity increased and the route wasn't as smooth as the last couple of days, but the views were great. A cramp in his right calf developed and he found relief by drinking fluids and eating his last banana from the trail angels. He stopped at Pulpit Rock and had chicken teriyaki for lunch.

Two miles later, he reached the Pinnacle and videoed vultures soaring over the farms and woodlots.

He added false coral to his collection of mushroom pictures. Dripping with sweat, he stepped out onto a road by a parked van and three men. The owner of the van, Steve from Tennessee, asked Sonny if he was thirsty. The trail angel introduced himself and the two thru-hikers with him. The tall one with the massive thighs was his son. A cooler was opened and cold pop, beer, and chocolate candy was offered. While Sonny made his selections, another hiker stopped by and the five of them sat down along the road and swallowed the refreshments. Before leaving, Sonny was allowed to 'grab some for later.'

There was a shelter over six miles away and he still had enough daylight left, but after 15.6 miles he decided that was enough for the day and stealth camped by a nice stream. Before the erection of the tent, he had to chase off a five-foot black rat snake that was hunting on the flat spot. Sonny's last meal of the day consisted of a bag of almonds, cheddar cheese crackers with peanut butter, and a can of beer.

DAY 93

Breakfast consisted of oatmeal with brown sugar and raisins and the rest of the sugar wafer cookies. Clif Bars and peanut butter centered cheddar crackers were place inside his front pouch for snacks along the way. During the night, three groups of hikers passed by his tent with their headlamps on, probably headed to the next shelter, which was over six miles away. Sonny had witnessed lightning and thunder while safely in his tent, but no rain ever materialized.

The trail started off very rocky and just short of ten miles later, he came to PA-309. According to his app and guidebook, the Thunderhead Lodge was only two-tenths of a mile to the west. Sonny found the complex and three other thru-hikers who informed him that the business was closed for the Fourth of July holiday, but water was available. The four of them found chairs, sat in the shade of a tree and sulked. A van pulled into the parking lot and they watched it park in back, out of the way.

When the driver got out, Sonny immediately recognized him. It was Steve, the trail angel from the day before who was there to wait for his son to show up. Sonny introduced Steve to the other three and they were given beer and chocolate. They all sat back down and some of them shared a joint. Steve indicated that it was going to be a while before his son would arrive so he asked the hikers if any of them would like a ride to a nearby gas station that had supplies and a small restaurant. All four hikers piled into the van and they were on their way. Like the others, Sonny loaded up on supplies and got a carryout fried chicken meal with mashed potatoes, gravy, and corn.

After lunch, all of the hikers thanked Steve again and returned to the trail. The path alternated between extreme conditions from smooth areas to very rocky. There were sections when, if Sonny hadn't seen the white blazes, he would have thought he was off the trail. He found relief from the heat and humidity when the rain fell on him. Along the way, he strained his left calf hopping down from a rock and he gingerly walked along as the lighting came to visit him again. Towards the end of the storm, he stopped briefly to examine a splintered tree that had been recently stuck by lightning. He was then faced with crossing the Knife Edge as the thunder grumbled in the distance. The rocky ridge was a one hundred yard, steep and pointy edge that was slippery and especially dangerous for someone nursing an injury. Sonny was not worried about snakes basking on the rocks, but he was concerned about a fall or a lightning strike since he was the highest point around.

After he survived that challenge, the weather improved and he took a picture of a painted skull on a rock that welcomed him to The Knob. He stopped after 16.9 miles and pitched his tent near the crowded Bake Oven Knob Shelter. The campsite was narrow, but it boasted a wooden chair with the seat cut out. Sonny presumed that the chair was used as a portable alternative to squatting in the woods. Still full from lunch, he ate a bag of almonds with a warm cherry Coke for supper. He did not have to rinse off before entering his tent for the night because the rain shower had already done that for him. He fell asleep after listening to far away firework celebrations.

DAY 94

The day began with a banana, dried fruit, cookies, and a vitamin pill. Sonny picked his way through the pointy rocks of the northern Pennsylvania trail until he came out of the woods at Lehigh Gap. From where he stood, he could see a river with a highway crossing it, railroad tracks, homes, businesses, and a steep rocky climb in the distance. He enjoyed the change of scenery and the descent. The skies were partly cloudy and it wasn't hot yet, but it was getting there. He made his way down to the PA-873 road bridge, videoed the crossing of the Lehigh River, and put off lunch until after the challenging ascent on the far side. All of his water bottles were full because he knew the next area had once been the site of zinc mines and the local water was contaminated with the metal.

He procrastinated as long as he could by taking a picture of a wingleaf primrose and then started the climb, just ahead of two day-hikers. There were short switchbacks and some straight-up sections, but all were rocky and the temperature was rising. He let the trekking poles dangle from his wrists and did a lot of hand climbing. Halfway up, when he stopped to rest, he overheard the man behind him warn the other guy to watch out because he had almost put his hand on a basking copperhead snake. Sonny knew that he had also used that same handhold and wondered how close he had come to being bitten. At the top, he took a picture of a rock that had a United States flag roughly painted on it. He looked down and admired the view and felt another small sense of accomplishment.

The ground leveled out and he stopped to eat his submarine sandwich. The next several miles were fairly level and he picked and ate wild blueberries and raspberries while enjoying the view of Palmerton. He took pictures of blue vervain, birdsfoot trefoil, and a cluster of pink flowers with five petals and a yellow center that he couldn't identify. At Blue Mountain Road, a trail angel had left gallons of water and Sonny filled all of his bottles.

He stopped after 18.1 miles at Delps Spring and noticed that sections of the heels were coming apart from the soles of both of his new shoes due to the sharp, rock-filled trail. The heat of the day caused him to be very thirsty, but not hungry enough to eat any supper. The spring at the campsite was dried-up, so Sonny rinsed off with his bottle water before entering the muggy tent.

DAY 95

It was another warm and sunny day. Sonny ate dried apricots for breakfast and drank much water. His left calf had a cramp and water supply options were limited. He stopped at Leroy A. Smith Shelter and ate a large meal. To obtain water, he had to go four-tenths of a mile down a steep hill. Because the spring was shallow, he used the bottom half of a plastic water bottle to scoop the scarce water from the puddle and poured it into the water bag before filtering it into his bottles.

The trail continued to be relatively flat and was either both rocky through the woods and lined with ferns, or just plain rocky through the woods. Wolf Rocks was a half-mile of boulders on the edge of a cliff. Sonny carefully made his way over the obstacles, but as he hopped off of the last rock, he strained his left calf again. He walked the last two miles of the 19.7-mile hike slowly so as to not compound the damage to his leg muscles.

A trail angel had left a cooler of Gatorade and cookies and Sonny ate and drank the gifts for supper. He talked to a man and woman who were staying in the Kirkridge Shelter for the night, but Sonny pitched his tent up the hill from them near a water spigot.

DAY 96

When the sun came up, Sonny was hungry and after he packed away his gear and loaded up with water, he went down to the shelter and prepared a meal of mashed potatoes with tuna fish and Gatorade. The couple stayed in their sleeping bags and asked Sonny if a bear had visited him during the night. They said that the bear came by about an hour after sunset and sniffed around the campfire and picnic table. Sonny recalled hearing something outside his tent about that time and had smelled what he described as a wet dog odor.

After breakfast, he eagerly headed north. In six miles he would arrive at a tourist town, buy supplies, and devour food prepared by others. The weather was sunny and cool and when he reached Look Out Rock, he savored the view, the thought of culinary delights, and Lily. Things were looking up. The trail spilled out onto a side street that intersected with PA-611 where he read a sign - Welcome to Delaware Water Gap. The first sign made him feel happy, but the second brought a smile to his bearded face.

He followed the direction of the arrow to Zoe's Ice Cream Parlor. The air-conditioned store with old-fashioned décor was playing music written way before his time and lured Sonny inside where he ordered and drank a root beer float in a tall glass with a long spoon. He then sauntered down Main Street searching for supplies and other eateries. The scent from Village Farmer and Bakery convinced him to try a pulled-pork meal with green beans, corn, a roll, and a glass of milk. He ate a small peach pie for dessert and bought a pecan pie for later. Somewhat reluctantly, Sonny left civilization behind and got back on the trail.

The four-lane bridge of I-80 crossed over the Delaware River and Sonny looked down upon a group of kayakers as he crossed into New Jersey. Seven states down, seven to go.

Later, he walked on the rock-filled shore of Sunfish Pond and although there were numerous displays of cairns and the water was clean, Sonny did not think very highly of it. Not only did the glacier-made lake not have a sandy shoreline that Sonny was accustomed to back home, but a sign indicated that camping and swimming was not allowed. He stealth camped after covering 16.4 miles, just past the Mohican Outdoor Center. Two architects, who were section-hiking part of the trail, were also tenting at the site. Sonny answered their questions about the trail until it got dark and then he slept on the ground, one more time.

DAY 97

The sunny and cooler weather predicted for the week was ideal for hiking and a small part of Sonny wished he wasn't taking a break from the trail to be with Lily - a very, very small part. He stopped and talked with four former thru-hikers who were setting up to serve hamburgers and beer for lunch. Any other day he might have stuck around for the trail magic, but he had other priorities and kept walking.

The Catfish Lookout Tower was closed to the public, but the views from its base were still impressive. Sonny took pictures of still-flowering rhododendron, showy goldenrod, and a large pond filled with water lilies created by a beaver dam. He finished the 7.6 miles for the day around noon at Blue Mountain Lakes Road. There he took off his pack, sat down, and called Lily to tell her that he was at the pick-up point. She answered after two rings and sounding a little exasperated, informed him that she was on I-80 about two hours away. He jokingly said, "Okay, I'll wait here."

"I changed my mind and went home to deal with the farm issues. I'll tell you about it later."

"No problem. Try to relax. Whatever it is, you're going to be alright."

"Sure."

Sonny ate a sub and washed it down with a warm cola. He placed his backpack against the base of a shade tree and set his phone alarm for ninety minutes. Using his gear as a backrest, he sat down on the ground, leaned back and closed his eyes. His alarm startled him awake and as he considered calling Lily, she called him. "I just left Kittatinny Visitor Center. The ranger there told me that I'm nine miles away from you."

"Great. I'll see you soon."

Sonny stood by the road anxiously waiting. Thirty-three minutes later the green Equinox stopped in front of him. Lily got out holding a cup of coffee and looked exhausted. Sonny decided it was best not to ask what took so long. Rather, he hugged her causing her to spill coffee on her sweatshirt. He thought she might cry, but instead she said, "It's been that kind of day."

He said, "I'll drive." She didn't argue.

The nine-mile road back toward the turnpike was laden with crater-sized potholes and Sonny learned first hand what took so long. By the time he had successfully guided the vehicle through the minefield, Lily had fallen asleep. Forty-five minutes later, he pulled into a slot of the parking deck behind the Historical Bethlehem Hotel. Originally, Sonny had thought about going to a less-expensive hotel, but when he looked at the beautiful woman sleeping in the passenger seat, he knew he would only get one chance at making a good first impression and was glad that he had changed his mind. The renovated elegant hotel with its large dome-top windows, boasted of 125 rooms and suites for lodging, a restaurant, halls for receptions and conferences, quaint shops, a swimming pool, and other amenities. Lily was still groggy when they entered the lobby, but came to life at the sight of a restroom and said, "I'll be right back."

Sonny approached the front desk, spoke to the receptionist and was relieved to learn that, due to a large wedding reception, only the least expensive traditional rooms were available. When Lily returned, Sonny handed her a keycard and said, "I got a room for you too. Next to mine."

"That wasn't necessary."

"Oh, really?"

"Yeah, I would have paid for my own room. But, thanks."

They settled into their rooms and while Lily rested, Sonny went to the laundry room and washed all of his clothes and Lily's hooded sweatshirt. He then showered and dressed, wishing he had brought along dress clothes. When he knocked on her door, Lily was also dressed casually and they began to tour the city on foot. They ended up seated outside at the Apollo Grill on Broad Street where they dined on bangers and mash with green beans, squash, carrots, and draft beer. After sunset, they held hands walking back to the hotel under the streetlights. They shared a brief kiss before retiring to their separate rooms. Despite feeling tired, neither one could sleep. Sonny iced his knees and channel-surfed the television while Lily pondered her financial situation. Lily considered calling Sonny and he thought about knocking on her door, but neither one did.

DAY 98

They had breakfast in the hotel and then continued to take in the city pedestrian style. At a leisurely pace, they visited museums about the Moravians and the booming steel industry that followed. The protestant Moravians had built a self-sufficient community in the area before the United States was ever founded. Later a college was created that was the first to offer an education to women. Between learning about local landmarks, Sonny and Lily perused the small shops and relaxed in a coffeehouse, but mostly they talked. Opinions and experiences were shared concerning families, agriculture, long distance running, thru-hiking, regrets, joys, and hardships.

About noon, they found their way back to the hotel where they each enjoyed a medium rare ribeye steak, garlic mashed potatoes, a vegetable medley, and beer.

Sonny ate whatever Lily couldn't finish. Afterwards, they went to their rooms to nap. Lily felt more relaxed after having discussed her problems with Sonny and she was able to fall asleep immediately. Sonny lay on his bed and iced his knees. Normally, when he had extended time off from the trail he would catch up on his videos by editing them into movies and uploading them on YouTube for his followers. He would also spend some time improving his hygiene by trimming his beard and nails. Access to healthy foods was a plus along with long rest periods for healing, both physically and mentally. He had a strong phone signal to connect with family members, but decided against talking to them. The quality time with Lily was paramount and he didn't want to have to explain his relationship with her to anyone, yet.

Lily had noticed that Sonny's shoes were taking a beating from the rocky trail. Near the heel of both shoes, the tread was pulling away from the outside edge. She had convinced him to call the outfitter in Front Royal and complain about the defects. To his surprise, the manager offered to send a pair of replacements. Sonny did not want to go out of his way to receive the new shoes, so he agreed to have them sent to a town in Massachusetts that the trail went through.

Eventually, Sonny fell asleep for a short nap, but was roused by a soft knock on the door. He answered and Lily said, "Sleep is important, but I think we should go back outside and make the most of the beautiful day."

They continued walking and talking. Near the conclusion of the day, which neither one of them wanted to end, they were seated outside an Italian restaurant on Main Street called Mama Nina. They began with drinking sangria and munching on bruschetta and Caesar salads. Lily ordered spaghetti with meatballs and Sonny chose the shrimp Alfredo. While the meals were prepared they started on a bottle of red wine and continued interviewing each other. Lily began. "Okay, I believe it is my turn to ask a question. "Who do you admire?"

Sonny took his time coming up with an answer. "I admire those people who can do things that I can't do, like musicians and singers, athletes and artists. But the ones who I admire the most are ones who got knocked down and stood up again. Anyone who was losing, but kept trying, like the underdog that no one believed in."

Lily suggested, "Kind of like you, at times?"

"I don't admire myself."

"No? I bet your kids do."

Sonny wasn't used to talking about himself and was slightly embarrassed. "Okay, enough about me. Lily, if you weren't a farmer, what else would you like to do?"

She didn't hesitate. "I used to think that I wanted to be an actress, but now the idea of owning my own flower shop appeals to me."

There was a brief lull in the conversation until Lily said, "What kinds of humor do you like best?"

"The funny kind."
Lily frowned so Sonny went on. "I like exaggeration and stating the obvious. Like, 'If you fire me, I'll never work here again.'"

Their meals arrived and after Sonny took his first bite, he reflected on his experiences during the past three months. The food he was eating was better than his normal trail cuisine. His hygiene had improved. Riding somewhere in a car was faster than walking. There was ample access to modern conveniences. On the other hand, the rewards gained from the struggles of the trail provided self-satisfaction and the joy of solitude. The darkness away from the city lights had displayed the stars and planets he was unaccustomed to. Lily noticed he had stopped eating and was starring at his food and said, "What are you thinking about, Sonny?"

He smiled at her. "I was thinking about how happy I am now."

She smiled back and they finished their meals in silence. Even though they were both full, they looked at the dessert menu to extend their pleasant time together. Lily said *if* she were going to get anything, she would want the chocolate soufflé. Sonny said the crème brule sounded good.

They slowly walked back to the hotel and rode the elevator to their floor. Outside the rooms in the hallway, they shared a passionate kiss and then Lily said, "I had a wonderful time, but you need your sleep, Sonny."

"I'm not tired."

"Yes you are. Goodnight."

Inside his room, Sonny stood and looked at a vase full of real-looking red roses.

"I should have gotten her flowers," he said to himself as he stripped naked in the bathroom knowing that it might be his last shower for a while. He took a good look at himself in the mirror that was hung over the sink and saw only muscles on bones. He had a farmer's tan and the places where the backpack straps rubbed his chest and shoulders were red and slightly raw. It took a while, but he used the scissors on the small Swiss Army knife and cut off his beard. After trimming his mustache, he used a bar of soap to lather his face before shaving it clean. When he was finished, he studied his body one last time, shrugged and stepped into the shower.

After drying off, he wrapped the towel around his waist and reluctantly began putting his gear into the backpack. As he folded his clothes he noticed that he still had Lily's sweatshirt. He could have returned it to her in the morning, but on impulse he decided to place it by her door with a note. After listening and looking both ways, he propped open his door with his backpack and stepped into the hallway clad only in a towel. The neatly folded sweatshirt was placed next to the wall across from the door where she might be able to see it through the door's peephole. He put the note on top of the clothing with one of the fake roses and returned to his room.

Lily stepped out of the shower and wrapped herself in an oversized white fluffy towel. She intended to dry her hair, but thought she heard Sonny's door close. She quietly crept to her door and looked through the peephole, did not see anyone, but spotted her sweatshirt. Against her better judgment, Lily opened the door, looked both ways and quickly tried to retrieve her hoodie. But the act of squatting down caused the towel to loosen and in the short time it took her to pick up everything, the door shut in her face. She was mortified by her situation that was made worse when she heard the elevator ding, signaling its arrival on her level. In a panic she pounded on Sonny's door. He quickly opened the door and backed up to let her enter. With the note, rose, and sweatshirt in one hand, she tried in vain to keep herself covered. The battle for modesty was lost when the towel, hoodie, and note fell to the floor. In a state of shock, she crossed her arms over her breasts, still holding the rose. Not realizing his own wardrobe malfunction, Sonny said, "Good God Almighty."

Trying to regain her composure, Lily said, "I got locked out. I didn't plan this. It was an accident."

Sonny stepped forward and took her in his arms and said, "I don't care."

DAY 99

Sonny slept longer than he had intended. When he reached over to the other side of the bed, he discovered she was gone. After he showered, brushed his teeth and dressed, he knocked on Lily's door.

They took the elevator down to the restaurant and occasionally made mundane conversation, but Sonny sensed that something was different now. He wanted to talk about the actions that had transpired between them the night before, but every time he started, Lily would change the subject. So, during the quiet breakfast, he uploaded his latest videos. Any sign of Lily had been carefully edited out.

There was a joint feeling of sadness in the air as Sonny drove her and himself back to the trail. After they parted, they would both savor the time they shared together in Bethlehem. But now, each one thought about what lay ahead. Sonny was rested, healed, and raring to go. Lily was leaving the good times behind and dreaded facing the reality of possibly losing her farm. Back at Blue Mountain Lakes Road, Lily sat in her vehicle and watched Sonny walk away.

She took out the note he had written her the night before and read it one more time. *Lily, I find you adorable. The time I have spent with you has been worth every mile, every mountain, and every blister. Sonny, XXOOX.* She wasn't sure if the tears were caused by happiness, fear, loneliness, or love. After a minute, she decided it was a combination of all and began the drive back to Indiana. Rejuvenated from much needed rest, good food and company, both returned to face the mountains of their lives.

Right away, Sonny spotted a red-spotted admiral butterfly along the still rocky path and took its picture. Much greenery surrounded him, but there were few blooms. The summer heat had arrived and he was sweating when he reached Sunrise Mountain Pavilion. The large rectangular shelter house, with its fourteen stone columns supporting the wooden shake-shingle roof, was located on a ridge with good views. After Sonny videoed the structure, Madison called. His phone signal was weak and he stopped to talk where he was, so the connection wasn't lost. "Hi Dad. I haven't heard from you in a while and wanted to make sure you were okay."

"I'm fine. Have you seen my latest videos?"

"Yes, I just watched them. It looks like you had a relaxing time in Bethlehem."

"I did. I should probably do that more often, but Baxter Park (Home of Mount Katahdin, the northern terminus of the A.T.) closes on October 15th and ..."

"Okay, Dad. Getting back to Bethlehem. I didn't see any other hikers in your videos this time."

Sonny was getting a bit annoyed by the accusations. "You saw the videos. I ate well. I checked out some museums. And I slept a lot."

"I'm going to hang up now, Dad. But before I do, just tell me one more thing."

"Sure, Madison. What is it?"

"How long have you been wearing lipstick?"

Sonny heard her laughing before the phone went dead. He quickly scanned his videos of the past two days and found the clue that only a woman would have noticed. At the end of the second day while at Mama Nina, Sonny had made a quick video while Lily was in the restroom. On the corner of the left side of his mouth was a smudge of red lipstick. He was tempted to call Madison right back and try to convince her that he had spaghetti sauce on his face. But his meal had come with a white sauce, while Lily was the one who had tomato sauce. Madison the detective would know the flaw of his argument and would use the evidence against him. Any further deception would dig deeper the hole he was already in. He threw up his hands in a surrendering gesture, laughed, and was glad she had called.

The trail turned less rocky and Sonny stopped for lunch at Culver Fire Tower. The lookout was locked but he enjoyed seeing the boats and cottages on Culver Lake while he sat on a rock and ate half of a sub and drank part of a bottle of Coke. Lily had given him homemade sour cream cookies with raisins and he finished them off before resuming the hike.

At one point, he came out onto a roadbed and wasted precious time and energy looking for a white blaze. A local woman, who was taking a walk, pointed him in the right direction. Even after a late start, Sonny had covered 19.5 miles and then pitched his tent by Mashipacong Shelter. There was no spring, but the metal bear box contained gallons of water. Sonny checked the time and thought that Lily must be back home. He ate the remainder of his lunchtime meal and as it got dark, listened to the sounds of distant firecrackers. He brushed his teeth and then walked away from the campsite to take a pee. While doing so, a man in pink leotards and a lavender sleeveless V-neck sweater did the same on a tree close to Sonny. The overly friendly man claimed to be a section-hiker who went by the name of Flaming Dragon. With an accent, the strange man said, "We should hang out like this more often."

Sonny finished, zipped up, and said, "I take it you're not an American?"

"What nationality do you think I am?"

"I'm going to say you're Gaelic."

The joke went right over his head. "No, I'm Canadian and I'm getting really tired of the week-long fireworks. One night should be plenty."

Feeling tired and agitated himself, Sonny said, "Yeah well, maybe when you win your independence from England, you'll celebrate too."

Indignantly the man responded. "We are an independent nation."

"Oh? Whose picture is on your money?"

The man had no answer and Sonny went to his tent for the night.

DAY 100

The skies were blue when Sonny began his daily hike. He should have been happy or at least satisfied, but instead he felt sad. When he realized it was day 100, he remembered the lyrics from the song by 3 Doors Down - *Here Without You.* The ear buds provided him the tune and he wondered if the emotions evoked were from knowing Ellen or Lily.

He continued on the trail that was flat but still very rocky. He photographed fragrant thumbergia and ate a banana, snacks, and Gatorade. About midday, he came to High Point Sate Park on the New Jersey and New York border. He entered the stone with wood-shake roof building, showed the ranger his thru-hike tag, and was rewarded with a free cold can of Pepsi.

Shortly after, he climbed a wooden observation platform for a view of Lake Marcia. A well-worn path, leading to the beach and snack bar, lured Sonny off of the trail. He corrected his mistake and then arrived at and entered the granite monument that stood atop New Jersey's highest point. He then climbed the 291 steps of the tower's spiral staircase for a look around through the dirty windows.

The rest of the day was spent walking through a lot of bogs. Fortunately, much of the low areas were improved with raised boards. When Sonny went to take a picture of blooming spotted wintergreen, he startled a turkey, which flew away. While walking past a large pond he videoed a white mother swan with five gray cygnets. Several hikers joined Sonny at a house belonging to the park system and filled their water bottles from a spigot. They all camped around the crowded Pochuck Mountain Shelter.

Sonny had sore feet after 19.6 miles and just wanted to relax, but he recognized some of the hikers and decided to be sociable. After speaking at length with Antelope, Lioness, Lemon, and Lime, they introduced him to a frail-looking, middle-aged guy from Columbus, Ohio. The intelligent and witty man was named Thesaurus. His misuse of words and phrases combined with a wry sense of humor made smart people chuckle. Sonny was heading to his tent when Perky got his attention and said, "See that tall guy over there with the two girls?"

"Here we go again. Yes?"

"His name is Plunger. Know why he got named that?"

"He's a plumber?"

"No. It's because he..."

"You don't have to tell me, Perky."

"It's because he jumps off of every tall bridge on the trail. Not the little ones over the streams. The bridge has to be a big one and the water has to be deep. What did you think I was going to say?"

"I don't know. But I'm going to say goodnight. See you on the trail."

DAY101

In the morning, Sonny still had hot spots on the balls of his feet. His knees were a little sore and he took some Tylenol. The comments from the Guthook app warned of sparse, or stagnant water and rocky trails with mosquitoes. Before starting back on the trail, Sonny saw that the power on his phone was low, so he plugged it into his one-pound rechargeable Anker battery to charge it.

Beautiful blue skies that provided scenic views meant that there were no clouds to buffer the heat of the blazing sun. The lack of rain allowed Sonny's blisters to heal, but also had a negative effect on the availability of drinking water. After going up and over Pochuck Mountain, he came to a swamp and a new-looking walkway. The Pochuck Boardwalk was one and a half mile long and included a 110-foot suspension bridge over a slow moving stream. The raised wooden path wound its way over the wetlands and reminded Sonny of those near the shores of Lake Erie. When he took a picture of wild bergamot, he saw that he had a text from August stating that he had acquired two tickets for The Ohio State Buckeyes vs. The Team Up North in November. It was one more thing Sonny had to look forward to after completing the A.T.

The breeze picked up and kept the mosquitoes away for the time being. It wasn't very often that the trail was easy, but Sonny knew it would get harder after lunch. He crossed the bridge and finished the boardwalk at NJ-94. There he met trail angel Dave, who gave him a peach and watched over his backpack while Sonny made a short walk to a hotdog stand. He sat on a picnic table under an umbrella and ate an appetizer consisting of a hotdog with onions, catsup and mustard, along with a bag of chips, and a cold can of Coke. From there, he crossed back over the state route and found the entrance to Heaven Hill Farm.

Originally a fruit and vegetable stand in 1982, the business had expanded. The massive brown barn and greenhouses now housed a farm market and garden center. It also had a bakery and sold ice cream. Sonny sat and drank a root beer float and then bought pastries for later. While leaving the property, Sonny disturbed a pair of mockingbirds who had a nest in a blue spruce. The birds were not happy to see him and showed their displeasure by squawking, displaying wingspans, and swirling their tail feathers.

Sonny sat down with Dave and ate grapes, pineapple, and cookies. The trail angel was a former hot air balloon captain who had completed a thru-hiked in 1982. He said he didn't have a trail name but would accept the title of Moose Man due to a run-in with the large animal while in Maine. After the break, it was time to get back to work and Sonny started up the incline. A mile later he began a steeper climb up a rock-strewn path known as Stairway to Heaven. The views were good, but as always, he had to work for them. Sonny took in fluids and continued to sweat.

In mid afternoon he stepped out onto Warwick Turnpike just as a section hiker and his wife were stowing their packs in the trunk of their car. Michael and Tammi were avid hikers from Pennsylvania who were intent on completing the Appalachian Trail, one section at a time. Michael said to Sonny, "I don't have any pop, but here's a bottle of water, if you want it."

Sonny graciously accepted and when he admitted to being a thru-hiker, Michael was thrilled. Sonny was envious of his enthusiasm. He felt like a member of the 1980's Russian hockey team watching the victorious USA players celebrate. Somewhere along the way he had lost his passion. Michael said, "Boy, I sure would like to walk awhile with you."

Sonny felt honored and humbled, but not sure if Michael was serious, so he challenged him. "Well c'mon, let's go then."

During the next half an hour, Sonny found out just how dedicated a hiker that man was. Michael turned to his wife and asked her if she would drive to the next crossroad and wait for him there. Tammi agreed and for the next 1.4 miles, Michael asked questions. Sonny felt the man could have easily walked faster than him, but held back to hear his answers. Michael's blue tee shirt was soaked with perspiration and his glasses needed to be wiped at intervals, but his easy smile radiated enthusiasm. His presence gave Sonny a boost and he was sad to see him leave, but the finish line was many weeks away and he trudged onward. He was always so grateful for the trail angels, but disheartened to think he would never see most of them, ever again. To boost his spirits, Sonny put in his ear buds. The first song that came on was by Cat Stevens - *The Wind*.

Towards the end of the warm day, Sonny came upon an iced cooler filled with bottles of Gatorade, cans of Mountain Dew, Genesee beer, and packages of string cheese. He and another man and woman sat down and refreshed themselves. Up on a ridge, he stepped over the New Jersey/New York border. Painted lines around a metal A.T. benchmark that was embedded in rock indicated the spot. At Prospect Rock, the highest point on the trail in New York, he took in a view of Greenwood Lake. The 16.9 miles of the day put him at Furnace Brook where he put up his tent next to a dried-up streambed. He rinsed off with his water bottle, laid on his sleeping bag, and reflected on the day's events.

DAY 102

Abrupt ascents and descents were trying, but one climb was made much easier by the installation of a rebar ladder. Cairns on the bare ridges replaced the white blazes in areas of nonexistent trees. Sonny was cooled by the wind while looking down on Greenwood Lake. A trail angel named Rooster, who had thru-hiked in 2017, gave Sonny water and fruit. The tall man was hiking to raise money for ALS. He had not met Lily, but had heard of her. Sonny made a video of him as he spoke of the charity and displayed his tee shirt that advertised the cause. Rooster signed off with his customary crow.

Late in the morning, Sonny found himself at Bellvale Farms. The white metal building with green metal roof was not serving lunch yet, but Sonny was able to purchase a quart of strawberry ice cream. He took a seat at one of the unoccupied picnic tables near the white picket fence and then brought out his folding titanium spoon and went to work on the appetizer. His next stop was at a stand called Hotdog Plus where he sampled the local cuisine.

In the afternoon he watched two does leap over rock pile walls and then casually cross the trail in front of him. As they flicked their tails and flapped their ears, Sonny assumed the insects were harassing them also. While coming down off of dusty stone steps, Sonny slipped backwards and startled a turkey. His eighth fall resulted in a cut left hand and a scrape on his right shin.

The humidity increased in the afternoon and the trail became very rocky. Following one last steep climb for the day, Sonny stopped after 14.2 miles. Near dark, he ate a supper meal of pistachio nuts with a can of 7-up while fighting off the mosquitoes, and then rinsed off before entering his sleeping quarters.

DAY 103

Before breaking camp, Sonny searched the ground for tracks of whatever large animal had noisily walked past his tent in the dark. The rain during the night that had erased the evidence was reduced to a slow drizzle, fueling another humid day. Several downed trees across the trail and a surge of mosquitoes made life difficult for the hikers. The arrival of the sun drove up the heat index and access sites to water were scarce. In two locations, Sonny found gallons of water left by trail angels, Susan and Hikeman.

After entering Harriman State Park, he waved down to the vehicles that were rushing underneath as he crossed the walking bridge over I-87. He videoed the Lemon Squeezer while attempting to pass through the landmark. The narrow rock passageway was inclined and slanted to the left. Sonny tried to complete the challenge while wearing his backpack, but found it too cumbersome. He removed and carried it in front while recording the event. There was a tough climb afterwards, but then the trail entered a grassy section with well-spaced trees and docile white-tailed does. Sonny ate handfuls of wild blueberries and took pictures of an adult eastern newt, a small garter snake, and rose spirea. At Fingerboard Shelter, he signed the login book and heated a chicken teriyaki meal and then followed it with a warm bottle of Coke. While leaving the lunch area, he spotted a marbled salamander.

Later in the hot afternoon, he stopped and talked with a hiker who had been taking a break with his dog. The large, fluffy white Great Pyrenees wore green saddlebags filled with its food and water. The dog's name was Ghost and he readily accepted the massage and praise applied by Sonny. Afterwards, while walking along a ridge, Sonny saw the New York City skyline and then he fell for the ninth time.

After 15.6 miles, he camped on a ridge with a view of the Hudson River to the east and a loud party to the west. He was very thirsty and drained much of his water supply before retiring to his tent. Even though he wore his earplugs, sleep eluded him for over an hour. The noise from the celebration below sounded like disco music and Sonny didn't recognize any of the tunes or lyrics. The DJ had it cranked up, but Sonny finally fell asleep when he imagined himself on a cruise ship.

Day 104

It was another warm morning. The weather app informed Sonny that he was facing a humid day that would reach 100 degrees. As he made his morning video while leaving the campsite, he fell for the third day in a row. The tenth fall left him with a scraped forearm. According to the comments on Guthook, the prices for food and lodging were going up. But at this point, Sonny didn't care about the costs, he only wanted to be comfortable. He knew that before the day was over, he would hit the 1400-mile mark and some of his necessities would be satisfied.

A day-hiker gave him a bottle of water as he passed by and then he met a hiker named Subway. The man was a retired policeman who lived nearby and had attempted the A.T. in 2017. He walked with Sonny through an area with a lot of stone steps and gave him advice about the upcoming portion of the trail. Subway told a story about two thru-hikers he had met in the area during a previous year. He said that his wife had first met the two hikers during an evening walk and as they talked, she became a food tease. She tortured the men by mentioning pizza and cold beer and then relayed the story to Subway when she got home. Subway decided to surprise the two hikers with pizza and beer trail magic. He figured that they would illegally stealth camp nearby and after buying the food, easily located the two tents in the dark. Using his cop voice, he demanded that the lawbreakers come out of their tents. When they emerged and saw who it was, they were greatly relieved and very pleased with the food. As it turned out, one of the hikers was also a cop and the other shared a talent with Subway, both played the bagpipes.

There was a stone observation tower with a metal roof on top of Bear Mountain. The climb up was much easier than the last tower he had ventured upon and the spotless windows allowed good views of the state. The close proximity of the Big Apple made the peak a popular place and it had restrooms, garbage bins, and vending machines. Sonny bought some pop and moved on.

For weeks he had observed what he thought were raspberry bushes along the trail. Throughout the months, he had seen the pink flowers develop into fruit and ripen into orange-red berries. He learned that they were wine berries that tasted marvelous, but were invasive.

At the Bear Mountain Recreation Area, he saw a scarlet tanager, walked by a picnic area and playground next to Hessian Lake, and then entered the Bear Mountain Inn and ordered food. The salad contained beets, walnuts, lima beans, and spinach. Sonny downed a few glasses of water while waiting for his meal to arrive. He sipped the glass of stout and slowly chewed the medium rare flank steak and french fries. Before he left the restaurant, he put away a vanilla malt for dessert and went outside to face the heat.

At its lowest elevation, 160 feet above sea level, the Appalachian Trail goes through part of the Trailside Zoo. When Sonny entered the attraction, he looked down on the large and crowded swimming pool. He wanted to go there and cool off, but felt that his choice of swimwear might be frowned upon. Instead, he continued on through the zoo and with envy, videoed the bears that were standing under a cool shower. After he took a picture of the box turtle, he left the place and walked to the toll road. He admired a 1924 stone building with its tiled roof and took pictures for his pipe dream of building a castle someday.

The air was warm and stagnant as he crossed the Hudson River on the Bear Mountain Bridge. On the far side, he turned left onto US-6 and walked on the side of the hot asphalt road until the white blazes instructed him to turn right and make a steep climb for one half mile. At the top, Sonny felt the sweat dripping off his head as he looked down the hill like a victorious boxer standing over a knocked out opponent.

He and a handful of other hikers patronized the Appalachian Market on Route 9 and filled their food bags. Sonny's day ended after only 13 miles at Graymoor Spiritual Life Center. He had intended to take a shower there and move on, but changed his mind and pitched his tent near the others. The Franciscan Friars allowed thru-hikers to utilize the facilities of the picnic area on their campus. The open area past the ball diamonds had a pavilion with power for charging cell phones. There was also water, porta-johns, and a shower.

After eating his supper, Sonny looked for a place to hang his bear bag. The devil tempted him to hang it from the large wooden cross at the far end of the ball diamonds. But after some consideration, Sonny thought that although he might be the only member of the Catholic Church in attendance, it would set a bad precedence, and so he hung the food bag from a tree, away from the pavilion. When the shower was available, he entered and washed his body. Afterwards, he wanted to just head to the tent and rest his sore knees, but first had to retrieve his charging battery in the pavilion.

The heat and hardships of the trail took a toll on all of the hikers. Despite that, some of the hikers were always happy, while others were temperamental. Sonny felt that he was part of the latter group. If he had always said what was on his mind, he wouldn't have had any friends. Everyone handled the stress in their own manner, but unfortunately, a few became irritable and relieved themselves on the others.

An elder pastor from North Carolina called Shepherd was having a heated debate about religious philosophies with a younger man named Earl Lee, who was the atheist son of a Texas Baptist minister. It got to the point where Earl challenged Shepherd to a fight, at which point, Sonny tried to calm things down by changing the subject. "Hey, Earl Lee. You know, if you got up before the sunrise every morning, they might call you 'Earl Lee Riser.'"

Shepherd saw the opportunity given to slip away unscathed and before doing just that said, "That trail name sounds familiar, Sonny."

Earl Lee, who still was in fighting mode, eyed his next opponent and said to Sonny, "You Yankees still think you're better than us."

Those who were standing nearby took a step back, but one of them said, "Let it go Earl. That war ended a very long time ago. Let's just focus on hiking to Maine."

"Naw, my pappy told me never to take any crap from anyone from Ohio. Sherman was from Ohio."

Sonny said, "That is true; you certainly know your history. General William Tecumseh Sherman was from Lancaster, Ohio, and is probably best known for his capture of Atlanta and the following March to the Sea."

Earl Lee sneered and said, "He didn't have to do that."

Sonny tried to reason with him. "Earl, did you ever win a close fight?"

"Yeah, lots of them. So what?"

"Well, then what happened?"

"What do you mean?"

"I'm guessing that after the other guy healed somewhat, he started thinking - 'If only I had tried a little harder, I would have won,' and pretty soon he wanted a rematch." Sonny continued, "But, if you had pounded the snot out of the guy, he would have avoided any future quarrels with you."

"So you're saying I should pound the snot out of you."

"I'm saying you're angry about something else, but you want to take it out on me."

Earl said, "You're right about that." But, as the angry man stepped toward Sonny, a large hand clasped Earl on his shoulder and stopped him cold in his tracks.

The hand belonged to a hiker who had just arrived at camp and Sonny was very glad to see him again.

Crew Cut said to the aggressor, "Take it easy. Sonny is a very good friend of mine and I'm sure all of this is just a big misunderstanding."

Earl sized up the longhaired marine and decided to call it a night.

Until sunset, Sonny and Crew Cut talked about everything that had happened since they first met, many miles ago. The marine informed Sonny of hikers who had left the trail for a variety of reasons. One woman had survived being bitten by a copperhead but decided that that was her signal to leave. A young and fit man, that everyone figured would make it to the end, face-planted somewhere in Virginia and called it quits. For a moment, Sonny felt a slight tinge of jealousy of those who were afforded the chance to abandon the trek. But he quickly pushed those thoughts away because he knew he would never forgive himself if he ever quit. Crew Cut also delivered more bad news when he told Sonny that Potty Mouth had yellow-blazed (completed part of the trail via motor vehicle) and was now in the area. Sonny knew that Perky, Ogle, and some others had flip-flopped (completed the sections of the trail in a disjointed manner) to catch up with tramily members, but they would later return and complete the skipped sections.

Just before darkness set in, Sonny said goodnight to everyone and took his phone and fully-charged battery to his tent. He called his family members and they updated each other about their personal current events. All of them watched his YouTube videos and offered encouragement. Sonny jokingly referred to them as merely cheerleaders, but he knew that it was the thought of them that pushed him on everyday. Lily sounded stressed as she relayed her meetings with the bill collectors and Sonny wished he knew the words that would comfort her. He fell asleep that night in a melancholy mood.

DAY 105

The day promised to be another warm and humid one, so Sonny started early to get in some cooler miles. Any fallen trees across the trail had been recently cut away. The conditions of both the trail and Sonny were evolving. Like the peaks and valleys that he walked through every day, his emotional state also rose and fell in dramatic fashion. At least with the terrain, he could look ahead in his AWOL guide and see what the future held.

He couldn't remember the last time he had shivered. The bitter cold was replaced with heat and humidity that left him sticky with perspiration at the end of cach day. He found it impossible to enter his sleeping bag without rinsing off first. At the onset, he had suffered from black bear paranoia, but now he had no problems falling asleep. He entered his tent every night confident that he had done everything correctly not to attract the varmints, and he was always very tired. Despite eating the freeze-dried meals and constantly munching on energy bars, nuts, dried fruit, and a variety of candy throughout the day, and pigging-out at restaurants and food stands, Sonny had lost a lot of weight. The bubble of hikers, that had crowded the trail early on, was gone. Only the serious and fortunate ones were left. For the most part, he walked alone and thought about the events of his life. The proud moments inspired him. But there were times, when he would go to that place in his mind, where he kept hidden away, all of his mistakes. During those periods, he would wallow in self-pity, embarrassment, and regret. He always considered himself a loner, but found that he did enjoy the company of others and tended to rattle-on whenever he met someone new. The soul searching, or as he referred to it, 'penance,' left him feeling drained. But after climbing out of the abyss, he would lift his eyes to the next peak in his future and again head north, one step at a time.

At Dennytown Road, sat a small stone hut with a spigot for filling water bottles and rinsing off. Sonny and six other hikers made use of the oasis and then sat down in a shady spot for lunch. While they were eating, a large bus and some SUVs pulled into the parking lot. Immediately, a large number of rambunctious junior high students with backpacks piled out of the vehicles and were rounded up by their leaders. An old thru-hiker verbalized what Sonny was thinking. "I hope they're not walking north."

The trail in the afternoon led across a cascading brook on stepping-stones near a beaver pond. A light rain provided relief from the heat as Sonny viewed the sandy beach of Canopus Lake. At the summit of Shenandoah Mountain, Sonny took a picture of the United States flag that was painted on the rock surface, in memory of September 11, 2001. Just before ending the day with 18.9 miles and camping at RPH Shelter, he slipped on some wet boards and fell for the eleventh time. It was a non-injury fall and he proceeded to erect his tent. The facilities included a white-painted block building with a roof-covered patio, a flower garden, and a privy. Sonny found out too late that pizzas could be delivered there.

Day 106

It had rained at night and Sonny's shoes and socks absorbed the wetness from the lush plant life crowding the slender trail. The first section that he hiked through at the start of the day was hazy, and the trail was littered with fallen trees from a recent storm. A maintenance crew had gone to work soon after and cleared the path for the ardent hikers. The days still began with the singing birds and ended at sunset, but they were getting shorter.

He crossed the Taconic State Parkway, paused to take in the views at a few spots along the trail and then came to Route 52. There he exited the trail and figured it was worth the time and effort to walk the half mile down the busy road to Mountaintop Deli. His judgment proved correct. He bought an egg and ham sandwich with orange juice for breakfast. Next, he had some ice cream and a bottle of Mountain Dew. A roast beef sub was bagged to go along with candy bars, a bottle of root beer, a muffin, and a Kind bar.

In back of the building, four other hikers were eating, charging their phones, and laying out their tents and clothing on the grass to dry in the bright sunshine. Sonny joined them at the picnic table. He had seen the younger men at a few of the campsites, but never conversed with some of them. Not that he could get a word in even if he had tried, for all of them always seemed to be talking at the same time. There was the dreadlock dude named Slang Banger and a serious guy who never smiled, called Webster, who was arguing with Thesaurus about the definition of a word. Then there was Doug who appeared to be talking to himself. Sonny dismissed Slang Banger as annoying, was curious about Webster, and thought Thesaurus was an interesting character. Sonny hadn't made up his mind about Doug yet. Thesaurus had a baby face that made him look younger than he was, but when he spoke, his appearance matured rapidly. Some of the hikers thought he was imbecilic, but Sonny felt he was closer to genius. Just during the debate with the others at the table, Sonny heard the man purposely misuse words and familiar phrases and most went right over the heads of the other three hikers. Sonny heard him say things like: 'I had to overcome much *diversity* in my life,' 'I'm going to sue you for *defecation* of character,' 'You're in for a *shrewd* awakening,' 'to *eat* his own,' and 'I'm going to knock you *scentless*,' to name a *phew*.

Sonny was the first of the group to leave and get back on the trail, but of course, the younger hikers soon caught up and passed him. He marveled at a white oak that had a diameter of five feet and grew in the middle of the trail. The streams were full and flowing, something he hadn't witnessed in a while, due to the drought. The trail led through another rock passage, but it was wide enough where Sonny did not have to remove his pack. Near Nuclear Lake, he was summoned by fellow hikers and invited to join them for a swim. It didn't take much convincing. Sonny stripped down and hopped in the cool water.

Twenty minutes later he felt refreshed as he followed the trail next to the lake. After walking by more stone pile hedges, he met a giant tree with a seven-foot diameter, another white oak. With an hour of sunlight left, he applied insect repellent and made camp alone, after covering 18.4 miles. Somewhere nearby, he heard the sounds of a city and anticipated its benefits.

DAY 107

In the distance, Sonny heard a train rumbling through, beyond the bog. Up and over a wooden bridge, he crossed the narrow Swamp River and continued on another long boardwalk through acres of cattails. He tried to call for reservations at an upcoming hostel, but was informed that the business had shut down for the year. Fortunately, he learned from the comments of other hikers on Guthook, that there was another place to stay in South Kent.

The Rustic River Getaway was not advertised, but went by word of mouth. Even though it was early in the morning, Sonny called in hopes of securing a room for the night. A woman named Karen answered the phone and Sonny apologized for the early intrusion on her life. She jokingly vowed that she would punch him when she saw him later.

At the far end of the swamp, in the middle of nowhere, Sonny stepped across the railroad and read the sign above the platform and bench that served as a train station. To the east, the tracks led to Southeast, White Plains, and New York. The route to the west carried passengers to Wassaic. He took pictures and then continued north until he arrived at a shady spot known as Hurd's Corner. There he found a cooler of bottled water and an empty six-pack of Magic Hat beer. He filled all of his bottles and his stomach with water from the containers and then made a video. He thanked trail angel Caroline for supplying the trail magic for over a decade at that location.

In a while, he used a wooden set of stairs that brought him safely over an electric fence into a pasture of Hereford cows. Concrete pillars on top of a hill supported a dark cylindrical water tower with a pointed top. The clear sky matched the color of the abundant light blue chicory flowers. A warm sun shone on the red clover and Queen Anne's lace and as Sonny made his way up a hill, he noticed the bovine were making their way to a shady grove. Every so often, a much-appreciated breeze would offer a respite from the humidity. Small details, like listening to the songbirds and seeing a purple and white bog orchid, boosted his spirits.

For a few miles later in the afternoon, Sonny hiked on flat ground alongside the roaring rapids of the Housatonic River. A sizable footbridge crossed the Ten Mile River before it flowed into the larger river. A mile later, he passed through the unpainted wooden-covered Bulls Bridge. He then stopped at Bulls Bridge Country Store, purchased supplies, drank some pop, and headed a half-mile down Route 7, away from downtown Kent, Connecticut. Before he reached his destination for the night, he watched a college-age woman run towards him on the other side of the road. She moved efficiently at a good pace and Sonny did not know at the time that she was also staying at the Rustic River Getaway.

At the given address, Sonny turned down a driveway towards the river. There was a newer large log cabin built on the side of the steep riverbank where the owners resided. Nearby was one of two rustic seasonal cabins with wood-shake siding. Sonny didn't see anyone around as he investigated the smaller cabin. He went to knock on the log cabin door just as a SUV parked in front of the green garage door. Sonny introduced himself as Phoenix to the lady driver, and Karen didn't punch him. However, she did prank him by downplaying the accommodations, saying that she had put him in the overflow cabin. The way she said it disappointed him, but he figured it would still be better than sleeping in the woods. She handed him the keys, told him that supper would be ready in an hour and pointed him towards a green footbridge. As Sonny walked on the flagstones and crossed the span over the ravine, it reminded him of Hocking Hills in Ohio, and he felt a little homesick.

Years ago, the small building had been used as a hunting cabin. Later, it was renovated. The main area was the kitchen, complete with a stove, microwave, and refrigerator. There was a sitting area with a fireplace that Sonny had no intentions of using. He parked his gear in the bedroom and then made use of the outdoor shower to wash his body and some clothing. Then he hung the wet clothes over the railings of the deck that provided an excellent view of the river. Someone had graciously left a bottle of beer in the refrigerator for him and he sat on the deck drinking it with a bag of pistachios. While relaxing and watching the Housatonic River flow away from him, Sonny created a video and then made phone calls.

First, he called his mother. She told him that all of the cherries had been picked, washed, and sold at his fruit stand or at the Bowling Green farmers' market. August had his entire family working in the orchard and they were resting up for the upcoming peach harvest. Henry and his family were enjoying the few remaining summer days of Colorado while they could.

Madison was pleased to hear that her father had found a good woman and wanted to meet her. The call to Lily went to voicemail. Sonny left a short message and said that he would call later. He then walked back across the bridge and found Karen and her husband Cliff busily preparing the meal.

The three other thru-hikers, which Sonny had never met before, were eating hamburgers, baked beans, and vegetables. Also in attendance was the woman runner that Sonny had seen on the road earlier. She was a senior at the University of Connecticut and was staying in the house for the summer with the owners. Sonny took two hamburgers and filled his plate with the other healthier items. There was a cooler with a selection of liquid refreshments for the guests. Sonny and another man accepted the two remaining grilled patties. In an attempt to be entertaining, one of the hikers told a joke about a talking parrot. When the polite laughter receded, Sonny said, "I know a joke about a talking dog. It was told by a priest named Father Matt during his homily many years ago."

More than one person urged him on. "Let's hear it."

So, Sonny began. "A man took a vacation to Ireland and after landing in Dublin, he rented a car and was driving to his hotel. As he drove through a residential area, he spotted a sign in front of a small house that read - TALKING DOG FOR SALE. The man's curiosity got the best of him so he parked the car and knocked on the front door."

"A gruff old man answered the door and said, 'What do you want?'"

"'I saw the sign and wanted to hear the dog.'"

"Before rudely shutting the door, the cranky man said, 'He's out in the backyard.'"

"The tourist walked around the house and entered the fenced in yard where a male yellow Labrador retriever sat. Worried that he was part of a prank, the man spoke to the dog. 'So you can talk?'"

"The dog said, 'Yep.'"

"'That's amazing.'"

"The dog elaborated. 'That's not the half of it. Let me tell you my story. I was born in Toledo, Ohio, one of a litter of eight puppies. From an early age, I learned to speak English and I decided to use my talent to help the government. They hired me on the spot and sent me along on several diplomatic missions with the humans. Many times I would be left alone with the foreign representatives who had no idea that I could understand what they were saying. Our government learned many top secrets in that manner. I got to travel all around the world and have a boatload of accommodations. Then one day, while on a mission here in Ireland, I met and fell in love with a blonde Lab.

We were married and had two litters of puppies. I'm retired now.'"

"The man was obviously impressed and told the dog. 'I'll be right back.'"

"He walked to the front door and knocked again. The crabby old man answered and said, 'What do you want?'"

"'I want to buy the dog. What's the price?'"

"The old man thought for a while and finally suggested, 'How about ten euros?'"

"The tourist was astounded. 'Ten euros. Why so low?'"

"'Because the dog's a liar. He hasn't done half of those things.'"

After the laughter subsided, cookies were handed out for dessert and Cliff told of the relationship he and Karen had with U Conn. Over a decade earlier, students from the college, which was a two-hour drive away, approached the owners and asked if they could cross the green walking bridge to study butterflies. The location on the west bank was suitable because it had filtered sunlight and desirable plants. Cliff told them, not only was it okay, but also suggested that they stay in an unused cabin. Every summer a different student arrived and spent the days counting butterflies by netting and marking wings.

The co-ed retrieved her net and gave a short presentation about her project. She was mainly interested in the northern metalmark. The topside of the one-inch wide endangered butterfly had faded brown and orange wings, but the underside of the green-eyed insect glittered with silver filaments. Sonny could tell the young men at the table were quite taken by the lepidopterist and hung on her every word. After thanking Cliff and Karen, Sonny grabbed another can of beer and went back to his cabin to call Lily.

He sat in a chair on the deck and elevated his feet while listening to the sounds of the river below. The beer was about gone by the time Lily answered his call. She seemed calm and resigned to the fact that she would lose the farm before the year was over. Sonny carefully listened to the details of her financial problems and they discussed viable options. Finally he suggested, "Maybe it's time for that change of occupation that you talked about."

Lily sighed, "Maybe. It is exciting to think about doing something new and it would be a great relief to get out from under this debt. But I'm going to hold on to hope for as long as I can and try to save the farm."

"I wish I could hold you right now, Lily."

"I wish you could too, Sonny."

"Just say the word and I'll be there."

After a pause she said, "Thanks, but you need to finish what you started and so do I."

"Well then, are you coming back here any time soon?"

"I don't know for certain, but I think so. Just not as frequent as before."

After they hung up, Sonny stayed seated and reviewed every thought that was whirling around in his head. He held out his hands and looked at them. They were not shaking, but he sensed that his pulse was elevated. He climbed into bed hoping to fall asleep quickly, but felt overwhelmed by dilemmas and suffered from insomnia. When he deemed the situation was hopeless, Sonny remembered the Serenity Prayer. He spoke the words to himself, a calm came over him, and he slept until the sun rose.

DAY 108

Before leaving the cabin, Sonny reviewed the AWOL guide for information about what lay ahead of him on the trail. The day would consist of several steep climbs and descents. He decided to visit the privy one last time. The elaborate outhouse was one of the nicest he had ever experienced. It was painted and decorated inside and out. There was a rack full of magazines and unlike a moldering privy that used decaying leaves, lime was applied to erase any odors.

Before crossing back through Bulls Bridge, Sonny again stopped at the store and Gulf gas station where he sat outside and drank a mango smoothie before getting back on the trail. He soon arrived at a kiosk that indicated the New York/Connecticut border. Nine states down, five to go.

He stopped at Mount Algo Shelter and ate a large lunch. Normally, when he intended to walk until near sunset, he would eat a bigger midday meal and then just snack the rest of the day. For a few hours, he hiked up and over several small steep peaks and then descended a treacherous section using oversized stone steps. After surviving the dangerous parts, he arrived at the bottom of the hill and was distracted by a couple of rock climbers that were repelling down a bald face. There, Sonny fell for the twelfth time and scraped his elbow, but he was rewarded with a five-mile flat stroll along the Housatonic.

He spotted a fancy daylily that somehow got planted between the trail and the river. At first, he thought it was orange, but when he got closer to take a picture, he found it was really pink and yellow. While relishing the low effort and scenic path, he listened to cawing crows, donned his flying-insect veil, and reminisced about a short story he had read in the plush outhouse, earlier that day. The tale reminded him of the sort of grandfather that he vowed to be.

An old man told his grandson a fable as they walked on a trail through the forest. "In every man there are two wolves that control his character and they are constantly doing battle with each other. One represents kindness, bravery, and love and the other embodies greed, hatred and fear."

The grandson looked up at his grandfather and said, "Which one wins?"

The grandfather replied, "The one you feed the most."

The rare horizontal trail ended and Sonny listened to music for the final steep climb of the day. *Highway Song* by Blackfoot helped to complete the 17.6 miles and got him to Silver Hill Campsite. There was no shelter and Sonny did not care because the site had everything else, save a shower. Along with a pavilion, picnic tables, a deck with benches and a porch swing, there was also a privy, a bear box, and ample tenting spots. The water table was far below the hand pump and Sonny watched a couple of other hikers try in vain to bring water up into their containers. After they had quit in frustration, Sonny gave it a try. The others told him that he was wasting his time. He ignored the critics and primed the pump by pouring some water on the rod extending through the upper cap. As he operated the handle up and down, he could feel the suction lifting the ground water up the well casing. It took a while, but then the jeering turned to cheering, and each of the hikers grabbed their bags and bottles and waited their turn.

DAY 109

Sonny started his day with a sore lower back. He relieved some of the strain by tightening the shoulder straps and the hip belt and then finished climbing the mountain he had camped on. The mosquitoes attacked him as he took a picture of a white wood aster and then he arrived at another rock passageway. The split boulder was wide enough to allow a backpack, but the floor of the inclined path was strewn with smaller rock obstacles and organic debris.

After lunch, Sonny heard the sounds of a loud speaker from down below in the valley. There were a lot of parked cars and at first, he thought an auction was taking place. But then he heard and saw racecars tearing up the track. He stopped for a break at Hang Glider View and watched the race. Although Lime Rock Park was far away and the cars looked like toys from his viewing point, the noise was still very loud. While he sat there, he thought about where he might stop and eat at an upcoming town, later in the day. Sonny figured that all of those race fans were going to flood the restaurants after the event, so he called ahead and made arrangements for a delivered pizza at a specific time and location.

Late in the afternoon, after hiking up in the mountain peaks all day, he came down, crossed the

Housatonic River again, and walked on the road past the Housatonic Valley Memorial High School. The level trail then intersected Water Street and a parking lot. There were two fit women from Long Island packing their gear into a vehicle who had just completed a 15-mile section of the A.T. and were handing out left over supplies to thru-hikers. Sonny accepted a bottle of water from Liz and Concetta and thanked the trail angels. He took their picture and then continued into Falls Village.

The package store, where the pizza was to be delivered, was located in the small town across the street from a large historical building. The crowded restaurant had white lap siding and black shuttered windows. Sonny had imagined that a package store was similar to UPS or FedEx. To his surprise, he learned that it was a liquor outlet. He purchased two tall cans of stout and put them in his pack. When the large east coast garlic pizza arrived, Sonny bought a bottle of Mountain Dew and then sat outside the store and demolished the meal. Feeling satiated, he retraced his steps out of town past the red New Haven caboose and headed north.

Sonny crossed the river over an iron bridge and turned into the woods. In a short time, he came to the Great Falls of Amesville. He videoed the cascading water with the dam in the background and then stripped down to his swimming underwear and went into the river. After the refreshing dip, he dressed and finished the 17.4-mile day by unknowingly camping illegally on the peak of Mount Prospect. As the daylight faded, he drank one of the warm cans of beer and looked ahead at the forecast of a full week of rain.

DAY 110

He exited his tent with a morning view of the northern valleys. During the night, the rain began and a strong wind blew water into the tent soaking his clothes. He wrung them out, put them on and walked until he reached the top of Raccoon Hill. There he photographed a rock formation known as the Giant's Thumb. Soon after, he took a picture of his trekking poles alongside the sticks on the ground that signified the 1500-mile mark.

It was far from lunchtime, but visions of sugarplums and other culinary performers, danced in his head when he reached US-44. In less than a mile, the route turned into Main Street and he took in the sights of the upscale New England town while the drizzle continued. Salisbury was a charming settlement, lined with many white-sided homes and businesses. Sonny passed by the brick fire and city hall building, a statue that stood at the point of a triangular green space, and a tiny sheep pasture. Finally, he found the bakery, went inside, and sat down to experience a cinnamon roll with a cup of chai latte. Next, he recorded a tribute to his daughter for her birthday and then traveled a few blocks away, entered the local grocery and loaded his pack with trail food including a freshly made roast beef sandwich. Before leaving town, he disposed of his trash including food wrappers from his pockets. In the process, he inadvertently threw away his ear buds.

Leaving the town, he prepared mentally for the four mountain peaks ahead of him. The lost ear buds were equipped with a microphone that had limited the wind noise when videos were made. It also allowed the user to privately listen to music and podcasts. Invasive sounds that intruded on the tranquility of other hikers were taboo. Sonny took a picture of scarlet bee balm and then began the first climb without any electronic inspiration.

The next mountain peak was called the Lion's Head. When he reached the top, he sat on a rock and ate his sandwich with a bottle of Pepsi. It was windy and through the filtered sunlight, Sonny watched the shadows of the clouds rapidly move across the green land below. The following steep ascent brought him to the highest peak in Connecticut, known as Bear Mountain. On the summit was a vast cairn with a flat top. There he was greeted by fellow hikers and a trail angel name Cumulus. The man with long, stringy, white hair and a beard proclaimed to be an atheist and offered fruit. Sonny readily ate the grapes, berries, and apples. Later when the rain returned, he wondered if he would be punished like Adam in the Garden of Eden.

Climbing down the mountain, he reached the west end of Sages Ravine and the stream opened to a deep pool where Sonny was tempted to enter. A steep climb took him to the Connecticut/Massachusetts border.

Ten states down, four to go. The rain stopped, the wind increased, and Sonny filled all his bottles from a fast flowing stream. He had put off obtaining water until he absolutely needed it because he did not want to carry the extra weight. But he was thirsty and after the filtration process was complete, he drank a bottle and then stripped down and rinsed off.

At the narrow summit of Mount Race he could see the next challenge. Two miles later he was there on top of Mount Everett making a video of the surrounding landscape and foundation of a former fire tower. For many miles ahead, it would be all downhill. Due to the steepness and rocky conditions of the trail, the progress was slow and for the first time, the sun went down before Sonny reached his destination. When it became too dark to see his feet, he strapped on the headlamp.

After 17.8 miles, he arrived at Glen Brook Shelter, switched on the less intrusive red light, and set up the tent.

DAY 111

The tough climbs from the day before left Sonny with a sore left knee in the morning. He pulled on the cloth elastic knee support and took a Tylenol pill. The rain, which had begun sometime during the night, continued as he stowed his gear away. He folded and rolled up the wet and dirty tent and then stuffed it into the top of his backpack. He thought it was going to be another depressing full day of climbing wet rocks, but then the sun emerged and he found a blooming cluster of butter-and-eggs. A squadron of mosquitoes welcomed him to a bog, where he had to watch his step on a boardwalk that was being repaired, and then the walkway was reduced to raised boards.

Many of the hikers that he had come into contact with that day, stated that they were going to an event in Great Barrington for the night. Five miles down the road on US-7, the town was hosting activities for hikers that included food, showers, and tent sites. The event sounded appealing to Sonny, but he had a new pair of shoes waiting for him at another town further down the trail. A couple that he knew from Bowling Green, Ohio, had been following his progress via his YouTube channel and were in the area and wanted to meet up with him. Sonny called them and made arrangements to meet them in Dalton where he had secured a motel reservation.

He took a picture of a stone marker that designated the Last Battle of Shays Rebellion in 1787 and then crossed the Housatonic River again. Following another climb, Sonny arrived at Ledges and looked back at the peaks he had conquered. He thought he had enough bars of power on his phone to allow uploading of videos, but it was not to be.

After 14.3 miles, he stopped at Tom Leonard Shelter. The structure had been severely chewed on by porcupines and none of the hikers slept in there that night. The off-and-on rain during the day caused his socks, shoes, and clothing to be wet the entire day. He noticed that some of the other hikers were hanging clothes out to dry and he did the same. Food supplies were low and he dined on pistachios, peanut M&Ms, string cheese, and the second can of warm stout.

DAY 112

Sonny carefully rationed the food supplies that were left. Before leaving the campsite, he ate his last banana while swatting mosquitoes. He had less than forty-three miles to reach the city of Dalton where his new shoes awaited him at the post office. The first part of the day was downhill and after he crossed over MA-23, he passed by Benedict Pond and stopped to check out the views at The Ledges. At a beaver pond, he felt the burn on the top of his raw toes as he crossed Swan Brook. There were several streams with good flow and he stopped at one to make water and tape his toes.

When he reached Jerusalem Road, Sonny looked to his left and saw a small red roadside stand with a white A.T. symbol painted on it. After a short walk, he surveyed the edible items for sale and then purchased several bags of chips, candy bars, and pop. Apparently, someone had unplugged the small refrigerator to charge their phone and neglected to plug it back in causing the soft drinks to be warm. He sat down at the picnic table under the large shade tree and began eating the snacks. He opened an orange can of pop that he thought was an Orange Crush. His taste buds anticipated a sweet flavor, but what they got was something akin to birch bark beer. The large label on the can said Moxie and boasted of being *Distinctively Different.* Being warm did nothing to improve the experience, but he drank it anyways.

His lunch was below the recommended daily allowance set by the Food and Nutritional board of the National Research Council/National Academy of Sciences and way under his stomach's standards. After the junk food meal, Sonny climbed over a fence into a pasture of Hereford cows and calves and spotted a rare honeybee. He noticed that the flies were bothering the cattle too. During the afternoon, the terrain alternated between peaks, pasture, and beaver ponds. Along the way he took pictures of staghorn sumac, hairy vetch, gold dust lichen, and a Weimaraner carrying saddlebags loaded down with food and water.

Sonny had often heard it said - 'The Trail Provides'. A young man who needed a new pair of shoes recently told him a story. After doing some research, the guy called an outfitter in New York City and was told they had exactly what he wanted. He paid for an expensive ride to the store, but didn't see the shoes anywhere on the shelves. To the salesman who took his call he said, "You told me you had the brand, model, and size that I wanted."

The sales man replied, "We have what you want. But we have to order it."

The young hiker was upset, but he needed new shoes so he looked over at the clearance rack hoping to find a pair that would work. To his delight, he found the exact brand, model and size that he wanted. And the price had been reduced enough to cover his transportation costs.

Sonny hadn't had that kind of luck lately. Twice during the day he found coolers next to the trail, but both times, the trail magic was gone and only the trash remained.

Late in the afternoon, a cool wind without rain helped him reach his 21.1-mile goal for the day. He came upon remnants of a stone chimney and a plaque that commemorated the donation of land to the Appalachian Mountain Club from the Mohhekennuck Club. A half-mile blue blaze trail led him to the Upper Goose Pond Cabin. The two story lap sided wooden building had a metal roof and the entire exterior was red. Electricity was not an option, but gallons of water were available to the occupants. There were nine other hikers spending the night, but Sonny secured a lower bunk on the second floor, changed into his running shorts, and then headed down to the pond for a swim. He ignored the two canoes lying on the shore and walked to the end of the wooden dock and then dove in. The golden hour had passed and darkness was setting in as he made his final video of the day with the three-quarter moon over his shoulder above the pond. Once inside his sleeping bag, Sonny quickly fell asleep. Suddenly he was awakened by a commotion from the first floor. A bear, that was outside inspecting the area set up for dish washing, caused the short-lived excitement.

DAY 113

Early in the morning, Kathy, the caretaker, and her young children, served pancakes to the hikers. Sonny re-taped his toes, packed his gear, and went down the stairs to the breakfast table. After he made an adequate donation for his stay, Sonny washed his dishes and then carried his backpack to the front porch. There he was met with a heavy downpour of rain. Sonny wanted to put in another good mileage day so that he would end up just outside of Dalton. If he could do that, then he would have adequate time to finish all of his necessary chores after he arrived. He needed to get his motel room, shower, and do his laundry, pick up his new shoes from the post office, catch a bus ride to buy supplies, eat somewhere, and purchase a new set of ear buds. All of that had to be done before his visitors showed up.

After ten minutes, Sonny lost his patience and headed back to the trail. He stopped only long enough to take a picture of an American chestnut tree that was being re-established in the area. The rain ceased, but the day remained overcast. Following a descent, Sonny crossed the Massachusetts Turnpike and US-20 and then began the climb over Becket and Walling Mountains. He caught a glimpse of Finerty Pond and then the terrain leveled out. When he reached October

Mountain Shelter, he stopped for lunch and felt confident that he could make it to the next shelter while it was still light. Unfortunately, when he got back on the trail, he went the wrong way. After a nice descent he arrived at a county road that looked very familiar. Upon realizing his mistake, Sonny's positive attitude disintegrated, he turned around, and then reclimbed the hill. Passing by many streams and beaver bogs, he videoed two white-tailed bucks looking back at him displaying their antlers.

Towards the end of the day, he felt worn out but resigned to make it to Kay Wood Shelter for the night. It was getting late and he knew it would require night hiking, but he pushed on until he arrived at a stream. On the far side, he saw a level spot covered with a thick layer of pine needles. In the distance he heard a thunderstorm approaching and although only 14.7 miles were covered for the day, he made the decision to stop and camp. He had just enough time to pitch the tent, eat a meal, and rinse off. Once secure in his sleeping bag, the storm arrived. Sonny forgot all about his mistake earlier in the day and smiled contently as the rain pelted his tent.

Early in his life, there had been so many occurrences that at the time felt like a complete waste of time. But now as an adult, he knew that those events had a purpose that prepared him for something larger, later in life. Up until ten years ago, he had been a long distance runner. His paternal grandfather, Brian Toth, had been a tough competitor who set the bar high for his descendants. Sonny's father, Alexander Toth Sr., was a cross-country high school state champion. Sonny had idolized his father, but despite always pushing his body to its limits, he was never as successful. During the difficult days on the trail, he still found himself looking up to Heaven saying to his late father, "I'm trying Dad. I'm still trying."

DAY 114

The rain that had come down for hours during the night was over, but the trail was still flooded in some sections and water was dripping from the trees and plants. As Sonny walked the few miles towards the next shelter, he was agitated by mosquitoes, but was grateful that he hadn't tried to traverse the slippery and rocky path during the rain at night. Slushing through long puddles made his toes burn, but three miles after the shelter, he found himself walking down Depot Street.

Passing by older well-kept houses on large lots, he reached the old downtown part of Dalton. On his right were businesses in three story red-bricked buildings. Onc was an ice cream shop called Sweet Pea's. To his left was an ancient paper mill with a noisy dam on the Housatonic River. He crossed the bridge on Main Street and found his way to the Shamrock Village Inn. Following the pack explosion in his room, Sonny shaved, took a shower, and washed his clothes. Next, he walked across the street to the post office and picked up his new hiking shoes. He carried them down to a restaurant and had breakfast. Still not satisfied, he enter another eatery and had dessert. After depositing his package back in his room, he learned from the motel owner that the bus stop was also just across the street. He went to the corner and soon was riding west towards a large shopping district. The bus driver dropped him off at a Verizon store where Sonny purchased a new pair of ear buds. From there, he walked to a grocery store and loaded up with supplies for himself and his fellow hikers. The bus arrived back at the motel just before the out of town visitors. Jim and Linda had driven from Ohio to visit their daughter who was serving an internship in nearby North Adams. They also had along with them two granddaughters.

After Sonny showed the group his hiking gear, they left the room and rode to an establishment named Jacob's Pub. Sonny ordered a draft beer and a large Reuben that came with a plateful of marcelled potato chips. After supper the young ladies went back to their room and Jim drove Linda and him to a spot on the trail north of town where Sonny placed plastic bottles of pop. He left a signed note asking the thru-hikers not to litter. The three of them then made a stop at Sweet Pea's where Sonny ordered a large hot fudge sundae. They sat outside where Jim and Linda ate more modest portions. He was given a ride back to the motel where Sonny thanked the couple for feeding him. Before retiring to his bed, he uploaded videos and walked to a sandwich shop to buy a sub for the next day.

DAY 115

Sonny awoke to a bright day, left the motel, and stopped in at a coffee shop where he bought a pastry and a cup of chai tea. From there he hiked a mile through a residential neighborhood and entered the woods. The trail magic that he left the night before was untouched, but he knew that wouldn't last long. Along the way, he passed by another beaver dam and a sizable associated pond. The atmosphere was still clear and Cheshire Cobble provided nice views of the Hoosic River Valley. Walking into the village of Cheshire, Sonny spotted an oasis.

The small worn-out building was painted baby blue, had an awning out front and a chimney in the back. The business was referred to as Diane's Twist and sold ice cream and other earthly delectable items. Sonny purchased a large soft-serve vanilla ice cream cone, a can of pop, a bag of chips, and a tuna sandwich to go. He carried the food to a shaded area, sat down at a picnic table and worked on the dripping cone. The day-old sub was then retrieved from his food bag and he finished that off with the pop and chips. After disposing of his litter in a trashcan, he cleaned his sticky hands and finished walking through the village.

A relaxing hike through some meadows turned into a long continuous climb. When he reached a pond that had a small cabin on the far side, the thunder and rain began. Rockwell Road brought motorized vehicles to the top of the mountain and Sonny crossed the route twice as he made his way up to the highest peak in

Massachusetts. Mount Greylock was home to Veterans War Memorial Tower and Bascom Lodge. The 93-foot monument, that resembled a chess piece or lighthouse, was the centerpiece of walkways and benches. On a clear day, surrounding states could be seen from it. Unfortunately, it was already locked up for the day.

The lodge was also built in the early 1930s and Sonny entered the large stone and wood building hoping to acquire a meal or snack before he left. In the wood-paneled lobby, he ran into Athena who stated that her tramily stopped for the day at the last shelter. Mark Noepel Shelter was a few miles back and Sonny had unknowingly walked right by the group of hikers. Athena had pushed on to the lodge for a good meal and a stay at the bunkroom on the second floor. When Sonny decided that 17.2 miles was enough for the day, Athena informed him that he needed to reserve a place in the restaurant. She showed him the way to a large room that had a fieldstone fireplace and open timber frame rafters. He spoke to the hostess who wasn't pleased to see him. She reluctantly allowed him to come to dinner, but said he had to be back in the restaurant in ten minutes when all of the other guests would arrive.

With no time to shower, Sonny hurriedly secured a bunk for the night and then returned to the crowded restaurant. He was seated next to Athena on the end of a table full of day hikers. But unfortunately, the snobby hostess was also the waitress. She treated the other customers well, but was very curt with Sonny.

However, the broiled pork chop on mashed potatoes and green beans dinner was delicious and despite her rude behavior, Sonny left the woman a nice tip. After a warm shower, he went to his bunk and soon fell asleep.

DAY 116

The forecast called for a chance of precipitation in the afternoon. Normally that scenario would inspire Sonny to move out and make as many miles before rain affected the trail conditions. But the Greylock Tower didn't open until a ranger drove up to the peak with the key. According to the receptionist in the lodge, the estimated time of arrival was between 8:30 and 9:00. Sonny used the extra time to eat a hardy breakfast and video the exterior of the granite tower and surrounding area. When the time came and went, he bought a pastry and a cup of coffee that he drowned with sugar and cream. From a seat on the fieldstone patio, he counted over fifty people who walked up to the tower and tried the locked door. After he was finished feeding his face, Sonny went back inside the lodge and asked the receptionist for an update. The polite woman called down to the ranger station and was told that somcone would be up there in thirty minutes or so to open the tower. Sonny thanked the woman, but suggested that a spare key should be kept in the lodge. He then went outside, put on his backpack, and headed north.

The rest of the morning was spent descending three thousand feet. Halfway down, Sonny stopped at Mount

Prospect Ledge and looked down on green fields, ponds, woodlots, and the town of Williamstown. He fell for the thirteenth time but was not injured.

By early afternoon, he was walking down Phelps Avenue in North Adams. There was a sign on a utility pole indicating trail magic just ahead at the Greylock School. When Sonny reached that point, he was waved over by many hands. Behind where an ATC truck was parked, local volunteers were cooking hamburgers on the grills. Tables were filled with vegetables, desserts, and cold pop. For entertainment, several youngsters were sitting in a circle banging on a selection of percussion instruments. Sonny sat down and ate as much as he could and then videoed Josh the organizer. Before leaving, Sonny thanked everyone and they sent him on his way with more food.

Leaving town, Sonny crossed MA-2 and then stepped upon a metal walking bridge that was painted green except for the interior which was white and decorated with numerous colored handprints. The span led him over the Hoosic River, a railroad track, and onto Massachusetts Avenue for a short distance. He entered the woods and climbed for two hours until he reached the Massachusetts/Vermont border. Eleven states down, three to go. At that point, the Appalachian Trail was joined with the Long Trail for 105.2 miles.

The sky became overcast and about the time Sonny hit the 1600-mile mark, the rain began. After 16.2 miles, he arrived at a very large beaver pond and set up his tent next to it near a spot called Beaver Pond Outlet. He ate the trail magic leftovers and the day old tuna fish sandwich while watching a pair of beavers repair the dam that he had recently walked across. After the sun went down, he laid in his sleeping bag and fell asleep listening to the singing tree frogs.

DAY 117

The rain had ceased, but everything around Sonny was still wet, including his shoes. Early on he missed a turn and continued on a trail that, for a very good reason, looked more like a streambed. For over a mile, he tried to avoid the mud and water by tediously stepping on stones. At a deeper stream, he removed his shoes and socks, crossed, and eventually, realized he had not seen a white blaze in a while. Referencing his Guthook app, he learned that he was far from the trail. Crossing back over the stream, he left his shoes on and splashed his way back to the trail. He pouted for the rest of the morning, but things improved when he stopped for lunch at Mellville Nauheim Shelter.

Some of the hikers there had enjoyed the trail magic he had left north of Dalton and thanked him. One young woman was also a vlogger and when Sonny complained about his limited storage capacity of his own videos, she recorded him on her own channel. Later in the day, he found a pink rock that someone had painted and left on the trail. The inscription - Always Stay Humble And Kind. With a bolstered spirit, he crossed a sturdy walking bridge over Hell Hollow

Brook as the white water rushed beneath. Following a climb, he was rewarded with a moderate view at Porcupine Lookout. There wasn't enough time left in the day to make it to the next potential campsite, so he stopped at Little Pond Lookout. The extra time left in the day was used to work out his video issues.

DAY 118

It was a cool and partly cloudy day. Sonny woke up early and continued to resolve his video problems. His food supply was getting low and he planned to go into a town in two days to stock up. Vermont was living up to its reputation for being muddy.

Around noon, Sonny climbed the Glastenbury Mountain Lookout Tower. The renovated structure had new hardware holding together the steel frame, aluminum paned windows, and wooden planked floor. Despite the haze, he could clearly see the elusive Greylock Tower in the south. After recording the views, Sonny climbed down the steps, had lunch near the foundation, and continued on.

With very few blooming flowers, the limited color shades of the environment made for repetitive scenery. He was beginning to run into SoBos (southbound hikers) that had started at Mount Katahdin about a month earlier. Even though they had completed nearly three states of difficult terrain, unlike Sonny, they were fresh and enthusiastic. He would ask each of them about the difficulty that lay ahead. Every one of them said that the White Mountains were beautiful. To one of them Sonny said, "Don't talk to me about the scenery. Tell me if you think I can make it."

With much conviction, the hiker said, "Of course you can. You made it this far."

He walked by a beaver pond that had a hut surrounded by yellow flowering lily pads. His fourteenth fall was caused by slippery mud, which was also what he landed in. After 16.8 miles he camped just north of Kelly Stand Road at the base of the next peak. He rinsed off in the east branch of Deerfield River and was soon fast asleep in his tent.

DAY 119

Another good hiking day, cool with no wind. Sonny ate oatmeal with raisins, drank a cup of Earl Grey tea with sugar and then started the climb up the muddy trail. Stratton Mountain had steep sides and a pointy top. By mid morning, Sonny had reached the lookout tower. Jean the caretaker, who stayed in the small cabin, greeted him. She asked him if he would evict the baby birds that were trapped in the tower while he was up there. The nuthatches were not born there, but while learning to fly, were carried up through the open floor hatch by the rising air currents. At the top of the tower, Sonny videoed hills of evergreens that went on forever as the fledglings banged into the window panes around him. One at a time, he was able to catch the nuthatches and drop them through the door on the floor. After climbing down from the tower, he scoured the area for dead birds. When he was convinced that they all had survived, he checked his phone and noticed that he had enough bars of power to upload a video. He also took the time to briefly check in with all of the important people in his life and then headed north.

The Stratton Pond Shelter was the largest of its kind on the Appalachian Trail. Sixteen people could sleep on its bunk platforms. It had a covered porch with benches on both sides and a picnic table in the center where Sonny sat and ate his lunch. Afterwards, the trail led him along the shore of Stratton Pond and across the bridge over Winhall River. At Prospect Rock, Sonny met section hikers, Jay and Hocks, who took his picture with the town of Manchester Center in the background. While talking with the pair, Sonny unintentionally Yogied (Derived from Yogi Bear - to convince others to provide trail magic.) items from Jay. The two hikers were going into the nearby town before the end of the day. Sonny said that he would be doing the same in the morning because he was low on food, and Jay gave him two Clif Bars.

Near the end of the day, Sonny crossed the three quarter mark of completing the Appalachian Trail. After 17 miles, he camped near a small, fast moving stream a half-mile short of VT-30.

DAY 120

Still feeling fresh from soaking in the stream the evening before, Sonny put on clean clothes sans deodorant. He made the short walk, put away his trekking poles, and retrieved the hitchhiking sign. The first car that came along pulled over. Sonny hopped in and introduced himself to Sean who worked for Orvis designing fly-fishing equipment. Five miles later he was in Manchester Center being deposited in front of Shaw's Supermarket.

He placed his backpack in a cart and pushed it towards the deli. When he had purchased as many edibles as he could carry, he went back outside and put the items into his food bag and then ate donuts and milk. He walked to the center of the upscale town, which was showcased by a busy roundabout, landscaped with small ornamental trees, and a perimeter of pink and yellow flowers. Inside the Mountain Goat Outfitter Store, he bought more dehydrated meals and then went over to a café on the busy corner. Seated inside, Sonny enjoyed an egg and sausage muffin sandwich with orange juice. Walking back towards the trail, he stopped in at McDonalds and had two hot fudge sundaes. Next to the fast food restaurant was another eatery where he ate a half chicken salad sandwich and a bowl of clam chowder. For dessert he downed a mango-tango smoothie.

Loaded down with food and back on the street, Sonny displayed his pink sign. He stood there a while, but eventually a hiker from London, England, named Michael, gave him a ride back to the trail. By the time he had made it up Bromley Mountain, fog had moved in. He could see the ski patrol building and the dormant ski lift, but it took a while to find a white blaze. While heading downhill, he was startled by ruffed grouse that noisily took flight from near his feet.

The rain came down hard, filled the streams, and created more mud. He was grateful for the wooden walkways, as were the porcupines that chewed on them. For the first time, he saw a pile of what looked like tater-tots on the trail. Later he learned that it was moose poop. The sun came out near the end of the day and Sonny took pictures of bunchberry and a flowering invasive orange hawkweed. Because of his fun time in the town, he was only able to cover 11.8 miles on the day and tented at Griffith Lake. Before going to bed, he ate a pound of deli sliced roast beef and a bottle of Coca-Cola.

DAY 121

Sonny started the morning off with a breakfast that included a banana, two blueberry muffins, and dried peaches. He also kept peanut M&Ms in his front pouch for snacking along the way. It was cloudy but not raining. The path was mucky and his socks, shoes, and pants were still wet from the previous day. He stopped to take a picture of the edible fungi, chicken of the woods, but did not harvest any. A sturdy suspension bridge carried him over the Big Branch River. Shortly, he discovered a recently placed cooler of trail magic at the parking lot on USFS-10. Under the lid and ice bag were cans of Coke and small cartons of chocolate milk. As Sonny was sampling the treats, Coco Bean, the smiling trail angel, showed up and handed him a Snickers bar to go along with the drinks she had provided. She had her curly-haired son strapped to her back and was about to take a shorter hike on the trail she had completed in 2005. Sonny thanked her and took pictures for his channel.

While back in the woods, Sonny heard but did not see, a large tree creak, crackle, and collapse to the forest floor with a resounding thud. At Little Rock Pond he intended to stop at the shelter for lunch, but he was distracted by people on the far side of the water and walked right on by the place. He settled for eating his chicken teriyaki and Coke meal near the end of the pond.

Part of the afternoon was spent in a fairyland. At Rock Garden, he videoed large boulders that had sprouted numerous cairns. A short while later at White Rocks Junction, smaller but more expansive stone structures adorned the ground. Legend had it that woodland gnomes worked feverishly on the projects whenever the hikers weren't around. The trail was lined with small rocks that passed by a stoned peace sign. At both places, Sonny started foundations for future pieces of art.

Bully Brook was a fast flowing, narrow stream with cascading falls followed by serene deep pools. Sonny avoided the falls and made water from a docile section of the flow. Following the 18.6-mile effort, he strategically camped at Minerva Hinchey Shelter on the downside of Bear Mountain. A lightning storm was predicted for early in the morning and he wanted to be heading for lower ground if that situation occurred.

DAY 122

The night before, when it was time to hang his bear bag, Sonny realized that he was no longer in possession of the orange string to complete the task. A few of the camping sites where he stayed had bear boxes and he gladly used them. But the last time he had retrieved the food bag from being hung in a tree, he had gotten out of his normal morning packing routine and left the string hanging from a branch. He had tried to charge his phone from the battery pack during the night, but both of his cords were wet and the process was unsuccessful. The mosquitoes and black flies were on the attack early and then he learned that his expensive Jungle Juice with 98% Deet insect repellent, was also missing. He donned the black veil and kept walking, albeit on the wrong trail. A half mile later, he realized the mistake and turned around. His day was off to a bad start and when the drizzling rain soaked his shoes, he decided it was about time for a night at a hostel.

During the descent, Sonny came to a ledge with a view of a small airport. It occurred to him that he never saw any factories in Vermont. He crossed VT-103 and then came to a narrow green suspension bridge that spanned the Cross Mill River at Clarendon Gorge. He made a video of the fast moving white water through the rock walls. A few hours later, he took a picture of a plaque on a tree that designated the 500 miles from Mount Katahdin. Governor Clement Shelter, with its impressive stone chimney, was where he prepared a dehydrated beef stroganoff meal. The can of Coke that he had, made his fellow hikers envious, so he tried to avoid eye contact as he drank it.

The next four miles were uphill and Sonny put in his ear buds, turned on his Spotify app, and listened to *Free Bird* by Lynyrd Sknyrd. He had covered 14.1 miles, but by the time he had reached Cooper Lodge campsite, the restaurant there was closed. He had never used a tent platform before and there was one site left. But Sonny gave it to a man with a dog and instead put up his tent on a flat sandy spot. Without his string, he again could not hang his food bag, but the man assured him that the dog would keep any bears away.

Before darkness came, Sonny climbed the steep and rocky two-tenths of a mile up Killington Peak, which was the largest ski resort in the northeast. There was a dilapidated fire tower and another structure for communication. As Sonny took in the view of the evergreen covered peaks around him, he could see that he was above the clouds. But they were fast approaching as the wind increased and Sonny hustled back down and barely made it into his tent before the rain hit.

DAY123

The forecast called for rain until late in the morning. Sonny packed away his nighttime gear and then rolled up his wet and sandy tent. The day was gloomy, but that would change when the sun emerged and he reached VT-4 in 6.4 miles, where the state route would take him to the comforts of a hostel in Rutland.

The Twelve Tribes Commune operated the Yellow Deli Restaurant and Hostel. Smoking and alcohol consumption were taboo and payment options included donations and volunteer labor. The hostel was located in the middle of the downtown section, but the vegetables were raised on a 160-acre farm outside of town. Prior to finishing the long morning decent, Sonny reached the 1700-mile mark and the sun came out. He crossed a walking bridge over a fast moving narrow stream and arrived at a trail parking lot. Out on the road, he stood with his sign and smiled at the blue sky and puffy white clouds.

A woman named Candy dropped him off at Mountain Travelers Outdoor Shop. There he bought dehydrated meals, insect repellant, and a replacement string to hang his food bag. He asked the manager to recommend a restaurant for breakfast and was sent to one across the road. Johnny Boys Pancake House met his needs and then he began to walk the final mile and a half into the center of town. The sight of a Ben and Jerry's ice cream shop halted his march. He procured a large vanilla malt, sat down outside, and afterwards unloaded days of trash into the available garage can.

There was a street party going on in downtown Rutland when Sonny came strolling in. He had passed by church steeples and noticed there was a large banner that was strung over the street between buildings. Many people were taking part in the celebration among the blocks of old brick buildings, some as high as four stories tall. Sonny missed the hostel, but he asked for directions from a native woman who then pointed the way for him. He found the restaurant and next to it was the door leading into the hostel. After the rules for staying were explained to him, he took a flight of stairs to one of the male bunkrooms and chose a lower bed next to the window. From there he had a view of the activities on the street and saw that there was a very large sandbox for the children, occupying the intersection.

The first thing he did was to take a shower and then put on his rain suit and flip-flops. After he washed his clothes, he put them in the dryer and went back out on the street, looking for a barbershop. The two he found had just closed, so he got a haircut at a beauty salon at a much higher cost than normal. He carried back food supplies from Price Chopper Supermarket and retrieved his dried clothes. By then, a storm was brewing and the streets were void of people and vendor stands. There was a front-end loader and a dump truck finishing the cleanup of the sand pile on the street. At the other end of the block, he entered the Hop'n Moose Restaurant and dined on craft beers along with other healthy entrées.

The storm was over by the time Sonny returned to the streets in search of a church. Immaculate Heart of Mary was begun in 1892 on a hill above Lincoln Avenue. The impressive gray stone church boasted high peaks, including a bell tower. Its tall interior had blue ceilings held up with pillars and white walls adorned with many stained glass windows and murals. Standing in front of the beautiful structure, he checked for Mass times and then made phone calls. He was expecting inspiration from encouraging voices, but all he heard were complaints. His mother told him about a roving flock of wild turkeys that kept climbing out of the ravine and decimating her gardens. August whined about how hot it was on his construction job. Madison said that none of her clothes fit her anymore. Henry felt frustration over deciding where to go on his family vacation. Sonny was feeling so worn out after talking to his family that he wasn't sure if he wanted to talk to Lily. She answered on the second ring with a cheerful voice. "Hello, Sonny."

"Lily, you are a breath of fresh air."

"Having a bad day, Sonny?"

"No. It's just that the sound of your voice alone, lifts me up."

"On eagle's wings?"

"Yeah. Just like that."

"Where are you now?"

"In Rutland. I'm staying downtown at the Yellow Deli Hostel."

"I stayed there. That's a cool place. Are you sticking around for breakfast?"

"I don't know if I'll have time. Mass starts shortly after they open the restaurant."

"You could go back after church."

"I could, but I don't like to backtrack. I'm always anxious about heading north."

"I understand."

"So, are you coming back anytime soon?"

"I might be able to squeeze in one more trip. I'll let you know, Sonny."

"I miss you, Lily."

Sonny went back to his room and took his still wet and sandy tent out to the back deck. He spread it out to dry near benches of potted tomato and pepper plants. Anything that was ripe was fair game. There was an occupied yurt at the far end of the large outdoor-planked surface. Back inside on a hallway wall, a large map of the United States was hanging with many colored pushpins that indicated the homes of thru-hikers. Sonny stuck a red one into the Grand Rapids, Ohio location. He then found his little sewing kit and went into the empty kitchen area, sat down, and began repairing the tears on the inside shin area of both pant legs. Just as he finished sewing, the room filled with several people. Sonny knew every one of the thru-hikers, including Athena, Fiona, Doubting Thomas, Antelope, Lioness, Lemon, and Lime. Following a fist bump reunion, they all told stories of the trail. At sunset, Sonny went outside and shook the sand from his dry tent. Before rolling it up he sprayed it and his clothes, with a bottle of Permethrin (tick repellent) that he found in the hiker's box (container where hikers take or leave items). He told the other hikers goodnight as he passed through the kitchen and then added, "Wouldn't it be cool if we all summited Katahdin on the same day?"

DAY 124

Before leaving the hostel, Sonny left an appropriate donation and then went next door to the busy restaurant. He sat at a table and after looking at a clock, told the waitress he only had time for coffee. She came back shortly with the cup of java, a plastic fork, and a carryout container filled with an omelet with tomatoes, onions and peppers next to a pile of brown rice. After downing the cream and sugar-ladened coffee, he left a tip on the table, stuffed his breakfast in the rear netting of his pack, and walked to the church.

After Mass, Sonny sat still and allowed most of the congregation to exit the building and then he took several pictures of the sunlight through the colorful windows and thought about castles. He ate his meal on the way to Rite-Aid where he obtained candy bars and crazy glue to repair his trekking poles. A young man named Drew drove him back to the trail and Sonny began a climb with clean clothes and dry shoes.

A mile later, he arrived at Maine Junction in Willard Gap. At that point, the Long Trail continued towards Canada and the Appalachian Trail headed east. Sonny followed the white blazes and left the Green Mountains behind. A short time later, he met another thru-hiker and struck up a conversation. Zip Code was a sixty year old, recently retired mailman from Pennsylvania. Sonny felt an instant bond as they shared their résumés. They had both intended to stop for a meal at the Inn at Long Trail, but by the time they realized their mistake, they had already walked three-tenths of a mile past it. Neither one of the hikers wanted to go back; instead they stopped at the ranger station in Gifford Woods State Park. Sonny filled up with a fudgesicle, one creamsicle, a Snickers ice cream bar, a small bag of almonds, and a can of Coke. Zip Code was scheduled to pick up a food package at the Killington post office the following day and was going to tent at the state park. Sonny still had a half-day of walking to do and moved on.

A bridge over a small gorge provided a good view of a waterfall that fed a large pond. Sonny followed the trail along the south shore of Kent Pond until he spotted a huge red barn. Referencing his Guthook app, he learned that the former farm building and white house were converted into a lodge. Sonny took the time to see in person what food was available at the site, but found that it was closed. He moved on until he reached Thundering Falls. The observation deck provided a front row view to video the cascading white water.

Next, he followed the 900-foot boardwalk over the Ottauquechee River and its corresponding marsh. Honeybees were having a nectar and pollen gathering frenzy on blooms of the spotted Joe-Pye weed. On Quimby Mountain, an aluminum ladder had been placed to help the hikers on a short, but very steep section. Sonny stopped and stealth camped by a small stream after 14.9 miles. Water was boiled for his meal and he noticed that his fuel canister was getting low. He sat down on a solid white rock that had highlights of green moss. From there he ate a chicken teriyaki meal again and supplemented it with pecans and a bottle of Mountain Dew.

DAY 125

Sonny's first meal of the day consisted of vanilla wafer cookies, dried peaches, one Tylenol tablet, and water. He knew that whenever he camped by a stream, the initial hike of the day would be uphill. Gnats pestered him by tickling his face in search of salt, but he was pleased that the weather forecast predicted no rain for the day. He knew that he was the first hiker on the trail because he continually walked into spider webs. Coming down from Ascutney Mountain, the lack of trees provided a breeze and good views. Sonny stopped for lunch after he took pictures of lupines, a monarch caterpillar, and a yellow swallowtail butterfly.

Late in the afternoon when he reached Pomfret Road, a sign pointed the way to a farmhouse that sold snacks in rear of the residence. Sonny worked his way down the road and found The Back Porch, which was run by former thru-hikers, Firefly and Loon. He climbed the steps, read the menu, and then bought a Whoopie Pie, two cartons of chocolate milk, a couple of cans of pop, two bottles of Gatorade, and candy bars. Sitting in a folding chair, he ate the pastry and milk and then headed back to the wooded hills where he found more stone pile walls. From some of the places, Sonny could see views of ski areas. Before he reached his goal for the day of 17 miles, a tramily greeted and then passed him. By the time he reached Thistle Hill Shelter, they already had their tents set up and were eating supper. He found a suitable spot and did likewise. After a meal of almonds and ginger ale, Sonny hung his food bag with his new string. He then went to the stream and made water and washed up. Upon returning to his tent, he rolled out his muscles to alleviate any lactic acid and considered going to bed early. But he really enjoyed the companionship of the group of hikers at the site and went to socialize with them at the shelter.

He knew and liked all of the hikers, save one. Most of them had stayed at the same hostel with Sonny in Rutland, but now Potty Mouth was back. The obnoxious ogre was telling coarse stories and didn't appreciate the interruption of his yarn nor the attention that Sonny garnished. It was evident that the group was tired of the lowlife and his narratives. Despite getting a dirty look from Potty Mouth, Fiona asked Sonny if he knew any jokes. "Okay, I have two jokes, but they are both long, so you'll have to choose one. There's the talking dog joke and the duck joke."

"They sound stupid, so I'm outta here." Potty Mouth said as he stomped away.

Sonny watched him leave and said to the group, "Perfect. Have you made your selection?"

After a short debate, the decision was made and Sonny began. "My father told me this joke many years ago. He said his barber at Craig's barbershop in Portage, Ohio, told it to him."

"There was a man who was holding a white duck while standing in line to purchase a ticket at a movie theater. When it was his turn, he told the manager in the ticket booth which movie he wanted to see and said, 'One ticket, please.'"

"The manager said in reply, 'I'm sorry sir, but you can't bring that duck into the theater.'"

"The man explained, 'Oh, you don't understand, I've had this duck since it was an egg. It won't make any noise and it is potty trained. I take it everywhere I go.'"

"The manager sighed and repeated, 'I'm sorry sir, but you can't bring that duck into the theater.'"

"The man then left the theater and walked to a nearby alley."

Sonny looked around and saw that they were captivated by his story so far, so he continued. "The man was used to the rejection from some businesses, so he always solved the problem by wearing baggy pants. He stuffed the duck down the front of his trousers and went back to the theater and obtained a ticket. He then went to the refreshment counter and bought a big tub of popcorn and a large cola. The theater was mostly vacant so he sat down right in the center. A few more people arrived, the movie began, and he enjoyed his snacks. Eventually, the duck became too warm and began to squirm around. So, the man pulled down his zipper and the duck popped his head out and calmed down. About the middle of the movie, an old lady who was sitting in the aisle seat, down the row from the man with the duck, began elbowing her friend seated beside her. 'Mary, Mary', said the first woman."

"'What?' said Mary."

"The first woman pointed her thumb at the man and said, 'Look over there.'"

"Mary looked at the man, became annoyed and said, 'Oh, for crying out loud, Martha. If you've seen one penis, you've seen them all.'"

"Martha adamantly replied, 'Oh no. *This* one, is eating popcorn'."

The group roared with laughter and their admiration for Sonny grew. He left them and went to his tent contented with the good feeling known as friendship. But he was concerned that he might have created an enemy.

DAY 126

The days were getting shorter and the birds allowed Sonny to sleep a little bit longer everyday, but his hiking time was reduced proportionately. Breakfast was a repeat of yesterday's fare. Most of the day promised to be sunny. But after that, there was a chance of rain for a week. The temperature was on the cool side, there was no wind, and he had nearly five miles of downhill hiking to enjoy.

Late in the morning, the trail left the woods and merged with Quechee Road. The route led Sonny into West Hartford to a bridge over the White River. He looked down on the young swimmers and sunbathers who encouraged him to jump from where he was into the water below. Back in his younger days, he would have accepted the challenge. But now as an older and wiser man, he walked down to the shoreline, stripped down to his swimming outfit and hopped in. Sonny watched from the water as a few of the other hikers made the leap. One woman named Orange Blossom asked if Sonny would make a video of her jump and then send it to her.

He sat on the rock cliff near the shore and waited for her to get into position. She climbed over the guardrail and waved at Sonny. Sonny waved back and she jumped. Her enthusiasm outweighed her experience. She did not point her toes to break the water surface, but rather landed on her butt causing a loud clapping sound. It must have really hurt, because when she surfaced, the only word that came from her mouth was a single-syllable bad one. She repeated the word until she finished swimming to the rocks.

The swim refreshed Sonny, but it was time to move on. He stopped at the Big Blue Barn for refreshments and then walked through the small town, went under I-89, and up into the woods. Swimming had made him hungry and he stopped at Happy Hill Shelter for lunch. He and Orange Blossom were the only hikers who stopped at the stone cabin. He sent her the entire video, but edited out her expletives for his daily video. She lay on the floor of the shelter and basked in the sunlight trying to decide whether or not to camp there for the night. Sonny quickly ate his lunch and moved on down the trail.

Two hours later, he came down out of the trees and found himself walking on a road headed towards Norwich. Most of the homes and businesses were typical of New England. There were some red brick buildings, but many were white lap sided with picket fences and stone foundations, walls, and chimneys. Coolers were set out near the road by local trail angels. Sonny helped himself to candy, nut bread, and watermelon slices. One resident allowed swimming at his home for all A.T. thru-hikers. Approaching thunder urged Sonny to keep moving, until a woman shouted out to him, offering homemade mango popsicles. Sonny walked up to the house and the lady named Barbara said she was sorry, but all of the mango popsicles were gone. She gave him a blueberry and banana substitute as the wind increased. A fruit smoothie was offered and Sonny accepted that too as the skies turned black. He thanked the trail angel and hurried into the town, passed by a tall steeple, and ducked into a business as the downpour started.

Dan and Whit's General Store had many supplies, but it was crowded. Sonny bought a container of orange juice and took it outside under the awning and drank the whole bottle. As he was leaving, he ran into Orange Blossom. She was heading to the library and planned on staying in town for the night. Sonny told her that he was going back to the trail. The rain let up a little and he walked past the town square and gazebo to the Connecticut River. Four busy lanes of vehicles skirted by on the wet surface as Sonny started on the bridge. At the halfway point, he stopped and took a picture of the concrete block with a ball on top and a granite VT/NH stone on the side to indicate the border. Twelve states down, two to go.

Hanover, New Hampshire, was home to Dartmouth College. When Sonny reached the downtown area, he asked some students on the street to recommend a restaurant. They named a couple of good sandwich shops that they frequented, but Sonny required red meat so they sent him to Market Table. The air conditioning chilled his wet body and he put on his hooded sweatshirt. The waitress served him a salad, a steak with baked potato, and seared vegetables. He drank a lot of water and a draft beer and made use of the restroom.

The white blazes took him though the town past the Big Green's football stadium and a Catholic church. Saint Denis was a beautiful stone structure that Sonny took pictures of for his dream castle portfolio. He loaded up on supplies at Hanover Food Co-op and then finished off the 16.4-mile day at Velvet Rocks Shelter.

DAY 127

Sonny felt good about being the first one to leave the crowded campsite until he wondered off the blue blaze trail and found himself down a hill next to the backyards of several homes. He climbed back up until he intersected the white blaze trail. As he followed the path, he used his Guthook app to double-check his direction and then turned around and headed north. There was no rain, but a heavy fog caused water to drip from every plant and his shoes were already wet. The climb up to Velvet Rocks was steep, but a knotted rope and bright orange signs by the Dartmouth Outing Club, aided Sonny's efforts. The descent brought him to a boardwalk along a marsh where he took a picture of the invasive purple loosestrife. From a trail angel's cooler, he took the last bottle of watermelon flavored Propel electrolyte water. During the ascent of the south peak of Moose Mountain, Sonny videoed long lengths of narrow plastic tubes that were attached to the sugar maple trees to drain the sweet water downhill for processing into maple syrup.

He noticed a green inchworm that hung from a single filament. Much like spider webs, the tickling oak leafroller's silk thread was a nuisance to the hikers. A Sobo hiker was filling his water containers from one of the two five gallon bottles left by a trail angel named J. Mason. The hiker informed Sonny that there was no water available for the next three mountains. Sonny thanked him for the information and then filled up his own bottles.

Lunch was eaten at Moose Mountain Shelter and then Sonny descended the south peak. He came to another beaver dam and carefully walked on rotting boards to pass by the pond. After completing 17.5 miles and with the sun barely hovering over the horizon, he pitched his tent on a ledge next to Grant Brook.

DAY 128

The noise from the brook drowned out the singing birds, but Sonny woke up at 5:45 out of habit. As part of his daily routine, he stayed in his sleeping bag and looked at his Guthook app and AWOL guide to see what was ahead. His mind drifted back to the beginning of his journey and he thought about how the trail and he had changed. The switchbacks of the south were gone. Now the trail went straight up and over the mountains of the north. He had lost weight and most of the fear of the unknown.

One glance inside his food bag told him he needed to resupply soon. He spoke with a Sobo hiker called Tadpole who said that the town of Lincoln was a good place to get supplies. A granite post that looked similar to a train whistle sign marked a spot that was once 412 miles from Mount Katahdin. But because of changes made to the trail, the information was inaccurate.

An hour into the climb, Sonny stopped for a short breather at Lambert Ridge. In another hour he summited Smarts Mountain and climbed the fire lookout tower. There he met a Sobo named Good Times who spoke reverently about the Whites. Through the paned glass windows they had good views all around including some peaks up ahead in the White

Mountains. Alone in the tower, Sonny uploaded his last video while he ate an energy bar and drank water.

Coming down from the peak, he met a young woman and four young men who belonged to the Dartmouth Outing Club and were performing maintenance on the trail. Sonny thanked them and took a group picture. Always on the alert for signs of black bears, he began noticing more moose droppings. He crossed the bridge at the south branch of Jacobs Brook and then warmed his last packaged meal for lunch on Eastman Ledges. Up on the south peak of Cube Mountain, he followed cairns and experienced a cool breeze and pretty clouds.

Bracket Brook had a good flow and Sonny filled his bottles. There were a large number of hikers camping on the flat spots by the water. Despite the warm temperature, some of them had gathered wood and lit a fire to heat their food. Sonny decided to eat his supper meal with them. Along with Gatorade, he ate the remaining handfuls of almonds and pecans while listening to Thesaurus and Webster continue their debate on the usage of the English language. Webster liked correcting other people and Thesaurus loved to toy with him. Most of the hikers were only entertained by the duo, but Slang Banger listened intently and took notes to be used later during his rap sessions. Sonny maneuvered behind the dreadlock dude and read the quotes plagiarized from Thesaurus: 'Don't *lick* a gift *whore* in the mouth.' '*Statue* of limitations.' 'Jump to *contusions*.' 'Knee jerk *retraction*.' 'Take it with a grain *assault*.' 'The plot *Dickens*.' 'Too many *crooks* in the kitchen.' 'You scratch my back, I'll *shave* yours.' 'Under the w*h*ether.' '*Roaming* at the mouth.' 'Are you ready to throw in the *trowel*?'

Potty Mouth was drinking beer and annoyed at not being the center of attention. He tried to insert his opinions and comments, but was met with groans. Athena rolled her eyes and Fiona moved closer to Doubting Thomas. The clinic ended when Thesaurus vowed to sue for PUNitive damages and Slang Banger saw a chance to display his talent. He fancied himself as a rapper from the hood, but was actually a thirty-something college dropout from a wealthy family. His poetry really was lousy, so he would spout borrowed lines to impress his peers. Most of the hikers tolerated the fraud, but after a week of campfire solo rap sessions, they had had enough. Unfortunately, as Sonny approached the gathering, he was asked by Ogle what he thought about rap music. In a mild attempt to be diplomatic, he said, "I really don't care for most of it. There's not a whole lot of talent involved. But I have to admit, some of the lyrics, if that's what you call them, are kind of clever."

Slang Banger took exception and challenged Sonny. "If it's so easy, let's hear what you can come up with, here and now."

Sonny shrugged. "Alright. Let's see. Okay, how about this? My feet are full of blisters. They smell just like your sisters."

Slang Banger looked indignant. But before he could respond, Tripper gave it a try. "Across the streams and through the forest... the words you use, only abuse and bore us."

More of the hikers took up the challenge. "You seem like a nice guy. I don't know why, you need to lie."

"Out here you roam feeling complacent. It has to be better than being at home living in your parent's basement."

Although visibly upset, Slang Banger kept his composure and returned the volley. "I'm not going to pout. But you leave me in doubt. You lessen my pedigree. You question my integrity. You disregard my clout. Ergo, I'm out."

Even though the sun had not set, the rapper retired to his tent and Perky said, "Maybe we were too harsh. I should have held my remarks."

Ogle took a hit from a doobie being passed around and said, "Wait. Before you call it a day, listen to what I have to say - Banger was here, but now he's gone. Only his name lives on. Those who knew him, knew him well. Those who didn't, can go to... Helena, Georgia."

Sonny shook his head and said, "Forget what I said. I'm going to bed."

He grabbed his pack and walked less than a half-mile to the next stream and put up his tent in a quiet space. The two big mountains that he had hiked over limited his miles to 13.9 miles for the day.

DAY 129

Inventory of his food bag took no time at all. There were only dried cherries, Gatorade powder, a Clif Bar and a few pieces of Lifesavers candy left. Several varieties of mushrooms were available for eating, but fear due to ignorance, held him back. Sonny ate the cherries with water for breakfast and made the rest last until early afternoon when he came out on NH-25. A right turn and three-tenths of a mile later, he was at Hikers Welcome Hostel.

The property had two houses. The first one, which had an exterior of unpainted wooden clapboard and stone, was attached to a barn. The other house was where the hikers slept. Sonny had no intentions of staying overnight because it was too early in the day to stop hiking. He had other needs and entered the barn to tend to them. Not only did he devour ice cream and sodas, but there were microwaveable sausage sandwiches for sale also. But because they were so small, Sonny ate more than a couple. Showers were available and Sonny paid for the privilege. He asked about the trekking pole repair station that was advertised as one of their services and was directed to a self-service bench littered with parts. After reviewing the collection, he tried a few mismatched pieces and then settled on using his super glue to solve the slippage problem. When his phoned was fully charged, he headed back to the trail.

Immediately, he came to a water barrier. The normal route of stepping-stones across Oliverian Brook was covered with water. Downstream there was a better way to cross and after walking out onto a gravel island, he shimmied across the stream on a fallen tree. Another steep, but shorter climb, took him over Mount Mist where he took a picture of fireweed. He called ahead to secure a reservation for the following night, but learned that most places were filled up already. Besides weekend hikers, an arts and crafts show in Lincoln brought in visitors. Luckily, one of the tourists had cancelled her reservation, so Sonny had a bunk for the night.

Near the end of the day, Sonny began looking for a location to stealth camp. At the last stream before Mount Moosilauke, he found a place - barely. The small clearing was not large enough to extend his stakes fully. The tent was touching the trail and the far side was right next to a drop off. But he was glad to have the spot because two day hikers informed him that there was nothing available up ahead. A hiker named Boot Straps offered him food, but he declined the offer and soaked his Knorr rice meal in his pot of water in an attempt to lessen the cook time. He fell asleep thinking about the food he would enjoy the next day in Lincoln.

DAY 130

During the night, the drop in temperature woke up Sonny, but he wrapped his sweatshirt around his neck and fell back asleep. Just after daybreak, *Safari Song* by Greta Van Fleet and *Working Man* by Rush helped him on the steep two-mile ascent of the next mountain. A mile from the peak, the trail leveled out a bit, but it was still rocky. Many of those rocks had been used to build cairns to show the way. Surrounding evergreen trees were stunted and non-existent as he went higher. The peak was over 4800 feet and he knew it was only a taste of what lay ahead. The view from the summit of Mount Moosilauke was excellent and Sonny hoped that it would be that good for his final mountain next month. The area was speckled with several day hikers and a steward who answered any questions they might have. The long descent was also spectacular, but made even more hazardous during the last mile where the trail ran alongside Beaver Brook. The long, narrow, and fast-flowing waterfalls were beautiful, but they made the rocks slippery. A large boulder had fallen into the ravine and taken a part of the trail with it. Fortunately, the maintenance crew had installed a rope to help get by the divot. Shortly after crossing the 1800-mile mark, Sonny heard road traffic.

At Kinsman Notch on NH-112, a pair of trout fisherman gave Sonny a ride to the hostel in North Woodstock. The trail angels, Sebastian and Duane, had their picture taken in front of the no vacancy sign at

Notch Hostel with Sonny. As per the rules, Sonny left his backpack and hiking shoes inside a shed in the backyard. The large white house had black shutters and an impressive front porch. The interior was divided into many rooms serving a variety of purposes. Sonny was relegated to the attic in the Moosilauke Room, but he was happy to be there. He took a shower and washed his clothes. Some of the hostels had secondhand clothes available to wear while the hikers were doing their laundry. Sonny dressed in clothes that might have been worn to the first Woodstock concert. While waiting for the dryer to finish, he reviewed the signatures on the lockers. When he found the name of Box Turtle, he signed his own, next to his idol's.

After a little research, Sonny selected one of the bicycles and rode down Lost River Road through North Woodstock into Lincoln. He passed the grocery store on his way to McDonalds where he ate a late lunch and uploaded videos. His next stop was to Saint Joseph's for Mass. No one looked down on him because of his vintage attire. An hour later, as he was leaving the white sided church, he asked a local couple where he could find a good restaurant. They gave a recommendation with directions and Sonny rode his bike to The Common Man. At the parking lot, he saw a large tourist bus unloading its contents. Sonny quickly locked his bike to a post and entered the establishment just before the flood of people. He was given a seat at the bar where he ordered a seven-seven and a meal. After the drink was finished, his prime rib, garlic mashed potatoes, green beans, and bread arrived and he asked for another glass of the same.

Still feeling the effects of the highballs, Sonny rode to Price Chopper and loaded up on trail food. He evenly distributed the plastic bags of food on the handlebars and carefully rode back to his home for the night, arriving just before sunset.

In the dark, he stood outside in the parking lot away from the people on the front porch and made his first phone call. "Hi, Mom."

"You can call me Annie Oakley now."

"Why? What did you shoot?"

"Do you recall our last conversation when I spoke contemptuously about turkeys?"

"Yes."

"Well, from my deck, I picked off two of those marauders in the garden and I only shot three times."

"Were you using your pistol?"

"Don't be silly, Sonny. If I had used the handgun, I probably would have missed twice. I had August adjust the sights on my varmint rifle. You know the .22 with the scope?"

"Mom, you do know that turkey season doesn't begin for another two months, right?"

"Don't worry, Sonny. The evidence is in the freezer."

Sonny hung up shaking his head and smiling. He called August whose oldest son had a dilemma. "I told him to pick one fall sport to try out for at his school, but he wants to play on two teams. What do you think he should do?"

"I think he should try football and soccer or cross country and soccer, but not cross country and football."

Next he phoned Henry. "Dad, I still haven't decided where to take the family on vacation. I have over a month yet to figure out a place that will make everyone happy."

"Send me a post card when you get there, Henry."

Madison was in a good mood. "The baby is growing. The nursery is ready. And Peaches is finally behaving herself."

"How are you doing in the heat?"

"I'm fine. But judging from your videos, I may weigh more than you do at this point."

Sonny hoped that the contentment he felt would continue with his call to Lily. She answered on the sixth ring and after Sonny relayed all of the good news about his family, she responded. "It sounds like there's a lot of optimism in your life right now. So, I'll keep things positive and not tell you about my problems."

"Lily, I'll listen to whatever you want to talk about."

"Well, Harry seems to have recovered from his back issues."

"You're saying he's back in full production?"

"Ha ha. Exactly. Makin' bacon."

"That should help your finances."

"It does some. Oh. And apparently, the kids are all grown up now because one of them is pregnant."

"Which one?"

"Sonny, you really owe it to yourself to visit a real farm and learn how these things work."

"I thought I already proved myself."

"You did and I have fond memories of the event."

"Maybe when this is over next month, I can come for a visit to your farm and you can further educate me about farm activities."

"I would like that."

"Will I see you before then?"

"One more time. I know a lady in Oquossoc, Maine who I'd like to visit. Text me the date that you'll be at Route 17 and I'll provide trail magic one last time.

Sonny lay on his bunk unable to fall asleep. He felt secure and comfortable and was tired from the six miles of hiking and an equal distance of biking. But in the morning, he would begin an 87-mile trek over the White Mountains.

DAY 131

After breakfast, Sonny grabbed his gear and sat on the front porch to consider his options. The trailhead was five miles away and he decided to take his chances hitchhiking instead of paying for a shuttle. But as he stood up, a SUV pulled up near the front steps and the woman driver got out and opened the hatch. A young woman south bounder named Wild Side put her gear in the back. Sonny asked the trail angel if there was room for him. Less than ten minutes later, he was thanking Ginger for the ride and taking a picture of the two woman to put in his daily video.

Simply put, the trail was rugged. It was steep, loaded with mossy rocks, evergreens, and an occasional waterfall. He stopped for lunch at Eliza Brook Shelter and made water. In the afternoon, Sonny was pleasantly surprised to see Zip Code again. The retiree had been tracking Phoenix from the sign-ins at the shelter log books and finally caught up with him. He also was worried and suggested to Sonny that they hike the Whites together. Sonny had camped with fellow hikers at numerous locations, but rarely hiked with them due to the difference of pace. But the safety aspect and the thought of not having to make all of the decisions by himself appealed to his good sense and was a relief.

Up and over the north and south versions of Kinsman Mountains, Sonny covered 11.5 miles for the day and camped at Kinsman Pond with Zipcode. The woman caretaker, who worked ten days followed by two days off, took their payment for the night's stay. It was only the third time during his journey that Sonny stayed in one of the shelters. He preferred the solitude of his tent, but made an exception because there was ample room. The two older guys shared the space with a young Sobo named Woodrow from Medina, Ohio.

DAY 132

The day started out sunny and the theme of the trail was steep. Sonny assumed that the terrain would stay that way for the rest of his journey and he was grateful for the steps made of wooden blocks that were anchored into a section of bare rock. After a two-mile descent, he and Zip Code stopped at Lonesome Lake Hut. The secluded two story lodge had an exterior of wood shakes and green trim. The interior was all pine with no heat or electricity. Young employees carried in all of the food on their backs. Thru-hikers were sometimes allowed to work-for-stay and any leftover food eaten by them didn't have to be carried away as trash.

After speaking to the employees, Sonny and Zip Code swept the floors and then sat down to a breakfast of scrambled eggs, sausage, oatmeal, and powdered milk. Afterwards, Sonny videoed the dining room with its picnic tables and wall of windows as Zip Code waited impatiently on the porch, peering through the door window with his arms crossed. Sonny was beginning to feel that Zip Code's main concern was to just get the hike over with. Sonny wanted to go home too, but first he wanted to savor and record the journey for his memories and inspiration to others. Outside in front of the lodge, he took pictures of the perfectly calm lake and its reflection of the mountain in the background. At Franconia Notch they crossed underneath US-3/ I-93 and then began another steep climb north, crossing rushing brooks, some with bridges. The overcast sky held on to most of its rain and there were no mosquitoes, but the fog limited the views. Somewhere along the way, Sonny lost his folding foam seat, but he didn't care because it was rarely used.

When they first began hiking together, the pair exchanged family information and stories. But soon after, Zip Code stopped talking and Sonny carried the conversation. They both missed their families, but each one dealt with the alienation in their own manner. Normally a quiet man, Sonny found inspiration and relief by talking about his home life. Zip Code was just the opposite. He never complained, but Sonny was under the impression that Zip Code preferred if they both would just shut up and walk.

Up on Little Haystack Mountain, the rocks had been removed from the trail and the level hiking from cairn to cairn was easy for a change. They continued on to Mount Lincoln where they were instructed by signs not to camp there. Hikers were encouraged to stay on the trail to protect the small vegetation that struggled to survive. Far above the tree line, Mount Lafayette was just under a mile in elevation, and a rare break in the fog teased the hikers with a slim view. After leaving the peak, Sonny spotted Box Turtle Rock, the landmark that was discovered in 2018 by a hiker with the same name.

The tougher climbs and descents equated to lower mileage. They only covered 13.3 miles for their efforts and made camp a mile short of Garfield Pond at an overlook. For his YouTube viewers, Sonny made a video showing how he hung his bear bag and Zip Code videoed Sonny pitching his tent.

DAY 133

Sonny took a picture of a purple mushroom and added it to his collection of the other fungi that were pink, red, orange, yellow, white, or tan. The trail was loaded with rocks of all sizes and angles that impeded progress. There were long stretches of sheer rocks made slippery with wet lichen. The trail was so primitive at times, if not for the white blazes, Sonny would have thought he was lost again. After working for two hours, the pair went over Mount Garfield. They entered Galehead Hut and sat down to a purchased meal of hot soup with rye bread and chocolate cake. The potato and dill concoction was more of a puree than a chunky style that Sonny preferred, but it still tasted good to him. They both bought Clif Bars and candy to supplement their diets.

From atop the pointy South Twin Mountain, both men were able to briefly communicate with their families. On the ridges, hikers were rewarded with views and short sections of smooth hiking. They finished the day after 11.6 miles near a waterfall at Zealand Falls Hut. There were thirty guests staying for the night and the workers gladly accepted the two hiker's offer of work-for-stay. Before suppertime arrived, Sonny and Zip Code wiped off the tables and then set out place settings for all guests and then watched them eat. When the guests had had enough and seating was available, the two hikers ate some of the leftovers. As the guests trickled away from the dining room, the places were cleared, tables, dishes and pot and pans were washed, floors were swept, and garbage was stored away. Some of the guests chose to loiter preventing the thru-hikers from finishing their chores and going to sleep. Sonny spent the time scrubbing the stove and food preparation surfaces. Eventually, all of the guests went to their bunks while

Sonny and Zip Code finished cleaning the last dishes and utensils. Normally, they would have had two hours of sleep in by that time. Finally, they were left alone in the dining room where they each chose a table to sleep under on the floor.

DAY 134

By the time the first guests showed up for breakfast, Sonny and Zip Code had stowed their gear in their backpacks to make room for the customers. The pair then sat down and ate along with the others, but they did not have to work because new thru-hikers arrived to work-for-food.

Before leaving the grounds, they walked over to see the falls from the top and then followed the trail and got a view from the bottom also. There was no wind and it was a good day for hiking. For the first six miles, the walking was relatively smooth and part of the trail followed an old railroad bed. One embankment of a train bridge was supported with cut stone blocks that were stacked up high from the brook. The two men crossed over more pedestrian bridges and Sonny spotted a small flying owl, but couldn't identify it. He fell for the fifteenth time, brushed himself off and kept going.

At the beginning of the Presidential Range, on Mount Webster, they looked down at US-302 in Crawford Notch where they had walked through two hours before. From there they proceeded to Mount

Jackson where the wind increased. The views just kept getting better with each new mountain. Early in the evening, they ended their day with 14.1 miles at Mizpah Hut. All of the huts had similar interiors and exteriors, but their layouts differed vastly. Sonny and Zip Code again signed up for work-for-stay and waited outside until they were summoned. Once again the power signal bars on their phones were nonexistent. No calls or texts went out and none came in. The number of Sonny's videos needing to be uploaded was beginning to build up.

There were a total of four thru-hikers signed up to work for the sixty guests. Two of them chose the breakfast shift. Sonny and Zip Code agreed to help with the supper meal, but complained about the previous night's labor that was in excess of three hours. The amount of chore time for a typical work-for-stay is around two hours. The young crew felt that the thru-hikers had been taken advantage of and took pity on them. Their assignment for the night consisted of washing windows and straightening up the library.

DAY 135

Again Sonny and Zip Code slept on the floor and then ate breakfast before beginning a six-mile climb. The wind and fog increased the higher they went and the trees became less stout. They worked their way through puddles and mazes of short evergreens and passed over Mount Pierce, Mount Eisenhower, and Mount Monroe. The substantial Lake of the Clouds Hut was crowded with ninety lodgers who had finished their meals and were prepping for a hike. Sonny and Zip Code left the wind outside and sat down to a free meal of oatmeal, pancakes, fruit punch, and cake. Sonny took pictures of the young employees as they used rope to strap cardboard boxes to a traditional wooden frame. They carried down the mountain, up to seventy pounds of garbage on their backs. The workers encouraged the pair to eat as much as they could to lighten the load.

As they resumed the climb, the angle and degree of difficulty increased. Sonny tried to take a picture of a cluster of yellow flowers from a single stalk, but the pummeling wind made the image blurry. A yellow warning sign touted the worst weather in America and resulting death from exposure. Above the tree line, they followed the cairns towards the obscured peak. A day earlier, they were a mile lower in elevation.

At 6288 feet, Mount Washington was the second highest point on the Appalachian Trail. The peak could be reached by driving up the road, riding the train, or hiking. As they approached the top, Sonny could hear people and a stone building materialized out of the fog. The Tip Top House was built in 1853 to serve as a hotel. In 1987 it was restored and used as a museum. The place was bustling with visitors and Zip Code went to mail post cards while Sonny made his way toward the Cog Railway. From that vantage point, he videoed single blue, red, and yellow passenger cars, each with its own train engine to push it to the top. The wind speed was so high that Sonny had to lean into it to stay upright. He watched the clouds fly at him and whenever there was an opening, a bright blue sky would replace the drab grayness. The sun would then pour down upon the green valleys and faraway peaks. Sonny and Zip Code found one another among the throng and took pictures to commemorate the day. They each posed in front of the blue train and then waited in a long line for their turns next to the Mount Washington Summit sign.

Inside the overly crowded visitor center, they followed the mass of tourists to the snack bar, squeezed in at one of the tables, and ate chili and hotdogs. It had been a long time since he had been around so many people and Sonny had the urge to get away.

They began the descent and watched the trains do the same. After crossing the railroad track they dropped below the clouds and the sights opened up to them. The fog left, but the wind stayed, and the views were spectacular. Peaks and valleys of muted green vegetation on gray stone dominated the landscape for miles under the forever blue ceiling. Much of the trail was through fields of rocks as they hiked by Mount Clay, Mount Jefferson, and Mount Adams. The scenery distracted their minds from the difficult hiking conditions. Towards the end of the day, they spotted the Madison Spring Hut down below and anticipated its comforts.

However, when Sonny inquired about work-for-stay opportunities, the young man in charge didn't give him a direct answer. Instead, he had the thru-hikers wait while he and the other employees presented their nightly pre-dinner skit to the guests. Close to a half hour later, he informed the pair that all work-for-stay positions had already been claimed. Zip Code asked if it would be possible if they could set their tents up on a flat spot near the hut. The request was denied and the two were advised to use a nearby tent site situated a half mile down a steep path. It was getting late, so Sonny and Zip Code began heading down to Valley Way campsite. Halfway there they spotted a stealth site barely large enough to accommodate their tents, but after 11.8 miles, that was where they spent the night.

DAY 136

The sky was clear, but Sonny awoke feeling sad, a little guilty, and helpless on his late wife's birthday. But there was nothing to do about any of it, so he stowed his gear into his backpack and the two hikers headed north. The climb up Mount Madison was rocky, windy, and hazy, but from the peak they could see the big mountain behind them. The descent brought them back into a land of tall trees, flowing streams, and across a bridge over West Branch Peabody River. Sonny stopped to record a northern saw-whet owl that perched a few feet away and then checked his phone for a signal. The 7.8-mile hike would bring them out onto NH-16 at Pinkham Notch, but there was no phone service at that location. Sonny kept checking and when one bar appeared, he called a hostel in Gorham. An employee answered the phone and said that all rooms and bunks were already full, but for a lesser fee, the owner allowed tenting in the yard. He went on to say that the owner was on his way in his Cadillac to pick up two hikers at the visitor center. Sonny relayed the information to Zip Code and then began to run the last half-mile. He arrived just in time to see the ride pull away.

Zip Code seemed a bit dejected and expressed a lacked of faith in Sonny's hitchhiking abilities. Sonny advised him to put away his trekking poles like he had done and then brought out the pink sign. Ten minutes later, a vehicle pulled over and the men were on their way into town. The trail angel from Connecticut, whose name was Jeff, was coming back from Mount Washington where he and his wife had spent the day hiking. The thru-hikers were dropped off in front of the hostel where Sonny thanked them and took a picture of the happy couple.

The colorful 1891 Victorian house was situated on a Main Street corner. It reportedly still had furnishings from the Libby family, but Sonny never got to see them. Besides being a bed and breakfast it also had a hiker barn connected to the home. Sonny and Zip Code entered the much less elaborate structure and met the owner. Paul was an enthusiastic man who took their money and showed what amenities came with camping in the yard. After they pitched their tents down in the ravine, they took turns using the shower and the washing machine. Sonny step on the bathroom scale and learned that he had lost forty pounds on the trail so far. When the chores were done, they walked into town and were seated at a restaurant. Zip Code ordered a large pizza and Sonny ate a slab of prime rib, a baked potato, peas, and carrots. Afterwards, they went to a small market and bought supplies meant to last a few days. They then stopped in at Subway and purchased foot longs for the following day. Zip Code carried his food back to his tent while Sonny crossed the street for dessert at Scroggins Cool Shack. From a table at the ice cream stand, he ate a banana boat and watched the tourists go by. His phone calls home were brief.

With the sun setting, Sonny made his last video of the day. When darkness came, most of the hikers went to their beds, but Sonny continued to upload onto his YouTube channel. During the process, he lay in his tent trying to relax. When the battery was nearly drained, he went inside to charge the electronic items. He sat at a desk chair and finished all procedures while everyone else slept. At two in the morning, Sonny finally went back to his tent to sleep a few hours.

DAY 137

In the morning, Sonny suggested to Zip Code that they have breakfast in town before they left, but he declined. Sonny walked to a restaurant alone and started with a cup full of cream and sugar with coffee. He followed that with bacon, eggs, toast and hash browns, with orange juice. When he arrived back at the hostel, Zip Code was all packed up and ready to go. Sonny packed his gear and the pair was given a free ten-mile ride back to the trailhead by Paul.

The rain had returned and they went inside the Pinkham Notch Visitor Center and looked around hoping the clouds would get it out of their system. When they had resumed hiking and had reached an elevation that provided phone service, Zip Code called home while Sonny recorded a chipmunk eating a mushroom. The sight made him hungry again. The fog and drizzle continued throughout the day as they scaled the Wildcat Mountains. On top of Peak D of the Wildcats, they took pictures of the gondola and then ate lunch. Sonny had his foot long submarine sandwich and washed it down with a bottle of Pepsi. They later stopped in at Carter Notch Hut for additional nutrition. The small shelter sold them vegetable soup and cake. They ended the damp and chilly day with 7.1 hard-fought miles on top of Carter Dome. Sonny found a decent, flat, and out of the wind site, but gifted it to Zip Code. Out in the open, on the trail, in the sand, Sonny put up his wet tent.

DAY 138

The cold wind slapped around his tent all night. Sonny wore his socks to bed and noticed in the morning that the tents stakes were nearly pulled out of the ground. But the sun was out and the hikers enjoyed good views from Carter Mountain Peaks and Mount Moriah. Fall number sixteen occurred when Sonny got his heel stuck between two rocks and fell over backwards trying to free himself. After 12.1 miles, they stopped at the Rattle River Shelter. Sonny erected his tent on an earthen platform and enjoyed a better campsite than the night before. He made water, washed up in the river, and slept well, knowing that he was out of the White Mountains.

DAY 139

The cool air of the night woke up Sonny, so he put on his sweatshirt and promptly fell back asleep. As the sun began to rise above the tree line, the pair of hikers passed a marker of sticks on the ground indicating 300 more miles. They had a short two miles to US-2 where they hoped to obtain a ride back to Gorham. Along the way they followed Rattle River and saw small trout. Once at the parking lot, Sonny put away his poles and took out his pink sign. A trail angel named Miss Mouse dropped them off across from the Libby House. The resupply was similar to the one three days earlier except that Zip Code joined Sonny for breakfast this time. Zip Code ordered pancakes, but Sonny had steak and eggs with home fries, toast, and orange juice.

They were given a ride back to the parking lot in a red Ford F-150 by a local hiker named Patrick. Crossing the Androscoggin River on the Shelburne Dam, Sonny paused to video the old hydro plant while Zip Code continued on ahead. Sonny found edible black trumpet mushrooms, but only took pictures of them.

Up until eight days earlier, Sonny had not walked continuously with anyone for longer than a few hours. But he had a lot in common with the guy. They were the same age, both were recently retired, and they missed their family members. Sonny had felt that the commonalities would bond them together. He had felt that shared decision making would ease the stress of the unknown and as a team they would be stronger which would make the final two states more enjoyable.

The initial satisfaction derived from the hiking together had expired miles ago. Zip Code became reticent and only wanted to finish and go home. His misery was contagious and was eroding Sonny's mental state.

Sonny was showing signs of fatigue, but did not know at that time the real reason. He thought that the lack of energy was due to the fact that he had burned away all of his fat. The smell of ammonia on his sweat-laden shirt convinced him that he was burning protein. He did not realize the full extent of Zip Code's homesickness. He thought that talking about family would help him, but it only made it worse. For Sonny, listening to music was inspiring and motivational. It had the opposite effect on Zipcode. Sonny tried to share music with him, but it was like torture. When Linda Ronstadt and Aaron Neville sang the duet - *I Don't Know Much*, Zipcode told him to turn it off. Sonny shut off the music and Zipcode made a decision and said, "Sorry, Phoenix, I have to make miles." Zipcode picked up the pace, passed Sonny, and walked away.

Sonny could feel the extra weight of his food bag as he climbed Mount Hayes of the Mahoosuc Range. Although the air was cool, the effort and humidity made him sweat. At Page Pond Outlet, Sonny scoured the water for moose, but all he saw were lily pads. He had kept an eye open for the large animal since Vermont. Like the black bears, the moose were a concern. Sonny wanted to see them, but on his own terms. Not too close. He wanted to take pictures, not fight with them. Dream Lake and Upper Gentian Pond were pretty, but did not showcase any large animals either.

Carlo Col Shelter was less than two hours away, but the sun was preparing to leave soon. Sonny spent his final night in New Hampshire at another tight stealth campsite after 15.5 miles. Inside his tent, he plugged in his phone to the charger. He noticed that the last song he had listened to for the day came from an album entitled - *Almost There.*

DAY 140

The weather was good, but rain was predicted during the night and into the following day. There were two famous difficult sections ahead that Sonny wanted to get through before for they became wet and more treacherous. He enjoyed an early success by going up and over Mount Success and then entered Maine. Thirteen states down, one to go. He repeated a saying that he had been hearing lately from other hikers - "No rain. No pain. No Maine."

Sonny could handle the rain, but he hoped the pain would be held to a minimum. Sections of easy hiking were scarce. Any place with soil had some kind of plant life struggling to survive and occupy space. The rest of the areas were covered with rock. Rebar ladders had been installed in some impossible hiking places on the trail. Some hikers, who didn't want to traverse the steep and slippery rock faces, created side trails. Sonny honored the LEAVE NO TRACE protocol and struggled on the dangerous surfaces of the designated pathway. He stopped and ate a large lunch at Full Goose Shelter, went up and over another peak, and then arrived at his first big challenge of the day.

Mahoosuc Notch was a notorious ravine filled with boulders and called the most difficult mile of the Appalachian Trail. Before attempting the task, Sonny spoke with a Sobo who was just finishing the landmark section. The healthy young man told Sonny that it had taken him two hours to complete the boulder maze. Sonny glanced at the time on his phone and assumed it would probably take him three hours.

After surveying the route, Sonny put away his trekking poles and thought it might be faster, but more perilous to stay on top of the heap of rocks. He began to rock hop from boulder to boulder. After each progression, he evaluated his next move. Halfway though the notch, he arrived at a point where his only option was to hang drop to a ledge below. He considered his center of gravity with the backpack and then lowered himself over the edge. The ledge below was wide enough for a safe landing unless his momentum made him fall backwards. As his fingers gripped the edge, he reviewed the plan. Upon release, it was necessary to slightly push away from the wall to stick the landing.

A moment after letting go, Sonny's feet smacked on the ledge. With his arms extended, he fought to regain his balance. When he felt secure, he took a deep breath and peered down below. Before bounding to the next surface, he shook his head at what he had just done. As he thought to himself that there must have been a better route, a hiker came from around the boulder and told Sonny that there had been steps available behind him. At one point, Sonny took off his pack and slithered through a tight opening. After only eighty minutes he finished the first challenge and began the second.

The Mahoosuc Arm was a mile and a half climb that rose 1500 feet. Any time that Sonny had gained in the Notch was lost on the Arm. At the top, Sonny was tired, but happy that it was over. The descent took him over the Speck Pond Outlet. He ended his 12.9-mile day at Speck Pond Shelter and paid the caretaker for a wooden tent platform. The site came with a bear box and was warmer than up on a windy peak. There was a group of college freshman spending a few days hiking and camping in the woods in lieu of the traditional campus tour. During the last week, Sonny had met students from Penn State and Dartmouth. These young adults were from Harvard.

DAY 141

In the morning, Sonny was confronted by an ugly day that was a mixture of a cold rain and fog. After packing away his wet gear he began the first climb of the day up Old Speck Mountain in a sullen mood. There was a tower on the peak, but he declined to go up it because the fog rendered the effort fruitless. While watching out for puddles, Sonny missed a turn and had to backtrack again. The lousy rain did bring some satisfaction in the form of waterfalls. Fast moving white water sliced through grooves in the rock. Wherever hardness of material won out over the invading fluid, the divide and conquer tactic resulted in a primitive battle of cascades.

His spirits were low during the long descent to Grafton Notch. But when Sonny reached the parking lot at US-26, things improved. At the trailhead, a trail angel with a white SUV asked him if he would like a sandwich. Mrs. Moose made Sonny a ham sandwich and gave him a cup of hot chocolate. She said that when she had looked out her window in the morning, she saw the miserable conditions and thought that hikers would appreciate a hot cup of coffee. But while at the grocery store, she bought more than coffee. Before Sonny had arrived, she already had fed other hikers and had given some of them rides to and from town. After quickly dispensing the first course, he was given seconds and also bags of chips, pop, and a banana. The meal and kindness satiated Sonny and he felt his strength return during the following ascent.

He stopped to take a picture of a yellow haired caterpillar as it crawled along. Like Sonny, the future moth had a goal, but they both had to survive the day and keep going. The local trail maintenance crew had made Sonny's trek much easier by building stone steps into long stretches of the hill. Before moving on, Sonny placed the caterpillar on a dryer spot near a whorled wood aster.

The winds on the west and east peaks of Baldpate were chilly. Between the two peaks was a bog with a narrow boardwalk through the center. A sign warned hikers to stay on the wood because the muck was deep. He saw evidence where one hiker learned about the depth first hand. Rather, first leg to be exact. Sonny met more college students fulfilling their orientation obligations. They were co-eds from Bowdoin College who were dressed in tee shirts and shorts. He pitied them, but they sounded like they were having a blast. Up on the foggy balds, Sonny followed tall cairns and battled the cold wind gusts. Later, after 10.4 miles, he got out of the wind and camped at Frye Notch Lean-to.

DAY 142

Sonny woke up in the middle of a restless night and put on his puffy jacket to get warm. The morning brought slight improvements. There were no birds anymore to roust him from his warm sleeping bag, but he still woke up at 5:30. The outdoor environment was still moist, windy, and cool. His clothes were still wet and his toes were raw again, but the sun was out. He looked forward to an overnight stay at a hostel in a few days, but had to make his food last until then. Up on the first peak of the day, Sonny texted Lily that he would meet her at the agreed location in two days at 8:00 am. After Lily confirmed the arrangement, Sonny started on a long descent.

The hoodie and puffy jacket he put on earlier were making him hot as he hiked over the rocks, roots, and mud. When he stopped to strip down to his tee shirt, he spotted a cluster of purple flowers that stood out among the drab plants. He added a picture of the closed bottle gentians to his collection of wildflowers. The waterfall circuit continued.

While eating his midday meal at Surplus Pond, Sonny noticed that some of the leaves of the red maples on the far edge were beginning to turn red. He had carefully scanned each of the alpine ponds, but had not seen a moose yet. The 14.6 miles for the day landed him at a tent site by South Arm Road with several likeable hiker friends, but also Potty Mouth.

DAY 143

The first task of the day for Sonny was to cross Black Brook on the available stones without getting his shoes wet. Once that was accomplished, he began a typical climb and was grateful for any stone steps and metal rungs and railings. Near some standing dead trees, he recognized the couple from Ireland that he had not seen in a long while. Lemon and Lime were analyzing two clusters of white fungi growing from the base of a tree trunk. Lemon assured Sonny that her husband had studied edible mushrooms for four years and was confirming the traits of the oyster mushrooms. Lime used his knife and cut off one of the clumps and told Sonny that he could have the other one if he wanted. They planned on cooking the delicacy with their supper meal. Sonny trusted the pair, but didn't feel confident enough to eat the fungi.

Sonny felt fatigued as he summited Old Blue Mountain. Much of the tight trail on the downside was made narrower by encroaching evergreen sprigs. At a stream he stopped to make water. He first filled his Platypus bag, screwed on his Wagner filter and Smart water bottle and then hung the assembly from a branch to let gravity do the work. Inventory of his food bag indicated three dehydrated meals, four packets of oatmeal, two Clif Bars and Gatorade. He warmed up beef stroganoff and sat down on the trail for lunch.

Sonny picked and consumed ripe blueberries as he walked and made a video of a male spruce grouse. Just before stopping for the day, he spotted a cooler along the side of the trail. Inspection of the contents revealed empty beer cans and other food items. Sonny chose an apple, a small bag of grape tomatoes, a bottle of water, and cookies. A sign stated that Greg and Geri provided the trail magic. As Sonny finished writing a thank you note, the trail angels who came to retrieve their cooler, approached him. They said that they had done a lot of hiking in the past and that the tomatoes were raised in their garden. Sonny thanked them in person and took their picture for his daily YouTube video.

He pitched his tent near Bemis Stream after hiking 12.4 miles and ate supper. A hard day on the rugged trail left him on the doorstep of trail magic from Lily and one day away from a restful night at a hostel.

DAY 144

Sonny looked out through the screen door of his tent and smiled. There was no sign of wind or rain, the sun was up, and the climate was cool, but not cold. However, his happiness was not derived from the weather conditions. Sonny had less than a mile walk until he saw Lily again. His phone calls and texts to the woman paled in comparison to the real thing. The night before, Sonny had alerted most of his fellow campers about the probability of a trail magic breakfast. He and the others planned to let Potty Mouth sleep in late while the rest of them snuck away, but somehow the lout learned of the scheme and broke camp with everyone else.

They forded Bemis Stream and then their hunger pangs caused them to arrive at ME-17 prematurely. Lily was not there yet and right away Potty Mouth accused Sonny of a prank. Sonny ignored the boor and walked down a ways to take pictures of the collection of hiker stickers adhering to the guardrail. Before tensions escalated, the green Chevy Equinox arrived and parked by Sonny. He hopped in the passenger seat and kissed the driver. Lily said, "I missed you too, Sonny."

Sonny smiled. "You may want to pull up a little farther by the bench. We could set up there."

"I see you brought your whole tramily with you today."

"Well, most of them anyways."

"Okay. Review their names with me."

"There's Fiona and her boyfriend Doubting Thomas."

"I recognize them. Both of them have lost a lot of weight."

"Yes, they have. Do you recognize Antelope, Lioness, Lemon, and Lime?"

"Oh sure. South Africa and Ireland."

"Correct." Sonny then pointed out Thesaurus, Webster, Perky, Ogle, and Potty Mouth.

""I've seen all of those guys before. That last one is trouble."

"I know. I think he already has been drinking today."

All of the hikers except one helped Lily and Sonny in some fashion or other. Potty Mouth planted himself on the bench and criticized everyone. The set up and cooking went smoothly and soon all were enjoying large heapings of scrambled eggs with bacon, hot coffee, cold milk, and orange juice while taking in the view of Mooselookmeguntic Lake. Afterwards, while Potty Mouth lay across the bench and napped, they all helped clean up and packed the supplies into the SUV.

When it was time to resume hiking, all but one gathered around Lily to thank and praise her. The smile on her face revealed the appreciation she felt, but it disappeared when her phone rang. She walked away from the hikers to talk in private with her bank for a few minutes. As a few of them headed north, Potty Mouth awoke from his slumber and lived up to his name. "Were you pricks just going to walk away and leave me here by myself?"

As he approached the group glaring at Sonny, Fiona spoke up. "You shouldn't drink so much."

"Shut up, bitch. I wasn't talking to you."

Doubting Thomas stepped forward to block his way and was punched in the stomach for his trouble. Fiona squatted down to tend to her boyfriend's discomfort as

Sonny dropped his pack and went to face the angry man.

Drunk and over confident, Potty Mouth clenched his right fist, drew it back, and attempted to hit him in his face. Sonny watched the telegraphed punch and deftly sidestepped it. The momentum of missing the target threw the aggressor off balance and caused him to fall face first into the dirt. Sonny did not hesitate, but instead leaped onto the prone man's back with both knees. The impact knocked the wind out of him and the older man pounded the back of his neck with his fist. He considered stopping there, but when Potty Mouth called him a bad word that suggested he had intimate knowledge of his own mother, Sonny grabbed the punk's right wrist. He then quickly shifted his position and sat on the back of his head with his knees holding his shoulders. With a solid base established, he used his right hand and pulled the wrist up to the shoulder. Potty Mouth screamed in pain, but continued with the insults and threats so Sonny punched him in the kidneys with his left fist until he heard him whimper. He thought about standing up and kicking him in the tailbone, but the adrenaline had worn off and fatigue was setting in. He stood up to catch his breath and then squatted down close so he was certain to be heard. "I am done with you now, but if you ever attack me again, I will show you no mercy."

Lily returned in time to see the end of the scuffle and was visibly upset with Sonny because his actions were reminiscent of her abusive husband. "I can't be with a violent man. Goodbye, Sonny."

Sonny and the other hikers watched her drive away. A couple of the men helped the battered man over to the bench and left him sitting there with his backpack and a bottle of water. Before walking on ahead, the thru-hikers all insisted that Sonny had acted appropriately under the circumstances. Before moving on, Fiona and Doubting Thomas hung back and walked with Sonny for a while. Doubting Thomas said he felt embarrassed by his attempt at chivalry and thanked Sonny for stepping in. Sonny praised him for wanting to protect Fiona. "I think you learned a lot today. Try to avoid fighting if you can. But if you have to, then be ready and try your darndest to win."

Doubting Thomas knew that Fiona had something that she wanted to talk to Sonny alone about so he picked up the pace and pulled away. As she gathered her thoughts Sonny looked up ahead at Doubting Thomas and said, "It looks like I've been replaced, Fiona."

"No one can replace you, Phoenix. Are you planning on stopping at Rangeley?"

"Yeah. I'll be going there early tomorrow morning. How about you? What are your plans?"

"Well. We're planning on spending tonight there and then take some more time off from the trail to see the local sights like we did in D.C. and New York."

"Just you and Doubting Thomas?"

"No. All of us here today and a few more who are in Rangeley already."

"Does any of this have to do with what happened today?"

"No. But it will be nice to lose Potty Mouth."

Fiona stopped walking and looked at Sonny with hopeful eyes. "Phoenix, I'd love for you to join us."

"I would like that, Fiona. But I need to finish this while I'm still able."

"But Sonny, I may never see you again."

Sonny nodded and offered his fist. Fiona bumped it and walked away quickly trying not to show her tears. Sonny said to himself, "Everyone is leaving me."

Walking along Moxie pond, he stopped to take a picture of pearly everlasting blooms. He stood there a long time thinking about the gardens at his home and wished he was there.

Lemon and Lime had made use of Long Pond and were swimming when Sonny caught up with them. He took their picture to prove to his viewers that the mushrooms they had eaten weren't poisonous. They told him that they had eaten the tasty oyster mushrooms with rice and ginger. Sonny walked along the rare sandy shoreline and imagined he was back in Ohio walking along Lake Erie.

The hiking conditions were tame for a change. Sonny visited several ponds along the trail. At Sabbath Day Pond and Little Swift River Pond, he stopped to search for moose, but found none. Still full from breakfast, he put off eating his midday meal. At South Pond, he witnessed jumping fish and stopped for lunch. After heating water and adding it to his beef stew packet, Sonny sat and ate in a flat-bottom boat that was resting on the shore. Afterwards he took off his clothes, put on his running shorts, and flip-flops and then rinsed his clothes and body in the pond. The wet clothes were hung on branches to dry while he made water. But feeling antsy, Sonny redressed in the damp garments and pushed on.

Utilizing his Guthook app, Sonny learned of a stealth campsite and stopped there after 13.3 miles. Using the last amount of powder mix, he made a container of Gatorade. The electrolyte drink and water were all he had left. The food bag that he hung contained only garbage. His memories of the day's events were a blur and he longed for better times.

DAY 145

Sonny woke up hungry and drank some water. After packing away his gear, he walked less than a mile to ME-4 where he had his picture taken sitting on a large rock in the parking lot by a day hiker. While he critiqued the image of his gaunt self, his ride showed up and took him nine miles to the Field Stone Hostel. He paid for one night, placed his pack in the empty bunkroom, and took a shower. It was a relief not to have the pack on his back, if only for one day. It wasn't the weight as much as the raw spot caused by the constant rubbing of his hip belt. The area on the backbone above his tailbone burned from the friction of the constant shifting backpack against his sweaty tee shirt.

After dressing in the cleanest of his dirty clothes, he walked to Lake Street. Saint Luke's was a white-sided church with a green steeple. After Mass he asked one of the members for a recommendation for breakfast and was given directions to the only place open. It was explained to him that there were two seasons. There was boating season and skiing season and Sonny had shown up during the lull between the two. He walked down the road to Keep's Corner Café and Bakery. The place was busy, but after a short wait, he began with over easy eggs, sausage links, home fries, toast, and orange juice. Still not satisfied, he ate a freshly made cinnamon roll with a glass of milk.

On his way back to the hostel, he walked by a flower garden and saw a few boaters on the lake in the background. The Pine Tree Frosty ice cream stand didn't open until noon so Sonny continued on to fetch his laundry. Along the way, he strolled past the quaint Rangeley Inn. The large light blue with white trim hotel was three stories tall and had a full-length front porch and a tavern. Sonny took pictures of flowers near the sidewalk including a yellow dahlia and a white hollyhock. After a short stop at the still unoccupied hostel where he changed into his rain suit, he proceeded to the Laundromat, placed his clothes in a machine, and then went for ice cream. By the time he had finished his banana split his clothes were clean. In the backyard of the hostel, Sonny hung his wet clothes on a rocking chair in the sunlight. He washed his silk sleeping bag liner by hand and hung that outside to dry also. Following a nap, Sonny placed a call to Lily that went unanswered. He went out and collected his dry clothes and lay down on the bunk again.

Before heading back out to walk up a hill to the IGA store, Sonny surveyed the free hiker food that was left by others on the kitchen table. While food was on his mind, he placed an order with the REI store for a delivery of dehydrated food. The meals were to be sent to Shaw's Hostel in Monson for the trek through the 100 Mile Wilderness.

After filling his shopping cart with enough food for a week, Sonny went to the deli and picked out a rotisserie chicken and a container of potato salad. Rain was falling when he exited the store, so he carried his bags under the awning and sat down on the sidewalk with his back against the building. He began uploading videos while he ate his meal with a bottle of Mountain Dew. After finishing the picnic meal, Sonny wiped his greasy hands with napkins, disposed of the litter, and then carried his bags back to the hostel.

The bunkroom had acquired another tenant for the night. Once a Player was on his way out the door to a sports bar for supper. Sonny unloaded his supplies on the table and put a few things in the small refrigerator. His heart wasn't into it, but he placed short calls to each of his family members. He told all of them that he was tired and was going to bed early, but he didn't. After another unsuccessful attempt to contact Lily, he sat at the kitchen table and ate half of a coconut custard pie with a glass of milk.

Before darkness fell, he decided to head back to the hill at the IGA to upload more videos. But as he walked away from the hostel, he noticed that the closed restaurant across the road was also up on a hill. He climbed that hill, sat on a plastic chair outside the business and resumed the uploading process. From that spot, he watched the sunset, saw the stars appear, and bats fly above him. By the time he was finished, it was 10 o'clock. He walked back in the dark and fell asleep before his roommate came home.

DAY 146

In the morning Sonny quietly took a shower and loaded his gear into his backpack. For some time he had cravings for canned peaches while hiking and after finding an opener, ate a full can. He finished the pie and the quart of milk and then looked in vain for the two plastic containers of cereal he had purchased. By then, Once a Player was up beginning his day. He noticed that Sonny was continuously looking for something. "Did you lose something, Phoenix?"

"I'm not sure. I thought I bought them, but maybe I lost them or left them at the store or something."

"What are they?"

"I could have sworn I bought some cereal yesterday."

"Wait. Was one Fruit Loops and the other Frosted Flakes?"

"Yes. Have you seen them?"

"I did. But they were on the table and I thought they were hiker food."

"Oh well. Mystery solved. I probably have too much food anyhow."

"Oh, I still have them, but I transferred them into plastic bags. You can have them back or I can pay you for them."

Sonny laughed. "Forget about it. Consider it trail magic."

The hostel owner drove Sonny, Once a Player, and two other hikers to a convenience store for breakfast sandwiches and then dropped them all off back at the trail. The mild incline led him and his heavy pack past Ethel Pond where the slope increased for two miles. Just above the tree line, Sonny looked back on the town of Rangeley and its surrounding lakes. The sun and wind fought to control the temperature as the lone hiker looked ahead and wondered when he would see the final mountain. The views were very good, but Sonny doubted he could see Baxter Peak. But he could see the peaks in his near future. A mile ahead was The Horn and beyond that, Saddleback Junior called to him. He continued on until he reached the transition point between peaks and sat on a rock out of the wind. While eating his lunch and resting, Sonny soaked up the warm sunlight and watched two eagles soar over the distant peaks and valleys. Since being dropped off at the trail in the morning, he had not seen any other hikers and he sensed the drop in population would continue until the end.

At times, Sonny relished the solitude, but then sometimes he felt discouraged. Up and over the final two peaks of the day he felt powerful as he looked back from whence he trod. But looking forward, he felt insignificant and weak under his full pack. He was a man of contradictions.

Near the end of the day, Orbeton Stream was in his way. While crossing on the wet stones, Sonny nearly lost his balance and fell. But on the far shore he let out a sigh of relief and kept going. Only the things that hurt him could stop him and that was all that mattered. He stopped after 14.2 miles at Sluice Brook and camped by himself. Part of his supper meal was a once large bag of potato chips. He had crushed them prior to transferring them to a quart sized plastic bag. During his wrap up video of the day's events, Sonny talked about the cereal incident, but didn't mention the thru-hiker by name. Instead, he jokingly referred to him as the Cereal Killer.

DAY 147

Sonny ate breakfast, packed his gear away and then began the first climb of the day up Lone Mountain. He only stopped long enough to pee and take a picture of white meadowsweet. The sky was overcast with a light rain that usually should have been good conditions for hiking, but the sore on his lower back irritated him. After conquering Spaulding Mountain, Sonny took a picture of a bronze plaque that commemorated the completion of the final section of the A.T. He had only two hundred miles left to finish his journey.

A large lunch, featuring chicken teriyaki, was eaten at a sunny location that boasted a view of Sugarloaf Mountain. The descent took him to South Branch Carrabassett River that he forded on a wooden plank and stones. He checked the time and determined it was possible for him to get past two more peaks before the sun left. With his ear buds inserted, he started the steep and rocky climbs listening to *Simple Man* by Lynyrd Sknyrd while snacking on peanut M&Ms. The wind had increased as he achieved South and North Crocker Mountains. After 13.8 miles, he found a stealth campsite next to a spring and selected a spot for the tent away from the dead trees.

DAY 148

The motivation for the day was knowing that once he was through the Bigelow Mountains, the terrain would become friendlier. The only real big mountain after that was the last one and Sonny told himself that he would crawl up that one if he had to. Sonny took a picture of the 2000-mile sign posted on a tree and since he still had plenty of food left, he passed up going into Stratton. He observed several large female American toads that had dug depressions into the sandy soil. The amphibians had then backed into the hole and awaited unwary insects that passed by. After crossing Dick Brown's Bridge, he began a long steady climb. During the sustained effort, he reminisced about the highs and lows of the last two thousand miles.

The journey was coming to an end, but his retirement would continue at other locations. He wondered if he would push away everyone who had a fault and end up alone or make every effort to find the good in all people and surround himself with hope.

What scared him most was not knowing if the decision was his to make. Did he have a choice, or was his destiny predetermined by inherited and environmental traits? Compared to his ancestors, he assumed his legacy would be less than spectacular and sometimes doubted that his life had a purpose. But then he would think of his family. His mother displayed strength and resiliency. He was in awe of his children and their accomplishments. And his grandchildren were the future. He recalled the short letter, which he wrote to the grandchildren on their first birthday, meant to advise and encourage.

Dear _____,

Nothing that is easy is worth having. There will be times when you will be afraid or feel that you can't do something. Keep trying. Find a way, because in the end it is the struggle that makes it all worthwhile. Try to be honest and helpful. Do the things that will make your family proud and surround yourself with good friends. If you do these things, you will find contentment. Whatever the level of your success, know that you are loved.

Grandpa Toth

To help get over the top, Sonny listened to Peggy Gordon sing, *By My Side*. He ate lunch at Horn Pond Lean-tos while looking down on Horns Pond. The climb over South Horn was shorter, but steeper. West Peak was above the tree line and the views were expansive, but Sonny could not see Mount Katahdin in the distance. But he could see the next peak and was there in less than an hour. On Avery Peak, the wind picked up again as Sonny inspected the stone foundation of the former fire warden tower. He then took a picture of the bronze plaque in honor of Myron H. Avery who was a major force in the completion of the Appalachian Trail.

As Sonny descended the final peak of the day, the rain began and he could feel the movement of the backpack rubbing on his lower spine. Nearing Safford Notch Campsite, Sonny noticed that a couple of hikers were gaining on him. He worried that he might miss out on a tent site if they passed him. Picking up the pace, he hustled through the boulder tunnel and found a level spot. While lying in his tent that night, Sonny thought about the rugged 14.6 miles he had covered. The raw spot on his back burned, but he felt that the discomfort was worth it. After climbing over so many peaks, he anticipated a smoother trail beginning in the morning.

DAY 149

The rain had stopped, but it was overcast and Sonny started the day with wet feet. He backtracked through the pile of boulders and began the easy two-mile hike up Little Bigelow Mountain. The walk on the level top was over a mile long, but that was followed by a three-mile harsh decline. A cool breeze canceled any thought of entering The Tubs (cascading pools) by Little

Bigelow Lean-to. Against his better judgment, Sonny chose to tread down a lichen covered rock ramp. At a moist spot, his feet flew out from under him and the trekking poles and water bottles sailed away. He landed on the raw area of his wounded back for fall number seventeen. As he picked up his scattered parts, it occurred to him that he was feeling weaker than normal.

At both Rocky Beach and West Carry Pond, Sonny heard the waves before seeing them. He stopped for pictures of showy orchids and yellow club fungi. Later in the afternoon, he saw a large brown wooden sign that designated the spot as The Great Carrying Place.

In 1775, five years before defecting, Benedict Arnold directed a thousand American soldiers to portage their canoes for thirteen miles towards an attack of Quebec. Sonny finished the 16.4-mile day at East Carry Pond. He camped next to a couple that had graduated from Bowling Green State University. After his supper meal, Sonny made water and washed up in the pond. Soon after, he went to bed feeling weary.

DAY 150

The nights were becoming cold again. There was still a fog on the pond when Sonny started hiking and he had on his hooded sweatshirt and glove liners. The ferry across the Kennebec River ceased operation at two in the afternoon, but the gentle trail assured him that he would make it there with time to spare. Near a bog, he found a very large turbinellus floccosus mushroom. The vase shaped fungus was white on the outside with an orange interior. Sonny took a picture and then walked on a sturdy three-plank boardwalk. He passed Pierce Pond, a series of cascading waterfalls, and then carefully crossed over Otter Pond Stream on a primitive three-log bridge.

All thru-hikers were required to be ferried across the dangerous Kennebec River. Over the years, some hikers had attempted to ford the river and a few of them didn't survive the venture. When Sonny arrived at the shore, he saw that the canoe was dropping off another hiker on the far side. While waiting for its return, he signed the waiver. Sonny put on a life preserver, loaded his pack in the center of the Old Town canoe, sat in the front, and helped paddle. Upon disembarking, Sonny gave Captain Greg a tip.

It was turning out to be a perfect day. The blue skies made the environment more attractive and the warm sun and cool breeze complimented the other. The peaceful evergreen forests against the stoic rocks with the invading fast flowing white water served to calm Sonny. But his lack of energy was beginning to worry him. He walked along the river a ways feeling relieved that he had made the crossing and then turned towards the small town. The town of Caratunk was home to a bed and breakfast and hostel with the same name. Sonny easily found the establishment, which of course, was a white lap sided structure with green trim. He sat on a rocking chair on the side porch and demolished two barbecued pulled pork sandwiches with two vanilla milkshakes.

Sitting down provided some relief, but as soon as the food was gone, Sonny lifted his backpack and headed north. He walked passed Pleasant Pond and then up and over Pleasant Pond Mountain to a stealth campsite after 19.2 miles. The tent site was on a slight slope, which would cause him to slide downhill all night, but it was only for one night. The feeling that he was experiencing was similar to that of a marathon runner in the later stages of a race. There were less than 150 miles to go and he hoped he had enough fuel in his tank to make it.

DAY 151

The weather was a repeat of the prior day, cool but warming. Although Sonny had his phone plugged into the charging battery all night, the power was draining. He limited his video making to extend the phone's life and was concerned about missing the opportunity of a moose sighting as he walked by Moxie Pond. There was only one peak on the schedule for the day and after summiting Moxie Bald Mountain he savored the views. A hiker named Popeye offered to solve Sonny's phone problem. After inspecting the device, the trail angel determined that there were too many items on the phone that were draining the battery. He turned off the unneeded ones and made Sonny's day even brighter. The two hikers took pictures of each other next to the summit sign.

Sonny made the descent and then after ten miles, stopped at Moxie Bald Mountain Lean-to. There on the picnic table, he warmed up mashed potatoes and added two packets of salmon to it. He ate the mixture with Gatorade and then went down to Bald Mountain Pond to make water. The rest of the afternoon was on an easy downhill grade. At the West Branch of the Piscataquis River, he put his trekking poles away and traded his hiking shoes for his flip-flops. A taunt rope that was stretched from bank to bank served as a hand railing as Sonny forded the small river. He continued on until he reached the East Branch of the Piscataquis River where he camped on the south side. Sonny observed that although he had covered 21.1 miles, the terrain was relatively easy and he shouldn't feel so tired. As he lay in his sleeping bag, he sensed that something was wrong with him.

DAY 152

It was another pleasant day and Sonny ate a quick breakfast and then rolled up his air mattress, sleeping bag, and tent. He carried his backpack to the bank of the small river while wearing his flip-flops. After rolling up his pant legs, he made the crossing and then put on his socks and shoes. While double-knotting the laces, he heard voices coming from across the waterway. One by one, the tramily that had left him a week earlier, assembled on the far bank.

Fiona was the first one to spot Sonny. She shouted out his trail name and immediately ran towards him with no concern about the water. Doubting Thomas followed closely behind her with the rest of the hikers in his wake. They treated Sonny like he had just scored the winning goal by mobbing him and jumping up and down. When the celebration waned, Sonny said, "I hope all of you have clean hands."

Perky said, "Well, it's too late now."

Ogle added, "There's only 120 miles left. What could go wrong?"

Fiona playfully punched Sonny on the arm. "Phoenix, you jerk. I though I'd never see you again."

Sonny rubbed his arm pretending to be hurt. "Ouch. Hey, what are you guys doing here?"

Doubting Thomas pointed at Fiona and said, "We saw some things, but *somebody* missed somebody else."

Lemon said, "We all missed you, Phoenix."

Antelope explained. "So we all decided to get back on the trail to see if we could catch up with you."

Sonny said, "Wow. You must have really pushed it to catch up with me. I could use some of your energy."

Their smiles gave him a boost and as they continued on the trail, he listened to their adventure stories of the past week. Most of the hikers picked up the pace to spread out during the 6.7-mile hike to ME-15. Some of them had arranged shuttle rides to the Monson, but others relied on hitchhiking. The latter group knew that they had a better chance of obtaining a ride in small numbers. Sonny was picked up and delivered to the A.T. Visitor Center by a trail angel named Sandy. He took her picture, thanked her, and then went inside and learned about permits and other pertinent information about the final leg of the journey.

Just down the street and around the corner was Shaw's Hiker Hostel. The operators of the complex, Poet and Hippie Chick and their children resided at the two story dark maroon house. Attached to the back of the home was Poet's Gear Emporium where supplies were sold. Across the yard with several tents, was another equally impressive house where Sonny and many others planned to spend the night. His cot was in the second floor bunkroom next to a window and a balcony. He placed his backpack on the floor, laid down on the bed, and immediately felt a sharp pain from the wound on his lower back. It felt like his spine was pushing against a sharp rock. He tried shifting his weight, but could only get comfortable on his side or stomach.

There was much to do before the day was over and Sonny got started. He put his dirty clothes in a washer, signed up for breakfast, and then took a shower. The scale in the bathroom indicated that he had lost fifty pounds. Once dressed in clean clothes, he and a few of the others walked to the Monson General Store. Sonny started with a leafy salad and a bowl of diced grapes, melons, and pineapples. He followed that with a Reuben sandwich and a quart of milk. Dessert was a quart of moose tracks ice cream. Everyone had things to do to get ready for the next day's hike and while most of them returned to the hostel, Sonny went and sat on a bench next to Lake Hebron. He could hear a group playing bluegrass music across the water. His failed attempts to upload videos caused frustration and the phone calls home didn't help. Although he was able to reach all of them, the signal was weak and conversations were brief and confusing. His call to Lily went unanswered.

Sonny shuffled back and entered the resupply shop where his order from REI was waiting for him. He also purchased other items from Hippie Chick and some of them were stowed away in a container that was to be delivered to him on an agreed date. Tomorrow morning he would be dropped off at the start of the 100 Mile Wilderness. The section of the trail was severely isolated from access to supplies, communication, and first aid. A ten-day supply of food was recommended. Many hikers only carried enough food for the first sixty miles and then had a container of supplies dropped off to them at that point.

Towards evening, many of the tramily headed down to Spring Creek Bar-B-Q, but Sonny wasn't feeling well and declined to go with them. He eventually felt strong enough to find supper. The short tour of the town provided him with views of a couple of churches with steeples and led him past the post office. Some of the buildings were built out right over the shore of the lake. Just past those businesses, he arrived at Lake Shore House. The lodging place also had a pub. Sonny worked his way through the hallways and ended up sitting at the crowded bar next to a carved wooden fish. He hoped that the ribeye steak, french fries, and glass of Guinness would improve his health. Disappointed with the results, he wandered back to his cot as the sun disappeared. As usual, he awoke periodically during the night to urinate. He took advantage of the stronger Wi-Fi at that time to upload videos. Between the frequent trips to the bathroom and the jolting pain of his sore spot, Sonny was awake enough to bring his video subscribers up to date at the expense of a restful night.

DAY 153

Sonny woke up feeling tired. After showering, he dressed, packed his gear, and then went downstairs and took a seat at the full breakfast table. Poet cooked and served eggs, sausage, bacon, and pancakes to the excited hikers. Water, coffee, tea, and juice were available and consumed in large quantities. Several shuttle trips delivered thru-hikers to the trailhead. Sonny made use of the second run. Along the way, Poet lived up to his name and recited a poem. He then instructed the hikers to think about their journeys up to that point and to savor the 100 Mile Wilderness. After the pep talk, the hikers exited the SUV and all but one charged onto the trail.

A posted sign cautioned hikers:

THERE ARE NO PLACES TO OBTAIN SUPPLIES OR GET HELP UNTIL ABOL BRIDGE 100 MILES NORTH. DO NOT ATTEMPT THIS SECTION UNLESS YOU HAVE A MINIMUM OF 10 DAYS SUPPLIES AND ARE FULLY EQUIPPED. THIS IS THE LONGEST WILDERNESS SECTION OF THE ENTIRE A.T. AND ITS DIFFICULTY SHOULD NOT BE UNDERESTIMATED. GOOD HIKING!

Sonny casually headed north, saying to the rocks and trees, "Here goes nothing."

All morning long, fellow hikers passed him by and wished him well. Once a Player told him that at some point he was going to do a fifty-mile stretch in a single day. At Sonny's mile and a half per hour pace, even the tramily left him behind. When they expressed concern or guilt, Sonny lied to them and said he would catch up to them later. At Bell Pond he stopped and looked for moose, but only saw ducks. He had the same results at North Pond, at a beaver dam, and Mud Pond. Little Wilson Falls was impressive. Sonny recorded the white water over a multitude of natural stone steps. At Big Wilson Stream, he resorted to his flip-flops and forded the slippery stone waterway. After nearly falling twice, he made water and ate lunch on the far bank and then crossed a set of railroad tracks.

By the time he reached Vaughn Stream, Sonny felt like he was sleep walking. For inspiration, he listened to Cat Stevens' song - *On The Road To Find Out.* Near the end of the day he found a nice tenting site, but foolishly gave it to another hiker. Farther up the trail, after 15 miles for the day, he found another spot next to Long Pond Stream. The site, which was between two large trees, hung out above Slugundy Falls. He struggled to erect the tent in the cramped area and then ate supper. Just before darkness set in, Sonny climbed down to the stream to wash up.

The mist from the falls had made the rock surface slick and caused fall number eighteen. Sonny's feet slipped out from under him causing him to land on his sore back and bang his head. His momentum continued and Sonny felt himself sliding towards the edge of the falls. In a panic, he held out his arms and legs creating enough friction to halt the slide. He then carefully inched away from the drop-off to a dryer surface. An injury inspection revealed that the accident had not helped his back any. Upstream away from the falls, he cupped his hands, and rinsed the blood off from a cut on his head above his left ear. He climbed back to his tent in the dark and tried to fall asleep.

DAY 154

The sunny day started off calm as he hiked past Barren Ledges on the fifth month anniversary of his trek. There were excellent views from the windy top of

Barren Mountain with no towns in sight, only green hills and ponds as far as Sonny could see. He made it over Fourth Mountain and then took a picture of his trekking poles alongside a 2100 displayed on the ground with sticks and stones. He pushed on past Rock Slide feeling worn out.

Late in the day when Sonny was out of water, he followed a blue blaze down to East Chairback Pond. His intentions were to make water and find a campsite down the trail a bit more. But near the shoreline, he spotted a nice flat area and decided to call it a day after only 13.6 miles. The sore spot on his back was getting worse and he felt very tired. For his last meal of the day, Sonny didn't even heat up the water that he mixed with the dehydrated food package.

DAY 155

After sunset, Sonny heard loons on the lake until he fell asleep. He was awakened before sunrise by grunting sounds and calls that he believed were from moose. But unfortunately, a hopeful survey of the lake in the morning only produced waterfowl.

He followed the side path back to the trail and took it downhill to West Branch Pleasant River. After fording the stream, Sonny began a gradual incline that turned into a series of small peaks. On top of Hay Mountain, he enjoyed the view, but worried about making it to his food delivery site in the morning. From the summit of White Cap Mountain he could see a hazy image of Mount Katahdin, over seventy miles away. But he was more concerned with covering the next seventeen miles. He was able to contact Shaw's Hostel and change the drop off time from nine to noon. He also added a few items to his list of supplies including two products he had never tried before: Aspercreme and 5-Hour Energy shots.

Coming down off of the mountain, Sonny videoed a few ruffed grouse that walked directly in front of him pecking at the trail as they scurried along. The trail leveled out and he spotted a hairy woodpecker pecking on the trees for insects. After 18 miles, Sonny put up his tent near East Branch Lean-to. A youth group occupied the shelter and the site was crowded with several tents. It was dark when he turned on his headlamp and went down to the East Branch Pleasant River wearing only running shorts and flip-flops. The noisy young teenagers became quiet as they observed Sonny make water and enter the river to rinse off.

To assure that he would make it to the road on time, Sonny set his alarm clock for 1:30 am. He had looked around at the other hikers while there was still ample light available, but none of them looked familiar. However, as he was falling asleep, he recognized a sound he had heard at the bunkroom at Shaw's Hostel. Over at a nearby hammock, a loud snoring blared into the otherwise quiet night. Sonny found his earplugs, but had a restless short night. An hour after midnight, he dressed and broke camp as quietly as possible.

A little ways down the trail, Sonny turned his headlamp from red to bright white. He walked along the pitch-dark path listening to singing frogs and insects with an eye out for white blazes. The air was surprisingly warm and the bright stars reminded him of a Van Gogh painting. He left his shoes on to cross the river on its worn stones. Up ahead, Sonny kept seeing someone with a headlamp, but he couldn't decipher if the hiker was coming or going. The mystery was solved on top of Little Boardman Mountain when the light transformed into a crescent moon.

DAY 156

By the time Sonny had reached Crawford Pond Outlet, the dawn revealed a blue sky. Following a brief rain, he reached Jo-Mary Road at the original scheduled delivery time of 9:00am. To his delight, a trail angel had paid to use the privately owned toll road and was open for business. A man dressed in a New England NFL jersey, had chairs set up near a vehicle loaded with food and a large American flag on display. He went by the name Patriot and he handed Sonny a menu with pictures of the large selection of food stored in numbered plastic bins. Like Lily, the enthusiastic man provided trail magic at several sites during the hiking season. While gorging himself with the free food, Sonny's container was delivered. He sat there eating and talking to Patriot and other hikers who showed up. At noon he rose and added his supplies to his food bag. He then reached back and applied the pain relieving cream to the unseen area. Poet had also sent along a foam strip. Sonny cut a notch out with his small knife and inserted the padding under his hip belt.

Sonny was dragging, but he pushed on, loaded down with food again. He tread on boards though a low area in the woods, went by Cooper Pond, and found himself at Sandy Beach at lower Jo-Mary Lake. For a short time, he walked on the sandy shore with lavender asters. Early in the evening, he stopped after 19.5 miles at Potaywadjo Spring Lean-to. He pitched his tent on an earthen platform and considered taking a nap. But instead, Sonny ate an early supper and then went to bed.

DAY 157

There was less than fifty miles to the north end of the Appalachian Trail. The sun was out. The sky was blue with a few puffy clouds. The temperature was warming. The pine scented breeze felt nice. The trail was dry and relatively flat. If there had been birds around, they would be singing. But Sonny was miserable. He put on a happy face for his videos, but the burning, swollen, open sore was killing him. The Tylenol and Aspercreme did little to alleviate his discomfort. He began to walk north.

His left Achilles tendon was starting to complain, but Sonny ignored it and occupied his mind with his other needs. He worried about securing one of the limited camping sites at Katahdin Stream Campground and obtaining a permit to summit Mount Katahdin. At one point, he wrapped his sweatshirt around his waist and then tightened the shoulder straps to relieve the pressure and rubbing of the pack on the oozing wound. At regular intervals, joyous, well wishing, unfamiliar hikers passed Sonny as he slowly walked along side the Nahmakanta Stream. One of them slowed down and hiked with him. Her trail name was Very Kind. She was the same age as Madison, married, but had no children. Her family had emigrated from India when she was a child. Even as a successful civil rights lawyer from Washington DC, she was still trying to earn the respect of her father. Her husband had been hiking with her but he had to leave the trail and she wanted to finish the section hike through the 100 Mile Wilderness and summit Mount Katahdin. As the daughter of medical doctors, she spent much of her youth in hospitals around sick people and she was concerned by Sonny's appearance. She offered him food, medicine, and encouragement. Sonny passed on all but the praise. When he told her he was going to stop for lunch along the bank of the stream, she did the same. He wasn't hungry, but was pacified by taking the pack off his back. They exchanged life stories and then continued on. When they reached Nahmakanta Lake she said she was going to stop and make water. Sonny had enjoyed her company, but thought maybe she wanted to part ways so he wished her well, said goodbye and continued on the trail down the beach.

The path wound into the woods but turned back to visit the lake at Gravel Beach and then again at West Beach. Sonny stopped to ingest and apply more painkillers. While he had his phone out checking the route on the Guthook app, he looked at pictures of his family and read old texts from them. He found a message from his mother that he had forgotten about. She had sent pictures of writings from his grandfather Brian Toth that Sonny had never seen before:

WHEN DOES THE PAIN GO AWAY?

I lost my wife the other day.
And I ask every man who's lost his –
When does the pain go away?

To the fortunate I say –
Give your wife a hug for me.
To the rest - I now know how you feel.
But when does the pain go away?

The night she died I slept in her bed.
And I asked for a sign.
Let me know you're okay.
I love you and want to see you again someday.

At her funeral I said, "I'll see you soon."
And, "I was more proud than sad today."
Since I'm needed here I have to stay.
But when does the pain go away?

SADNESS CAME TO VISIT ME AGAIN

I no longer see you in my dreams, but I still hear your encouragement.

When I ask for your approval, I see you smile.
And just when I got comfortable...
Sadness came to visit me again.

As time goes on, I am content knowing that our
reunion is closer.
Are you proud of me?
Life has offered me many pleasant distractions.
But just when I had control...
Sadness came to visit me again.

The next mile was a blur. His mind cleared a bit
when he ran into a dog with a hiker who was one of
Sonny's faithful followers of his YouTube channel. M.C.
Ballpein and Nails warned him of a steep seven-tenths
mile climb just ahead. Sonny had been on numerous
hills of greater stature and difficulty, but he really
struggled trying to get to the top. Like hitting the wall
while running a marathon, his body was failing him. He
imagined the hill to be his life's accumulation of sin and
he was doing penance to cleanse his soul. Near the top,
fatigue took over and Sonny could no longer lift his
legs. His mind was drowning in negative thoughts and
sensing failure, he covered his face with his hands and
wept.

He tried to call family and friends, but there was no
service in the isolated area. Through his ear buds he
listen to *Bookends* by Simon and Garfunkel. In a
dreamlike state, he drifted to the right and picked his
way through the rocks and brush. The low feelings
were amplified by the music in his head and he didn't

notice or care that he was off the trail. His senses told him that he was headed towards Mount Katahdin, but it was in the direction that the crow flies. When he reached the cliff, *One Is The Loneliest Number* by Three Dog Night was ending and the dungeon of depression began to overwhelm him. He stood within ten feet of the edge with the urge to look over and saw the actuality of a fall, so far below. His ear buds offered *4 + 20* by Stephen Stills and he could not feel his feet when he took a step forward. The blinding sun obscured his reality and he thought back to the day that Ellen had left him forever. While he relived the details of that horrible day, *Can't Get Used To Losing You* by Andy Williams flooded his senses and he took another step toward finality. When *Unchained Melody* by The Righteous Brothers came on, he held out his arms as if to fly and began to step forward. He could clearly see the rocks below calling to him, like the mythical sirens, but then strong arms embraced him from behind and pulled him back to safety. He immediately yanked out the ear buds and turned to face his savior, but there was no one there.

DAY 158

Sonny woke up not knowing where he was at first. He didn't recall eating a meal or setting up his tent. While making a short video of himself still in his sleeping bag, he noticed that he had swollen bags under his eyes. There were pictures on his phone of Mount Katahdin, presumably from nearby his campsite. The Guthook app informed him that he had hiked 12 miles and was on Nesuntabunt Mountain. He tediously ate breakfast and packed his gear. He chose not to buckle his hip belt and held his pack away from his back as he began to hike on the cool morning.

Following along Pollywog Stream, he noticed that he was running low on water, but kept moving. The crossing of the stream was made easy by a logging road bridge. After walking six hours, Sonny had only covered six miles and stopped for lunch at Rainbow Stream Lean-to. There was no one else there. He made water and then boiled some for his beef stroganoff meal. Following a visit to the privy, he generously applied Aspercreme and took more Tylenol tablets. Sonny knew he had a fever and every time the cold wind blew, he wished he were at home soaking in the hot water of his bathtub.

After only 10.3 miles, Sonny was done for the day and he stopped at Rainbow Lake Campsite. The better tent sites were probably on the east side of the trail because some hikers headed that way. Sonny was the only one who put up his tent on the west side, close to the trail. The ground was rocky and not conducive to driving stakes in far. He held them in place with rocks and then, skipping supper, he climbed into his sleeping bag and shivered uncontrollably. Just as he was falling asleep, the wind blew hard enough to cause half of his tent to collapse. Sonny left the comfort of his mummy sleeping bag and went outside and bolstered the tent supports with more rocks. After climbing back into his sleeping bag, he placed his cold hands on his thighs to warm his fingers and noticed that his right leg felt like it was on fire. It finally dawned on him that he had an infection and needed to go to a hospital, soon. The road that led to Millinocket was 11 miles away and that night Sonny prayed that he would be able to cover the distance in only one day.

DAY 159

Sonny woke up feeling worse than the previous day. He couldn't stop shivering and the top of his right leg looked like bubble wrap. After putting on all of his warm clothing, he forced himself to eat and began walking. A short time later he heard a familiar voice from behind him, calling out his name. He stopped and glanced back as Very Kind studied his appearance. With a worried look she said, "You don't look so good, Phoenix. I'm going to walk with you today."

Sonny responded unconvincingly, "I'll be okay. You don't have to do that."

"I have plenty of time. I just have to be in Millinocket by the evening."

"Suit yourself."

"Let me try out your trekking poles. Use your hands to help lift the weight off of your back."

While Sonny traveled as fast as he was able, Very Kind would walk ahead a ways and then wait for him to catch up. He felt like he was back in high school doing interval training and was reminded not to dwell on the difficulty of the entire workout, but to focus only on one segment at a time. Each time Sonny caught up with Very Kind, he was rewarded with a short break and the process repeated itself for hours.

The sight of Hurd Brook Shelter was an enormous relief. Sonny and Very Kind sat down and ate their respective meals. The rest provided him with a small amount of energy and he hoped it would be enough to make it out to Golden Road. From there, he had a chance for a ride to the tiny hospital in Millinocket. After he finished what would be his last supper for a while, Sonny got to his feet and once again, lifted his pack. But before he could put it on his back, Very Kind took it from him. She said that she wanted to see if she could carry the load in front, in addition to the one already on her back. Sonny tried to argue, but she reasoned that it was just an experiment for future hikes. Up to this point, Sonny had carried all of his gear from Amicalola Falls. He had not sent anything home and he did not slack pack. He knew she wasn't being honest, but was only trying to help. Two thoughts ran through his feverish brain. Someone had once told him that one of the kindest things you could do for other people was to let them do you a favor. And, even Jesus had Simon of Cyrene help carry the cross. Sonny swallowed his pride, nodded his head and felt somewhat defeated. Very Kind handed back the trekking poles, hugged his pack and set out to finish the last three and a half miles of the 100 Mile Wilderness.

Sonny staggered after her. Long and powerful strides carried her away from him and the feeling of abandonment returned. But like before, she would stop and wait for him to catch up. With a mile left, Very Kind handed Sonny his backpack and said she would run up ahead and buy food for him at the Abol Bridge store. He told her he craved pop and chips and ice cream. He watched her run away with her pack strapped to her back and he envied her strength.

Eventually, he reached the road. There were no signs of any vehicles, but when he looked to his right, he saw Very Kind hustling back toward him. She had plastic bags filled with snacks dangling from both arms and a bowl of ice cream in each hand. She said, "Pick one of the flavors. I'll eat the other."

Sonny grabbed one and they both quickly finished off the melting treats. He then started on the pop and chips. Very Kind said, "Let me see your hitchhiking sign. I want to try it."

While Sonny sat on the ground devouring the junk food, Very Kind stood on the edge of the road holding up the pink sign. Gingerly, he got up and said, "I think I hear a truck coming."

The joyous sound of a diesel engine increased and hope returned. Around the curve came a large black pickup truck and Sonny felt elation and relief when it decelerated and stopped. He opened the passenger door for Very Kind and greeted the driver and then placed his backpack in the bed of the truck. When Sonny returned to the cab and climbed in, Very Kind was not there. Sonny was startled and asked, "What happened to the young lady that was with me?"

The driver looked confused and only shrugged his shoulders. Sonny felt disappointment and with misty eyes said, "I never got to tell her goodbye."

Much of the road was filled with potholes and the pain in Sonny's lower back and upper right leg caused him to wince with every bounce. The driver introduced himself as Robert and said he worked for an outfit that reclaimed vintage sunken logs. Sonny gave brief details of his recent odyssey and asked to be delivered to the hospital emergency room. Robert told Sonny that he was in luck because the only reason he was making the forty-minute drive, all the way to Millinocket, was to buy cigarettes. Sonny confessed. "Normally, I don't approve of smoking, but today I'm very grateful that you do."

While thinking about Very Kind, Sonny asked. "Hey Robert, I have to know. Did you pull over and give me a ride because you saw the hitchhiking sign or because a woman was holding it?"

Robert's face took on a quizzical look. "When I came around the curve, the first thing I saw was the bright pink sign and I stopped without even thinking about it."

Before Sonny could question him further, Robert added. "And Phoenix... there was nobody with you. *You* were holding the sign."

Sonny looked down and shook his head. "I must be hallucinating."

Robert jokingly suggested. "Maybe, she was an angel."

Sonny looked at Robert and said, "Are you an angel, too?"

Robert laughed. "I've been called many things, but never an angel."

Near the emergency entrance, Robert parked the truck, retrieved Sonny's backpack, and helped him out of the cab. He tried to walk Sonny inside the building, but Sonny insisted that he be left on the bench outside the door. Against his better judgment, Robert relented and placed the backpack on the bench. Sonny thanked him again and Robert drove away. While he sat there thinking about Very Kind and contemplating the existence of angels, Sonny passed out and slowly slumped to the ground.

When he awoke, he found that he was inside lying on a cot and the nurse that was tending to him said he needed surgery and that an ambulance had been dispatched to take him to a larger hospital. After

Sonny's mind cleared a little, he asked, "How did I get in here?"

The nurse became very talkative. "Oh. I thought you knew. It was quite the scene. Your *father* carried you in here. At least that's who he said he was. He looked a lot like you, but much older. We were amazed at his strength. He said he was proud of you and that everything would be okay. It's too bad he couldn't stay. I thought maybe you wanted to talk to him."

Sonny said, "I do."

When he became inundated with grief, the nurse left him alone in the room. She returned a little later and blood work and a CAT scan were performed. Sonny asked if there was any way he could take a shower before the ambulance arrived. He was led down a corridor to a small shower and given toiletries and a towel.

While waiting for his ride, Sonny learned that the original intentions were to ship him to Bangor. During the past couple of hours, a female accident victim there had damaged muscles removed from one of her buttocks. The surgeon there had just gotten out of the operating room and after looking at Sonny's cat scan, was too fatigued to perform the same procedure again. About ten pm, when the young men loaded Sonny into the back of the patient transport vehicle, they told him it would be a long three-hour ride. Sonny jokingly asked if they wanted him to drive and then soon after, fell asleep. He woke up in Portland as they unloaded his gurney.

The extra two-hour ride was worth it. Sometime around three in the morning, a young surgeon and his intern determined that muscle removal was not necessary. Instead, the infected area was sterilized and lanced. Then the pus was forced out through the opening and the wound was washed, packed with gauze, and covered with a large bandage. During the procedure, an ultrasound device was used to see if all of the purulence had been removed. Both the surgeon and the intern laughed when Sonny asked if he could have a picture to hang on his refrigerator like pregnant women often did.

DAY 160

The hospital was overflowing with patients and because no rooms were available, Sonny was deposited near a nurse's station along with many others. While lying there trying to sleep, Sonny looked around at the other patients. He witnessed a hospital counselor consoling a young male war veteran. The soldier had had the lower half of both legs amputated. Sonny felt humbled and undeserving of even being in the same recovery room as the man. Apparently, someone else in the area felt that way too. After walking to and from the restroom by himself, Sonny was discharged and advised to get a room somewhere else. He was given a voucher for a discount at a local hotel that also provided transportation and then ushered to the pharmacy. Sonny hadn't eaten for a while and decided to stop in at the cafeteria for breakfast before calling for the ride. He sent a brief text to his family and fellow thru-hikers.

****

Fiona and Doubting Thomas were with their tramily at Katahdin Stream Campground, five and a half miles away from Mount Katahdin, when they got the news about Phoenix. The group was planning on summiting that morning. They were excited and sad at the same time. Like every thru-hiker before them, they experienced the same dilemma. They were glad it was over, but they didn't want it to end. As they watched the sunrise and discussed the final leg of the adventure, Fiona offered a solution. "What if we delay the end?"

Athena said, "How so?"

The others moved in closer to hear Fiona give the details of her plan. "I'm not ready for it to be over yet. And I have a friend who is still out there. We all do. I knew Phoenix was falling behind us. I just didn't know the extent of his injury. He was taken to a hospital, but I know that when he's well enough, he will be back on the trail again. I know most of you can't hang around for that. You have jobs and families and another life somewhere else and you can't wait around to see him finish. I get it. I understand. But that is exactly what I'm going to do."

The hikers exchanged glances and one by one they responded. Thesaurus spoke first. "I'm sorry, Fiona. I have to get back home now. But I would have loved to have been here to witness the *Plight* of the Phoenix."

The humor helped to ease the tension and all were concerned about the well being of their fellow hiker. However, all but one of the hikers followed suit and said that they were going to finish the journey and then go back from whence they came. Watching the others depart was rough on Fiona, but having a friend at her side made it much more tolerable. "Okay Fiona, but what do we do until Phoenix comes back?"

"Thanks for staying, Thomas. For starters, I know some places that I would like to go and see in the Midwest."

She could have said she wanted to go Alaska and he would have gone with her. "Are you thinking about visiting Phoenix at his home in Ohio, if he goes there?"

"No. When I see him the next time, I want it to be a surprise and I want it to be on the summit. I was thinking of someplace in Indiana. Is there somewhere that you would like to go?"

"There *is* a village in New York by the Finger Lakes that I would like to show you."

"Isn't that the area where you grew up?"

"It is. My parents still live there in Watkins Glen."

"You want me meet your parents?"

"Not if you don't want to. We could go somewhere else."

"Are you kidding me? I want to meet them and see where you lived and all that."

"You might be disappointed."

"Tom. Stop underestimating yourself. Take me there, now."

After hitchhiking to Millinocket, the young couple rented a car and drove southwest. Although only a few of the trees were changing into their fall colors, the ride through New Hampshire and Vermont was relaxing. Somewhere in the state of New York, the sun went down.

****

After swallowing a sulfa drug to kill bacteria, he took a short taxi ride to the downtown Clarion hotel. Once in his room, Sonny removed his clothing and climbed into the bed. He woke up hungry, some time in the early afternoon. After putting on his raingear and flip-flops, he stuffed all of his dirty clothes into a washer down the hallway and then left the hotel. Across the street was a convenience store where he purchased a sandwich and some fruit and ate them in his room.

After lunch, he transferred his wet clothes into the dryer and began to upload videos. Shortly, he retrieved his clean clothes and then took a shower being careful not to get his bandage wet. Following a nap, he dressed and rode the elevator to the restaurant where he ate haddock and steamed vegetables. Returning to his room feeling sleepy, Sonny made one phone call. Madison answered after the second ring. "My God, Dad, are you okay? I just watched your video about the hospital."

"I'll be alright. They gave me some strong antibiotics."

"Well, that's good, but what about your bandages? Who's going to change your gauze?"

"I'm going to do that after I'm done talking to you."

"I take it that Lily isn't available to help you."

Sonny paused. "I'm not sure if Lily will ever be available for me."

"That saddens me, Dad. It sounded like she had potential. I was looking forward to meeting her."

"I'm sad too. But some things just weren't meant to be. Anyhow, I need you to call your brothers and grandmother and give them an update so they aren't worried about me."

"Maybe you should just come home so that we can take care of you."

"I'm hoping to stay in Maine until I'm strong enough to finish what I started."

"Okay, Dad. Heal fast. I still wish you would come home."

After the call ended, Sonny realized he hadn't asked his pregnant daughter how *she* was doing. He stood sideways in front of the full-length mirror and pulled off the outer bandage and some hair, along with it. He placed the roll of fresh gauze within reach and began tugging on the long strip of gauze that was stuffed in the wound. He did not know at the time that he could have soaked the absorbent material to soften the dried blood. Each pull issued a burning pain and fresh blood began to flow from the cross-shaped cut. Between each yanking session, he would look over his shoulder in the mirror at the mess, take a few deep breaths and then continue the extraction. By the time he was finished, the open gap was spilling blood down his legs and onto the floor. The tile under his feet looked like the floor of a butcher shop. After applying an anti-bacterial ointment, he took the new gauze and began to tediously stuff it into the wound. When it was full, he covered it with a fresh bandage and then cleaned up the murder scene. He looked at the clock on the nightstand and couldn't believe that the change of dressing had taken so long. Madison was right, *again.* Sonny picked up his phone and bought an airplane ticket to Toledo and then went to sleep.

****

Doubting Thomas turned into a cul-de-sac and parked in the driveway of a quaint craftsman style house. A few outdoor lights emphasized the manicured lawn with trimmed bushes and the flowerbeds that were weed free. As they walked towards the house, they held hands and Fiona admired the landscape. Doubting Thomas said to her, "My parents do all of the work, themselves."

At the front door, he nervously rang the doorbell as Fiona stood behind him. A couple in their late fifties answered the door. The man was tall and had dark hair like his son. The woman was slightly shorter with dyed hair and a pleasant face. They had not seen their son in nearly six months. He had lost sixty pounds of fat and his newly acquired muscle mass was impressive. Now with facial hair, he resembled a lumberjack. They did not recognize him until he spoke. "Hi Dad. Hi Mom."

In a state of disbelief, his father said, "Tommy, is that you?"

The mother pushed past her husband and embraced her son. Tears of joy filled her eyes. Doubting Thomas was embarrassed by the show of affection and said, "Mom. I want to introduce you to someone."

For the first time since opening the door, the parents noticed the young lady standing behind their son. "This is Fiona. She walked the trail with me."

The two women hugged while the men shook hands. Fiona followed the family into the small home that displayed arched doorways, fine wood trim, and built-in cabinets and shelves. Even though it was late, Doubting Thomas' mother insisted on making supper for all. Fiona helped the mom cook while the two men set the table and opened a bottle of wine. During the meal, the two young hikers told stories about their journey and stated that they planned to stay put and rest awhile before going to Indiana. Fiona confessed that her real name was Shelly, but wanted to retain her trail name at least until after she had finished the journey. Doubting Thomas sensed that his parents were so enthralled with Fiona that they would not have questioned the young couple if they had intended on sleeping together. But out of respect he stated, "Fiona is going to sleep in my bedroom tonight and I'm going to sleep on the couch if there are no objections."

The joyful look on his mother's face intensified, if that was even possible.

DAY 161

Much like the last trip home due to injury, Sonny had a layover in Charlotte. From the North Carolina airport, he phoned his daughter. "Wow, Dad. You're halfway home already."

"Right. I got up early, packed, and had breakfast before taking the shuttle to the airport. I'm still weak though. And sore."

"Sounds difficult, but I'm sure you'll be fine."

"Of course, I will. Quitting is easy."

"Stop it Dad. You're not a quitter. Besides, you still have more than a month before they close Baxter Park."

"Madison?"

"Yes, Father?"

"How's your baby doing?"

"She's doing fine. Oops."

"Uh oh. I take it you haven't had the gender reveal yet."

"No. A nurse let it slip during my last appointment. So, we were going to tell everyone after you finished the trail."

"It will be our secret."

The airport food tasted better than usual. Sonny had collapsed his trekking poles and hid them inside his backpack. He worried that some of his gear might be confiscated, but none was. During the flight, he found it uncomfortable to place his weight on his right buttock and leaned to the left, which worried the woman passenger beside him. His grimacing and explanation did little to alleviate her concerns.

Outside the terminal door at the Toledo Express airport, Madison heard applause and watched as a soldier walked by, dressed in battle fatigues. A few minutes passed and she began to think that somehow her dad wasn't on the plane. But then a very thin man with a short gray beard carrying a backpack came limping towards her. His condition brought tears to her eyes and she carefully hugged him. After placing the backpack in the backseat of the white Jeep, Madison slid the passenger seat back as far as it would go and then helped her dad into the vehicle. While assisting him with the seatbelt, he looked down and she noticed the droplets from his eyes land on his lap as he struggled to speak. "Fifteen miles. I was only fifteen miles from Katahdin. I could see it, but I couldn't get there..."

Madison knew that she wouldn't be able to drive if she looked at her father. She stubbornly kept her eyes on the road in front of her and said, "I'm taking you home, Dad."

****

Following a late breakfast, Doubting Thomas asked his parents if they needed help with anything around the house. They both shook their heads and encouraged him to take Fiona on a tour of the village and surrounding areas.

Any other year the young couple would have wanted to hike the nearby trails, but settled on driving past the high school and walking along the downtown streets by the variety of shops. They ended the day having supper again with his parents in their home.

DAY 162

The day's activities were similar, but Doubting Thomas went out of his way to proudly introduce Fiona to the townsfolk he knew. Unbeknownst to the other, each parent had taken their son aside and expressed great fondness for his girlfriend. Doubting Thomas assured each of them that he felt the same way about her.

****

The sun introduced a beautiful late summer day in Ohio. Birds and butterflies were putting on a flying clinic and the honeybees were packing copious amounts of pollen and nectar into their hives. The breeze through the open window invited him to come out and play on the fertile land, but Sonny stayed in bed enveloped in self-pity.

He dreaded having to change the gauze again, but around noon he was hungry and had to pee. After pushing off the covers, he threw his legs over the side of the bed and his body followed. Still dizzy and weak, he made his way to the bathroom. Madison had made some calls and then had passed the suggestion on to her father. Sonny took his daughter's advice and this time, he stood in the shower and soaked the gauze before attempting to remove it. There was less blood flow and pain during the withdrawal, but the repacking procedure was still cumbersome.

From the chest freezer in the garage, he found a container of homemade chicken noodle soup and the microwave oven brought the leftover meal back to life. After finishing the entire contents of the large bowl, he placed it in the sink and then went out on the deck and sat down with a cold bottle of Gatorade. An hour of sulking passed by and although he tried, he could not free his mind from thoughts of the trail. He already missed the people, the places, and even the bad days. The feeling of acceptance by his peers was gone, and he sensed that he had let them down. When the time came to call his family, he wanted to put on a happy face and sound optimistic, but he wasn't even close to that frame of mind yet. That would have to wait awhile. Finally, he decided to have a conversation with the one person who could make or break him. He placed the call and held his breath. Lily answered on the third ring. "Oh my goodness, Sonny. I just watched your last video. Are you going to be okay?"

Sonny heard the empathy in her voice and took a moment to bathe in it. "Lily, I never should have entered the 100 Mile Wilderness in the condition I was in."

"You stubborn man. You let your pride dominate your life."

"It's all I have left."

The accusation stung Lily. "When you were in Monson, why didn't you use your phone and take a picture of the infection?"

"I guess at that point I wasn't thinking straight. Yeah, I knew it hurt, but if I had seen how bad it looked, I might have gone to see a doctor sooner."

"You might have? Sonny, I think you need a life coach or something."

"Or some*one*."

Lily didn't respond to Sonny's suggestion so he changed the subject. "Well, enough about me. Tell me about your problems."

"It doesn't look promising. Compounded interest can work for you as well as against you. In my case, I'm drowning in debt. Not everyone who says he wants to help me is on my side."

Sonny wanted to jump in to show his support, but he bit his tongue so that she would continue. "Shortly after my husband died, a local farmer named Jim came around and I agreed to let him help me with all of the work and then share in the profits. After a while, he let it be known to others, that he wanted more than just a business relationship with me. I had no interest in intimacy and bluntly told him so. Afterwards, he began stealing from me and was very clever about covering his tracks. By the time I figured out what was going on, it was too late. I had nothing in writing as far as our agreement went and there was little money left to hire an attorney. Now the scoundrel is trying to buy my farm for pennies on the dollar and the bank sounds interested in the deal."

Sonny wanted to suggest that maybe a life coach would be in *her* best interest too, but he still wanted to win her back and knew that sarcasm would not help his cause. The venting helped relieve the stress that was eroding Lily's spirit and she continued to let it out. "I don't have any family like you do, Sonny. Besides the people I have met on the trail, my neighbors John and Alice are my closest friends. I trust them."

Sonny knew the ball was in his court and it was time to state his case. "I want to be your friend, Lily. You can trust me too."

There was no response. When Sonny couldn't stand the silence any longer he said, "Are you there, Lily?"

"I'm here, Sonny. Keep in touch."

"I'll do more than that if you let me. I love you, Lily."

"Goodbye, Sonny."

Sonny listened as the line went dead and then stared at the phone in disbelief. He sat it down on the table, leaned on the railing, and gazed at the flowerbed talking to himself. " I shouldn't have said those words over the phone... I should have told her in person."

He hobbled back into the kitchen and grabbed an IPA from the refrigerator. After sitting down on his recliner, he took a gulp of the beer and then promptly fell asleep.

DAY 163

Growing restless, Doubting Thomas and Fiona departed and continued west. Halfway through Ohio, they left the turnpike and got onto US-6. At Wapakoneta Road they turned right and drove through Grand Rapids to get a sense of the small town that they had heard Phoenix talk about so much. They did not stop for fear of running into him and continued into Indiana arriving at Brown County near sunset.

****

Sonny woke up early the next morning and discovered that a little of his strength had returned. After a hardy breakfast of bacon, eggs, toast, and orange juice, he cleaned the bathroom and swept the floors and then rested. Following the break, he washed his bedding, took a shower, and changed the gauze. He noticed that it only took about half the amount of gauze to fill the wound. That observation and the fact that he had more energy proved one thing - he was getting better. Without becoming too hopeful, he allowed himself to look ahead at the weather forecast for Millinocket, Maine, in the upcoming two weeks.

His mental soundness was returning also. He was tired of being despondent and decided to be sanguine and deal only with the issues that he had control over. That decision alone gave him a feeling of power. It was time to talk with his family. He called his pillar of strength first. "Hi Mom. I'm home."

"Hello, Sonny. Welcome back. Hey, I watched your videos and talked to Madison. Do you think you'll be well enough to help me with the apple harvest in a couple of weeks or am I on my own?"

"No can do, Mom. I'm an invalid. You might have to increase your workload for a while."

"Are you trying to kill me, Sonny?"

"I don't think a mere mortal like myself could do that, Mom."

"Well son, you have another job to finish first. Don't worry about it. Those apples will be there when you get back."

"Thanks, Mom."

Sonny called his eldest son next. "Hi, Augie. I was hoping to catch you on you lunch break."

"You did, Dad, but it's almost over."

"Okay, I just wanted to let you know that I'm feeling better and will eventually finish my hike as soon as I can."

"I had no doubt that you would. But before you go back to Maine, we want you to come over for a family cookout some afternoon."

"Thanks, Augie. I appreciate the incentive."

Sonny phoned Colorado. "Hi, Henry. How's it going?"

"We've had a few snow flurries already so our gardens aren't looking so good."

Sonny again resisted the urge to suggest that Henry move his family back to Ohio. It was only recently that he resigned himself to the fact that his youngest son was pleased where he lived. Sonny was happy for him too, but sad in knowing that he would probably never be close to Henry's children. "But everyone is doing well?"

"Yeah, we're all good here. How are you feeling now? You looked pretty sad in your videos."

"I was pretty sad in many ways. But now I'm much better."

"So then you *are* going back to finish it this year?"

"I am."

"Well, good. We're looking forward to seeing the video... I wish I could be there, Dad."

"Me too, Henry. Me too."

The call to his daughter went to voicemail and Sonny left a brief message. "Hey, Babe."

Madison called back a minute later. "Hi, Dad. I had to let Peaches out. She was going berserk because there was a squirrel in the yard."

"How will she be when your baby arrives?"

"I think she'll be okay. I held a friend's baby in her presence and she wasn't jealous, just curious."

"That's a relief."

"You sound better, Dad. Did Grandma or Augie tell you about the cookout we are planning?"

"Yes. I'm looking forward to it. I'm getting stronger. So, maybe in a few days I'll be ready to return to Maine."

"Don't jump the gun. There's still plenty of time left. Pick out a nice day and climb that final mountain, Dad."

DAY 164

Meanwhile, down on the farm in Brown County, Indiana, Lily's neighbors were having a conference. John was over at Alice's home expressing concern. "We need to do something. I've never seen her this down in the dumps before."

"I agree, Johnny. But what else can we do? The bank is coming after her farm."

"I'm not sure, Alice. All I know is I don't want Jim to own it. I don't trust him."

" I don't trust him either. I never did, but I didn't want to say anything. I thought he was better than what she had before, but that was just wishful thinking."

"Okay, Alice. I think we're on the same page here. I have a plan, but I'm going to need your help."

****

After a short visit to the small town of Nashville, Indiana, Fiona and Doubting Thomas decided that a college town was more appealing. They spent the rest of the day in Bloomington and learned from some locals of a popular winery. Each night ended with a long soak in the hot tub where they discussed the day's events and planned others.

DAY 165

After breakfast, they drove to Oliver Winery, sampled the goods and toured the grounds. A few bottles of their favorites were purchased and then they drove back to the cabin and napped. That night, Fiona shared her plan with her boyfriend, but told him she had to go alone.

DAY 166

Early in the morning, Fiona drove on winding gravel roads through the rolling farmland following her GPS directions. Although surrounded by field corn, soybeans, and woodlots, there was no doubt she was at the right place. The long and curvy driveway was lined with trees that displayed two by six inch vertical white blazes. She slowly advanced towards the landscaped homestead. The two story farmhouse was old, but well maintained. She parked out front and climbed the steps onto the gray wooden porch floor and rang the doorbell, but no one opened the ornate vintage door. Fiona peered into the picture window and saw an ironing board, but no people. Undeterred, she walked around past flowerbeds to the back of the house. There were bed sheets and other articles hanging from the clothesline. Fiona felt a pair of socks and learned that they were still a little wet. She then proceeded to the old red barn, walked past the large opened door that smelled of manure and entered the workshop though the opened man door. At the far end of the workbench, sparks were flying. Lily had on a pair of safety glasses and was sharpening a mower blade on the grinding wheel. When she saw Fiona, she turned off the grinder.

Fiona said, "I was in the neighborhood and I saw the white blazes, so naturally, I followed them."

Lily smiled. "Let's go in the house. Would you like some tea?"

They sat in a room on comfortable chairs with a coffee table between them. Fiona complimented Lily on the room's décor. Lily said, "Thanks, I've been making subtle changes, a little bit at a time. Oh and Congratulations! Welcome to the club."

"Actually, I haven't finished the trail, yet."

"Why? What's wrong?"

"There's nothing wrong with me. I'm waiting for a friend. He's injured now, but I know he'll be back when he can and I want to see him summit the last mountain peak."

"This friend of yours must be really important to you."

"He is. I wouldn't have been able to accomplish the journey without him."

"He sounds like a saint."

"No. He's no saint. Everyone has flaws. But he's a good human being."

"Some flaws can't be repaired."

"Lily, that scene you walked up on; you only saw the tail end of it. Phoenix was defending others and me. First, Doubting Thomas tried to step in against Potty Mouth, but my boyfriend hasn't had much fighting experience."

"That's what worries me about Phoenix. He looked experienced. My late husband was abusive of me for our entire marriage and I'll never be with another man like that."

"Phoenix is not abusive. It took a lot for him to turn violent that day. I'm glad he did because it was necessary. He had always been gentle and kind every other time. I wish you would give him another chance. He's a good man."

Lily thought for a while and then offered, "I have watched all of his videos and I even talked to him four days ago. I have to admit, I do feel sorry for him."

"He doesn't need your pity. He needs your love."

"Oh."

"Other than his family, the only thing I've ever heard him talk about was you. You should be more than flattered. He might not have used that exact word, but I think he adores you. A girl can't do any better than that."

"Fiona. You are wise beyond your years."

"Thanks. I've matured these past months. The trail has taught me a lot."

"The thing is, I miss Phoenix. But I'm afraid."

"Lily, we're all afraid. That's what makes us human."

Lily sat quietly for a moment and then nodded her head. "Here I was thinking that he was more stubborn than me."

"After having watched him struggle enough times, I think a better word would be *determined*."

Lily walked Fiona to the door where they said goodbye with a hug. "Fiona, I'm glad you stopped by. I'm going to contact Sonny and try again."

The late summer Ohio weather was perfect for the afternoon cookout at the family homestead in McKee's Corners. Tables and chairs were set up in the yard near Sonny's mother's flower gardens overlooking the ravine. The main course of fried chicken, mashed potatoes, and sweet corn was enjoyed with green beans, fruit salad, and apple pie. Sonny had been strategically placed in a chair at the head of the table with his back to the house. His elderly uncle, Father

Sam was positioned beside him and had been assigned the task of keeping him occupied while the table was cleared. The two men had a great relationship and during discussions, no topic was ever off limits. Sonny said, "What's the best part of being a priest?"

"That would be helping people and saving souls."

"Not hearing confessions? I would think hearing confessions would be the best part."

"Hah! No, but it is a close second."

It was Father Sam's turn to tease. "Sonny, had I known back in May that I'd see you again before you summited Mount Katahdin, I wouldn't have given you that heirloom stone until now."

"I had to carry much heavier burdens than that stone along the way."

"Well then, leave them atop of that mountain too."

"I will."

"How soon were you planning on going back to Maine?"

"I've been looking ahead at the weather forecast and the middle of next week looks promising."

"You look healthy."

"Thanks. You're too kind. I'm still not feeling great, but I think I'm in good enough shape to do the last miles."

"As a former runner, I'm sure you remember what it feels like to see the finish line."

"I do. I've seen it and I can't wait to get there. After a two-week layoff, I thought the end would be anti-climatic, but it's not."

"Sonny, I think you're ready to go back now."

Father Sam stood up, picked up his spoon, and tapped on his glass to gain everyone's attention. Although he knew the words by heart, he opened the Bible that he had brought along for the occasion. In a loud voice he said, "Take away the stone."

All eyes were on the retired priest as he continued. "Sonny, if you didn't already have the trail name of Phoenix, I think an appropriate one would be Lazarus. Like Phoenix, Lazarus also rose from the dead. Twice you were knocked off of the trail, but both times you were healed. This gathering today wasn't about you finishing your journey. That celebration will come at a later date. We assembled here today, with all apologies to St John, to witness your rising from the dead per se."

He closed the Bible and said to Sonny, "Lazarus come out."

Right on cue, Madison stood and replied, "By this time there will be a stench."

All of the grandchildren looked on in bewilderment as the adults chuckled. Madison added, "Dad, we have a surprise for you."

Sonny said, "I thought I heard a car pull up to the house, but I'm too full for pizza."

August walked over and stood next to Madison. "Don't turn around yet, Dad. This is better than pizza."

"Okay, I'll play along. I'm guessing it's a cake."

Sonny's mother got up, stood next to her two grandchildren and said, "The cake will be served after the surprise."

"Does this have anything to do with the commotion I heard inside the house about ten minutes ago?"

Madison said, "It does."

Behind him, Sonny heard activity and both August and Grandma warned the grandchildren at the tables not to give away the secret.

Madison said, "Dad, do you have any more guesses?"

Sonny thought that there couldn't be anything better than a visit from Lily, but he was wrong. "I have no idea."

"Well then Dad, turn around."

He slowly turned and saw that standing in front of him was Henry, his wife, and their four children.

Sonny was speechless, but Henry said, "We came here to pick apples."

After countless hugs by all, Sonny was introduced to his youngest grandchild. Even the older grandchildren, whom Sonny had spent little time with, didn't really know him. But because Henry had spoken about his father so often, the grandchildren immediately bonded with him.

Cake and ice cream were served. There were nonstop conversations and after the sunset, they all sat around the fire pit. Eventually, people tired and drifted away. Sonny and Father Sam were the last two staring at the orange embers. When Sonny looked up at the stars, Father Sam asked, "Is this what it's like on the trail?"

Instead of giving a direct answer, Sonny asked a question. "How do you feel right now, Sam?"

"I feel happy and proud and fortunate to be part of this family. I am experiencing a joy that I rarely have and I don't ever want it to go away."

Sonny looked at his uncle and said, "That, is what it is like."

Sam nodded, but didn't say anymore. He got up, quietly walked to his car and left Sonny alone with his thoughts.

DAY 167

Henry and his family moved into Sonny's home and would spend the rest of the week getting reacquainted and picking apples. While cleaning up after breakfast, Sonny's phone rang and Henry's oldest child answered it for him. "Here, Grandpa. I think it's your girlfriend."

Henry and his wife said that they could finish the dishes without his help and shooed him away to talk in private. Out on the deck he said, "Hello? Lily?"

"No, Phoenix. It's just me, Fiona."

"Oh, hey, I'm not disappointed. It's just that when I was handed the phone I was told... Well never mind. How are you, Fiona? What was it like on the summit?"

Fiona lied. "It was a glorious day. We all wished you could have been there."

"I would have loved that."

"So, when will you go back?"

"One week from tomorrow I will fly into Bangor, spend the night in Millinocket and then hike to Katahdin Stream Campground the next day. The following day is supposed to be sunny and clear."

"That's cool. You should be able see for miles when you're up there. Doubting Thomas is still complaining about our lack of views on that day."

"Send me a picture of your summit when you get a chance."

"Sure. You do the same for me. I'm going to miss you, Phoenix."

"I feel the same about you too, Fiona. Maybe, we can all meet at Trail Days next year."

"I'll plan on it. And Phoenix, I wouldn't give up on Lily. She's a smart lady."

Hands of all sizes picked apples until early afternoon. After lunch, while Sonny rested, Henry gave his family a tour of the countryside up and down the Maumee River. Following his nap, Sonny went out to his barn and worked on his antique Farmall tractor until evening when Henry returned with his family. The kids had wanted to see one of the Great Lakes, so

Henry had driven them to the sandy shores of East Harbor State Park.

After supper, Sonny's phone rang and he grabbed it before anyone else could. Henry commented, "Anything to get out of doing the dishes again."

This time, Sonny checked the caller ID as he went out to the deck. "Hello, Lily."

After her greeting, Sonny remained silent to allow Lily to speak first since she was the one who had called. "Sonny, I'm sorry. I overreacted. I'm not going to make any excuses for my behavior. I hope you can forgive me."

"Forgive you? Lily, you know how I feel about you. I just wished I could have told you in person. Maybe in a couple of weeks I can stop by for a tour of your farm."

"That would be wonderful. I should still own it by then."

"Great. Maybe then you can talk to me about your abusive husband."

Lily didn't respond right away and Sonny thought that he had made another mistake. "Sonny, if you have the time, I'm willing to talk about him right now."

By the time Lily had finished relaying her past and present problems, she and Sonny were on good terms again. After Lily hung up, Sonny noticed that it was so late that the house was dark and Henry and his family had gone to bed.

DAY 168

At breakfast, Fiona and Doubting Thomas were still chuckling about the conversation with Sonny. "Okay, Fiona. We have a week left. Where do you want to go next?"

"I was thinking we could explore the Hocking Hills area of southern Ohio for a few days and then head back to your house, Tommy."

"You called me Tommy."

"I really like your parents."

"Do you think your parents would like me?"

"Maybe after we climb that mountain, we could go to Iowa and find out."

DAYS 169-174

At first Sonny thought that Henry and his wife were only feigning interest in the operations of the farm. But after days of tours, demonstrations, and discussions, he knew that their curiosity was genuine. They worked well together as a team and by the time they left, all of the work was caught up. It saddened Sonny to see them leave.

DAY 175

Madison gave Sonny a ride back to Toledo Express Airport, and then he caught an early flight to Charlotte, North Carolina. He had lunch during the layover and then flew to Bangor, Maine. From the airport, he put on his backpack, and hiked a mile to the bus terminal and purchased a ticket. During the long wait, Sonny walked over to Subway and bought his lunch for the following day on the trail. He then went over to McDonalds and ate supper there. While waiting at the bus terminal, he remembered the song that was stuck in his head over two weeks ago when he made his way home. He put in the ear buds and listened to that tune, *Flagpole Sitta,* by Harvey Danger. After a two-hour wait, Sonny boarded the bus that drove an hour up I-95 to Medway.

Stepping off of the bus, he was greeted by an older man who drove him to the hostel in Millinocket. The shuttle driver whose trail name was Old Man, not only operated the AT Lodge, but was Hippie Chick's father. Sonny entered the red historical house and went to his private room on the second floor.

DAY 176

After rising early enough to eat a bowl of cereal and a pastry, Sonny went outside near the carved statue of Gomer Bear to make his morning video with the AT

Lodge in the background. The details of the two story red building with off-white trim were much clearer in the daylight. Old Man came out of his office and they both got into the SUV. During the ride to Golden Road, the former thru-hiker told Sonny that it had rained a lot during the past week, warned him of a flooded area, and advised him to take a side trail. He was dropped off where he left the trail over two weeks earlier.

As his ride pulled away, Sonny looked back south and had a feeling of deja vu. He walked down the empty road and as he contemplated buying more food at the Abol Bridge Store. The need became more apparent when he realized he had left his lunch back in the hostel's refrigerator. Despite the overcast sky, Sonny could see Mount Katahdin above the West Branch of the Penobscot River. He finished crossing the Abol Bridge and entered the store and restaurant. After buying a sandwich and a soda, he decided to stay long enough to eat a second breakfast of scrambled eggs, pancakes, and juice.

Back on the trail, Sonny noticed that more of the maples were turning red and there was no wind. He crossed the Baxter State Park boundary and a short bridge over Abol Stream and then registered at the kiosk. The trail was so quiet that he only heard his own breathing and footfalls during the easy hike past ponds and beaver dams. After following the Penobscot River, the trail turned and headed along the Nesowadnehunk Stream at a rock outcropping called Pine Point. The trail followed the stream for six miles and along the way, Sonny made a video from the top of Big Niagara Falls. He observed two men catching small trout in the pool below the raging water. At Little Niagara Falls, Sonny sat on a rock at the top of the falls and ate his lunch.

The next landmark was the location of a nineteenth century toll dam for the logging industry. Looking out from the east shoreline of the calm surface of Daicey Pond, Sonny spotted a man in a canoe, but no moose. Towards the end of the day's ten-mile hike, Sonny walked on a brand new bog bridge constructed by the Maine Conservation Corps. He interviewed and thanked Doug and his crew for the trail maintenance that had made the hike more safe and enjoyable.

Sonny finished the ten miles and arrived at Katahdin Stream Campground early in the afternoon. The low clouds blocked the view of Mount Katahdin, but Sonny knew it was there. Since the shuttle back to Millinocket would not arrive for another three hours, he explored the grounds and ended up at the ranger station. Inside of the screened porch was a table of sign-up sheets for campsites, shuttles, A.T. registration, and a weather forecast. There was also a scale model of Mount Katahdin on display and a list of acceptable behavior while at the summit. A pile of well-used slack packs was available for those hikers who were so inclined. When a ranger stopped by, Sonny obtained a summiting permit for the next day. He then sat on the porch and rested until the shuttle arrived. When he climbed into the SUV with three others, he was reminded of what thru-hikers smelled like.

After dropping his gear off in his room, Sonny went back outside. He crossed the street and walked a block, past the white gazebo, to the corner eatery. Scootic In was a two story yellow-sided building with green trim that had been a restaurant for over 100 years. He obtained a window seat and ordered a salad, a medium rare ribeye steak, mashed potatoes, and a roll. While he looked outside at the people on the street and scanned the faces in the room, Sonny sipped his Manhattan and thought about the upcoming final hike.

DAY 177

After his shower the night before, Sonny thought he would have a hard time falling asleep, but that wasn't the case. In the morning before leaving the security of his bed, he lay there reviewing the remaining 5.2 miles. The hike would start off easy enough, but it would become increasingly steeper and then large boulders would serve as the final obstacles. A young woman thru-hiker had described the final barrier as, "Like the Notch, but vertical."

He repeated the mundane breakfast of the prior day and carried his gear outside. At the designated departure time of 6:30, Old Man, Sonny, and three other hikers left the AT Lodge and headed to Katahdin Stream Campground. Along the way, the vehicle slowed at a couple of reliable moose sighting sites.

Each time, Sonny readied his phone to record the lifetime event, but was always disappointed. The happy hikers were turned loose at the ranger station where they signed up for the return shuttle and then headed north. In a short while Sonny was alone on the trail again. There was a light breeze and puddles from the prior night's rain. The few clouds floating above the state of Maine, dissipated like the opening curtains on the stage of life. Sonny crossed over a bridge and then strolled past a row of small camping shelters.

As he hiked the mild terrain of the Hunt Trail, Sonny made a video thanking his family, friends, and trail angels with special mention of Very Kind and Miracle Lily. Once again, he encountered a warning sign:

YOU ARE ENTERING MAINE'S LARGEST WILDERNESS
   YOUR SAFETY IS YOUR RESPONSIBILITY
   SET A TURN AROUND TIME AND STICK TO IT
   YOUR DESTINATION IS YOUR SAFE RETURN TO THE TRAILHEAD
   RESCUERS CAN BE MANY HOURS IN ARRIVING.

Sonny crossed a walking bridge over Katahdin Stream next to a small waterfall. A minute later, the sight and sound of much larger cascading falls impressed him. The intensity of the slope increased and Sonny was again grateful for stone steps. Even after the convalescent period, he felt the fatigue setting in and knew that he would have to pace himself to reach the summit of Baxter Peak. At 5267 feet, it was the highest point in the state of Maine and with each step, Sonny thought about all of the other mountains he had climbed to get there. At O Joy Brook, he rested a short period and then continued the climb above the tree line. The day before, hikers who had summited, had complained about the ice on the trail and lack of views. Sonny was pleased with his choice of summiting day as the clear and deep blue sky enhanced the faraway sights.

The steep incline with large boulders and ledges, increased the workload and the resulting sweat. Occasionally, there were metal rungs anchored in the rock of the difficult spots. The Hurt Spur was a section where the terrain briefly flattened out and gave a reprieve to the hikers. Sonny rested there and looked behind him at the advancing hikers scattered down the trail. He turned around and watched a similar scene moving away up the steep path and then he followed them. The next mile and a half section was also difficult, but Sonny knew that it would get easier once he reached The Gateway. The excitement drove him on until the terrain became less steep and he entered a field of rocks known as the Tablelands.

Sonny paused to video the distant sights of numerous lakes in the south and the mountains of the north. He continued picking his way through the rocks until he reached Thoreau Spring where he stopped only long enough to splash water on his face. There was one mile left. Sonny tried to savor every step as he reminisced about all that had happened to him during the journey. He envisioned the changes in scenery, the famous landmarks and the people he had met. He remembered the scents of the forests, the sounds of nature, and the doubts and fears he had overcome. He thought of his loved ones and the one he hoped would love him in return.

Up ahead he could see the finish line getting closer. Sonny remembered that one of the reasons he had taken on the challenge was to inspire future generations. He made a short video to his grandchildren telling them they could succeed in life if they worked hard and kept trying. As he approached the summit of Mount Katahdin, Sonny saw the iconic brown wooden sign and a smattering of hikers who were loitering among the rocks and savoring their accomplishments. His ear buds provided him with Mason William's, *Classical Gas,* and he was now close enough to recognize some of his fellow thru-hikers that he hadn't seen since meeting them in the springtime. He thought, "This must be what Heaven's Gate is like."

During his final steps, the other hikers applauded Sonny. He touched the sign with one hand and said, "I made it, Ellen." From his pocket, he removed the stone and placed it on the ground.

Fiona and Doubting Thomas were waiting for him at the summit, but hiding behind a large cairn towards a ridge called the Knife's Edge. Sonny didn't see them at first and they allowed him to spend personal time, alone with his thoughts reflecting on his journey, before approaching.   The sight of them brought a big smile to his face. "Fiona, how did you know I was even going to make it back?"

"Phoenix, last spring I remember a frightened girl who just wanted to go home, but you wouldn't let her. You convinced her to stay and climb one more mountain. You did something for her that she didn't do for herself. You believed in her. And she believed in you. I had no doubt that you would finish the beast."

"That frightened girl is long gone, Fiona."

Sonny and Fiona broke with acceptable protocol and hugged. Fiona said, "There may be a bigger surprise coming your way in the near future."

Sonny looked around. "There aren't many things that can top this."

The three friends had numerous pictures of themselves taken on top of the iconic brown Mount Katahdin sign. In comparison, they were only specs in the center of an expanse of countless peaks under the bright blue sky. But at the moment, they felt like giants. For an hour they meandered around congratulating one another and applauding whenever another thru-hiker summited. After a quick lunch, they absorbed the views and the feeling of accomplishment, one last time.

Like any graduation ceremony, there came the moment when it was time to go home. Reluctantly, they silently trickled away in single file, back down the same way they had come up.

By the time the three of them had reached the ranger station, there were no other hikers around. Park employees repairing a roof on a shelter confirmed Sonny's concern that the shuttle had already departed. They walked out to the mosquito-infested road and hoped for a ride. Shortly, a pickup truck with Alabama plates pulled to a stop. The cab was full with Bill, Kevin, Connie, and their luggage, but the bed was available. The jubilant hikers climbed in the back and were driven back to Millinocket. The trail angels parked across from the Scootic In where they went for supper after Sonny took their picture. The hikers agreed to return to the restaurant as soon as they had dropped off gear at their respective hostels.

Before leaving the hostel, Sonny met with Old Man and signed up for a morning shuttle to the bus stop in Medway. He then attempted to pay his lodging bill for the two nights, but Old Man said, "It's already been taken care of."

Sonny said, "What do you mean?"

Old Man pulled out a paper from under the counter, looked at it and said, "Do you remember a man named Michael that you met in New Jersey?"

"Not sure."

"He said he hiked with you a short ways."

"Oh yeah. I remember him."

Old Man handed Sonny the paper with the trail angel's name and phone number. "He covered all of your expenses for your stay."

As Sonny walked back to the restaurant he called the number.

"Hello."

"Hi. Is this Michael?"

"Yes it is. Who is this?"

"Michael, my real name is Sonny, but my trail name is Phoenix."

"Phoenix, tell me you finished!"

"I did. And then when I got back to Millinocket and went to settle my bill I was told that you already paid for it. Thank you. That was quite generous."

"You're welcome. I hope to stand on top of Mount Katahdin someday too."

"I think you will."

Sonny went into the restaurant and saw the three trail angels sitting in a booth. He waved to them and was again seated at the window. Fiona and Doubting Thomas joined him and drinks were ordered. Sonny told the waitress to put everything on his tab and to send a round of drinks over to the booth as well. Sonny ordered a two-pound lobster that came with a small bowl of melted butter, coleslaw, and rice pilaf. He then sipped his seven-seven and exchanged stories with the two lovebirds.

The celebration ended and all of them promised to meet the following May at Trail Days. During the walk back to his room, Sonny called his family and briefly told them that he was tired, but happy, and he would try to upload the last videos before he slept. He called Lily and wanted to talk longer, be he sensed that she was worn out from working hard to save the farm. Before hanging up she said, "Do you remember how you felt at the summit?"

"I'll never forget it."

"Good. Come and see me sometime and bring that enthusiasm with you."

****

Sonny went home and began the process of returning to his civilized life. He received good checkups from his dentist and general practitioner and wore clothes that were too small for him six months earlier. Sometimes he would take a shower even when he didn't need one or stand in front of the refrigerator staring at the cold beverages and selection of food as the cold air flowed over his feet. It would be a long while before any feeling returned to the balls of his feet. Sonny didn't take the time to watch his videos yet, but he did look at the many pictures he had taken along the way. He was most interested in the stone structures that increased his fascination with castles.

One evening, Sonny took his mother, his daughter, Madison, and her husband to dinner at Mancy's in Toledo to celebrate his accomplishment. August and his family met them there for the memorable night. Sonny's mother informed him that she had friends who followed his journey on YouTube. One of them named Cindy invited the two of them to dinner at the Oregon Inn. They accepted and the group of friends treated Sonny and his mother like celebrities.

Sonny's physical and mental health returned quickly. He was gaining the weight back and his strength and stamina were put to work on his land. After calling Lily one evening, his desire to see her again was at its peak. Early the next morning, he drove to Brown County, Indiana. The day was perfect. They held hands as they strolled around the rolly farm. He put on work clothes and helped her do the most difficult chores. They cooked meals, ate and cleaned up afterwards together. They drank local wine, discussed many topics and rediscovered passion.

The following day the happiness continued. They worked together well and shared ideas to enhance their futures. But at suppertime, Lily stated that even if she lost the farm she wanted to stay in Brown County. Sonny suggested that if the bank took her land, she should leave the area and start over somewhere else. Lily set her utensils on the table and said, "This is my home. I may lose my house, but I will always live around here."

"Lily, you have no family left. You worked hard, but it didn't work out. If you can't save the farm, let it go and come to Ohio with me."

"Sonny, if you were losing your farm, could you move down here with me?"

Sonny pondered the question and answered it honestly. "I would give up my farm to be with you."

Lily looked pleased until he added, "But I couldn't leave my family."

For the rest of the evening there was a cloud hanging over their heads. Bedtime came early and Sonny slept on the couch. Things weren't much brighter at breakfast. Negotiations resumed and they agreed on most matters, but the impasse of who should move, remained. Sonny decided it was time for him to return home and Lily agreed. On the front porch Sonny said, "I'm sorry, Lily."

Before closing the front door, Lily said, "Me too. Goodbye, Sonny."

The drive home seemed longer than it was. Sonny kept reliving the activities of the past two days and wished they had turned out differently. He fought the urge to turn around and go back to find a compromise. He questioned which of the two of them was right and then decided that they both were.   Lily had a similar conversation with herself. Both of them felt miserable and each tried unsuccessfully to not think about the other by busying themselves with chores.

Sonny decided it was time to put away his hiking gear that was still resting in a bedroom corner. He opened the top of his backpack, turned it over and carelessly dumped the contents on his bed. He grabbed the quart-sized bag that had served as his first aid kit and carried it to the bathroom. After placing all of the left over supplies into the medicine cabinet, Sonny was left holding a small folded piece of paper. He thought that it was probably a phone number or email address, but when he unfolded it, he remembered getting it in Pearisburg, Virginia. He stared at the numbers, crumpled the paper, and then dropped it into the wastepaper basket. When he was finished cleaning the house, he sat down for lunch with his laptop. After checking his email and Facebook, Sonny began a game of Sudoku. Halfway through the puzzle, he quit and Googled, Virginia Lottery.

The winners of the kind of ticket that Sonny had purchased would clear one million dollars after taxes. He felt silly reaching into the trashcan, but knew it would always bother him if he didn't check the numbers. He went to one of the winning number sites and entered the date of the drawing and compared his numbers. Momentarily stunned, he clicked on another site and typed in the date. The feeling of elation was surrounded by doubt and he checked a third site. The numbers were a match. So, Sonny did what most people would do in that situation. He called his lawyer.

Many people who have fantasized about acquiring a windfall already knew what they would do with the money. Sonny was in that group. First, he presented Father Sam with a tithe for the Haskins House. The eighty-acre farm was a work-for-stay organization for first-time pregnant woman who needed a place to stay. Sonny valued his family's opinions and had called each member and had lengthy discussions about his intentions. Next, he purchased ten overpriced acres on the Maumee River and took his ideas and collection of stone building pictures to a local architect. During communications with Lily, he never mentioned his winnings or his plans for it. They both ached to be with the other, but each of them stubbornly refused to budge on the matter of where they should reside. At the end of their last phone conversation, Lily said goodbye with finality and days later, after much contemplation, Sonny made a decision.

Before leaving on his trip to Brown County, Indiana, Sonny mentally reviewed the items that he would bring along. He had his wallet containing the check, phone, car keys, drinks, and snacks, a change of clothes, and lastly a bottle of wine from the Lake Erie islands that he thought Lily would enjoy. He picked up the small cooler and overnight bag and when he reached the foyer, the doorbell rang. He sat his things down there on an oak bench and opened the door. In front of him stood a woman. She was pretty and slender with shoulder length light brown hair and green eyes.

"Lily, what are you doing here?"

"I forgot to tell you. I love you."

They embraced and kissed passionately. When they came up for air, Lily said, "Are you going somewhere?"

"I was going to see you."

"Really?"

Sonny took out his wallet and handed her the document. "Yeah, I want to give you this to save your farm."

Lily stared at the check and then slowly tore it up.

Sonny asked, "What are you doing?"

"I don't want you to move away from your family, Sonny."

"I don't want to either, but I will, to be with you, Lily."

"I sold the farm."

"You did?"

"Yes, Harry and the kids now belong to John and Alice. I was right about them. They're getting married."

"That's wonderful. But what about you? Will you stay here with me?"

"I would like that and I don't think your children would mind the arrangement, but your mom might. So, I was looking at a place to rent in Grand Rapids. There's an apartment there that is above one of the stores and overlooks the canal."

Sonny said, "Mom is more liberal than you think."

Lily noticed the wine bottle that Sonny had planned to take to her at the farm in Indiana. "You had good intentions, Sonny. Maybe we should celebrate."

They sat on the deck and when the wine bottle was empty, Sonny stood and offered his hand to Lily. She stood up and placed her hand in his and said, "I'm willing to take a chance that your mom won't be visiting today."

Sonny responded by leading her to his bedroom.

AFTERWORD

Shortly after moving into the upstairs apartment in Grand Rapids, Lily purchased the old building, secured the proper permits, and began the renovations. Beginning with the foundation and working up, the historic structure became plumb, level and square. After a new roof was installed, the mortar joints of the exterior bricks were repaired and then scoured with muriatic acid. Electrical and plumbing systems were replaced, but any fixtures that were functional, were saved. The hardwood floors and decorative trim were refinished and interior walls were located to better suit the purpose of a flower shop. Sonny and August worked with Lily and the contractors to assure that the final inspections were passed.

Early in December, as Lily was making final preparations for the grand opening, she heard the doorbell ring for her apartment. She wasn't expecting any deliveries but nevertheless, Lily scurried to answer the door. On the other side of the threshold, a heavily pregnant woman stood with a worried look on her face. Lily said, "What's wrong, Madison."

"I got tired of sitting around at home so I came over to help you. But now I can't because I think my water just broke."

Lily looked at the front of Madison's outfit, stepped outside and shut the door behind her and said, "Give me your keys."

She helped Madison into the passenger seat of the white Jeep and told her to call the Wood County Sheriff Department to explain the situation. Lily safely broke several laws leaving the village and the deputy who normally sat in front of the fire station, pursued them down Wapakoneta Road with flashers on. Before they reached US-6 the officer had gotten the message to escort them to Saint Henry's Hospital in Bowling Green. Along the way, Madison called her husband, father, and doctor, in that order. Lily was still a little rattled when she pulled to a stop in front of the emergency entrance. As Madison was loaded onto a wheelchair, she smiled at Lily. Still shaking Lily said, "How can you be so calm?"

As they wheeled her away, Madison said, "I trust you."

Before the day was over, baby Ellen came into the world. The first time Sonny held his new grandchild, he told Madison that his life was now complete. Madison winked and responded with, "Almost, Dad."

In the springtime, the baby was baptized at Saint Louis Catholic Church in Bowling Green. Afterwards, there was a reception at the proud parents' home. Everyone except Sonny drove directly to the party. He headed to the construction site on River Road. Up until that time, Lily had been preoccupied with her thriving flower shop, which had become one of the canal village's prime attractions. Sonny slowly pulled into the winding driveway and Lily said, "I've been by it, but I never had time to stop."

"Well, today's a good day to look it over. Nobody works on Sunday."

"Oh, by the way Sonny, I just got a wedding invitation from a town in Iowa."

"So did I. Are you going?"

"I want to."

"Good. Maybe we could go together."

Lily gave Sonny a strange look and he parked at the circle in front by the fountain. As she got out of the car and looked around Lily said, "It looks like you spared no expenses."

"I kept the original design, but after you tore up that check, every room got a little bit bigger."

The crews had made good progress and the exterior was finished. Gray stone walls held stained and beveled glass windows and solid ornate wooden doors. Lily looked on in amazement as Sonny continued the tour. "The steeplejacks just finished the tile roof. I enjoyed watching them working on the turret. The tower on the other end has an open area at the top with a good view of the river during the day and stars at night."

"This is wonderful, but what are you going to do with your current place?"

"Oh, that's the best news yet. Henry is buying the farm. I'm in seventh heaven, Lily."

"Sonny, it looks like all of your dreams are coming true."

"Right. Hey, the reason I brought you out here was to help me figure out the landscaping."

"Sounds like fun. I think I could make some time for that."

"Great. We should get over to the party, but since were here, let me show you the inside."

Sonny unlocked the sturdy door and welcomed Lily into the foyer. She peered into the next room that had a high ceiling, but was unfinished. When Lily looked back towards Sonny, she saw that he was holding his left hand over his heart.

"Sonny, are you okay?"

Sonny kept his hand where it was on his chest, held her gaze and smiled. "Never been better."

The quizzical look on Lily's face turned to astonishment when she noticed the diamond ring on his pinkie finger. "Oh my goodness."

Sonny placed the ring on his palm and held it out to her. "Lily, my heart feels empty without you. The dream that I want to come true is that you never say goodbye to me again."

Lily took the ring, slid it on the ring finger on her left hand and the trail magic continued.

THE END

Made in the USA
Monee, IL
31 May 2021